TRANSFORMERS

DARK OF THE MOON

PETER DAVID

Based on the screenplay by
Ehren Kruger

BALLANTINE BOOKS • NEW YORK

A Del Rey Mass Market Original

Copyright © 2011 by Hasbro, Inc. All rights reserved.
Copyright © 2011 by Paramount Pictures
Based on Hasbro's Transformers® Action Figures
Excerpt from *Transformers: Exodus* by Alex Irvine copyright © 2010 by Hasbro

All rights reserved.

Published in the United States by Del Rey, an imprint of The Random House Publishing Group, a division of Random House, Inc., New York.

HASBRO and its logo, TRANSFORMERS and all related characters are trademarks of Hasbro and are used with permission. © 2011 Hasbro. All Rights Reserved. © 2011 Paramount Pictures Corporation. All Rights Reserved.

DEL REY is a registered trademark and the Del Rey colophon is a trademark of Random House, Inc.

ISBN 978-0-345-52915-2
eBook ISBN 978-0-345-52916-9

Printed in the United States of America

www.delreybooks.com
www.transformersmovie.com
www.hasbro.com

9 8 7 6 5 4 3 2 1

Del Rey mass market edition: June 2011

TRANSFORMERS

DARK OF THE MOON

CYBERTRON—
THE WAR YEARS

We were once a peaceful race of intelligent mechanical beings. But then came the war between the Autobots, who fought for freedom . . . and the Decepticons, who dreamed of tyranny . . .

I am Optimus Prime, and I remember my world from ages long gone and mourn for what my planet had been. I wonder whether it could ever be restored to the glory that had once permeated every inch of its glorious surface, and I am saddened to realize that the answer is very likely a resounding "no."

Once . . .

Once the sky above had been a shimmering, cloudless blue.

Once the surface had been a vast stretch of gleaming silver composed of an array of flat metal continents that were interlocked with each other in perfect geometric shapes. Between the continents were vast valleys that served both as the homes of the population of Cybertron and as a place to take refuge should anyone be foolish enough to try to attack our small but hardy world.

We have lost the gleaming. That is our greatest loss: the loss of the gleaming.

The once-silvery world is now burnished and dark and gray, carbon-scored with countless battles that have ranged above the surface, upon it, and below it. The sky is permanently blackened through the haze of smoke that resulted from the constant explosions and battles that had ranged from one pole of Cybertron to the other.

The incessant battles have been destructive to far more than just the exterior of the world. It has suffered on every level. Once Cybertron had been teeming with life, the paragon of scientific research and development in its particular corner of the galaxy. The technological advances were beyond anything that was known for any other race. Nor had its advancements been limited to science. The arts were treasured as well. The residents of Cybertron wrote poetry . . . mostly of the great achievements by their ancestors.

We scream defiant howls of challenge in combat. We scream through the air, inflicting brutal punishment and damage and death upon each other. We scream in pain, and we scream in death.

Once we were a proud civilization. Now our very world is a victim of war, wounded and dying, and the only thing we have left to be proud of is simply surviving from one day to the next. And how much pride can we take in that when we think of all that we have lost?

I tread across the battlefield. To my immediate right runs the edge of a valley that is steeped in the shadow of death. I step carefully around random pieces of deceased brethren. It seems that every day sees the fall of another brave warrior. Will there ever come an end to it? Well, yes, obviously. It will end when all of one side or the other is dead. What would happen then? Would it be possible to rebuild and perhaps restore Cybertron to its former glory? Those very words have been asked by my devoted followers. I nod in confidence, as a Prime is expected to do, and assure those who believed in me that Cybertron can and will survive—has to survive—and it is upon them to make certain that it does so.

What else am I supposed to say? That Cybertron is doomed? Surely they could see that with their own eyes. But they need to believe in something greater than simply endeavoring to survive another round of assaults from their enemies. There has to be more to living than simply not dying. There has to be—and it is my job to make sure that it is provided even though I suspect it may be hopeless. This is no longer a world. It is simply a battlefield with pretensions of something more. Pretensions that will never be realized.

A noise rips through the air above the field, jolting me from my melancholy reverie. I see an aircraft, a large one that is moving far faster than its considerable size would have made seem possible.

I know the craft. I know what it contains and its importance to our future.

There are six Decepticon fighters howling after it.

Out of reflex, I whip my Energon sword into a defensive position. "No," I say, and then louder, "No!" I wave my sword in a vain attempt to try to draw attention to myself. But the Decepticons are paying me no heed. They have their sights locked on to a far more formidable target.

The aircraft being pursued is far larger than the Decepticons that are chasing it, but the attack vessels have the advantage of both number and speed. Apparently aware of that, the aircraft is determined to shake its hunters rather than try to fight it out. It dives into the canyon that is to my immediate right. Without hesitation, the six smaller vessels dive in after it.

I start running, desperate to keep the larger aircraft in sight and perhaps provide aid if it is remotely possible.

This particular valley is a maze of towers and outcroppings. The larger aircraft darts into their depths, threading the needle of obstructions as the smaller ships follow behind, fast and hard.

The common wisdom would have been for the aircraft to try to gain even more speed. Instead it slows abruptly, twisting sideways to avoid blasts from the pursuing vessels while permitting a couple of them to get closer than they had expected, faster than they were prepared for. The aircraft flips its wings quickly, first in one direction and then in the other, slapping the pursuing vessels broadside and sending them crashing into the canyon walls. They erupt in balls of flame. Flying shrapnel is hurtling in all directions, cutting through yet another vessel, riddling it with holes and destroying its ability to maneuver. It flips end over end and strikes a tower, bending around it with a screech of metal.

On flies the larger aircraft, picking up speed, diving even lower into the canyon. Two more ships go after it.

It should have been impossible for the large aircraft to accomplish what it does next. It fires its reverse thrusters, and the ship flips over 180 degrees. It is suddenly flying backward, staring directly down its barrels at the ships pursuing it. The airship fires off a few quick shots, blasting aside the two ships, sending them colliding into each other. Then it flips back, narrowly avoiding smashing headlong into an outcropping before zipping around it and going faster than ever.

It is everything I can do to keep up, to be able to see what is happening. Five of the six pursuers are gone, and I allow, just for a moment, hope to swell within me.

Then I recognize the remaining Decepticon fighter, and dread fills me once more.

It is Starscream, leader of the air command. I know all too well that once Starscream is locked upon his quarry, he will never give up. In fact, he probably could have destroyed the target at any time. To Starscream, this is more of a game than a challenge.

But it is a game that he is still going to win, and furthermore, it is a game that he is tiring of.

"Starscream! Stand and face me!" I shout.

It is impossible to determine whether Starscream hears me. If he does, he ignores me. He probably even chuckles to himself inwardly at the desperation of my plea, a desperation that I could scarcely keep out of my voice.

With the section of the canyon coming to an end, there is nowhere else for the airship to go. Now it is simply going to be a matter of speed. The airship angles straight up a split second before reaching the end of the trench, hurtling vertically toward the outer atmosphere. Starscream does not slow a whit as he goes after it.

I have never felt more helpless. My grip tightens in frustration on the Energon sword. I can only watch as the battle plays out toward what seems an inevitable conclusion.

Higher and higher speeds the airship, and suddenly it puts on a burst of speed that threatens to leave Starscream behind. There is what sounds like a howl of outrage from the Decepticon, or it might just have been the screech of the air being rent asunder. Either way, for one glorious moment, it seems that a miracle might well occur and the airship will manage to elude its pursuer.

I should have known better.

Starscream locks on and fires. A single pulse from his cannon catches the aft wing of the fleeing ship.

The result is instantaneous and catastrophic. The blast tears off a stabilizer. It sends a shudder through the airship, and seconds later the cargo door blows open. Debris spills down from it, tumbling to the dirty gray surface of Cybertron like metal rain. The airship tries to compensate but fails completely. Instead, with no control at all, the airship spirals off into the darkness of space, the distant stars gleaming at it silently.

With his job done, Starscream banks sharply away. Again it could well be my imagination, but I think I may have heard mocking laughter as Starscream departs.

The Decepticon wouldn't even do me the simple courtesy of facing me in battle. Either he is worried that I would destroy him or, more likely, he is arrogantly convinced that he would destroy me.

Which means he wants me to live. He wants me to be saddled with the awareness of what has just happened and my helplessness at preventing it. He wants it to eat at me, to make me dwell as long as possible upon the catastrophe that had just befallen the Autobots.

Disappointment hangs heavily upon me. I am all too aware of the importance of that ship that had been blasted away into space. It represents a horrific loss not only to the Autobots but to Cybertron itself.

I am not one to give up, ever. Yet three words go through my mind, three words that I dare not utter lest one of the other Autobots hear me and fall into despair to hear their Prime speak so.

And those three words are: WE ARE LOST.

Earth—1961

i

Doctor Aaron Brooks had come to a conclusion: He was wasting his life.

How in the world he had wound up in the Mojave Desert, staring at a bunch of screens that were in turn linked to row after row of radio telescopes, looking for . . .

Nothing. He was looking for nothing.

He glanced around the room at others who were just like him. Half a dozen scientists who had gone into various fields, such as astronomy or theoretical physics. All of them had once been young students, looking forward to careers of accomplishment and exploration.

And one by one, they had wound up here.

If they were anything like Brooks—and he knew they were—they had joined up with the same ambition to do something remarkable: to be the very first to find a signal from outer space that was a sign of intelligent life elsewhere. There was little doubt that it would be the greatest moment in humankind's history since the invention of the wheel.

Yet as year rolled into year, Brooks had monitored magnetic beats from pulsars or the background radiation left over from the big bang itself, searching for one signal out of a billion. He had felt the enthusiasm he initially had for the project slowly, steadily being sucked out of him. The most depressing thing was watching the same realization creeping over the other scientists in the control room.

Ah, the control room: crammed with the latest technology, lined with screens and instrumentation that could chart everything and anything that came within the considerable range of the telescope array. Once it had seemed vibrant and alive to him. Now it just seemed sterile. It was where dreams of close encounters went to die.

He was going off shift soon. The setting sun was casting its red glow across the desert, and soon Aaron Brooks would witness yet another day of disappointing emptiness come to an end. Just one more, the latest dropped on the stack of—

That was when the center lit up.

A Klaxon sounded, so deafening that Brooks leaped straight up out of his chair, mashing his knee on the underside of the console. He grabbed his earphones and shoved them hard against the sides of his head. He needed to hear the signals for himself, even as a message scrolled across the lit screens with as much dispassion as if it were listing stock market prices:

UFO DETECTED. COLLISION COURSE.

Aaron Brooks was the team leader, his predecessor having dropped dead two months earlier (of boredom, some had morosely joked). Even though everyone knew what to do, even though they all had trained for a situation just like this one, still every eye turned to Brooks. They seemed to be seeking confirmation from him—or perhaps they were hoping that he would shake his head, laugh, punch a button that would shut down the alarms, and inform them that it was a false positive or a test or even just a sick joke to shatter the ennui. They would all yell at him if that last one were the case and then would mutter that they knew the whole time he was just mess-ing around and they hadn't been fooled, not for one second.

Every one of these men, wearing the unofficial uniform of black slacks, white short-sleeved shirt, and thin necktie, was a professional. None of them was going to outwardly panic. There would be no throwing of papers into the air, no screaming of, *Oh, my God, we're all going to die!* No one was going to soil himself or vomit up the tacos he'd brought in for lunch. Nevertheless, Brooks said firmly, "Stay on task, people. We have a job to do." *Even though it may well be that no one is going to be alive to know whether or not we did it.* "Station One, confirm contact."

"Confirmed," Ralph Simmons said from Station One, and rattled off what his sensor apparatus was telling him.

Methodically, Brooks went from one man to the next until all six weighed in with identical readings. Then Brooks turned to Kelly—tall, bookish, the seismologist who knew this stuff cold and could come up with conclusions without having to run numbers through computers—and simply uttered two words: "How bad?"

"If it hits us? Very. Bad," Kelly said with his typical understatement, adding the second word as if it were an afterthought.

Brooks turned to Newman, the expert when it came to tracking collision courses. "Is it going to?" Brooks had looked at the same numbers as everyone else, but there were still variables: too many plus or minuses within the margin for error to be certain. Newman was the only one who might have a lock on it.

Newman wasn't looking at him. He was running the numbers. He wasn't inputting anything or even writing anything down; he was just staring.

Then, slowly, he turned and leveled his gaze on Brooks.

"Too close to call," he said.

Dead silence.

"Nobody breathe," Aaron Brooks said in what he realized might well be the last order he ever gave.

ii

(The object—or, as half a dozen men would now describe it, the contact—hurtles through space, as it has for uncounted years. It is a dead thing, frozen and dark. All this time, all this way, it has managed to avoid falling into the grip of the gravity field of any astronomical body. Despite the vastness of space, this has not been as easy a feat as one might think. If it had endeavored to accomplish this by design, such a task would have been formidable. Since it has transpired by luck, it is nothing short of miraculous. It seems to be a compelling argument for the notion that there is some unknowable, unseen being who is guiding matters along—although whether it is because of some grand master plan for the betterment of the universe or just perverse personal amusement, it would be impossible to say.)

(Whatever the reason, though, luck has obviously run out for the object; a collision is imminent. And the target appears to be a blue/green sphere dead ahead, the third sphere in orbit around the Type G2V star hanging a mere 93 million miles away . . . a vast distance under most circumstances but a mere stone's throw in astronomical terms. Moving at 33,000 miles per hour, when the object hits—depending upon where that should occur—the results will be catastrophic. If it hits the water, tidal waves or an underground seismic event will certainly result. If it strikes

land, then the outcome will be a crater the size of several cities and perhaps another seismic event, possibly enough to split or sink a continent. Or it might not even reach ground. It could well superheat in the atmosphere to in excess of 40,000 degrees Fahrenheit and explode with a ferocity two hundred times greater than an atomic bomb. This had happened before, ripping apart eight hundred square miles of Russian forest, leaving 80 million trees flattened in a radial pattern.)

(Except this object might well detonate above a major city, leveling hundreds—even thousands—of skyscrapers and snuffing out the lives of millions of people. There are only so many times that a single planet can escape cosmic catastrophe.)

(Closer it comes to the blue/green sphere, and faster, and yes, it is going to be a city, a city that a group of scientists in the Mojave are powerless to warn because it's going to take too long and an evacuation would require hours, perhaps a full day, and they have only minutes left. All they would have time for is to pray to the deity that has seemingly abandoned them to a random and capricious fate.)

(And then a small, silver-gray mass of rock—that doesn't have anything on its plate except affecting the tides and serving as inspiration for both romantic poets and suckers for werewolf legends—puts itself between the blue/green sphere and the intruder. With no atmosphere in which the intruder can superheat, with no population to die, it has nothing to lose. It is an undead soldier throwing itself upon a grenade to save the troops.)

(Mission accomplished.)

(A journey that began oh so long ago is brought to an abrupt and terminal halt.)

iii

"Lunar impact!" Aaron Brooks shouted. He didn't bother to poll the other men but instead simply called out, "Confirmations?"

"We have impact!" "Lunar impact, confirmed!" "Way to go, baby!" The shouts were coming quickly, overlapping one another, laced with cries of relieved laughter and all the tension that they had managed to keep bottled up in the face of an impending crisis. They were clapping one another on the back, congratulating one another as if they themselves had somehow managed to move the moon directly into the intruder's path.

Brooks sagged into his chair, his chest heaving, putting his hand to his head and realizing that his hair was now drenched in sweat. As he waited for his pulse to return to something approximating normal, Newman walked straight over to him, all business. Brooks wasn't surprised at Newman's detachment. The man lived and breathed numbers and had ice water in his veins. To him, the object striking the moon was an interesting outcome to a mathematical exercise in trajectory and nothing more.

"It's not a meteor," he said with certainty.

Forcing himself to take a slow breath and then exhale just as slowly, Brooks said, "So when the computer's saying UFO, it really means . . ."

"Yeah," Newman said. "The telemetry leaves no question. Whatever that thing is that hit the moon, it's not a meteor or a fragment from a comet or anything that's understood by anyone, except maybe those lunatics out at Area 51. We have a genuine unidentified flying object."

"So you're saying there may be an alien corpse lying on the far side of the moon right now."

"Or several alien corpses. Or maybe . . ." His voice trailed off.

"Or maybe what?"

"Or maybe alien weapons."

"You," Brooks said immediately, "read too much of that sci-fi crap." But even as he said it aloud, the truth of Newman's speculation burrowed into his imagination and promptly began to eat away at what little peace of mind he had left.

At that moment, Brooks's aide, an attractive young British woman—Carla Spencer—came running up to him and pointed at a blinking red line. "Mr. Webb's ready to take your call now," she said breathlessly. "They kept trying to put me off, and I told them they would bloody well speak to you now if they cared about the future of their bleeding planet."

Brooks couldn't help himself; he laughed. Spencer, normally brimming with British reserve, chuckled in response as she realized how she'd come across. Brooks felt as if he were truly seeing her for the first time. He had always been a single-minded workaholic, and there was nothing that focused someone on matters other than work more than a narrowly averted catastrophe. He reached for his receiver, but just before he pushed the button to connect it, he said, "You wanna go out for a drink after work?"

"Desperately," she said.

He nodded, then put the phone to his ear and, just before he started talking, decided that perhaps boredom was underrated after all.

iv

James E. Webb, a barrel-chested man whose hair had not started graying until after he became NASA administrator a mere two months earlier, glared at the phone on his desk as if it had tried to bite him.

Outside his office window, the White House was illuminated against the evening sky. He had been awed by it when he had first settled into the job in February. Now all he could do was stare at the building and think about how he was letting down the main man occupying it. Or perhaps (he hated to think, darkly) the main man had in fact been letting *him* down.

Shortly before taking office, Webb had had dinner with his immediate predecessor, Doctor Hugh Dryden. Dryden had only been an interim replacement, following Doctor T. Keith Glennan. Both of the men who had preceded Webb were scientists: Dryden's field had been aeronautics, and Glennan was an engineer. Webb, by contrast, still wasn't sure if he was the best fit for the position, since he was a former marine fighter pilot turned lawyer. He had been candid with Dryden, whom he respected, and wondered aloud whether he had the proper skill set for the job.

Dryden simply stared at him over the tops of his round spectacles and said, "Never doubt you're the right man at the right time. Most of your job isn't dealing with scientists. You're dealing with politicians. This isn't a job requiring scientific acumen. It needs a pit bull."

It hadn't taken Webb long to realize that Dryden had been absolutely right. Since taking office he had had to deal with one senator after the next, all of them small-minded men, united in only one thing: They were all positive that they had far better uses for government money than giving it to NASA. Not that they could agree on what that use was, although more often than not, they all felt it should be earmarked for programs in their home states. Most of the Republicans wanted to cut taxes and felt that a disproportionately large amount of the money that such cuts would require should be taken from NASA's budget. Most of the Democrats simply wanted to redirect the NASA budget into social programs, reasoning that America should be more interested in feeding and clothing children than in wandering around in the depths of space's unforgiving vacuum. And then there was the idiot who he had just hung up with, a congressman so superstitious that he wanted to introduce a bill asserting that NASA could never put the number thirteen into any spaceflight mission because terrible things would happen as a result. Incredible, the notions that people staked their decisions upon.

And it wasn't as if the president had been particularly helpful. Webb had to admit that that, at least, was understandable. He had come into office on a wave of expectations, brimming with youth and vigor. That was a hell of a lot to live up to, and on any given day he was probably being pulled in a hundred different directions at once—and NASA wasn't necessarily a priority.

His office intercom rang, and he punched it. "Yes?"

"Doctor Moore's people calling back."

"Right, right." Moore's assistant had called him minutes earlier, when he'd been hip-deep wading through the superstitious foolishness of the congressman. Unfortunately, the "honorable gentleman" was someone who was in a position to choke off NASA's money, and so Webb had to focus on what was important rather than whatever Moore was calling about. Webb had informed his secretary to tell them to call back in five minutes. He briefly considered blowing them off again, thinking that maybe once, just once, getting out of the office earlier than 9 P.M. might be accomplished.

Instead, giving in to the inevitable, he said, "Put it through." Moments later, the phone rang and he picked it up. "This is Webb," he said briskly.

Moore was speaking quickly, so quickly that Webb had to tell him to slow down and repeat everything he'd said. Then, when he did so, Webb told him to say it a third time. He'd understood him the second time; he just wasn't sure he believed it.

Webb's secretary walked in with some letters for him to sign and stopped dead. Webb's face was ashen. He was saying, "Are you sure? How long ago?"

Normally she wouldn't have been able to hear a voice on the other side, but the caller, Doctor Moore, was speaking so loudly that it came through the receiver: "*Impact detected. We have impact confirmed. Contact at 2150 PST.*"

Webb was scribbling something on a sheet of paper while Moore continued talking about all manner of specifics, which the secretary wasn't entirely following. Then Webb gestured for the secretary to come over and tapped the piece of paper. She looked at it, and her eyes widened.

It read, "Get me McNamara."

v

It was less than an hour after the agitated conversation in Webb's office when a black limousine pulled up to the front of the White House. Credentials were quickly displayed, and the marine guarding the gate quickly waved the limo through.

Minutes later the limo discharged a man who couldn't quite believe the insane direction this day had taken. He was wasp thin, with round glasses and short dark hair that was meticulously parted and slicked down.

At that particular point in time, if he had run into Bob Lovett—the man who had been the president's first choice for the cabinet post that he now held—he would have been sure to thank Lovett with a brick upside the head. No one should have to deal with something this strange. The fact that he could say with complete honesty, " 'Strange' is my middle name," didn't make things better.

Robert Strange McNamara, the secretary of defense, hurried through the corridors of power of the White House, hastening toward the Oval Office. His boss had already settled in for the night with Jackie and the kids and hadn't been thrilled at the prospect of an emergency meeting. He was even less thrilled when McNamara—with all due respect—had declined to go into detail as to what exactly was going on. On the off chance that the phone line was not secure, he didn't need word of this leaking out.

It wasn't as if McNamara didn't have enough things on his mind. The situation in Indochina was deteriorating, the Soviets were making noise, plus there were very early indications—and he prayed that it was just rumors, nothing more—that the Cubans were up to something with missile bases. That would be just what they needed: missiles parked practically in their backyard. What a ready-made crisis that would be.

And yet, incredibly, all of that paled in comparison to what they were faced with now. It made worldly considerations seem positively mundane.

He approached the main entrance to the Oval Office and was waved in by the Secret Service. McNamara had been running, but now he stopped and chose to take a few moments to try to restore his breathing to normal. The brown leather briefcase he was carrying had been thumping against his leg as he ran; he was probably going to have one hell of a bruise in the morning.

He rapped briskly twice on the door and stepped in. Kennedy was looking out the window, apparently deep in thought. Without even turning, he said, "Good evening, Mr. Secretary."

"Good evening, Mr. President."

Allowing slightly less formality, the president said, "Working late, Bob?"

"Just came from Webb's office, actually."

"Let me guess: He's giving us heat because of the Russians."

"Well . . . that does continue to be an issue."

Kennedy sighed. "He's tired of NASA being so far behind. Don't think that I'm unsympathetic. And don't think that I haven't been hearing about it, Bob. People are steaming over Yuri Gagarin. Everyone's bellowing about national pride, and yet no one actually wants to loosen the purse strings to make it happen. We're in a race, Bob. Although"—he shook his head—"the people who *are* worried are concerned to an insane degree. You have no idea how many of them have told me they think that the Russians are going to get to the moon and set up gigantic guns so that they can shoot at us. Can you imagine that? Weapons on the moon."

"I can imagine it pretty well, actually, and that's the reason for my coming in, Mr. President." He crossed the room and settled the briefcase on a table. Reflexively he glanced under the desk to make sure the president's son wasn't hiding under it again. The last thing he needed was to have a child discussing this with his little friends. He opened the briefcase and pulled out a file folder, holding it up. "Designation top secret. We believe a UFO spacecraft has collided with the moon."

Slowly Kennedy swiveled around in his chair to face the secretary of defense. Kennedy was far too good a poker player to permit incredulity to play across his face. He allowed, in this case, a slightly raised eyebrow as he looked at the report McNamara was spreading across his desk. "A UFO."

"Yes, sir."

"At first glance, my assumption would be that that notion is insane."

"Then with all respect, Mr. President, I would suggest that, in this instance, there's more than meets the eye."

He laid out the information for Kennedy, walking the president through the specifics. He did so in exactly the way Webb had done with him and made it clear that Webb was available to come in and discuss matters further. Fortunately, the scientists who had made the discovery had been comprehensive in breaking down their research for digestion by nonscientists.

McNamara had initially been concerned that Kennedy would simply dismiss the notion out of hand. Certainly there had been men who had occupied that office who would have done exactly that. Hell, Nixon would have laughed him out of the Oval, so thank God *that* election had turned out the way that it had.

Instead, after initial skepticism, Kennedy had taken in everything McNamara was telling him. The secretary could even see the beginnings of quiet excitement in Kennedy's bearing. The more he heard, the more evidence that was presented to him, the more galvanized he became.

Yet when McNamara concluded his case . . . when he finally stopped talking . . . Kennedy didn't respond immediately. Instead he sat there for a time, steepling his fingers, and he seemed to be staring inward. McNamara could practically hear the wheels turning inside JFK's head.

Finally he said, "Tell NASA to move heaven and earth. I want a manned mission." To himself as much as to McNamara, he added, "We need to get Bobby in here. We need to sell this to Congress."

" 'This'?" The word concerned McNamara. "Are you

intending to tell Congress . . . ?" His hand drifted toward the top-secret material.

Kennedy snorted, and his Boston accent became even broader. "I tell Congress, and the only thing they'll launch is investigations into the sanity of everyone involved—including me. Hell, they'll probably claim the Pope put me up to it. No, we're going to have to sell this thing without telling people what we're actually selling. We may also want to confer with Dave Bell on this. The OMB is definitely going to want to weigh in, and the sooner we get Bell on board, the better. But we minimize this thing, Bob. 'Need to know' is our watchword. Well . . . watchwords. *Nobody* can know that *this* is the impetus for what I'm going to be proposing. Not even Lyndon."

"Have you considered, sir," McNamara pointed out, "that Lyndon—or even someone else—may be sitting in that chair when it actually happens? It could take twenty years . . ."

"We don't have twenty years. And if we did, and someone else is in this office when it happens, then I'll wait until the men are approaching the moon and I'll tell the president myself." He stared at the papers atop the desk. "This is not an easy endeavor we're discussing, Bob. This undertaking . . . it's on par with the effort that went into the building of the Panama Canal. Or the Manhattan Project."

"Yes, sir. On the other hand, for all we know, whatever's landed on the moon could wind up making the A-bomb look like a firecracker."

Kennedy nodded with a smile that was anything but mirthful. "Which brings us back to weapons on the moon. Suddenly seems a little less paranoid than I would have thought."

"Yes, sir," said McNamara, who had been thinking exactly the same thing.

vi

On May 25, 1961, before a special joint session of Congress, President John F. Kennedy gave what he considered to be the single most important speech of his presidency, if not his life. Only a handful of people truly understood the subtext of what he was discussing, and they were sworn to secrecy under threat of treason.

One of them was Aaron Brooks. He sat with his arm draped around Carla Spencer, who nestled against him on the couch, listening attentively.

"First, I believe that this nation should commit itself to achieving the goal, before this decade is out, of landing a man on the moon and returning him safely to the earth. No single space project in this period will be more impressive to mankind, or more important for the long-range exploration of space, and none will be so difficult or expensive to accomplish. We propose to accelerate the development of the appropriate lunar spacecraft. We propose to develop alternate liquid and solid fuel boosters, much larger than any now being developed, until certain which is superior. We propose additional funds for other engine development and for unmanned explorations—explorations which are particularly important for one purpose which this nation will never overlook: the survival of the man who first makes this daring flight. But in a very real sense, it will not be one man going to the moon—if we make this judgment affirmatively, it will be an entire nation. For all of us must work to put him there."

Neither of them dared say aloud what was going through their minds, because they had had hammered into them, by no less than Director Webb himself, the necessity of keeping silent about the impetus for what they were hearing. Let the rest of the world believe that this was in response to the Russians. But Brooks and his people, they knew better.

Still, the matter could be addressed without actually being addressed.

"Do you think they'll go for it?" she asked.

"I certainly hope so," Brooks said. "Because I'm telling you right now: I don't think we can afford *not* to."

HOUSTON, TEXAS—
JULY 20, 1969

"I'm at the foot of the ladder. The LM footpads are only depressed in the surface about one or two inches, although the surface appears to be very, very fine grained, as you get close to it. It's almost like a powder. The ground mass is very fine."

The voice of Neil Armstrong paused. In Mission Control in Houston—in a large room filled with technicians, engineers, and the best and brightest the aerospace industry had to offer—everyone was quiet, tense, and focused on the job at hand. They were all too aware of the weight of history pressing down upon them. No one wanted to be the one who, lapsing in his duties, was responsible for anything going wrong in the mission designated Apollo 11.

"I'm going to step off the LM now."

Another pause, one that the fanciful would have said stretched from the very first moment humanity's most distant ancestors stared up in wonder at the pale globe in the sky through to all the descendants to come who would look back upon this moment as one of the seminal achievements of the race.

A framed picture of John F. Kennedy, hanging on the wall, looked on in silence.

Thirty-five seconds ticked past. It was the longest thirty-five seconds anyone in the room could possibly have imagined.

And then Neil Armstrong's voice came through, announcing that he had set foot upon the moon, and the place went berserk.

It was thoroughly unprofessional, but it was a brief indulgence that Bruce McCandless could understand. He did not, however, join in the burst of excitement and the cheers that were going on around him. In his position of being in charge of Capsule Communications—otherwise known as CAPCOM—he couldn't afford to allow his focus to waver for so much as a second. His was the voice of Mission Control, and he had to stay on top of every single word Armstrong was saying.

Someone was tapping him on the shoulder. McCandless glanced to his left and saw a PR flack from NASA consulting a sheaf of papers. He looked confused. "Did Armstrong just say, 'One small step for man' or 'One small step for *a* man'?"

" 'For man.' Why?"

"He was supposed to say 'a man.' " The flack double-checked the papers. "That's the line that was vetted."

"What difference does it make?" McCandless was getting impatient.

"It makes a huge difference grammatically. Talking about an individual man makes sense, but just saying 'man' as in the whole of humanity makes the line self-contradicting."

McCandless was incredulous. "Oh, for God's sake. We just put an astronaut on the moon. You seriously think years from now anyone's going to care about whether or not he said a participle?"

"It's an article, actually. And reporters are already asking. Could you tell Armstrong to say it again, correctly?"

"Get away from me," said McCandless, because Armstrong's voice was coming through again."

"Yes, the surface is fine and powdery. I can kick it up

loosely with my toe. It does adhere in fine layers, like powdered charcoal, to the sole and sides of my boots. I only go in a small fraction of an inch, maybe an eighth of an inch, but I can see the footprints of my boots and the treads in the fine, sandy particles."

McCandless nodded and said, "Neil, this is Houston; we're copying." He noticed that the flack was now standing between reporters from Reuters and *The New York Times*. Everyone looked confused. The flack was saying something about static obscuring the word "a." McCandless rolled his eyes. Some people had no sense of priorities.

He waited for Armstrong to reply, to keep him and, by extension, everyone in Mission Control apprised. But instead of the mission commander's voice coming back to him, he began to hear increasing amounts of static. "Neil, we're getting signal interference. Do you copy? Come in."

Nothing. The static only grew louder and more annoying.

McCandless kept his voice level, but there was quiet intensity in it as he called out, "What the hell just happened?"

Everyone was hearing—or not hearing—the same thing McCandless was. One of the technicians called out, "Seems to be a transmitter malfunction."

"Well, get it back up. Get our men back in contact!"

ii

Need to know.

That had been the golden rule of the operation ever since JFK had first said the words in the Oval Office.

Among everyone in the building that housed Mission Control at that moment, only three men needed to know what was about to happen on the moon.

None of them was actually *in* Mission Control.

Instead, while the technicians endeavored to fix the problem that had just dropped upon them from nowhere and McCandless tried to keep his concern bottled up as he waited for the techies to get matters sorted out, three men were huddled in an antechamber that almost no one in the building even realized existed.

All three men were wearing black suits, crisp white shirts, and black ties. Their appearance had been carefully conceived to leave no lasting impression on anyone who might see them.

They were all named Johnson.

None of them was related.

"Eagle," said Johnson into a small but powerful microphone, "you are dark on the rock. Mission is a go. You have twenty-one minutes."

Standing next to Johnson, Johnson clicked a stopwatch on Johnson's mark. The twenty-one minutes began running.

THE MOON—
JULY 20, 1969

i

"Twenty-one minutes, copy that," said Neil Armstrong. He glanced toward Aldrin, who nodded by tilting his entire upper torso.

They started moving as quickly as they could.

All the practice that they had done in swimming pools, trying to simulate what it would be like to move in a low-gravity environment, had been fine as far as it had gone. But the preparation could only take them so far, and now, faced with the reality of the moon, Armstrong realized that there was going to be a learning curve in being able to bound across a gray, powdery surface with a fraction of the earth's gravity.

As they moved as quickly as they could across the Sea of Tranquility, heading toward the short ridge they needed to scale, Armstrong could only imagine what CAPCOM was going through. McCandless must have been out of his mind with concern. He felt bad about it, and the week before liftoff, there had come a moment where he was almost tempted to tell McCandless not to be concerned if there was an extended absence of communication shortly after touchdown. But McCandless was simply too smart a guy. He would have asked what Armstrong meant by that, and one question would have led to another, none of which Armstrong would have been in a position to answer. So he kept it all to himself even though the prospect he was facing seemed almost too gargantuan for any human being to conceive, much less keep secret.

Although Armstrong was the first one on the surface of the moon, it was Aldrin who made it first to the top of the lunar ridge. The height would provide them with enough elevation that they would be able to see down into the section of the moon's far side that was their true destination.

Armstrong heard Aldrin gasp upon seeing something and, with a final vault, landed on the top of the ridge next to him. He did not make a sound in the same way Aldrin had, but he fully understood why Buzz had reacted that way.

Until that moment, Armstrong had not quite been able to shake the notion that maybe, just maybe, this entire side mission was some manner of twisted joke, coming down from a secret branch of the government whose only job was to mess with the heads of United States citizens. It would certainly have explained a lot about why the country was the way it was. But all remaining doubts went right out of Neil's head as he beheld— spread out below them, half-buried in the lunar soil, just beyond the edge of available sunlight—what could only be the ruins of a vast spacecraft. The ship had clearly been blown apart on impact, creating gaping holes in the outer hull.

Armstrong finally managed to say, "Where do you think it came from?"

"I have no idea," said Aldrin.

"Let's go," Armstrong said. "We don't have time to waste."

"Roger that," Aldrin said ruefully.

Armstrong and Aldrin made their way down the ridge as quickly as they could. There was no easy path, and in short order they were climbing over the wreckage as they moved toward the holes that would provide their means of access.

Armstrong had to think that if they had a signal, the medical boys would be going out of their minds trying to figure out why his vitals had probably just gone through the roof. This was almost too much for one human mind to embrace. Not only the first man on the moon but the first to make definitive physical contact with something that was extraterrestrial?

He stepped through one of the holes, being extremely careful to make sure there were no jagged edges that could tear his suit. That would be the last thing he needed. Aldrin came in right behind him, holding a light to illuminate the eerie interior of the vessel. "Houston," said Armstrong, "we are inside the ship. Extensive damage. Hull's been breached. Appears to be empty—"

That was when the ground literally went out from under him.

The floor of the ship gave way beneath his feet. It caught him completely by surprise, for everything had seemed solid until that point. Bits of lunar dust and debris were falling through, and then so was Neil Armstrong.

It was the low gravity that saved him—the low gravity and the quick thinking of Buzz Aldrin, who was standing just beyond the crumble zone. He grabbed Neil by the arm and pulled him clear before he could disappear into the gaping hole.

The lunar debris continued to fall past as Armstrong found his footing. Aldrin had the presence of mind, even as he helped stabilize Armstrong, to shine his light down into the depths of the hole.

"Thanks, buddy," Armstrong said.

Aldrin didn't hear him. "What the hell?" he breathed.

Armstrong looked down to see what the light was playing against.

Even though it was exactly what they were looking for, he still couldn't quite believe it.

It was a mouth. A gigantic mouth that appeared to be in the face of a huge mechanical creature. A robot, perhaps, or . . .

. . . something more?

It took Armstrong a few precious seconds to find his voice, and then he finally managed to say, "Houston . . . we've found extraterrestrials. No signs of movement or life."

"Jesus," came the stunned reaction from Earth, and there was some hastened muttering briefly audible. For some reason, Armstrong found that comforting. The black-clad special ops men had been living with this knowledge for far longer than Armstrong and Aldrin, who were relatively recent additions to the need-to-know roster. If even the go-to guys for the hush-hush stuff could reflect astonishment in their voices, that made Armstrong feel better about his amazement. Then they continued, *"We copy,"* which was somewhat unnecessary since the startled exclamation of the Savior's name pretty much confirmed that they'd heard him. *"You've got seven minutes. Take photos and samples and get 'em home safe."*

Seven minutes? The statement ripped through Armstrong's mind. He checked his mission readout and realized that the information was correct; time had slipped away from him in the face of what they were experiencing, and now they were hemorrhaging time.

They did as they were bidden, grabbing as much evidence of what they were witnessing as they could. It required two minutes of what they had remaining to them, and then they headed for the hole through which they had entered. Another precious minute gone then as they emerged from the ship and moved as fast as they could toward the ridge.

And then Armstrong saw it on the distant horizon line: the first glimmerings of the sun's rays.

Sunrise was coming. Sunrise on the far side of the moon, bringing with it sunlight that would not be filtered by atmosphere.

There might not be a problem. After all, Tranquility was in direct sunlight. But there was no certainty that the daylight temperature on the far side might not be hotter than expected. It was possible that despite the insulation, Armstrong and Aldrin could literally broil inside their suits. They might well be safe if they remained in the alien ship, but then they could be trapped there far beyond the limits of their oxygen supply. To play it safe, they had to get going immediately.

They moved as quickly as they could.

As if they were beings from myth wearing legendary seven-league boots, the two astronauts bounded across the surface of the moon. They were going far faster than they had when they'd initially hit the lunar landscape, yet because of the oncoming sunlight and the possible threat it was carrying with it, they felt as if they were moving even slower. Up the lunar ridge they sprinted— or as close to sprinting as they could considering they were moving like tortoises—and now they were feeling the glare of the oncoming sunlight on their faceplates. Armstrong's heart was pounding against his chest, his breath ragged in his lungs, and in his imagination he thought he could actually hear the sun roaring toward them like an express train.

They hit the top of the ridge, and suddenly the ground started to crumble under Aldrin's feet. He tumbled backward, and Armstrong grabbed at him.

He just missed.

Buzz Aldrin fell backward into the direct sunlight bathing the far side of the moon.

"Buzz!" Armstrong shouted.

He lay there for a moment and then slowly got to his feet. "No problem," he said. "Temperature's a little hotter, but nothing unbearable."

Armstrong sighed in relief.

"Should we go back?" Aldrin suggested.

"No. We don't know the long-term effects of the far side, and there's only so long we should keep CAPCOM hanging."

"*Eagle, do you read?*" came the concerned voice of Johnson. "*It's been—*"

"I know what it's been, Houston," Armstrong said wearily. "We're clear. Repeat, we're clear. Although the flight surgeon's probably going out of his mind; our bio-med readings must be—"

"*They're all reading normal, Eagle,*" Johnson assured him. "*We've taken care of that.*"

Armstrong didn't quite know how they would have gone about feeding false data to the med heads in Mission Control and decided he was fine with that. He already knew more than he wanted to.

And as he and Aldrin got to their feet, Armstrong said with wonderment, "We're not alone, after all, are we?"

Buzz said, "No, sir. We are not alone."

ii

Aldrin had never heard anyone sound quite as relieved in his life as when CAPCOM reestablished contact. McCandless was a good guy, one of the best, and Aldrin hated what the man must have been put through during that interminable blackout. At least the astronauts knew what was going on; McCandless had been in the dark. He deserved better than to be going out of his mind with worry.

Couldn't be helped, though.

Everything else about the mission had been utterly routine. That was what happened when the best minds in aerospace put their heads together and mapped things out. It was amazing how quickly one's world could shift. One day walking upon the moon is the stuff of science fiction, and the next day the entire world knew it was science fact.

But there was other previously believed fiction that had to remain in the realm of speculation, at least for now.

As the lunar capsule hurtled toward the earth, planning its angle for reentry with perfect precision, Aldrin realized that he was devoting only a portion of his attention to his assigned tasks. It wasn't happening in such a way as to endanger their safe return, but every so often his thoughts kept drifting back to what he had experienced on the moon's far side. He thought about that vessel with the pitted hull and that gigantic machine buried deep within. The machine with a face . . . presuming it was a machine at all. But if not . . . then what? A once-living creature that looked like a machine? Was that even possible?

What a silly question to ask. If there was one thing Aldrin had learned in this endeavor, it was that anything was possible.

The earth loomed before them, welcoming them home. Welcoming the first men to walk on the moon.

Not just that, he thought in awe. *The first men to make contact with an alien civilization.*

And then he thought of all the reports he'd heard over the years about so-called alien visitations. Reports that he had once dismissed out of hand as the results of overly imaginative fools or drunks.

Or . . . are we? he wondered, and then returned his full focus to completing the job at hand.

iii

(The great ship, or at least what is left of it, continues to rest upon the moon. But something remains deep

*within it, undisturbed by the recent visitors from a small
planet. Deep within the ship, beyond where the astronauts could safely journey—at least not without elaborate climbing equipment that they simply didn't
have—there sits an enormous vault. It is vast, like a
crypt, and it houses the remains of a massive mechanical
being.)*

*(And surrounding the strange being are five pillars
with mystical markings, arranged around like the spoils
of war in a Celtic king's barrow. His face is noble, and
his eyes emit a faint blue light.)*

(And he waits.)

WASHINGTON, D.C.— SEVERAL YEARS AGO

It wasn't all that long ago that Sam Witwicky would have been intimidated by the idea of a visit to the Oval Office, a photo op with the president, and being awarded a medal of freedom, whatever the hell that was.

But that was before he had found himself repeatedly facing death at the hands of gigantic killer robots. When someone survived all of that, it tended to put things in perspective. Short of the president suddenly sprouting guns from his arms and trying to shoot him or his medal going berserk, turning into a robot and trying to strangle him—neither of which seemed impossible, given the vagaries of Sam's life—it required quite a lot these days to throw Sam Witwicky off his game.

At least that was what he thought.

Then, as he was hastily ushered out of the Oval Office so that the president could pose for more photos—this time with the British ambassador—he discovered that his game wasn't quite as set as he thought it was. He discovered his one area of vulnerability.

It shouldn't have been that much of a surprise.

Emotionally, Sam had shut down when Mikaela had left him. He kept telling himself that he couldn't blame her. She hadn't signed up for the life of constant assault that seemed to have enveloped the two of them. She told him that it was nothing personal, that she was still crazy about him. That it wasn't him; it was her.

And he had nodded and kept his smile frozen into place, but he knew that it wasn't really her.

It was him. All him.

He had even told his parents that he was done with relationships. His mother actually looked a bit relieved, which was mildly disturbing, but his father had just snickered and said, "Yeah. Sure. Right." Then his mother had punched his father in the arm and insisted that he wasn't being sympathetic to his son's pain. And his father had just shrugged and said, "I wasn't trying to be. I just know better, that's all. Sooner or later—"

"Never," Sam had told him firmly.

"Whatever," his father had said.

Now, as it turned out, it looked like his father had been right, after all.

The girl he was looking at was breathtaking. She'd come in with the rest of the delegation from the British embassy, but she looked like she'd stepped out of a Victoria's Secret catalogue. She had long, gorgeous brown hair that draped around her slender shoulders and down her back. There was an aura of utter self-confidence about her, a worldly-wise attitude. It said to him that she was someone who wouldn't be fazed by anything, up to and including skyscraper-tall Decepticons bent on annihilating all life on the planet.

Sam had to admit that he might be just imprinting upon her what he wanted her to be. After all, she hadn't even given him the slightest glance, so there was no reason for him to be conjuring up all these . . .

She turned and looked at him with the most piercing blue eyes he had ever seen. Her lips were thick and lustrous, and she appeared amused to see that he was staring at her.

You're staring at her! Holy crap, Witwicky! Get it together!

He cleared his throat, trying to effect an attitude of composure. "Hi."

"Hi," she said. She imitated his tone, but her crisp British accent made even the most trivial words sound exotic.

"I'm Sam Wickwitty."

She frowned slightly. Even when her forehead wrinkled, she looked gorgeous. "I thought it was Witwicky."

"It is."

"You said Wickwitty."

"No, I didn't." He paused. "I did?" When she nodded, he continued, "Well, at least one of us knows my name." Then he paused again. "You know my name?"

"Yeeess," she said, sounding amused. That was good. Girls liked guys who made them laugh. "Your name was on today's list."

"It was? I mean, yes," and he squared his shoulders. "Yes. It was. I fight aliens from outer space." He winced because that sounded remarkably stupid, and the last thing he wanted to sound at that moment was remarkably stupid. "And you are—?"

"Carly. Carly Spencer. Actually, Carly Brooks-Spencer, but I go by the shorter version these days. So . . . you fight aliens from outer space, eh?"

"You into things like that, Carly?" he said with what he imagined was a certain amount of confident swagger.

"Somewhat. Runs in my family, actually, going back to my grandparents. I was named after my grandmother Carla."

"Really?"

"Yes."

He waited for her to go on, but she didn't. Instead she simply continued to regard him with what seemed mild curiosity mixed with amusement.

He'd been wearing the medal around his neck for the photo shoot but had since transferred it into a small box. Determined now to keep the conversation going and also wanting to impress her, he held up the box and said, trying to sound nonchalant about it, "Just got this. From POTUS. POTUS means president of the United . . ."

He tried to flip open the box with one hand and in doing so almost dropped it. He half twisted to reach down and grab it with his other hand and as a result swept around and banged an elbow into a crystal vase that was standing on a pedestal.

From which it promptly tumbled off. Sam grabbed for it, but it deftly managed to slide right between his hands, eluding his desperate grasp, and hit the floor. It shattered into what looked like a thousand pieces.

Oh, God. Oh, God.

Sam looked at the demolished vase and for the life of him couldn't decide which was worse: that he had just destroyed what might well be a priceless antique or that he had done so in front of this girl he was totally failing to impress on any level.

How could things possibly get worse? he wondered, and as he did, he was quickly provided with the answer.

Carly was reading a small sign on the wall near where the vase had previously been standing. "Wow. A gift from Winston Churchill."

Perfect. A British woman who worked for the embassy had just seen a clumsy American demolish a present from arguably the most renowned prime minister in the history of England.

He heard the pounding of feet from down the hallway, and at that instant, with his all-too-brief moment of glory spiraling down the toilet—or, in deference to the young lady, the loo—Carly gave him a conspiratorial look that he would come to know and love in the months and years to come and said, "I can create a diversion if you want to run."

Sam stayed right where he was and grinned lopsidedly. "Um . . . did Churchill ever fight aliens?"

She didn't have the chance to answer before the Secret Service showed up, their guns at the ready, but as it turned out, the answer was no.

At least, not that anyone knew for sure.

WASHINGTON, D.C.—
FIVE MINUTES FROM NOW

i

Carly had let Sam sleep for as long as she possibly could. She'd tried to wake him up earlier, but he had moaned so pathetically that just as she always did, she took pity on him and let him sleep a little bit longer.

Their apartment was modest, a duplex furnished in an eclectic style that Sam casually referred to as "early whatever we can afford." They certainly had a decent location, which in real estate was everything, with a balcony that opened out onto a view of K Street. Particularly nice were the hardwood floors, although there was a lovely area rug under the coffee table in the living room. The floors had been a major selling point because, as Sam had put it to Carly (prompting a confused look from the realtor), "Hardwood is better. That way, we won't have to worry about constantly having to smooth out tire treads in the carpet."

She strode into the bedroom and surveyed the bed with clinical detachment. It was a crumpled mess of sheets and blankets, with a single foot sticking out from under the end. That foot was a blessing; otherwise she wouldn't have been sure what position the sleeper was lying in or even if he was there at all. As it was, she wasn't a hundred percent certain he was alive. She listened for a moment, and then a ragged snore from someone deep within the sheets verified that yes indeed,

the man of the hour from two years ago was still suck-
ing oxygen.

Since Sam was getting off to a slow start this morning,
it had given Carly the opportunity to go out and acquire
something to get him off in the right spirit on this particularly important day. She had settled on a gigantic white
stuffed bunny that had been gathering dust in the front
window of a card store down the street. Approaching
the bed, she gyrated the toy around so that it looked as
if it were dancing. As she did that, she called to him in a
singsong voice, "My hero needs to wake up! Motivate!
Today"—she paused dramatically, shoving the rabbit
down so that it would be face-to-face with Sam when he
emerged—"is the day!"

"Mondays suck," came back Sam's voice from under
the covers. At least it was two coherent words, which
was something of an improvement. It certainly beat the
grunts she'd gotten earlier. He pulled the blanket off his
head and squinted in the offensive sunlight that was
pummeling his face. His hair was matted and askew,
and his five o'clock shadow was well into 11 P.M. and
still growing. Rubbing his eyes but still not quite lifting
his head clear of the pillow, he stared at the plush face
that was mere inches from his. "What's this?" He
sounded as if he were gargling gravel.

"For luck!" Carly said with far more cheer than
should have been legal, as least as far as Sam was concerned. "It's your new lucky bunny! You're getting a job
today!"

"I'm not so sure about that."

"No worries. I'm sure enough for the both of us."

He certainly couldn't deny that. Propping himself up
on one elbow, he rubbed away the last of the stubborn
sleep that was in his eyes. "Um, Carly? Love the
thought, but . . . just this." He pumped the rabbit's foot

as if shaking its hand on a receiving line. "It's supposed to be just the rabbit's foot."

"Well, this is a bunny," Carly said, undeterred by her tenuous grasp of superstitions. "Easter bunny, really, on sale," which made sense since Easter was some weeks back. "And they rip off his foot? I mean, that's just cruel!"

That was also something Sam couldn't argue with, which was usually the case with Carly. She was so filled with both determination and exuberance that often what he needed to do was just hold on with both hands and pray that he could keep up with her.

She pulled back the blanket because he wasn't doing it fast enough and went on. "Anyway, it's to start you thinking positively. Wear your nice tie. Do you need twenty dollars for lunch?"

That last one hurt. She hadn't meant for it to; Carly didn't have a vicious bone in her body. She was just trying to be helpful. Still, as she flounced out of the bedroom, no doubt on her way to accomplish her ninth chore this morning while he had yet to get out of bed, he yelled after her, "You're killing me! I'm just your American boy toy!" The fact that she laughed carelessly at the characterization certainly didn't help. "Do you know how demoralizing it is to have saved the world—*twice*—and be groveling for a job?"

"People don't know you saved the world, Sam."

That much was true. Yes, he'd received the medal, and yes, he'd had his photo op, but the exact nature of his involvement with the Autobots and Decepticons—and the way he had consistently found himself smack in the middle of their eternal pitched battle—had been kept strictly under wraps. During the photo op he'd simply been referred to as a "valued adviser" in the recent ugliness, and even the inscription on his medal was suitably vague.

Sam had been more than happy to go along with the government's preference that his participation be kept under the radar. He wasn't some glory hound seeking the limelight. He didn't feel the need to get plaudits from crowds. Of all the things Sam had wanted to acquire in his lifetime, celebrity simply wasn't one of them.

She was right. People didn't know.

And if she'd just dropped it there, it wouldn't have been an issue.

But instead Carly's voice went on to say, "I mean, *I* do. I believe you."

Whatever residual sleepiness Sam might have had instantly evaporated when he heard that. He bounded out of bed and went to the bedroom door. The floor was cold beneath his feet, but he didn't care as he stood in the doorway and called to her, "Whoa! What does that mean?" He grabbed his bathrobe and tossed it on carelessly.

"What do you mean, what does that mean?" She was in the kitchen, cracking eggs, preparing breakfast. Carly was not a believer in grabbing a muffin at a local doughnut store and calling that a morning meal, which was typically Sam's method of operation.

"I mean it makes it sound like you don't believe me."

"How does saying I believe you make it sound like I don't?" She was using that same tone of both amusement and confusion that she was so adept at.

"It was just . . . the way you said it." The more he spoke, the more ridiculous he sounded even to himself, but he couldn't help the way he felt.

"I was just saying I wasn't there, Sam. I'm sorry. It was a bad choice of words."

He was willing to accept that, but still, he was on the defensive and couldn't pull back from it. "The govern-

ment knows. They could have set me up with something." He slumped against the door frame and, more to
himself than her, muttered, "I should be working with
the Autobots."

"Well, they paid for your college," she pointed out.
The eggs could now be heard sizzling in the pan. "The
president gave you the hero medal."

With a sigh, he glanced across the cluttered apartment toward the medal, which was mounted on a
plaque on the wall, along with a photograph of Sam
shaking hands with the president. They were meticulously cleaned and the only framed objects on the wall
that were hanging perfectly level. The amount of reverence he displayed for maintaining those objects was in
stark contrast to the general dishevelment in the rest of
the apartment.

"And as I recall," she continued, "that wasn't even the
highlight of your day."

He had to smile at that, sinking back onto the bed and
recalling the bizarre circumstances under which he and
Carly had met.

They hadn't started dating immediately. She had a
busy schedule and also traveled quite a bit, plus she was
seeing somebody else. But he'd been persistent and the
other guy hadn't known what he had and was dumb
enough to let her go, so eventually they'd gotten together. Or at least they'd gotten as close as Carly had allowed them to get.

Minutes later, when Carly came back to him, having
eaten her freshly scrambled eggs and now in the process
of putting on makeup, he was still sitting on the edge of
the bed, caught up in the pleasant recollection of one
of the truly great days of his life. She kicked the edge of
the bed, startling him from his reverie. "Move on!" He
looked up at her blankly, and she said, "Where's your
confidence, eh? Why I fell for you?" She finished put-

ting on her lipstick, capped the tube, and then affection-
ately ran her fingers through his messed-up hair. Automatically she started smoothing it down. "You're
amazing," she said confidently, "and it's just taking the
world a while to catch up. Getting a job is hard for
everyone."

He reached up, squeezed her hand, and then stood
and headed for the bathroom. "You going to shave?"
she said. "I love watching you shave."

"Yes, I'm going to shave, and what are you, five years
old?"

She sighed wistfully. "I loved watching my daddy
shave when I was five," she said as she followed him
into the bathroom.

"Great. Don't remind me."

"You have a problem with my daddy?"

"Nooo," he said as he got the electric razor out of his
cabinet. He shook it a few times out of habit to make
sure it didn't turn into something else. "It's just that in
one week, my parents are going to be here, on their road
trip party bus world tour." He looked bleakly into the
mirror of the medicine cabinet. "I have to have a job by
then, or my dad will spank me."

"He can't do that! That's *my* job!"

She hoisted herself onto the sink and wrapped her legs
around Sam. They were strong and muscular, and he felt
as if he were melting. Her voice became silky, teasing.
"*I'll* give you a job. Tonight, romance me with a nice
dinner. And then," she said, starting to lean forward,
"maybe I'll give you your bonus—"

Carly brought her tongue forward to lick the inside of
his ear . . .

. . . and then she screamed.

Mood killer, Sam thought as he grabbed at the side of
his head, wondering if his eardrum had just been shattered. *Why the hell did she—?*

He didn't even have to complete the thought. He should have known, or at least suspected, the answer immediately.

He looked down and saw a ten-inch-tall blue alien robot staring up Carly's skirt.

She aimed a kick at him but came up short as he darted backward. As the robot got out of the way, Sam shouted at him, "*Brains!* What are you *doing*?!"

"Just watchin'," Brains said defensively, bobbing his head so that his wiry "hair" waved around like a field of wheat.

Sam lashed out with his foot and had more luck than Carly had, catching Brains squarely across his torso. The robot zipped backward, and Sam endeavored to recapture the mood with Carly. But it was the romantic equivalent of trying to shove the toothpaste back into the tube. Carly, visibly shuddering, walked out of the bathroom. Sam followed her. "Carly—"

She wasn't listening. "I'm late, but the creepy one . . . yesterday, I found him in my underwear drawer."

Sam didn't want to be in the position of having to defend the little perverts, but still . . .

"They're stuck here! They're stranded. Someone's gotta look out for them."

She stopped and turned back to him, automatically smoothing her skirt and then reflexively looking down to make sure no one was taking in a show. "So," she said ruefully, "not a normal boyfriend, then?"

"Thought that's what you love about me."

Carly tapped his nose with a finger. "We are not to the L word yet. Maybe a bit closer when you're covering your half of the rent." Then she kissed him on the cheek. "Bye, bye, baby."

She headed out, and moments later her high heels were clacking down the stairs to the front door.

The moment she was gone, there was an insistent knock at the balcony door. Sam turned and strode over to it quickly, knowing what he was going to see before he opened it.

Sure enough, there was Wheelie, rolling back and forth impatiently next to Sam's huge wet mastiff, Buster. Neither robot nor dog seemed particularly thrilled. Wheelie, however, was more vocal about it.

"It's inhumane, is what it is!" Wheelie complained. "Make us live in a box, on the balcony, right next to the beast, like a common animal!" He slapped at Buster, who responded with an annoyed bark.

Sam was not brimming with sympathy at that moment. "Okay, you and your creepy sidekick cannot be in here without permission."

Buster, apparently having no patience for conversation, bounded into the room. Wheelie grabbed on to his fur and rolled in behind him, as if he were water-skiing. He rode him a few feet and then released his hold, allowing momentum to glide him over to the television. He turned it on and immediately let out an aggravated squawk. "Who messed with the TiVo? *South Park* sucks! What's this Kar-duh-SHEE-uhn crap?" he said, mangling the name "Kardashian." Then with more interest he said, "*Star Trek,*" but he quickly followed it with a disappointed "I've seen that one." Struck by a thought, he wheeled around to face Sam. "Here's an episode I'd love to see. The *Enterprise* is cruising along, and suddenly it comes face-to-face with a Prime. And the *Enterprise* starts changing around, and the nacelles become cannons, and it says, 'So you've found me! At last . . . we finish this!' 'Cause it's a Decepticon, get it?"

"Yeah, I get it. Look—"

"And the two of 'em start whomping on each other—"

"Will you listen to me!" Sam shouted, managing to get Wheelie's attention. "I'm serious! I don't need this relationship going the way of . . ." He stopped and then rephrased it. "You know how long it took me to get over Mikaela!"

Wheelie seemed put out at the mere mention of her. "The warrior goddess dumped you, she dumped us. Now we're the only family you've got."

Sam crouched down and pointed an angry finger at Wheelie. "No. We are *not* family. *You* are a political refugee. I am your . . ."

"Refuge-or?"

"Whatever. The point is, I've finally found someone who appreciates me for me. And I'm not going to let you screw that up."

" 'Cause you figure you can screw it up yourself?"

For an answer, Sam brought his fist down on top of Wheelie's head and thumped it as hard as he could without damaging his hand.

Wheelie didn't even seem to feel it. "Travesty's what it is. They don't even offer us a position?"

In spite of himself, Sam said, "Yeah. I was saying the same thing."

"I tell you, we know how you feel. Wasted talent. Even Brains can see that."

Sam glanced over at Brains. The little robot had a box of screws he'd pulled out from under the sink and was busy chewing on them and spitting out the heads.

Great. I have no job, my girlfriend probably thinks I'm a loser, my parents are going to give me no end of grief, and the only ones around who see things the way I do are a couple of metal midgets with a fetish for hardware and my girlfriend's panties. Maybe I'm the one around here with a screw loose.

He walked over to Brains and grabbed the box away

from him. Brains gave a protesting bleep. "Okay, stop with the screws," he said, then stepped back to address both of them. "Look, you guys like it here? Just treat Carly with respect."

Wheelie spun back and forth, which was his mocking version of a salute. Brains, who was preoccupied with watching MSNBC, spun his head around and muttered, "Buy, sell, buy, buy, sell, hold. Short."

Exasperated, Sam headed for the shower and hoped that Brains wouldn't start flushing the toilet the way he had the last time.

ii

Sam, wearing the one and only suit he owned, strode out into the street while making what seemed the umpteenth adjustment to his necktie. He took a mental inventory of how the day had gone so far, couldn't find a single positive, and wondered, *How could things possibly get worse?*

From nowhere a horn started blasting from down the street that was so loud, it sounded like a lighthouse, complete with foghorn. Sam turned to find the origin of the hellacious noise and was horrified to see his parents, Ron and Judy Witwicky, navigating a gargantuan RV right down the middle of the street. Three parked cars lost their side-view mirrors as his father steered the beast with the skill of a blind man.

I have got to stop wondering about things getting worse.

As the RV drew closer, Sam, out of habit, checked the front to see if it was carrying a Decepticon emblem. How strange had his life become that he was seeking out evidence that a vehicle was a disguised alien robot in order to make sense of it?

There was a large parking space available in the street, mostly because Ron felt that that whole business about

not parking next to fire hydrants was more of a guide-
line than an actual law. ("If there's a fire, I'll move it!"
he frequently said.) Once he had maneuvered the behemoth into its illegal space, Ron clambered out the
driver's side while Judy hopped out of the passenger's
seat. She threw wide her arms as if she were a falcon
about to take flight and cried out, "Oh, Ronald! Look at
him! He looks just like a little man!" She clapped her
hands together, ran to him, and started patting his face
repeatedly, thus ensuring he would have curious red
marks on his cheeks for his interviews. Then, for her fi-
nale, she shoved his cheeks together so that his lips
wound up pressed forward like a goldfish's.

Having inflicted enough damage on her hapless son,
she turned around and surveyed the area. "Where's
Carly? Show me that beautiful girl. Where is she?"

Not here, thank God. "She's at work, Mom. She got a
new job. What are you doing here . . ." *An entire freakin' week early!*

"Just speeding up the trip," she said, as if the answer
should have been obvious. "Wanted to see you. And"—
she lowered her voice and chucked a thumb toward the
RV—"I could not last another month in that thing. It's a
nightmare. Relived the entire Civil War."

He wasn't sure if by that she meant that they had attended a Civil War reenactment or she and Ronald had
split the thing into North and South sections and then
fought the entire time.

Ron sauntered toward his son, obviously thinking
that his wife was busy extolling the joys of traveling
everywhere in a conveyance so large that it had its own
ZIP code. "Like the dream machine, huh?" He winked.
"Could be yours someday, kiddo."

I can't wait to have it run me over. "Thanks, Dad. I'm
getting the chills," Sam said with his best forced smile.
"Guys . . . you should have called."

"Then we couldn't surprise you!" his mother said.

Sam wasn't exactly seeing the downside of that.

Mom, meantime, was busy straightening the lapels of his jacket. "Oh, Ron, look how handsome! See, I *told* you he'd find a job."

"Took long enough," Ron said. "We were getting worried."

"Guys, I can't talk. I'm gonna be late . . ." He paused. *Lie to them. Tell them you're going to work. It's their fault, not yours. If they had shown up when they were supposed to, you wouldn't have had to lie. So just make something up . . .*

And then the other side of his brain, the one that was aware that his parents certainly posed far less of a threat than a rampaging Megatron—although to give them their due, they were right up there—kicked in.

You're an adult, Witwicky. Man up. There's no good way to disabuse them of the notion that you're gainfully employed. Best thing to do is just rip it off, like a bandage, in one shot.

". . . late . . . to my interviews."

His parents looked as if they were deflating, and that was when Sam remembered just how painful ripping off those bandages could be.

"Oh. Interviews," they said in unison.

Feeling bad for having disappointed them but confident that it would be only a short-term disappointment, he put a hand on each of their shoulders. "Look, this is gonna work out great. This way you'll be here to celebrate with me tonight when I get the job. So go tour the museums, okay? I'll be back tonight. Welcome to D.C."

His parents nodded gamely, and Sam, knowing he had done all he could to make a bad situation better, headed to the garage. Wishing yet again that they had an electric door opener, he gripped the handle and pulled. The door grunted in protest and then, making it clear that it was not happy about doing so, moved upward with a screech of metal.

For half a second, in his mind's eye, he was staring at a beautiful yellow Camaro, and he was a teenager once again, falling in love with his first car . . . a car that returned that adoration in ways he could not possibly have anticipated.

Then reality caught up with him, and he stared, depressed, at the garage's current occupant: a dilapidated Datsun. There were dings all over it, the paint was peeling, and the rear bumper was being held on with wire.

But hey, at least it ran.

Sometimes.

He climbed in behind the wheel and turned the key. The engine started to turn over and then started again, and a third time, and then began to choke itself out.

"Oh, no. No, not now, not today . . . *please not today.*"

Except of course it was going to be today, because it was becoming abundantly clear that today was simply *that* kind of day. And it just wouldn't be *that* kind of day if his parents weren't there to witness every bit of his humiliation.

He begged the car to cooperate every time he turned the key, even though the engine was getting weaker and weaker with each successive attempt. But the car gods had never responded well to begging unless one counted making things worse as a response.

"Sam!" came Judy's voice from behind him. He sagged forward, thudding his forehead lightly on the steering wheel. "Where's Bumblebee?"

"You tell me, Mom. He's off on his missions." He punched the dashboard in frustration. "Had to buy *this* for backup."

Ronald Witwicky stepped in behind his wife and said the absolutely perfect thing: "Uh huh. So your *car* has a job."

As it turned out, that was actually the high point of Sam's day.

SOMEWHERE IN IRAN

In any war, there are calms between storms. It has been several years since the last Decepticon attack. And while the world knows of our existence, it remains a source of controversy. We now seek to assist humans in their early conflicts. To defend the free and protect the innocent. Usually at their request. Sometimes of our own volition . . .

i

The sun was no more blistering on this particular day than it ever was, yet Lieutenant Sulimani, for some reason, was sweating.

He was manning his guard post as he typically did outside the gated industrial facility. He didn't actually know what went on in there, although he had heard rumors that as a result of the facility's activities, he wouldn't be able to have children. Considering the way the world was these days, he didn't necessarily see that as such a bad thing. On the other hand, he'd also heard that you could indeed have children, but they would be hideously mutated. After giving the matter a good deal of thought, Sulimani had come to the conclusion that he didn't actually want to know. It wasn't going to change his situation, and he wound up sleeping better at night. Fewer strange dreams.

He felt as if he were having a strange dream right now. In the distance, visible through air that was shimmer-

ing with the incessant heat, there was the distinctive
cloud of dust that always meant vehicles were approaching. Typically they were army vehicles, and had that
been what was approaching now, Sulimani would have
thought nothing of it.

Instead, as the caravan drew closer, he was able to
make out a very familiar lead car: a Mercedes.

He rubbed his eyes, still allowing for the possibility
that it was a dream or perhaps a mirage. Then he looked
to his partner on the other side of the gate, Lieutenant
Faraj. But Faraj clearly saw it as well.

"The defense minister's car?" said an astonished Sulimani, seeking final confirmation that he was not losing
his mind.

Faraj was nodding, looking no less perplexed. "Why
did no one warn us?"

That was not the question that was puzzling Sulimani.
He was willing to believe all too readily that someone
had simply fallen down on the job in the chain of communication.

What he couldn't fathom was where on earth the cars
following in the convoy had come from.

Sulimani was something of an automobile buff, always had been. He loved to look at pictures of them,
since that was naturally all that was available to him,
and he would often imagine himself behind the wheel of
some exotic muscle car, tearing through the streets of
America, which he had heard from reliable sources were
smooth and black and without an abundance of pot-
holes, checkpoints, and bombs.

He had long ago resigned himself to the fact that he
would never get to see close up any of the cars he lusted
over.

Yet here they were now, coming, as if the defense minister had for some reason decided to bring a car show
along with him in order to entertain the guards.

He recognized every single model. Rolling in behind the Mercedes was a yellow Camaro, a red Italian sports car, and a silver concept Corvette. Not a single one of those cars was remotely appropriate for the battered desert roads that served the facility, and yet here they were. Even more astounding, none of them showed the slightest signs of the sort of wear and tear one would normally expect the road conditions to impose on such vehicles.

"What the hell are they made out of?" he wondered aloud.

The sweat running down his forehead was becoming even more pronounced. Obviously, there was some matter of security at stake. The defense minister had to be coming here to perform a surprise inspection, and surprises—especially in this part of the world—could have dire consequences.

Immediately, Sulimani and Faraj opened the gates, swinging them wide in welcome. Then they snapped to attention, saluting, as the row of vehicles rolled in.

The moment the cars came through the gate, however, everything changed.

Literally.

The beautiful red sports car was the first one to undergo the metamorphosis. In rapid succession, so quickly that the guards could scarcely follow what was happening, parts twisted and gears emerged. The sports car was making noises that sounded like a combination of an oncoming locomotive and a series of head-on collisions.

It grew, higher and higher, until a shadow fell upon the guards because it was blocking out the sun. Seconds earlier it had been an idling sports car.

Now incredibly, impossibly, it was a towering flame-red robot with gleaming swords for hands.

Shaking off their astonishment—which was, in and of

itself, one hell of an achievement—the two guards tried to unsling their rifles so they could bring them to bear.

They never had the chance. Unknown to them, that was actually fortunate. Had they managed to open fire, the bullets would have ricocheted and most likely hit them.

Instead, the robot simply brought his swords up and placed the points at their chests, nudging ever so slightly. If they didn't fall backward, they would be impaled. Their knees bending, they dropped the rifles that they never had a chance to aim and fell onto their backs.

The titan leaned over them and spoke with surprising softness.

"We won't be long," it said.

ii

While Mirage took the point and incapacitated the human guards as carefully as he could, the Mercedes, Camaro, and Corvette—Wheeljack, Bumblebee, and Sideswipe, respectively—were still in stealth mode. Truthfully, they could have simply stormed the gates in their robot forms, smashing the barriers underfoot and reveling in their superiority. But there was no reason to pull out all the stops if it wasn't necessary. "Like killing a mosquito with an elephant gun," as the humans might have said.

That, and the less the humans saw giant robots tearing around their planet, the better it was probably going to be in the long run. At least that was Wheeljack's thinking, and since the learned Autobot was respected for his technological and scientific savvy, his opinion carried a good deal of weight.

Now that they were in, however, there was no point continuing the subterfuge. "Well, Autobots," Wheeljack said. "Let's inform them of the consequences of violating global sanctions, shall we?"

Within seconds, as the guards watched goggle-eyed, the rest of the disguised cars assumed their robotic forms. Accessing his arsenal, Wheeljack produced several new cannons and handed them out to his peers. "Here, lads," he said convivially. "Might be a bit spicy. They're fresh out of R&D."

Bumblebee eyed his with curiosity, while Sideswipe cradled his as he would an infant. A very large, lethal infant that could inflict untold damage upon anything it was aimed at.

Then he swung it around and took aim at the facility. His onboard sensors swept it and found an unpopulated section. He pulled the trigger, and the cannon hammered the east wing. Brick and mortar flew, and a gigantic belch of flame leaped skyward.

It was all the incentive that the remaining workers in the facility required. They came tearing out in all directions, screaming, their arms raised over their heads, making no attempt to seem as if they were planning to put up a fight. That suited the Autobots just fine; it was impossible to teach human beings a lesson if they were all dead. The more survivors there were to inform the Iranian government of the ultimate folly of its actions, the better off everyone would be.

The Autobots set to work with a vengeance, and within minutes the entire facility had been reduced to rubble.

And just before they left, Mirage turned to the two guards, who had not moved from the spot where they had fallen. "See? Not long at all. Have a nice day," he said.

The guards, who didn't understand him but would have agreed to anything, nodded.

RUSSIA

*For there are missions for which we are more suited . . .
to stand in harm's way.*

There were times when it seemed that the compound
adjective "war-torn" had been coined specifically for
Chechnya, and this was one of those times.

In one of the more notorious insurgent zones, rebels
were busy planting a bomb in a disabled car. They
thought they were unobserved.

They were mistaken.

From high above, a helicopter pilot radioed, *"This is
Pale Rider-6. Confirmed visual on four targets placing
roadside IED. You're cleared to engage."*

Seconds later, a black 4×4 pickup, a GMC TopKick,
came rolling up and glided to a stop alongside the men.
They watched it warily. Two of them thumbed the
safeties off their sidearms, ready to open fire on whoever
might emerge from within.

Instead they were witness to the same astounding
conversion process that had been witnessed in Iran,
not to mention terrorist strongholds all over the
world.

Looming over them, Ironhide looked down. If he
could have smiled, he would have.

"What's up?" he said.

ii

Still, while many trust in our human alliance, others believe we are to be feared. So, given this debate, we deem it best to call little attention to ourselves.

Furthermore, there are greater concerns than the humans can readily comprehend. There are Energon detectors in Earth's cities now. There are long-range defense systems watching the skies. And for years, it has been far too quiet. For in my Spark, I know . . . the enemy shall return.

The words came to Colonel William Lennox from all the way back in basic: *They also serve who stand and wait.*

He was clinging to that old saying now and holding tightly for all he was worth. The truth was that he didn't feel like he was serving his country at all, no matter how many aphorisms claimed that he was. He hated standing and waiting.

By all discernible measures, he was succeeding in his career track. He not only had been steadily promoted but was currently being trusted with matters of greater and greater delicacy. Matters having to do with the security not only of his country but of the entire world.

Yet he felt he was dying by inches, being sent from one nondescript building to the next—this one in the heart of Russia—for one dead-end meeting after another. Always it was with informants who claimed to have intel that was vital to American interests. And every single time, they had nothing that U.S. intelligence didn't already have in its own files, often more accurate than what was being presented to him.

He felt like his talents were atrophying in this endless pursuit of dead-end leads. Sure, one in twenty resulted in some action, but the intervening nineteen were boring the crap out of him.

It seemed like yesterday that he was doing what he was born to do: fighting a furious ground battle against an enemy that was threatening everything he held dear. He had been in a desert and the ground had been erupting beneath his feet, and then some kind of metal creature such as he never would have thought possible had emerged. Metal tentacles had been whipping everywhere, and there was an endless series of explosions, so loud that even to this day he still suffered from tinnitus.

It had been his, and the world's, introduction to the alien race called the Decepticons. From then on, the world around humanity had been transformed into a vast battle arena for creatures seemingly beyond comprehension. Lennox, alongside Sergeant Robert Epps and so many others, had fought desperately, bravely, and, in far too many cases, fatally.

In those first insane hours, Lennox had been giving no thought to his career track. He had been too busy just trying to stay alive. If, however, he had been inclined to give any real speculation to it, he never would have come up with his current assignment. It would have seemed astoundingly anticlimactic.

Too often, his workday began and ended in places just like this one: long hallways, dimly lit by flickering fluorescent bulbs, and silence hanging like a shroud.

If I were dead, how would I know? Lennox wondered. *Maybe I didn't survive even that first battle. Maybe I only think I did, and now I'm sitting here dead, and the only way I'll be able to move on is if I admit what happened and leave the world behind.*

Might be worth a try.

Seated behind his colorless desk in the colorless office,

Lennox said aloud to no one at all, "I admit that I'm dead. I'm ready to move on. Come and take me."

He then waited with his fingers interlaced, his hands upon the desk.

Seconds ticked by, and then, to his surprise, he heard a distant, rhythmic tap of footsteps echoing down the hall, growing louder and louder.

"I'll be damned," he said.

The door creaked open, and a washed-out heavyset man with a gray flecked beard stood at the threshold. Even though he was indoors, his black overcoat was buttoned all the way up. He was holding a briefcase in his gloved hand. The light overhead continued to flicker, making it seem to Lennox as if he were watching an old silent movie.

Without a word, he entered the room and sat. Obviously, this was not a heavenly host sent to gather up Lennox and bring him home. No, this was the man with whom he was supposed to meet. It was Lennox's job to make an immediate assessment of the man and get a feel for what, if anything, he might represent as a source of information.

The man was methodically removing the contents of his briefcase on the desk in front of Lennox. He lay down photos and documents neatly in meticulous rows, even stopping to jog the pictures so that they were parallel to one another. Once he had done so, he placed his hands just so on the desk and said with a bearlike growl, "I am Voskhod, general counsel, Ukrainian Department of Energy." He spoke very carefully, his English hardly fluid but perfectly understandable. "My government will officially deny that we are having this conversation. However, at one of our decommissioned facilities, a discovery was made, which I fear may be alien in nature."

Of course he would say that. He knew that that was what Lennox was looking for. It had, after all, become Lennox's specialty, the thing that he was best known for in the intelligence community, even though his expertise grew not from a lifelong interest in the subject but from simply having a knack for being in the wrong place at the wrong time.

Just because Voskhod was saying "alien," however, didn't make it so. In fact, it probably wasn't. Making the sort of snap judgment he was paid to make, Lennox was sure he saw before him just another tired, washed-out Soviet bureaucrat, probably looking to sell something. Pictures of lights in the sky, perhaps, or samples of pieces of metal that couldn't readily be identified.

Another dead end. Another waste of a fighting man's talents.

Fighting off boredom, Lennox began sorting through the pictures and documents.

He frowned.

Suddenly fighting off boredom was not a problem. He was no longer remotely bored. These were not the images he had expected to see.

He looked up questioningly, silently asking, *Is this what I think it is?*

As if reading his mind, Voskhod nodded. "The facility is named Chernobyl."

And Lennox felt a pulse of the old excitement beginning to beat within him. Even though he knew there was the potential of a threat, even though he knew his life might be at risk once more, all he could think was, *About freakin' time.*

iii

Upon approaching the city of Prypiat, Ukraine—the city that had once been home to thousands of power plant workers—the first thing one noticed was the silence. No birds sang there. No children played. It was like one of those postapocalyptic cities in the movies. One might have expected to see Denzel Washington walking around with a rifle slung over his shoulder and a determined look of survival on his face.

At the edge of the city, a Ferris wheel was rusting on its chassis, and rotting bumper cars were peeking out from beneath the overgrowth. It was a city abandoned, a city of the dead. It was clear from everywhere one might have looked that it had been the scene of a hastily beaten retreat.

Faintly, when the wind blew in just the right direction, one could hear Russian classical music drifting through the air, serving to break up the monotonous silence. Supposedly the music was played to entertain the cleanup crews so that the surreal isolation did not drive them mad. Whether it managed to succeed in that goal was open to debate. There were many who felt that the music simply elevated the environment to entirely new levels of creepiness.

Looming over the scene of devastation was the Chernobyl nuclear reactor, entombed in a towering concrete sarcophagus.

A light snow was falling, adding to the seeming permafrost that already covered the landscape. And now something shattered the silence with far greater force than the strains of Russian music. Thundering along the road came an ice-covered semitruck with a trailer hitch, arriving outside the gates of the plant. A custom red and blue paint job could be seen through the ice and salt splatter.

The cab door opened, and Colonel Lennox jumped down. A NEST technician named Willis climbed out the other side. "Uninhabited since '86," Lennox said to Willis. "Don't expect it to be livable again for twenty-thousand years."

Even though the radiation had fallen precipitously from its lethal levels of 1986, Lennox and Willis weren't taking any chances. They were clad in radiation suits.

Voskhod, who was waiting for them, was not. Instead he was dressed identically to the way he had been when he'd met with Lennox the other day. Voskhod was looking around the city that he had once called home, and there was unspeakable sadness in his eyes. Except . . . Lennox might have been imagining it, but there might have been hope in his expression as well.

"Mr. Voskhod," Lennox said, making no attempt to hide his concern, "where's your radiation suit?"

Voskhod shrugged as if he had neglected to bring an umbrella when a light shower was predicted. "It would not matter. For me, it is only a matter of time."

Lennox didn't know what to say to that. As always, when unsure of what to say, he opted for saying nothing at all. It was hard to go wrong when following that strategy.

They entered the reactor sarcophagus together. Unlike the city outside, the interior of the power plant was surprisingly clear and orderly in places. Men had come back to work there and had slowly brought some of the utilities back online.

But as the group descended, they began to see the effects of that terrible day in April 1986.

"There were energy experiments going on in this reactor," Voskhod said casually, as if he were leading a tour down the middle of Hollywood Boulevard. "Its fuel quite literally melted down. Remains fossilized, like lava."

It was true. Lennox had been stationed in Hawaii for a time and had walked fields that were composed of lava that had cooled and dried centuries ago. This had the same feel to it. The closer the men drew to the core, the more they encountered the hardened fuel.

"Every year," Voskhod continued, "our cleanup efforts probe deeper. Only days ago, we found . . . *it.*"

There were several men waiting for them, all dressed in radiation suits as well. One of them stepped forward upon their arrival and bowed slightly. Voskhod indicated him as he said, "Yuri will lead you below."

Willis moved past Voskhod, carefully checking the readings he was receiving on his instrumentation. Lennox started to follow him, but Voskhod pulled him aside before he could go past. "And Colonel . . . one other thing . . ." he said in a voice filled with caution.

Before Voskhod could continue, there was an echo of movement from above. A shadow flitted through the rafters, catching Lennox's attention. He squinted in the dimness, seeking the source. "Don't tell me you have birds living in here?"

Voskhod was looking up as well, studying the ceiling. Suddenly he seemed nervous where he hadn't before.

"It can wait," he said.

iv

The group descended into the core, the heart of where the meltdown had originally occurred. The accident that had shaped an entire generation's views on atomic energy had begun right here, and Lennox realized that he was holding his breath for extended periods as they moved around within the ruins of the reactor.

"There," Yuri said, pointing below and to the right. Willis, the NEST tech, came forward with his instruments. Everyone in the group was shining flashlights around so that the entire area was bathed in illumination.

The excavation crew had cleared away a section of the "lava" just as Voskhod had claimed. In doing so, it had revealed what appeared to be a charred case on which were emblems that Lennox was reasonably sure he recognized.

His communications channel open, he said, "Optimus, we have a visual. Objects in some sort of metal harness. There's also a case. Guys," he said, turning to the Ukranians, "those markings on the case . . . they're from the Soviet space program, yes? Why are these markings from the Soviet space program?"

He did not have the opportunity to get an answer, however, because the entire room began to shake violently. Lennox staggered but didn't quite fall. "Willis! Talk to me! What are we dealing with!"

"Energon reading, sir!" the NEST tech shouted, even though his voice was coming loud and clear over Lennox's headset. "It's strong! Below us! Closing fast!"

Lennox had heard and felt enough. The environment had suddenly turned unstable. Remaining here, particularly with a bunch of civilian scientists, was not an acceptable option. "Everybody abort! Move topside! Now!"

That was when the room erupted in a blast of dirt and rubble, and for a moment Lennox was back in Qatar, with the ground being torn apart by the attacking Scorponok.

But this looked different, felt different, and, most particularly, sounded different. He was hearing whirling tendrils coming up from below. It sounded like something was . . . drilling.

He didn't have to see the entirety of what was coming for them to make an educated guess as to where its allegiances lay.

"Take cover! Decepticon!" he shouted, trying to make his voice heard above the arrival of the attacking creature.

Metal tentacles emerged from the floor, grabbing two of the scientists who had simply been trying to get away.

It thrust them upward, and they screamed for mercy, but their appeals were in vain as the tentacles crushed them against the ceiling, killing them almost instantly. More and more of the creature was emerging from the floor below, from underground.

Lennox flattened himself against the wall as the tentacles whipped past him, just barely missing him. He was trying to discern what it was that he was seeing, but it was beyond huge, beyond vast. It was hauling itself out now, bringing itself into full view. As near as Lennox could determine, the closest analogue the thing had to species that dwelled on the earth was a giant squid. Its body, or at least what Lennox could make of it, looked like a massive torpedo, with a half dozen or more tentacles extending from it. And on the end of each tendril was some manner of whirling cutting apparatus that had chewed through the rock-hard lava as if it were cotton candy. His pure guess was that the thing was, tip to tip, about a hundred yards long and thirty feet in diameter.

And it was barreling straight toward the surface.

"Optimus! Whatever this thing is, it's heading your way! Optimus, do you read me? *Optimus!*"

v

Optimus Prime was waiting.

Even as the creature from below, which had so ruthlessly mowed through several hapless scientists, punched through the roof of the once-potent nuclear power plant, the blue and red tractor trailer rearranged its surface, parts clanging together, overlapping and taking on the size and stature of the leader of the Autobots. The trailer he had been hauling changed as well, making itself over into a horseshoe-shaped weapons pack mounted on his back.

In seconds Optimus Prime was standing poised and

ready, confronting something that had absolutely no business being there.

It was a Driller, and it dwarfed Optimus. It was the size of a football field, and Prime, for all his stature, was comparable to a bunch of football players. If the field decided to annihilate the players, they wouldn't have much of a chance.

Drillers were of Cybertonian origin, semisentient at best. They were essentially beasts of burden that obeyed simple commands and developed fierce loyalty to whoever their particular masters were. Typically they were used for mining operations, but not this one. This one had been bred for use in military operations and was much larger than any typical Driller, bigger than any Driller that Prime had ever seen.

Quickly Prime extended his arm swords and sliced deep into the Driller's tendrils.

The Driller was holding what Prime recognized as a fuel rod, but it slid from its tentacles and clattered to the ground. Surprised by the attack, it slipped back a bit into the hole it had come from. Despite its military breeding, its instinct was to recoil in the face of danger or, at the very least, in the face of a being as powerful as Optimus Prime. Even though it was many times larger than Prime, its impulse was to submit to him and the authority—and weaponry—he wielded. The only way it would battle him would be if some guiding mind told it to.

And then a cockpit in the Driller slid open, and a form became visible within it. It seemed to look about, surveying the area. It was massive and gray, with a cannon on the end of its right arm and a single gleaming red eye set into its head, which had curved horns at its temples.

"Shockwave!" said an astounded Optimus Prime.

Shockwave, utterly focused on his mission, was every bit the calculating scientist Prime remembered from ages gone by. Typically, Shockwave had no time for useless emotions such as fear and surprise. His mission, whatever it might be, was of paramount importance, and anything that stood in his way was considered an obstacle. He wasn't going to be lured into destroying Optimus Prime out of enmity or spite or a burning need for vengeance. Instead he would fight if he had to, destroy Prime as necessary, or simply avoid him if it served the mission. It was absolutely nothing personal.

He leveled his blaster arm, and Prime knew that the plasma energy he was capable of unleashing would be powerful enough to incinerate an M1 tank.

Lennox and the surviving humans had emerged from the plant below; their timing could not have been worse. Optimus immediately pulled two massive shields from his weapons pack and shouted, "Lennox! You and your men, get behind me! *Now!*"

He didn't have to tell them twice. They hurled themselves behind the protection offered by the towering Autobot just as Shockwave fired his plasma blast. It fried the air, slamming against Prime's shields with thunderous force. The Autobot was rocked by the impact but managed to remain upright.

Prime's onboard cannons locked on to the newly presented enemy and opened fire.

Shockwave withdrew into the cockpit as the blasts exploded all around him. Another Decepticon, simply out of pride or from a determination to take advantage of the situation, would have pressed the attack. But Shockwave's pride was centered entirely in his ability to accomplish whatever mission was before him. As for taking advantage, he was quite confident that another opportunity would present itself. There was simply no reason to jeopardize the mission at this point.

The cockpit slid closed, hiding Shockwave from both

view and assault. Seconds later the Driller had withdrawn, sinking down into the ground that was its first home and burrowing away, beyond Prime's ability to pursue.

There was no point dwelling on the fact that Shockwave and the Driller had made a getaway. Instead, his attention immediately shifted to the fuel rod that the Driller had dropped. Lennox was holding it, turning it over and staring at it uncomprehendingly. "What the hell was that thing? And why was it after this?"

"It's impossible," Optimus said. "This is an engine part . . . from a long-lost Autobot ship . . ."

vi

Alexi Voskhod sat alone in his car. He clutched a crucifix and a family photo to his chest. In the photo, two young children were standing in front of a Ferris wheel, with their mother behind them, her arms draped around their shoulders.

He had taken the photo himself. It had been on a family outing the day before Voskhod departed on an important business trip.

It was the day before the power plant would melt down and the Ferris wheel would be reduced to a large piece of junk, and Voskhod's family would be wiped off the face of the earth.

The day before his life would lose all meaning.

"May God have mercy on me," Voskhod whispered.

A shadow passed over his car. Naturally, he didn't see it when it was on the roof, but then it moved across his hood and he spotted it. A small flying creature was zeroing in on him. It swooped past and then angled around and came straight at him. Voskhod had a brief glimpse of two red eyes glittering with pure malevolence.

Apparently God's mercy, long delayed, had finally come.

"Thank you," he whispered as Laserbeak unleashed his firepower on the car and shot it—and Alexi—to pieces.

WASHINGTON, D.C.

i

How did it go, honey? Did all the interviewers fall in love with you? Were they all fighting for your services? Is there going to be a bidding war? Are you finally going to be able to start kicking in for the rent?

Oh, where to start, Carly? Where to start? Interview after interview in which they're asking me about my job skills, and I'm saying stuff like "I'm a team player," and "I'm good under pressure," and "I've got experience with robotics." And none of it really means anything to them because they don't know the kind of high-tech government teams I was a part of, or the pressure I was under, or the gigantic freaking robots I was busy driving around or fighting alongside or running from or bringing back to life. Oh! Oh, and then there was the interview that was actually going pretty well until Mom stuck her head in and said, "We're just running to the drugstore, dear. Lunch isn't agreeing with your father." Which pretty much ended that interview. You know what? Maybe it's better if I just drive a marlinspike through my head. Best-case scenario, I manage to pick off the brain cells that contain the memory of this day and get rid of them. Worst case, I kill myself. You know what? On second thought, maybe I have that backward. Maybe killing myself is the best-case scenario . . .

Walking out into the sunlight after the very last of the series of horror shows that constituted his job hunting that day, he blinked like an owl faced with a barrage of spotlights and realized that he had the makings of the worst headache of his life, if not in the history of humanity. The only thing that was on his mind at that point, or at least what was left of his mind, was getting back home, shucking off (and possibly burning) the lousy suit, and waiting for Carly to come home. She was the only good thing in his life, and he didn't like to contemplate what his existence would be like without her. He'd probably wind up like the male equivalent of a cat lady, except instead of a bunch of cats, he'd have little robots running around all over the place.

He smiled at the thought of her waiting at the door for him. In his imagination, she was wearing a diaphanous gown, with a cold washcloth in one hand to cool his fevered brow and a large chocolate chip cookie in the other.

He stopped. *I've got to start coming up with fantasies that have harder ratings than PG-13.*

Then the chime of an incoming text message caught his attention. He pulled out his phone and looked at it:

LATE ADD: FINAL INTERVIEW OF THE DAY: ACCURETTA SYSTEMS.

Apparently the employment agency had decided that there was enough time in the business day to subject him to a little more humiliation.

He clicked shut the phone, sighed heavily, dismissed the last vestiges of his fairly tame fantasy, and climbed aboard his parents' RV. "Home?" said his father from behind the wheel, displaying the singular lack of enthusiasm that was the hallmark of most of his interactions with his son, particularly where Sam's career was concerned.

"Got another interview, actually."

"I have a good feeling about this one!" his mother burbled, which was what she had said with equal enthusiasm about every one of the preceding interviews. Sam decided that either the woman had boundless optimism or he was witnessing the early onset of Alzheimer's and she was just forgetting everything that had happened during the day. If the latter was the case, he envied her. Would that he could forget.

ii

The nameplate on the desk read BRUCE BRAZOS, and under that was his title: EXECUTIVE VP OF PERSONNEL.

The desk was decorated with pictures, which Sam knew wasn't all that unusual. The thing was, typically such photos were of family members or friends. In the case of Bruce Brazos, they were all of him. Brazos on a fishing trip, proudly holding up a trout. Brazos wearing a karate outfit, striking a martial arts pose. On one level, Sam had to admit grudging respect for a man so in love with himself that he was his own number one fan. On another, though . . . just how pathetic *was* that?

The office itself was fairly nondescript, but at least the man *had* an office, which was more than Sam could say for himself. So who was he to criticize?

Brazos, in his mid-fifties, was an intense sales-type guy. There were rolls of paper towels that were less self-absorbed than he was. He had a file folder in front of him that had Sam's name carefully printed on a tab. "Okay," said Brazos. "I got myself a Sam Witwicky, recent college graduate." He took a moment to clap slowly, mockingly, showing just how much weight Sam's major credit carried with him before continuing. "Previous experience next to zero, but . . . hmmm . . ." He had opened the folder and was looking at the only piece of paper in there aside from the form Sam had filled out earlier. "He's got a letter of recommendation from one of our board members."

"That's nice, but . . ." Sam frowned. "I'm blanking. Do I know someone on your board?"

Brazos leaned back in his chair and proceeded as if Sam hadn't spoken. He folded his hands across his stomach and thumped on his chest with his thumbs. "Here's the deal . . ."

Oh God. There's a deal, thought Sam.

"You know who we are," and then, as if Sam didn't know, he continued. "Accuretta Systems. Global leader in telecom, aerospace. Seventeen billion in profit last year. We contract for DARPA, NASA . . . you name it." He then leaned forward, the chair creaking under him, and tapped the top of his desk for emphasis. "You perform here, doors open for you anywhere. Kids sat in your chair who run Congress now, who own major corporations. You know what they have in common? Me."

And yet you're stuck in personnel, so, y' know, sucks to be you. But he didn't say that aloud, which was probably wise. He was starting to realize that it was comments like that that were going to keep him unemployed.

Brazos was far too interested in what he himself had to say to pay any attention to how Sam was reacting. "First job outta college is critical, kid. You either take a step onto the right career path or you fall into the life-sucking abyss. All depends on how you respond to two little words."

Buzz off?

"Impress me."

Well, that was better than "buzz off." Sam cleared his throat and said with growing uncertainty, "Um . . . now?" He wasn't sure what the guy was looking for. He didn't think that surviving a firefight between Decepticons and Autobots was going to be a marketable job skill, plus how could he demonstrate that for Brazos without getting the guy's office shot to hell? Maybe he should pick up the guy's photographs and start juggling them.

Once again, as if Sam hadn't spoken, Brazos kept talking. "You a go-getter? A ramrod? A take-charge kinda guy? We're not looking for that here. I want a machine."

Damn. I should have had Wheelie apply.

"Follows my orders," Brazos said. "Questions nothing. But no brownnosing, no suck-ups. I hate that."

Then Sam realized that Brazos wasn't looking at him anymore, but instead past his shoulder. Sam turned in the chair and saw that Brazos's attention had been caught by a young woman who was walking away from a coffee station, carrying a red cup presumably brimming with coffee. She walked past the glass windows that lined the outside of his office. Noticing that he was looking at her, she tossed off a wave. Brazos automatically waved back, but even as he did, he picked up his phone and punched a number as if it had done something to him personally. Sam didn't know who the lucky individual on the other end was, but without preamble Brazos demanded, "Why is Jane using the red cup from the red floor when we're on the yellow floor?" There was a muted response from the other end, and Brazos said, "Thank you," brusquely before he hung up. Then he focused his attention on Sam and shook his head, displaying his incredulity over the state of affairs under his watch. "Total anarchy around here."

Sam crossed and then quickly uncrossed his legs. "The listing said 'administrative aide' . . . ?"

"You start in the mailroom," said Bruce Brazos, as if he were informing Sam that he had just won the lottery.

"You know who else started there? Me. The CEO. And me. You know what a mailroom *is* at a company like this?"

"A large room where they sort the mail?"

"It's the freaking cerebral cortex!" Brazos said in such a way that Sam suspected he hadn't even heard his response, which was probably fortunate. "Sensitive documents 24/7. Land of total omerta. And I need a machine I can trust. So I'm giving you ninety seconds here. Impress me."

Sam made a mental note to look up "omerta" when he had the chance. And considering what he knew he was about to say, he reasoned he was going to have plenty of leisure time on his hands to crack a dictionary. "Y' know," he said slowly, "I'm really looking for the right job. I just . . ." He shook his head. "Thanks, but I don't think it's going to work."

He stood up, shoulders bowed, not even bothering to reach across the desk and shake hands. He was mildly curious as to who it was who had recommended him but didn't feel strongly enough about it to pursue it. Without another word, he turned and headed for the door.

"What's that?" It might well have been the first time Brazos was responding directly to Sam rather than just listening to himself talk. "*You* don't *think? You?* You know how many Ivy League Phi Beta Kappas would kill to set foot in my office?"

Sam paused long enough to scrape together what was left of his self-respect. He straightened his shoulders, turned, and said proudly, "Mister . . . I saved your life. Twice. I can't tell you when, where, or how, but rest assured, I have done shit that matters. And I'd kinda like a job where I matter again. Thank you." He pumped a fist. "Keep it yellow. Goodbye."

He turned, reached for the door, and started to open it. To his surprise, Brazos was fast enough to make it around the desk and shove his hand against the door, slamming it closed. "What's your story, Witwicky? Walking out on my interview? No one's ever done that before."

Sam didn't think he really needed to add much to the sentiment that he didn't want the job. How was he supposed to elaborate on it? *I really,* really *don't want the job, you pompous windbag?*

Yet again, Brazos didn't bother to wait for a response. Clearly suspicious, his face inches away from Sam's, he said, "You really *don't* want this job, do you? You want the job after it. And one after that. But this job's the one in your way. And that's why you're gonna be good at it. That's right, no secrets here. 'Cause I look at you and see a younger *me.*"

Sam was backing away from Brazos, wondering if they were on a high enough floor that if he went crashing through the window, he would fall to his death. Anything was better than the notion that he was going to age into Bruce Brazos.

He bumped into a chair and flopped into it. Brazos leaned on either armrest, effectively pinning Sam where he was. "Nine A.M. tomorrow. I need that mailroom desk filled or . . ." He hesitated and then, for the first and only time, dropped the macho, greed-is-good routine and admitted, ". . . it's my ass." Then, rallying, he said, "So welcome to gut-check time, Witwicky. 'Cause I say I just found my new company man."

What just happened here?

iii

"I have no idea what just happened there," Sam told his parents. "I don't know how much it pays. I don't know who the recommendation came from."

They could not have cared less. Instead, his mother was too busy making noises about how her baby was all grown up and his father was extolling the virtues of starting low on the corporate ladder and working your way up through sheer grit and determination, which Sam obviously had because it was what all Witwickys had, and Sam was a Witwicky, so he had it. QED.

And even Sam had to admit on the trip back to his place that having his parents being jubilant and extolling his virtues was far superior to having them offering halfhearted support in the face of ongoing rejection.

Once there, he climbed into his car, deciding to take one more shot at starting the stupid thing up. This time it roared to life as if it were the most natural thing in the world. Of course it did. Now that he didn't have an appointment, failing to start up wouldn't have been an inconvenience.

He backed out of the driveway. His parents were standing on the sidewalk, waving, his mother shouting to him, "Go give Carly the good news!"

Sam gave his mother a thumbs-up and thought, *Finally. Something that even my parents can't wreck by saying the exactly wrong thing.*

"Yeah," called Ron. "Tell your sugar momma her boy toy's finally pulling his weight."

Spoke too soon.

He had entered the address of Carly's new place of business—where she had been hired as an assistant events manager for some high muckety-muck—into his GPS, and the handy little device guided him right to it, navigating him around some traffic tie-ups along the way. It was no Bumblebee, of course, but at least it got the job done.

Still, when he arrived at the destination, he briefly thought that either the GPS had steered him wrong or perhaps he had entered the address incorrectly. "This can't be," he muttered, staring at the building looming in front of him.

But having established that he was in the right place, he parked the car and slowly approached the astounding building that lay before him.

Set back across a granite plaza, it was a towering structure that was a symphony of glass and steel. I. M. Pei, the so-called master of modern architecture, would have been proud of it, assuming that he had not in fact designed it himself.

Sam entered the foyer. It was cavernous. They could have fielded an arena football team in there. In a daze, he wandered up to the receptionist and said, "Um . . . Carly Spencer?"

Without a word she pointed down a vast hallway. He turned and looked and saw, to his surprise, that Carly was standing at the far end, talking on a cellphone. Even more curious, there were two exotic cars on display on either side of her. It made Sam wonder if her job there was to be part of an exhibit on various kinds of totally hot bodies.

Seeing him, Carly held up the phone, pointed excitedly at it, and said, "Your parents told me! You really got a job?"

She doesn't have to sound quite so surprised . . . aw, who am I kidding? Even I'm surprised. My parents calling her and blowing the news for me . . . that doesn't surprise me.

Hanging up, she threw her arms around him and gave him a quick squeeze. "See? What'd I tell you? The bunny!" She kissed him quickly on either side of his face and on his forehead, punctuating each one with a word. "You. Are. Welcome."

He barely felt it, because he was still feeling a considerable amount of awe thanks to the environment. "Yeah . . . uh . . . you said you're this guy's new assistant events manager. You didn't mention he owns Space Mountain. What's his name?"

"Dylan Gould."

Carly hadn't been the one to speak. The confident male voice came from behind him, and he turned to face the single most ridiculously good-looking man he'd ever seen. He was wearing a vintage leather racing jacket, a dress shirt, and a silk tie. He had wavy black hair and perfectly proportioned features and was clearly the kind of guy men wanted to be like and women wanted to be with.

He held out a hand. "Dylan Gould," he repeated. "Please. Carly told me all about you."

"Thanks," said Sam, who couldn't help thinking that Carly had told him absolutely nothing about Dylan. Was it just that she didn't think it important? Or was she keeping it to herself so that Sam wouldn't feel inferior, which he very clearly was. He glanced back at Carly. He could see it in her expression: *Isn't Dylan just dreamy?* Then, just as quickly, Sam shook it off, telling himself that Carly wasn't looking at Gould in any particular way. It was just his raging paranoia and feelings of inferiority showing. "Nice, uh, place you have here."

"Ah." Dylan actually had the nerve to sound modest. "Before she came in to help run the collection, it was in complete disarray. Now my restorations are on track. I'm showing at the top Concours shows again. This woman"—he took her hand and squeezed it—"she's my secret weapon"

Yeah? My secret weapon is a Camaro that turns into a giant robot. Top that, hotshot.

Carly was busy returning modest for modesty. "Mr. Gould, please. You're so hyperbolic. All I've done is get you organized."

"You've done more than that." He brushed a stray

strand of hair from her face. "You've brought your radiance. My duchess."

"Uh huh. Okay," said Sam, and he quickly stepped in and took Carly's other hand. "Nicknames. That's fun."

Gould affably released his hold on Carly's hand and took a leisurely stroll toward one of the cars. Carly squeezed Sam's hand as if to say, *Just calm down. He's only my boss, okay? Granted, he's handsome and confident and every woman's dream, but that doesn't mean I wouldn't want to just take him and—*

Sam shook the concerns from himself forcibly. He simply had no knack for making himself feel better.

"When I stole her away from the British embassy," Gould said, "I told her: Helping manage a country is easy. Try managing a priceless collection of art. Take this Delahaye." He pulled on a racing glove and slowly ran his fingers over the car's exterior. He did it so lovingly that Sam kept waiting for him to start licking it. "The rich patina . . . the lines," Dylan continued, his voice low and throaty. "Elegant. Sensual. Built to evoke the body of the ideal woman. You know why? Designed by Frenchmen."

"Uh huh," Sam said. "Are *you* French?"

"No."

"That's good!" he said with probably far more relief than he should have.

"Come with me," Dylan said eagerly.

If I want to live?

"You've got to see my garage." Dylan was gesturing for them to follow him through a bay door. At that moment, Sam would have preferred to go just about anywhere else, including directly into the targeting sights of Megatron. Instead, feeling like one of the walking dead, he stiff-leggedly followed Dylan. Carly was at his side, still holding his hand.

Sam realized as they entered the garage that Dylan Gould collected cars the way some people collected stamps or action figures. His garage consisted of row upon row of cars: classic cars, exotic cars, classic exotic cars. If it was worth more than most people made in two years, Dylan had it in his collection. It was enough to give Jay Leno feelings of inadequacy, much less a guy who owned exactly one car that ran only when it felt like it.

"My dad had a ten-dollar desk and a dream," Dylan was telling them. "Built it into an empire. We're one of the largest accounting firms in the U.S. I started up the venture side before he passed. It's a gambler's game, really, Sam. Invest in the future; try to bet on winners. Collecting cars"—he gave a little shrug—"it's just to keep my sanity."

Yeah, I'm really worried about you keeping your sanity considering I feel like I'm about to lose my mind. "Uh huh. I get it," Sam said, making only the slightest effort to keep the annoyance out of his voice. "You have more money than Congress. Must be nice."

His attempt at sarcasm obviously failed, because Dylan was continuing to drone on about his cars. While he did so, Sam allowed his attention to be drawn away by a wall full of photographs featuring Dylan posing with a host of assorted politicians, actresses, business leaders, and more actresses. Sam recognized all of them.

The only one he was disconcerted to see, however, was one of Dylan posing with his arm draped around Carly. And in the photo, she sure didn't look like she was uncomfortable with Gould being so close.

Carly noticed that Sam was staring at the picture. There was concern on her face. Unsure of how to react, Sam gamely said, "You guys look great!"

Apparently thinking that Sam was referring not to

the picture but to his staggering collection of vehicles, Dylan said, "You an aficionado, Sam? What do you drive?"

Sam shifted uncomfortably from one foot to the other. It was actually the question he'd been dreading ever since he'd first set foot into this display room for *Motor Trend*.

Carly chose that moment to step in with a quick rescue. "Sam used to drive this amazing Camaro."

"One of a kind," Sam said quickly, nodding his head so fast that he looked like a bobblehead. "Lotta special features."

"Outstanding ride," Dylan said with approval. "Like your taste. I mean," and now the comment was clearly directed at Carly, "it's quite evident."

The words hung there like smoke, and Sam clapped his hands together and rubbed them briskly. "So! I just came by to take Carly home. *Our* home. Duchess? Back to our chariot?"

That wasn't an entirely unfair description. His car looked like a chariot, all right: one that Ben-Hur had kicked the crap out of during the big race around the Roman Colosseum.

Sam led Carly out to it, telling her in broad strokes about his new job while trying to find ways to avoid saying something as buzz killing as "working in the mail room." When they reached his rust bucket, he opened the creaking door for her. As she slid in, he glanced behind them and saw, to both his chagrin and his horror, that Dylan was standing a distance away. His face was impassive, but Sam was certain that—even from here—he could see contempt in his eyes.

Quickly he slammed the door, almost catching Carly's foot. She barely yanked it clear in time. He didn't notice. Instead, he came around and clambered into the driver's seat, firing an annoyed look in Dylan's direction. "See what he's doing? He's judging me by the car. *Never judge a man by his car.*"

"What is *with* you?" Carly said with obvious irritation. Nearly getting a broken ankle because her boyfriend almost shattered it with a car door was hardly going to put her in a good mood. "He's my boss! This job pays for our food, our rent . . ."

"No, I get it," Sam said. "It's cool. *Duchess.*" He heard the anger, the jealousy in his voice, but he couldn't help it. He felt like he was drowning in it.

Carly sounded skeptical. "Come on. You're not threatened by him?"

"Threatened? What's threatening?" He tried to sound dismissive and casual and failed spectacularly at both. Instead, he ran down an imaginary checklist. "His money? Power? Good looks? What? None of the above? Check!" he said triumphantly.

As if he had settled something, he turned the ignition key. Naturally, the only response from the engine was a sound like a dying swan.

Sam moaned and slumped back in his seat. He wouldn't have blamed Carly if she had stormed off in disgust. Disgust for the way he was acting, disgust for the car.

Instead she said, with as much patience as she could muster, "Sam, he's not the first man ever to smile at me. I think I can handle it."

"I don't care that he smiles at you."

"Then what?"

Sounding like a petulant child but unable to help himself, he said sulkily, "It's the smiling back part."

In a loving but mocking tone, she said, "Okay. No more smiling, I swear. Never again. Only for you."

The way she said it helped underscore just how ridiculous he sounded. It made him feel a little better about it all. Not a lot better, but a little.

He got out of the car and popped the hood. "Give it a shot," he said, and when she turned the key and failed to start the engine, he studied the array of wires to see if he could find the problem.

Sam heard a footfall behind him and knew who it was. "It's a rare model Datsun," he said without looking. "Very vintage."

Dylan Gould was both a car enthusiast and probably a multibillionaire. Guys like that had no reason to mince words, and Dylan was no exception. "Looks like a train wreck," he said bluntly. As he spoke, he reached in under the hood and started making a few adjustments and connections with his bare hands. Sam was about to tell him to keep his mitts off the car, but the words died in his throat. Why should Gould not touch it? What was he going to do? Break it?

Continuing to poke around, Dylan dropped his voice and spoke so softly that only Sam could hear him. "Carly told me you've been struggling jobwise. Just so you know, I'm on the board of Accuretta systems. So I put in a call. Sent in a recommendation."

Sam suddenly felt as if a fist had clamped around his heart. "You—?"

Dylan nodded. "Keep it between us, okay? She's so proud of you. Way to go." He gave Sam a friendly pat on the back. "Lucky man." Then he stepped back and called, "Try it now, Carly!"

Obediently the car roared to life on the first try, sounding better than ever.

His job done, Dylan walked away, leaving Sam feeling more utterly defeated than he had ever been in his life. His feet leaden, he dragged them back to the car and sagged into the driver's seat like a balloon leaking helium. "What is it?" Carly said, concerned.

"Nothing." He pointed in the general direction Dylan had gone. "Good guy."

"Y' know the problem with him, though?" She rubbed his shoulder. "He's not you."

She kissed him, but even that wasn't enough to bolster Sam's spirits by that point. He threw the car into gear and drove off, the setting sun hanging low in the sky behind him.

VIRGINIA,
JUST OUTSIDE D.C.

i

We move among humanity, and most of the time no one realizes that we are there. We hide in plain sight. It makes sense that the humans with whom we have most closely allied ourselves would adopt our methods . . .

The sign on the gate outside the nondescript federal building read "Health and Human Services." It wasn't on the main road, but people drove by it every day. They were ordinary citizens who never gave it so much as a second glance or the slightest thought. Had they done so, they might have wondered why it was that something so relatively mundane looking was surrounded by not one but two twelve-foot fences, with concertina wire running along the top of the interior fence. They might also have done a double take over the notion that a building ostensibly containing something as utterly benign as Health and Human Services would be guarded by armed soldiers.

Then again, they might not have. America had been in a state of perpetual alert for over a decade. Orange security signs were permanently posted outside tunnels or at bridges. Armed soldiers on guard might have been part of day-to-day life in downtown Tel Aviv, but they were never a part of the suburban American landscape prior to the beginning of the twenty-first century. Now they were a common sight everywhere from airports to train stations to, in some cases, shopping malls. So it was entirely possible that civilians would have shrugged their shoulders and thought, *Sign of the times,* that something as benign as some government human services building required additional protection. After all, terrorists would attack anything that left itself open, and so maybe everything had to be guarded indiscriminately.

Indeed, the only thing that might have gotten a reaction from any passersby would have been the gorgeous Italian sports car that pulled into the HHS building and was promptly waved through by the guards. At most, though, they would have speculated that government payrolls needed to be trimmed if someone working in a low-level HHS job could afford a car quite so choice.

ii

Once he was moving down the access road and was safe from the prying eyes of humans—or at least humans who might be stunned by the sight of a car turning into a robot—Mirage shifted into his preferred form, stretching his arms and legs as if he had been cramped inside a large suitcase. Ratchet, Bumblebee, Skids, and Mudflap were ahead of him down the road, having returned from a mission, and were likewise changing into their upright robotic bodies. They walked toward huge hangar doors, passing V-22 Osprey and Blackhawk helicopters, the sorts of vehicles that were not exactly standard issue in a government HHR building. Then again, if the Autobots were not capable of providing services for humanity's health, who was?

Bumblebee heard the roar of an approaching motorcycle and turned to see Lennox rolling up. Lennox skidded the motorcycle to a halt and said, "We've got some company, Bee." When Bumblebee didn't respond, Lennox chuckled. "Wish *my* vocoder was damaged."

"Senator," came an angry female voice, "I suggest you

remember that when the NSA needs funding, they call me." The voice was accompanied by a staccato clicking of heels, and seconds later a severely dressed woman strode across the floor with a phone pressed against her ear. She sported thick black glasses, and her hair was tied back. Bright red lipstick stood out against her pale complexion. She was wearing a gray pantsuit, blue shirt, and necktie. If she had looked any more severe, she would have come with a whip, silk ropes, and a safety word.

As she moved, she kicked off her high-heeled shoes and dropped a pair of sneakers in front of herself. She barely slowed as she slid her feet into them and kept talking without missing a beat. An aide who was running behind her picked up the heels and slid them into a bag as if he had done so a hundred times before. She didn't seem to notice him.

"When the CIA's gotta take out a target, they ask first for my permission. And when the president wants an opinion on what members of Congress are politically vulnerable in terms of undiscovered criminal conduct, mine is the number he dials. Because I keep a list. Right here in my pocket. And whenever I see it, it reminds me of you." She paused then, and Lennox could hear the outraged bellowing of the person she was talking to coming through the phone. The reason Lennox could hear it was that the man was yelling so loudly that the woman had pulled the phone slightly away from her ear so that she wouldn't go deaf. He was saying something about her not having any proof of her "outrageous calumnies."

When he paused for breath, she slipped in quickly with, "Never use your own credit card, Senator." That apparently silenced him, and she said confidently, "I look forward to your vote on the bill."

With that final riposte, she snapped shut her cell

phone and then turned to Lennox. Clearly her mood wasn't about to improve as she focused on the matters that had prompted her coming to the base. "He 'demands' to see me? He *demands*? It should be *me* demanding *him*! The CIA is up my ass about that mystery raid in the Middle East. So you better come clean. Was your unit involved?"

"Um . . . not sure, ma'am," Lennox said, being evasive.

She was not amused. "As director of intelligence, I'm a real big fan of intelligent answers."

"Can't tell you definitively. Y' know how teenage kids sometimes sneak out of the house at night."

"Colonel Lennox." What little patience she might have had was dwindling rapidly. "Are you in command or aren't you?"

"Yes, ma'am," Lennox said as he continued walking toward their mutual subject of interest. "But aliens . . . they're tricky. They work with us, not for us. Sometimes they just do what they think is best."

"Stop with the 'ma'am,' " she said in frustration. "Enough with the 'ma'am.' Do I *look* like a ma'am?"

"Yes, ma'am," he said out of reflex, and then took the time to process what she'd asked. "No, ma'am, I mean . . ."

There was a steady clanking as Wheeljack strode up to them. Lennox had never been more grateful for an interruption. Mirage and Ironhide were coming up behind him. "Oh, good, you're here," Wheeljack said. "I do hope you have answers for him. I've never seen him so upset."

Mirage nodded in confirmation. "He won't talk to me, to Ironhide, to anyone."

Lennox and the newly arrived woman walked past them to Optimus Prime. He was in truck mode, with the alien artifact—the thing that he had informed Lennox was a fuel rod of some kind—sitting on a pedestal in front of him.

"Optimus," Lennox said, "you remember Charlotte Mearing, our director of national intelligence?"

No response. Lennox looked up at Wheeljack, who shrugged. It was odd to see such a human gesture being made by a gigantic alien robot. Then he realized that, no, the odd thing was that he was *talking to a gigantic alien robot*. It served to remind him of just how utterly out of whack his frame of reference had become.

As the lack of reply stretched into seconds, Mearing glanced at Ironhide. "What's this, the alien silent treatment?"

"Seen that," Ironhide said. "This is not that. This is worse."

And suddenly, in a heartbeat—the fastest alteration Lennox had ever witnessed—Optimus Prime shifted from truck into robot and leaned straight in toward Mearing. *"You lied to us!"* he thundered, sounding angrier than Lennox had ever heard him short of when he was squaring off against a Decepticon trying to kill him. To underscore his fury, he kicked over the pedestal, sending the fuel rod clattering to the ground.

Mearing coolly glanced at the fallen pedestal. "Is that for effect?" she asked, not in the least nonplussed.

He pointed at it. "Everything humans know of our planet, we were told all had been shared. So why was this found in human possession?"

Lennox had once happened to fall into a poker game in which Mearing was involved. He had spent the next two hours getting utterly pounded and had resolved never to get pulled into another such endeavor because Mearing had nerves of steel and a poker face that made the Sphinx look scrutable. Those attributes were on full display now. "Optimus, I assure you, at Langley, the bureau, we were in the dark about this," she said so smoothly that Lennox could not have told whether she was being honest or not. It sure sounded like she was on the up and up, though. "It was director-only clearance at Sector Seven until now . . ."

She signaled to an aide who had been remaining at a respectful distance but now hurried forward upon receiving her slightly sardonic instruction, "Please bring me my bag that contains the worst information known to mankind."

The aide came forward, and there were three men accompanying him. None of them was young. Lennox recognized only one of them, but when he did, he drew in a sharp breath and fought the impulse to genuflect.

As they approached, Mearing said, "This was a secret few men knew. And fewer still remain alive."

One of the approaching old men was looking at Optimus with a guarded expression, and Lennox could decipher it immediately: He was trying to assess whether the robot presented a threat. The other two men, however, were regarding the Autobot with expressions that conveyed both reverence and camaraderie.

"Optimus Prime," Mearing said as the elderly men approached, "this is Doctor Johnson, an early mission director. This is Bruce McCandless II, former astronaut who was CAPCOM for the first mission to the moon. And this is Buzz Aldrin, one of the first two men to set foot on the moon."

"From a fellow space explorer to another, it's an honor," said Aldrin.

"The honor is mine," Optimus replied.

Lennox felt a brief wave of relief. At least Optimus wasn't so pissed off with them that he wasn't attending to simple social graces.

McCandless spoke up. "I can fully understand your anger about being kept in the dark, sir," he said to Optimus. "I was initially kept out of the loop as well," and he cast an annoyed look at Johnson.

"Out of what loop?" said Optimus Prime.

Clearly irritated that she was discovering something this momentous so long after the fact, Mearing said, "Our entire space race of the 1960s, it appears, was in response to an . . . event."

"We were sworn to secrecy by our commander in chief," Aldrin said. "Our mission was for mankind and science, yes. But there was also a military component, which is where Doctor Johnson came in, being a military astrophysicist. Our mission was to investigate a crashed alien ship. Its cargo hold was empty, as near as we could tell, presuming it *was* a cargo hold. No survivors aboard."

"The Soviets managed to land unmanned probes," Johnson said. "Must've somehow picked up that fuel rod."

Mearing's aide had produced a small DVD player that he handed to her. She held it up, opened it, and pressed play. A grainy video began to play on it, showing scientists hard at work.

"This is security video obtained by Mossad in '86, which we've transferred over onto DVD," she said. "Apparently it was being fed into a remote location, for reasons that will quickly become obvious. We believe the Russians deduced the rod was a fissionable fuel assembly, believed they had mastered it, and tried to harness it at Chernobyl."

On the small monitor, the Soviet scientists were throwing a switch. Instantly gauges spiked with a rising whine, and the scientists were patting each other on the back in mutual congratulations. That lasted for all of five seconds before they clearly realized that they had set events into motion that were going to be cataclysmically horrific. They scrambled to shut it down, and absurdly,

Lennox wondered if they were going to make it. Then the screen went blindingly white.

"Obviously," Mearing said drily, not in the least caught up in the tragedy that she had just witnessed, "not the best use of judgment. The Russian ministry, of course, disavows this incident ever occurred."

"As I mentioned, I didn't know about it during the first mission," said McCandless. "But once the first contact was made, CAPCOM and mission controllers were brought on board so we wouldn't have to worry about being out of touch with the astronauts for lengthy periods of time." He glanced in mild annoyance at Aldrin.

Aldrin rolled his eyes. "It's been forty years, Bruce. Let that out of your teeth, wouldja?"

"Fine, fine, okay," he grunted, and then continued. "We landed six missions in total. Obtained thousands of photos and samples, locked 'em away for all eternity. There was no way to disassemble the ship."

"But you searched it entirely?" said Optimus. "Including its crash vault?"

McCandless and Johnson exchanged concerned looks. Aldrin said, "I can't speak for subsequent missions, obviously, but we barely had twenty minutes in the ship."

"It wasn't a ship," Prime said. "Not *just* a ship." He paused, and his voice sounded thicker with emotion than Lennox was accustomed to. "Its name was the Ark. I watched it escape Cybertron myself. It was carrying an Autobot technology that would have won us the war. And its captain . . ."

"Who was its captain?" said Mearing.

It took Optimus a few moments to get the name out; that was how painful it was for him to recall the events of which he was speaking. "The technology's inventor: the great Sentinel Prime. He was commander of the Autobots . . . before me."

"Then . . ." It began to fall together for Lennox. "The Decepticons are hunting for whatever happened to that ship."

Optimus Prime nodded. "It's imperative that I find it before the Decepticons learn of its location. You must launch another moon mission. And," he added gravely, "you must pray it is in time."

NAMIBIA

An old Russian oil tanker truck was rumbling down the cracked, dry, and dusty road of the African savanna, making such a racket as it approached that a flock of swans was startled into taking flight.

Seconds later they were nothing more than a flock of pulped flesh and scattered feathers, blasted into oblivion courtesy of Laserbeak, who had annihilated the flock mainly because he was feeling itchy after having not killed anything for at least a day.

The tanker rolled up to Laserbeak, and then it began to change, just as the Autobots had in their various missions on behalf of humanity. There were two differences: First, the tanker had no interest in aiding the hairless apes that populated this misbegotten world, and second, his metamorphosis was taking much, much longer. It was almost painful to witness, like watching a former Olympic sprinter who was now wracked with arthritis and trying to navigate a flight of stairs.

It required a full minute for the mass of twisting metal to assume the dreaded form of Megatron, and even then he was almost unrecognizable. Hunchbacked, leaking Energon from his devastated face, the once proud leader of the Decepticons made for a sheltered clearing while dragging a sack. Trailing along behind him was a head with spidery legs. Megatron had the feeling that he once knew the head, back when it had sat perched upon the body of one of his followers. But time and lack of interest had erased the name from his memory. Now it was little more than a dog whimpering at his side. He had taken to calling it Igor for no particular reason.

Megatron thudded heavily to the ground and loosened the cords on the sack. What tumbled out would have looked to any non-Decepticon eye like a living nightmare. They were hatchlings: a cross between organic and metallic life, partially developed protoforms dripping slime.

He leaned over the hatchlings so that the Energon dripping from his face fell down upon them, providing them with the sustenance they needed. He kept talking to them as they squabbled over the food. "Don't be greedy. Don't be greedy. Greed is not a plan."

The disembodied head was putting in its own bid for nourishment, scrambling around and trying to get anything it could that fell to the side.

There was a roar in the air from overhead, and Starscream slammed to the ground in front of Megatron, kicking up a huge cloud of dust as he did so.

"My brave and wise master," he said. "Starscream hears your call! It pains me to see you so wounded, so helpless, so weak—"

Igor let out an incoherent, scolding babble directed at Starscream. *"Hurgl! Snurgl!"* That was followed by something more discernible: "My master! Mine!"

Having no patience for such moronic distractions, Starscream kicked the head, which rolled away. Then he turned his attention back to his master. "No harm meant, my lord! It's an excellent strategy: hiding. Hiding and scheming. Going very well."

A third of Megatron's face was missing, but now a mouth formed upon it made from sheer Energon. "Silence, you insipid fool!" Megatron said with a snarl. "You know what you are told, which is nothing. While I lay prisoner here those many years, beneath their wretched dam, Soundwave was watching over this planet. Perhaps you remember a ship called . . . the Ark."

Soundwave, as if out to display his many talents as the foremost spy of the Decepticons, seemed to appear in the camp out of nowhere. Laserbeak landed on his shoulder and gave off what sounded like a sadistic purr.

"It has been found, Lord Megatron . . . by the Autobots."

"Then we will race them to it!" Starscream said. "We will get it before them! And if they arrive while we are there, we will confront and destroy them! We—"

Megatron growled in a way that immediately silenced Starscream. "Let the Autobots do our work for us," he said. "Let them bring the ship's cargo to me. And as for your 'human' collaborators, Soundwave." He glanced toward the sky. Despite the fact that it was daytime, the faint outline of the moon was visible. "It is time to ensure their silence." And then his Energon-created mouth vanished.

Laserbeak squawked in delight at the prospect.

HOUSTON, TEXAS

Madeline Singer, all of seven years old, was playing jacks in her backyard when she spotted the most adorable robot toy she had ever seen. It looked like some sort of animal, down on all fours, with a pointed tail on one end and a long neck attached to a head with glowing red eyes on the other. She didn't know where it had come from. One moment it hadn't been there, the next it had. But she was at an age at which she didn't question such little miracles. Instead she laughed with delight at the way the little thing lurched toward her with a stilted gait.

"Hello!" said Madeline, springing to her feet, causing her golden ringlets to bounce around her face. She ran toward it, and it stopped in its tracks. It looked neither right nor left but just stayed there. "Who are you?"

It didn't answer.

Experimentally she stepped backward and was thrilled to see that the toy mimicked her as it moved toward her in synchronization with her backward step. She stopped. It stopped. She moved back a few more steps, and it followed her. She clapped her hands and then knelt so that she was on eye level with it. "Would you like to come to my tea party? We can have it upstairs in my room. We have to be quiet because my daddy is taking a nap, though. Okay?"

The robot nodded eagerly.

The little girl led him inside.

Her mother, Julia, was on the phone in the kitchen, sounding particularly irritated as Madeline walked past. "Look, any kid who pukes in my Volvo no longer gets to carpool with me!"

"Mommy, I have a robot I'm taking upstairs for a tea party."

Without even looking her daughter's way, the harried mother waved her off. "What? No, Bob and I have a party. The NASA gang's finally sending up the Atlas X. No, don't worry about me. I'll drink my way through it."

She continued to chat as she finished preparing dinner. After a few minutes, she called Madeline down for dinner and asked her to wake up her father on the way down.

Another thirty seconds passed during which time she shut off the carrots cooking on the stove top and slid the meat loaf out of the oven.

Then Julia heard a sound that would stay with her the rest of her life: a scream of mortal terror ripping from her daughter's throat.

Instantly she dropped the phone and sprinted up the stairs, taking them two at a time. She reached the upstairs landing and saw Madeline on the floor outside her parents' bedroom, her hands to her face, still screaming. The door was wide open, and as Julia ran toward it, she heard Bob screaming, "No! No, you don't have to do this! We can still work together!"

And then his pleas were cut off by the shattering sound of small arms fire.

Now Julia's screams joined her daughter's.

In the bedroom, a robot crouched over the unmoving, perforated body of Bob Singer. Then it turned its attention toward the terrified mother and daughter.

Laserbeak chattered happily.

WASHINGTON, D.C.

So this is what it's like to be an Autobot. To be able to move around and be capable of doing so many things, but nobody notices you because you just blend in with everything else.

Those were the thoughts going through Sam's mind as he pushed his mail cart through the aisles of cubicles in Accuretta Systems. Once in a very great while, a coworker might address him by name, or at least try to ("Thanks, Sid"; "Much obliged, Sol") or thank him for delivering some letter or package she or he was waiting for. Especially grateful on this particular day was Mickey in cubicle 27A or, as Sam thought of him, the baseball nut. He kept his cubicle decorated with everything from bats to balls to mitts. When Sam handed him a small box, Mickey started telling him about how it was a signed ball he'd gotten off eBay, and how if his wife knew how much he spent on this stuff she'd kill him, and on and on until Sam finally found a way to excuse himself so he could continue on the rounds that he really didn't want to do anyway.

In most instances, Mickey notwithstanding, Sam would acknowledge the overtures with a nod of his head or a casual wave.

But his thoughts remained on other things, such as the Autobots, and why he wasn't working beside them, and how was he supposed to be placing any value on work such as this when only a few years ago he'd been saving the world.

In the course of his seemingly endless rounds, he noticed that there was one guy—some young Asian fellow—who seemed to be watching him. But when Sam turned around to look directly at him, the guy walked away and Sam started to wonder if he'd been imagining it.

As Sam returned his empty mail cart to the mailroom and headed for his office, he tried to think of the last time he had felt this level of despair and decided it was the time Optimus Prime had died while saving him from that demented Decepticon who had wanted to remove his brain. Granted, Sam had been instrumental in restoring Prime back to life. But at this point he was starting to think that had he realized how little use he'd wind up putting his brain to, Optimus could have saved everyone a lot of trouble by just letting the so-called Doctor have the damned thing.

He sank onto his creaky chair behind his desk. It wasn't as if he even had his own office, since he shared the cramped space with two eager-beaver interns and one beaten-down devil who had been working in the mail room since stamps were twenty-nine cents. Fortunately, they were all still out doing rounds or whatever the hell they were supposed to be up to.

"So I hear this is where the CEO started."

Startled, he looked up and saw Carly standing there, leaning against the door frame.

All he wanted to do was crawl under the desk, but he didn't want to let on to Carly how mortified he was to have her see him there. So instead he said, with forced joviality, "It's true. This was his desk." He started pointing to other objects. "His stapler, his Wite-Out, his rubber band ball." Sam stood and gestured around the room, his "excitement" becoming deliriously over the top. "There's an energy in this place. Hold it. Feel it. It's electric!"

Carly folded her arms and smiled wryly at Sam's carefully modulated histrionics. "Had a meeting downtown. Okay to stop by?"

He didn't bother to say what he was thinking, namely, that it was a little late to ask if it was okay. "Not sure. I mean, there's probably some company policy about it. Unfortunately, my five-hundred-page employee conduct manual isn't exactly a page-turner."

"Sam, it's a job! At last!"

"Oh, yeah." He was unable to keep out the sound of bitterness. "Autobots are off protecting the world, and I've organized four-ring binders. This is *so* much better."

"It's not about what's better or worse! It's about doing what . . ."

He wasn't listening. Instead he was noticing that the same Asian guy who had been watching him earlier was now moving very, very slowly past his office, making such an effort to appear casual that he was instead amazingly conspicuous.

"May I help you?" Sam shouted so abruptly that Carly jumped slightly. Her head whipped around to see where he was looking even as his personal stalker hustled away. Sam turned back to Carly and said in exasperation, "Creepy Asian guy keeps—" Then, seeing Carly's confused expression, he waved it off to make it clear that it wasn't worth dwelling on.

Perfectly happy not to dwell, Carly opted to pursue something she considered cheerier than this office or Sam's clear frustration over not running around saving the planet. "Listen, this Saturday; Dylan's throwing a client party at his house. It's a work thing, but he's invited you, too."

He moaned. She couldn't be serious. She couldn't be asking what he thought she was asking.

"I want you to come. Say witty things, laugh at my jokes." She tilted her head in that way she had, accentuating that beautifully slender neck of hers. "It means a lot, okay? Please?"

Sam wanted to tell her that there was simply no way in hell he was going to do it. That it was too much to ask, that it wasn't fair to him. She knew how fragile he was feeling right now.

Fragile? For crying out loud, Witwicky, stop being such a wuss. Your gorgeous girlfriend is asking you to be there for her for a party. Man up, wouldja?

"Uh . . . okay, I guess." Then he frowned, something suddenly occurring to him. "How'd you get over here?"

"Oh. He gave me one of his cars. He wants me in something a little more"—she looked for the right word—"professional."

"Hang on. He's giving you a car?"

"Loaning," she emphasized. "For *business.*"

He was standing, and now he leaned against his desk, trying to seem indifferent and failing. "Exactly what kind of car?"

"A Mercedes. SLS AMG. Cute gull-wing doors . . ."

Sam could feel the blood draining from his face. "Do you know how much that car costs? Two hundred thousand dollars! Know how long it would take me to afford that? Sitting here? Fifty years!"

He was now pacing back and forth in the small office. Carly's head was moving side to side, watching him, as if observing a tennis match. "What am I supposed to say to him? 'No'?" Trying to talk Sam off the metaphorical ceiling, she added, "He said it's for both of us to use!"

"And where will the both of you be driving in it?"

She laughed at the absurdity of his interpretation. "The both of you and me." Then, when she saw that her laughter wasn't helping the situation, she grew serious.

"Don't you get that there's no him and me outside of a business context?"

Yeah. Funny business. He's making moves on her, and she's so naïve that she doesn't even realize it. And he's making it sound like he's just trying to help me? "That's touching. Mr. Car Museum Guy, just *so* concerned about my welfare."

He'd still been pacing, and she reached out and grabbed his arm to halt him. Meeting his gaze levelly, she said, "Look, you're frustrated, I know. I've been there. My British embassy job, soooo glamorous: printing ID badges all day."

He stared at her and realized that she still wasn't getting it. It wasn't about the job. To some degree, it wasn't even about her. This was about Mikaela. Even though it had been years, he was still carrying the baggage of her dumping him, and he was terrified of the prospect of Carly doing the same thing. Sure, the reasons would be completely different, but the outcome would be exactly the same: He would be abandoned once more, his only company being a couple of demented former Decepticons and a drooling dog.

But he didn't want to say that because he knew exactly what Carly would say in response. She'd say that it wasn't fair to her that she was getting grief because of actions taken by somebody else. And what was he supposed to say to that? That she was wrong? That she had it coming? He'd be driving her—no pun intended—straight into Mr. Perfect's arms.

Meanwhile she was still talking about the entire job thing. "It's called 'paying your dues.' And then good things happen."

As if to underscore that good things were not exactly on the horizon, Bruce Brazos strode in. The typical radar that Sam's office mates displayed where Brazos was concerned was obviously functioning, because within seconds of his entering, the interns and the depressed lifer sprinted in behind him, taking their positions behind their desks like soldiers scrambling to get in line for inspection.

"Boys!" Brazos called out. "I need lunch hour filing done, stat! Who wants to score some Bruce Brazos points?"

"Me! Me!" shouted the office lackeys, waving their arms as if they were desperately trying to flag a passing cab.

Brazos smiled as if he were some manner of puppet master making the marionettes dance to his tune. Then his gaze fell upon Carly, and suddenly Sam had a feeling of what the snake's expression had been like in the Garden of Eden when it has first spotted Eve.

"Witwicky! My man!" Filled with false good cheer, he approached Sam as if his interest was in him when it was so obviously focused elsewhere. He draped an arm around Sam's shoulders, but he wasn't looking at Sam at all. "Whoa, hello. Who have we here? Sister? Facebook buddy? Twitter tweeter?"

"My girlfriend. Carly." Then he mentally kicked himself for volunteering her name. The less Bruce knew about his life, the better Sam liked it.

"Nice to meet you," Brazos said, slithering toward her and devouring her with his eyes.

"Nice to meet you, too," said Carly. "Sam was not kidding: You do have a smashing head of hair." She quickly turned so that her back was to him and she was facing Sam. "See you at home. Keep up the good work. Oh . . . brought you a present." She reached into her bag and produced a mug.

A red mug.

With a package of red Twizzlers protruding from it.

Bruce reacted in a manner evocative of Dracula being confronted by Van Helsing waving a crucifix. He recoiled, stopping just short of hissing. If he'd been wearing a black cape, he would have brought it up over the lower half of his face.

Sam smiled inwardly. He'd never been happier than at that moment that he was working on a yellow floor.

Oblivious to Bruce's reaction, Carly walked out of the office, her hips swaying as if she were striding down a catwalk in Milan. Sam suspected that she was putting some extra oomph into it just to drive home to Brazos how lucky Sam was or, more precisely, how unlucky Brazos was.

As it turned out, Brazos was so clueless that apparently he thought it was some sort of come-on. He leaned in toward Sam and said, in a strictly *entre nous* manner, "I don't know how serious you kids are, but you set me up with that fine English toffee: instant promotion."

Sam Witwicky slammed the mug onto the desk with such force that the Twizzlers flew out of it in all directions. Brazos was startled, jumping back, as Sam spoke in a voice choked with low fury. "Or . . . harassment suit. If you push me."

Brazos studied him as if trying to assess just how serious Sam was, and then he gave him that patented Bruce Brazos insincere grin. "Witwicky, you warrior. God, I like you." He dropped the stack of files on the desk. "Have 'em filed by three."

Sam couldn't tell whether Bruce genuinely considered this some sort of reward for having the nerve to stand up to him or a punishment to remind Sam just exactly who was in charge.

With the opportunity to score Bruce points cruelly snatched away from them, the interns returned to their desks, casting envious glares in Sam's direction. One of them picked up a remote and turned on the office television. The grainy screen lit up to CNN. It was depicting a rocket ship blasting off, identified as the Atlas X, from Vandenberg Air Force base.

Sam barely glanced at it, not particularly seeing how it had anything to do with him.

He had no way of knowing that among the crowd watching the liftoff at Vandenberg, Charlotte Mearing was leaning toward William Lennox and saying to him, "Well, Colonel Lennox: One giant leap for robotkind."

If Sam *had* known that, he'd probably have paid much closer attention.

THE MOON,
SEVERAL DAYS LATER

It is similar to visiting a graveyard.

I move across the surface of the earth's moon, Ratchet beside me. Several of the small creatures created by NASA called "rovers" accompany us. It would be akin to humans being accompanied by chimpanzees, but I respect the humans' consideration.

On some level, I am hoping that I will not find what I know I will find. Yet there it is, the wreckage spread out before me, just as the astronaut Aldrin described it. I remember witnessing its departure, certain that I would never see it again and that I was watching the final hopes of the Autobots departing Cybertron with it. How curious are the vagaries of fate to bring us to this point where we are reunited after millennia.

Even with the ship destroyed, a shattered remnant of what it once was, I know exactly where to go in order to find my old commander.

I nod to Ratchet, and he follows me into the Ark. According to Aldrin, he and his companion were frightened and awed by what they saw. All I am filled with is a sense of sadness and loss. All this time, I had held out some vague hope that perhaps, just perhaps, somehow the Ark had survived. Seeing our brethren frozen in death, seeing the definitive end of such fantasies, brings only pain.

We approach the crash vault as if we are entering a sacred tomb. And why not? To us, it truly is sacred.

The astronauts never found the keypad that would allow entrance to the crash vault and, even had they done so, would have been unable to activate it. I go directly to it, and moments later seven glyphs set into a wall are glowing at me. I tap in the code, and the vault swings open.

Within lie the remains of Sentinel Prime.

Ratchet and I bow our heads, a sign of respect.

How far has the greatest of us journeyed . . . in order finally to come home.

(Were Optimus Prime and Ratchet not so preoccupied with their mission, they might well notice the three Decepticons scuttling across the lunar surface after them. Three animalistic Dreads, hiding behind every outcropping, every ridge. They should certainly be aware that upon their departure from the moon, the Dreads are clinging to the side of the rocket as it takes off, flattening themselves against the hull. But they are not, in fact, aware.)

(It is fortunate indeed that, uncertain of how much Sentinel Prime would weigh, the humans overcompensated for the fuel allowance. Had they not done so, the additional weight of the Decepticons would have caused the Atlax X to burn through its allotment, the ship would have crashed or burned up in the atmosphere, everyone aboard would have died, and events would not have been allowed to play out to their tragic conclusion. But they had, and so they did.)

WASHINGTON, D.C.

i

Sam couldn't take it anymore.

At that point it wasn't the job that was getting on his nerves or the prospect of Carly being swallowed up by Car Museum Boy and becoming yet another acquisition of his.

No, in this instance, as he stood in an elevator at Accuretta, it was the Asian guy who had, for no reason that Sam could determine, slowly morphed into a passive-aggressive stalker. It always seemed to Sam as if the guy were just there all the time, lurking in the corners, hiding in the shadows. But every time Sam would look directly at him, he would scuttle away like a cockroach departing the premises when the lights were turned on.

Apparently, however, matters had come to a head, because the Asian guy was now standing in the elevator with Sam, staring at him. There were several other people in the elevator with them, so obviously nothing was going to happen, but still, this had just gotten ridiculous.

The elevator slid to a halt, and everyone but Sam and his stalker stepped off. Sam was about to follow, but suddenly the guy moved directly into his path and then came to a halt. This had the result of blocking Sam from exiting just long enough for the door to slide shut. The elevator continued on its way.

The stalker turned and for the first time confronted Sam directly. "Mailroom boy! Can't hide from me! Don't respond to my e-mails? I tried friending you on Facebook ten times!"

Sam had no idea what he was talking about. The only e-mails he ever responded to were from family members. He just assumed that every other e-mail he received was from people in South Africa telling him that they wanted to trust him with a delicate financial matter requiring that he provide them with all his banking information. So he just deleted pretty much everything that came in without bothering to read it.

Facebook? He had a Facebook page? People were trying to friend him? He had friends?

"Uh . . ." Sam wasn't remotely sure what to say. "I'm sorry . . . do you work here?"

"Shhh!" The Asian guy put his fingers to his lips. "No names! Not safe! Not here!" Apparently having no grasp of such notions as personal space, he stepped in close to Sam and whispered, "I know you. I know who you are. Spotted you the day you came in for a job interview."

Aw, come on. Just how much crap am I supposed to have to deal with? Not enough that I have a lousy job and some rich guy is giving my girl expensive cars. Now I'm on the radar of some office freak?

Mercifully, the elevator opened again, and Sam managed to shove the guy aside and get into the hallway. He walked quickly down it and didn't even have to look behind to know that the guy was following him, hurrying to keep up.

"No! You're him! Little guy from the news!"

"Little guy? Dude, I'm five-nine! That's like average, okay?"

He ignored Sam's protest. "FBI manhunt. Whole world was looking for you. I got you with aliens. You showed up in the background of six different photos, two continents, with aliens. That was you, in Egypt! Because *you know aliens*!"

He could just as well have smacked Sam in the face with a two-by-four. *That* was why he'd referred to him as a "little guy." Because he'd studied photographs in which Sam was visible alongside the Autobots. Standing next to Optimus Prime, Kareem Abdul-Jabbar would have seemed like a midget.

Sam was so stunned that the guy was able to yank him into the nearest men's room. Belatedly Sam tried to pull away, but the guy was seized with such manic energy that he couldn't do a thing as the guy pushed him back into the handicap stall, which provided the two of them some room, and then bolted the door. Then he faced Sam, who was starting to wonder in a not very good way just how much of a fan of aliens this guy was.

Becoming almost manic in his speech, the guy said, "I'm Wang. Deep . . . Wang."

Okay, that could be taken a lot of ways, none of them the least bit appealing to me. Not that there's anything wrong with that.

Seeing Sam's confused expression, Wang continued, "Deep Wang. Deeeep Wang." He rolled his eyes because of Sam's apparent obliviousness to history. "Deep Throat? Deep Throat?"

"You're a porn star?" Sam was totally lost.

"Don't you know history?" Wang said in mounting frustration. "Went to Ivy League school! Watergate! Deep Throat! I'm talking code to you!"

Actually it was more like gibberish to him, although some of what Wang was talking about was starting to sound vaguely familiar. He'd seen a movie about it with Robert Redford and Dustin Hoffman.

Wang was still going, pointing around ominously. "They watch . . . they listen. Everywhere. Can't go to the government, but you! You can! This shit is going down. It's Code Pink, you hear me?"

"As in breast cancer awareness?"

"As in Floyd! The dark side! Why you think no one's been up there since 1972?"

"Sir, I know you're speaking English, but it's not normal English."

Then, to Sam's alarm, Wang undid the tops of his pants and dropped them around his ankles. *Not good. Not good.*

But Wang reached down and ripped off an interoffice envelope that was taped to his leg. He forced it into Sam's hands. Sam counted himself lucky; there were far worse things Wang could have shoved at him.

"My manifesto!" said Wang. "They're whacking us out! They want us all silenced! Everyone who knows . . . what's on the dark side!"

There was the sound of hinges squeaking. Someone else had entered the men's room.

Wang heard it, glancing nervously in that general direction. His voice barely above a whisper, he said, "Your alien friends are in danger. You know: the good ones. It's up to you."

With that pronouncement, he burst out of the stall, doing up his trousers. Sam stuck his head out and saw to his horror that Bruce was standing near the entrance to the men's room, staring at Wang in confusion. Instinctively, Bruce snapped into a Krav Maga defensive posture, but Wang brushed it aside and, grabbing Brazos by the shirtfront, shoved him up against the wall.

"Yo, dawg! Getting up in my shit?" Wang said, his voice going up an octave. "Who you working for? *Who you working for?*"

When a stunned Bruce wasn't able to provide any immediate response, Wang shoved him aside and bolted from the men's room.

It left Sam and Brazos staring at each other in a moment that would have qualified as the textbook definition of the word "awkward."

The moment extended seemingly to infinity.

Finally . . .

"Bruce," Sam said formally, as if they had simply bumped into each other in the hallway.

"Sam," Bruce replied in a "I really don't want to know" voice.

Sam then practically sprinted out of the men's room. He kept going until he finally made it back to his office, a place he never would have thought in a million years he would be glad to see. It was only upon reaching his desk that he realized he was still holding the envelope that this Wang guy had handed him.

Immediately he dropped it into the garbage can next to his desk. It was the only reasonable thing to do. The guy was obviously some sort of psycho who was fluent not in English but in conspiracy theory.

But still . . .

He knew about the Autobots. Not what they were called, certainly, or their background, but he knew about them. And he had deduced Sam's connection to them. So whatever else the guy was, he sure wasn't stupid. There was a fine line between genius and insanity, and Sam wasn't all that certain where on the tightrope of that divide this guy was standing.

But still . . .

If the Autobots really were in danger . . . if this Wang guy knew something that needed to be conveyed to Optimus and the others . . .

What kind of friend and ally would Sam be if he refused to at least give the guy's concerns a cursory glance? Just out of concern for the safety of the bots.

He reached down and extracted the envelope from the trash can. Undoing the string that kept the interoffice envelope closed, he removed the contents of the "manifesto" and began to study them.

And several words leaped out at him.

"The dark side . . . of the moon?" He knew that that was a misnomer. That the correct term for it was the far side, since it was perpetually facing away from the earth, even though it received just as much sunlight as any other part of that lifeless sphere. Still, there was no denying the exotic sound of it that to a nut job like Wang would have an undeniable appeal.

He looked over the rest of the material, and the longer he did so, the more he was forced to realize there were two possible opposing conclusions to be reached here:

Wang was insane, and no one was in any danger except Wang himself should the men with the butterfly nets get anywhere near him.

Wang was perfectly sane, and everyone was in danger.

There was only one way to find out.

ii

It was one of the few instances in which working in the mailroom proved to be a major plus. Sam had a comprehensive directory to the place at his fingertips. It took him only minutes, operating on the assumption that the guy's name really was Wang, to track him down. There were three guys named Wang working for the company, but checking their bios, two of them were approaching retirement age. Only one seemed to be the right fit, and he wasn't just some random nut job. He was Jerry Wang, vice president of satellite R&D, and he worked over in the aerospace division.

Leaving the pile of unfiled documents on his desk, Sam hurried one floor up, toward the company's executive section. Wang's office, and indeed the entire department in which he worked, couldn't have been more different from the environment in which Sam spent his days. No cramped spaces or cubicles here. Everything was wide open, and the offices—each of which had large windows looking out over Washington—had big, brassy nameplates on the outside. Sam's eyes scanned them quickly, but as it turned out, he didn't need to find it. He heard Jerry's voice before he spotted the office itself, and that drew him right to it.

Jerry was speaking loudly and with obvious concern: "But I did it! I did what you want!"

Sticking his head around the corner of the doorway, Sam saw that every available bit of wall space was occupied by lunar maps. Jerry was standing on the far side (the dark side?) of the office, gesticulating, speaking seemingly to nothing. Was the guy so far gone that he was really ranting to midair?

Sam rested his hand on the door, and it creaked open slightly more. Instantly, Jerry spun to face Sam, and it seemed as if he were repositioning his body to hide something. "You! Why are you bothering me? Can't you see I'm working?" He raised his voice as if he were talking to the back row of a balcony. "You total stranger, lost office bitchboy!"

"But . . ." He frowned. "I'm Sam. Bathroom. We were in the stall together? You pulled out your—"

Jerry jumped as if he'd just been tickled with an electric cattle prod. "We're not boyfriends!" and his voice went even higher. "You lie! One phone call, I'll have you fired! I'm a PhD, VP, R&D, A-OK boy." He pointed at the door. "Knock first!"

Sam blinked, confused. It wasn't just Jerry's crazed attitude, denying that he knew Sam after spending all that time seeking him out; that was bewildering. Even the office setup was strange. He had two computers: one white, one jet-black. Who needed two computers?

"Is something . . . wrong?" Sam said slowly, beginning to have an uncomfortable feeling.

"Never met you, Caucasian orphan child. Leave me be!"

Jerry was leaning with one hand on his desk, and Sam noticed that he seemed to be trying to signal him with his eyes. He was indicating mutely that Sam should look down toward the hand.

Sam did so. At first there didn't seem to be anything odd. His hand was next to the mouse of his black computer.

Then Sam looked closer and thought he could feel his heart stopping.

The mouse had teeth, which were sunk into the fleshy part of Jerry's right hand, which was flat on the desk.

"Uh . . ." Sam gripped the edge of the door frame as the world seemed to tilt under him. "I'll come back." Then he amended that by saying, "Wrong office."

He backed out as quickly as he could and sprinted away. Any remaining doubts that he might have had about Jerry Wang were gone.

There was a Decepticon in Wang's office.

iii

The instant Sam Witwicky was gone, Laserbeak dropped his computer camouflage and resumed his normal state. He leveled his malicious gaze upon Jerry.

Jerry pointed in the direction in which Sam had just fled. "Don't know him! I'd never say anything! I sabotaged the mapping satellite like you told me! I put a blind spot in the program as a bonus. They can't see a thing!" He gulped. "What more do you want from me?"

Laserbeak hissed fiendishly, "Suuuuuu-i-ciiiide . . ." With that, he turned his attention to the white computer and extended his talons. They tapped over the keyboard and the words "I'M SICK OF THIS PLANET. I HATE IT HERE.—JERRY" appeared on the screen.

Seeing it, Jerry sank into his chair as if the air were being slowly released from him.

"Mission abort, moon man," said Laserbeak. "Decepticons no need you anymore."

And suddenly Jerry was back on his feet, and Laserbeak realized belatedly that the human had pulled two pistols out from under his desk. Apparently he had some fight left in him. "Ooooh! What up now, bro?" Jerry said defiantly. "Who wants some chicken dinner? Somebody played with the wrong Wang today!"

The human's amusement value expended itself almost immediately. With a grunt of annoyance, Laserback slapped Jerry, knocking him back into the office chair. He sat there, stunned, and Laserbeak grabbed the chair and sent it crashing into and through the large office window.

"What up? *You* not up," Laserbeak said. "You down. All the way down."

iv

Sam's mind was racing almost as fast as his heartbeat.

Everything Jerry had been saying now made complete sense. It wasn't paranoia if they really were out to get you, and that was clearly the case here. There was no telling how long Decepticons had been watching him or what the hell he had gotten himself into.

Sam knew only two things for sure: One floor above him a man was being menaced by a Decepticon, and he, Sam, had to get word to the Autobots.

Then, as he dashed past a conference room, he heard a distant scream and, to his horror, saw what looked to be Jerry Wang plummeting past the window.

Now he only knew one thing for sure.

He didn't even remember getting back to his office. One moment he was looking out the window of the conference room, and the next he was back at his desk, grabbing his jacket in one hand and the manifesto envelope in the other. He turned to leave and discovered that Bruce, looking extremely agitated, was blocking his path.

"Witwicky! Mission critical! The stall thing . . . forget it. Don't ask, don't tell. We got sticky HR, but weird. Look . . . we had a jumper. That whack job, Wang. I coulda called it. We're all lucky he didn't take more of us with him. So here's the drill. I'm spearheading press. You"—he thumped Sam's chest—"clean up. Wang's everywhere. Get a powerwash team ASAP. Strip his name off his parking space, box his personals, send his kids something nice."

That was when cubicles started to blow up.

v

(*Laserbeak has learned the art of disguise from the master himself: Soundwave. A computer is no longer going to be of any use to him. It is too stationary. Tracking his target to the lower floor, he scans an office copier, and in moments he has assumed the exact shape of the equipment, save that he is black instead of white.*)

(*He makes his way along the wall, making sure to stop every time a human happens to pass by. It isn't in his interest to attract the attention of any Autobots by turning this human place of business into the site of mass slaughter.*)

(*Unfortunately, even Laserbeak has his limits. When an unsuspecting office worker tries to lift his lid and make a copy, Laserbeak's arms extend and he unceremoniously throws the guy against the far wall. Deciding that subterfuge has reached its limits, Laserbeak—still in his disguise but capable of accessing his weapons—starts blasting aside cubicles, clearing the way so that he can get to the human who had been talking to Wang. Because he thought he recognized him, and if the human*) *was who Laserbeak thought he was, this is an opportunity worth seizing.)*

(The human he was seeking spots him just as he draws within range. There is another human standing in front of him, blocking his egress, but the target is looking over the other human's shoulder, and his eyes widen. "Behind you! The copier!" the target shouts, and shoves the other human obstruction out of the way. The former obstruction tumbles over a desk, knocking aside stacks of papers, before ending up crashing into a wall and being buried under all the piles.)

(Upon drawing nearer, Laserbeak's red eyes zoom in on him.)

(It is he.)

(It is Witwicky.)

vi

"You," said Laserbeak. "I know you. Laserbeak never forgets." Then, getting down to business, he snarled, "What did the moon man have to say?"

Sam backed up, then suddenly spun, took several running steps, and threw himself forward like a diver. He landed belly down on a mail cart and hurtled away.

With a roar of fury, tossing aside the last vestiges of subtlety, Laserbeak reverted to his normal appearance, pounding across the floor after the runaway Sam.

He let loose a blast, clipping one of the wheels of the fast-moving cart, and it tumbled over, spilling Sam to the floor. There was a cubicle to his right, and, recovering quickly, Sam darted into it. The cubicles were empty, thanks to most employees running outside to discover what had happened to the late Jerry Wang.

Laserbeak sped around the corner and fired into the cubicle Sam had just entered. He was annoyed and surprised to discover that Witwicky was no longer there;

instead he had clambered upon the desk and over into the next cubicle.

Hoping to cut him off, Laserbeak took the low road, dashing around the cubicle and into the next one. He had Sam cold; the human was standing upon the desk, one foot poised to climb over to the next one.

Sam lashed out with his other foot, kicking the cubicle partition. It wasn't exactly built for such heavy-duty impact. The cubicle wall fell over on top of Laserbeak, sending his blast awry. He tore through the cloth of the partition, but Witwicky was already gone.

All right, then. The high road it was.

Laserbeak leaped up onto the desk and clambered to the top of the cubicle.

But just as he started to climb over it, Sam was suddenly there in front of him, wielding a baseball bat. Laserbeak had just enough time to see an assortment of baseball memorabilia in the cubicle, and then Sam swung the bat with considerable force. It slammed broadside across Laserbeak, sending him flying over the array of cubicles. He crashed through a window at the opposite end. Huge shards of glass fell to the street below. Laserbeak almost went with them, but he managed to snag the sill with one of his claws at the last second.

Hissing and spitting with pure fury, he hauled himself back into the office and charged up the middle aisle. At the far end he saw a door wide open and Sam's baseball bat lying in front of it. Clearly he had dropped it in his panicked flight.

Laserbeak vaulted over the baseball bat and through the door.

He skidded to a halt.

Around him were rows of machinery. He was in the server room.

What there was not was any sign of Witwicky. There

was also not, as near as Laserbeak could tell, another exit from the room.

He spun around toward the way he'd entered and had just enough time to see a quick image of Sam's smiling face as he slammed the heavy door shut from the outside. Sam had never been in there; instead, he'd held the door open, hiding behind it, and waited for Laserbeak to go past.

There was a loud, decisive click of a heavy-duty bolt slamming home. Laserbeak charged the door, crashed into it, and fell back.

"Well, craaaaap," he said.

vii

In Sam's apartment, Carly was doing her level best to ignore Wheelie and Brains as they peered over the counter, watching her every move as she prepared dinner. She supposed she should be grateful. At least they weren't on the ground trying to stare up her dress again or staging another impromptu panty raid in the bedroom.

"It's so frickin' complicated," Wheelie was saying to Brains, although who knew if Brains was listening to a thing he was saying? "I'm still trying to figure it out. The chickens they eat. The monkeys they don't. The cows they eat. The bears they don't. Fish, yes; whales, no. Cats no, rabbits yes. Pigs sometimes, and the dog . . . unfortunately, he's safe. There's no rhyme or reason to it."

Carly sighed, pulled a bowl down from the cabinet overhead, then reached under the sink and got a box of screws. She poured a portion of it into the bowl and set it down on the counter. They immediately started devouring the contents of the bowl. She hoped that this time they would remember to stop eating once they finished the screws. It was annoying having to buy replacement bowls all the time.

"Sure you don't want to run back to your club-house?" she said. That was the term she and Sam used to refer to the structure on the back balcony, since they figured that "doghouse" wasn't going to go over well with them.

"Nah," Wheelie said between bites. "View here's better." He made a bizarre whirring noise, and his eye shuttered in what Carly suspected was an attempt to wink.

He was coming on to her.

She shook her head at the bizarreness of it all. It was like being propositioned by a microwave oven. At least he wasn't humping her leg again as he had when he first met her, calling her "New Warrior Princess." How weird had *that* been?

Suddenly the door to the apartment burst open, and she heard Sam's panicked voice shouting, "Carly, we gotta go! Get in the car! Go!" He appeared at the kitchen door, pale, gasping for breath. "Decepticons! They're back!"

She couldn't believe it. Actually, it wasn't that she *couldn't*. When she had assured Sam that she believed everything he'd told her, she had meant it. But still . . . it had all been in the abstract somehow. It had been so unreal to her. Now, with the potential reality of it staring her square in the face . . .

Wheelie and Brains, as irritating as they could be, were just that: irritating. They weren't vicious. They weren't trying to kill her. They weren't sprouting guns or arm cannons and firing off hundreds of rounds at will. They weren't doing any of the horrific things that Sam had recounted Decepticons as being capable of doing.

And the way they were reacting now—shrieking and making a panicked dash for the door—indicated that they certainly didn't want any piece of their former allies. The transference of their loyalties from Decepticons to humanity probably wouldn't sit too well with . . .

. . . With who? With what? Was Megatron, the creature Sam had described to her in such vivid detail, on his way, ready to step on their home and mash it to pieces?

She looked at Sam, trying to bottle up her rising fear, and suddenly she wanted to scream at him, *Oh, my God, what have you gotten me into?*

Instead she dropped what she was doing and grabbed her bag on the way out, moving almost entirely on autopilot. They dashed to the garage, the entire time Sam muttering, "Please let it work, please let it work," and it was only when he climbed behind the steering wheel that she realized he was referring to his staggeringly unreliable Datsun. Wheelie and Brains were already in the back, jumping up and down, screaming for him to get the useless bucket of bolts in gear, which was certainly somewhat ironic, considering the source.

Then, despite all odds, the engine roared to life. Apparently the fixes that her boss had made to it had held. Sam backed the Datsun up out of the garage, turned to Carly, and looked at her expectantly.

And she thought, *Wait? Why am I running? These creatures may be coming for him and for the two little freaks, but not me. They don't know me. I wasn't part of their war or any of the insane things that Sam was involved in. That was years ago, before I came on the scene. The apartment may not be safe, but Sam . . . he's going to be a magnet for them. Wherever he goes, sooner or later they're going to show up, and if I'm anywhere nearby, I'm going to wind up collateral damage. I didn't sign up for that. I should go on foot to a nice hotel or maybe stay with friends. I don't . . . I can't . . .*

All of that went through her head in mere seconds.

She looked at Sam, and something seemed to pass behind his eyes. Wheelie was still babbling while Brains was making squealing noises, and Sam said sharply to them, "Shut up. Both of you." Then he shifted his gaze back to Carly and said, "Do you have someone you can stay with?"

She blinked. "What?"

"They'll come looking for me, not you. They don't know anything about you. It's safer for you if it stays that way. Just keep your head down, okay?"

"She's not coming?" said Wheelie.

"No. That would be stupid," he said firmly. "Carly, no time for a whole big goodbye thing. Just go. Hurry." Either he felt nothing or he was forcing himself to turn off all his emotion for her sake.

He started to back up.

Carly ran alongside, yanked on the passenger side door, and pulled it open. She clambered in as Sam said in confusion, "What're you—?"

"I'm a big girl, Sam. I can make my own decisions. I don't need you making them for me. Just shut up and drive," she said.

"No way," he said firmly. "No way in hell."

She looked at him challengingly and said the one thing she knew would work: "Dylan wouldn't leave me behind."

He stared at her. Then he slammed it into reverse as he said, "Dirty pool, Carly. That's dirty pool."

"I thought you liked it when she did stuff that was dirty," said Wheelie.

"Shut up!" they shouted in unison, and Wheelie withdrew and sank onto the floor of the back of the car.

VIRGINIA

i

Sam gave Carly a quick rundown on what had happened at the office even as he drove as if his life depended on it. She gasped when she heard of the death of Jerry Wang and was visibly trembling when he described to her the lethal game of tag he'd had with a Decepticon.

"Laserbeak," said Wheelie. "Nasty customer even for one of us . . . I mean, one of them. You're lucky you didn't end up in eight separate pieces, scattered all over the—"

"We really need less talking from you," Carly said sharply, and he withdrew once again.

Sam steered the Datsun onto I-66 West and opened her up, praying that the engine wouldn't stall out in protest. "Look, Carly, it's not too late to—"

"You're not dropping me off anywhere," she interrupted. "I'm not bailing on you, okay? I'm not bailing. I'm not leaving you. I'm not . . ." She hesitated and then said, "I'm not *her*. Okay? You understand?"

Sam caught his breath. Then he let it out slowly and said, "Yeah. I understand."

"Good. So what's the plan? I mean, there is a plan, right?" she said in a hopeful voice. "Something beyond 'Mother of God, the Decepticons are coming, let's get the hell out of here.' "

"Yeah. There's a plan. We're going to the HQ for NEST."

"Who?"

"NEST stands for Nonbiological Extraterrestrial Species Treaty. It's a military alliance that was created to handle . . . stuff like this. They're just outside D.C."

"Okay." She nodded. "So if, or when, these creatures show up in force, it won't be a lot of people running around screaming and all manner of things blowing sky high. There's actually contingency plans in place to deal with it."

"Lots of plans, yes."

She visibly relaxed. "Good."

Sam paused and then added, "But in the interest of full disclosure, the odds are pretty good that there will also be a lot of people running around screaming and all manner of things blowing sky high."

She tensed up again.

ii

Minutes later, when the car rolled up to a rather mundane-looking gated facility, Carly started to wonder if this wasn't all some sort of joke. Or worse: Maybe he was trying to make himself look like a dynamic man of action, bringing her along on an adventure, so that he wouldn't feel so threatened by Dylan. Because she had a definite idea of what a military base should look like, having been to quite a few in her time. And this most definitely was not it.

Sam barely managed to get the car to screech to a halt just short of crashing into the gates. Two guards immediately emerged, their weapons half raised.

Sam hurriedly rolled the window down. "Open the gate! We've gotta talk to Colonel Lennox! We're reporting a Decepticon! The Decepticons are back!"

"Sam, where are we?" she said nervously.

One of the guards, looking not the least in the mood for an elaborate prank being staged by a jealous boyfriend, said warningly, "Sir, this is Health and Human Services—"

"Right, packing M4s; don't give me that. Lemme talk to Optimus," Sam said.

"Sir, you've made some mistake," the other guard said. "Step from the vehicle, please."

Carly really didn't like the way this was shaping up. She hated the thoughts going through her head. She despised the notion that it would even occur to her that Sam was staging this whole business just to try to add some excitement to his crushingly mundane life. But the thing she liked least of all was the idea of being arrested while trying to assault the department of Health and Human Services. Hell, these days you risked being detained just by attempting to board an airplane if you happened to have a four-ounce container of Liquid Prell in your bag. Who knew what they'd do to you if you tried to crash security in an actual government building? And what was her defense going to be? Her boyfriend thought there were giant robots in there? She might never be heard from again.

"Sam," she said, trying to keep the lack of confidence out of her tone. "Are you sure you're at the right place?"

"Trust me," he said, and then turned back to the guard. "I'm Sam Witwicky. Don't you know who I am?"

"Sir, if you don't have the right paperwork, we don't care if you're the president's daughter," said the guard. "You're not getting by on our watch."

"What part of 'Decepticons are back' do you not understand?" At which point, thoroughly out of patience, Sam hit the gas and sped forward.

He didn't get very far as fortified roadblocks—the type designed to prevent car bombs from approaching buildings—snapped into place to halt his advance. They came up both in front of him and behind, sandwiching him in place.

Abruptly alarms started blaring, and Carly was sure that they were connected to some sort of security breach alert. As it turned out, she wasn't entirely wrong.

"We've got an Energon reading!" one of the guards shouted.

All attempts at politeness vanished from the nearer guard. "Get out of the car! Now!"

They didn't wait for Sam and Carly to comply. As other guards came charging out of the darkness of the evening, the first two yanked the doors open and bodily pulled the two young people out of the Datsun. One of the guards peered in through the back window. Wheelie was shaking so hard that Carly could hear the metal of his body clattering. Brains was busy chewing on the buckle of one of the seat belts.

"Got aliens inside the vehicle!"

"Freeze! One move and you're dead!"

Sam tried to shout above the rising ruckus. "Just tell Bumblebee! Is Bee in there?" The guard who was busy pushing him to the ground had his radio out, informing unseen persons what was transpiring, and Sam tossed off a shout into the radio: "Anyone hear me? This is Sam Witwicky!"

Then Sam grunted as they wrestled him to the ground. They hadn't done so with Carly since she had offered no resistance, but they were keeping her arms pinned behind her so forcefully that she was afraid they were going to wrench them out of the sockets. Sam, meanwhile, was still struggling as fiercely as he could. One of the soldiers had his knee firmly in his back to immobilize him while another was pulling out zip ties from his belt to bind his wrists.

The gates burst open, and a tall yellow robot stepped into view. He pushed the guards aside as gently as he could, but for him "gently" was a relative term, and the guards went flying even at his lightest touch. The robot ignored them and instead put out his hand so that Sam could haul himself to his feet. The remaining guards stepped back, forming a semicircle, but none dared come near Sam as the robot loomed over him protectively. Then the robot cast a single glance toward the soldiers who were still holding Carly. Immediately they got the message, silent as it was, and released her.

She should have known. She really should have known, and inwardly she berated herself for doubting Sam even for an instant.

Carly couldn't help herself. Even after all this time, she gaped at the behemoth because it just wasn't easy getting used to it. "Hello, Bumblebee," she said. "Long time, no see."

Sam wasn't quite so convivial. It was humiliating being knocked around like that, plus considering all that he had accomplished, it certainly didn't seem the proper treatment for a hero. Brushing off the dirt from his chest and shoulders, he said scoldingly to the Autobot, "What's with you, huh? I know your black ops stuff's important, but we never see you anymore. You can't even spend one night in the garage? Just hang?"

Bumblebee continued to be the least verbal of the Autobots, his vocal apparatus having never fully recovered from having been damaged in battle. Typically, when he did endeavor to communicate, it was either with indecipherable squawks or through his radio. Now, though, he just looked sullen and apologetic, staring at the ground rather than directly at Sam. Carly wasn't sure, but it looked like he was scuffling one of his feet.

Sam picked up easily on the visual cues but wasn't the least mollified. "Yeah, I hope you feel bad! You *should* feel bad. Look at this thing I'm driving now," and he pointed at the Datsun. "I feel bad every day."

Through the open gates came running another soldier, one who, by the way the others reacted, was clearly in charge. "Stand down, everybody stand down," he called out somewhat unnecessarily since no one was aiming a rifle at Sam any longer or trying to slam him around. Then he approached the two civilians. "Sam? And . . . ?" He paused and then came up with, "Carly?"

"Have we met?" she said, confused.

"Colonel Lennox." He shook her hand briskly. "No, we haven't. But you're in Sam's file. Also, Bumblebee's mentioned you."

"Has he?"

Bumblebee's radio suddenly switched on. There was a brief crunch of static, and then Joe Cocker's voice filled the night air, crooning, "*You are so . . . beautiful . . .*"

She smiled. "Flatterer."

"Fine, fine, all is forgiven, you big lug nut," said Sam. Then, looking around, he called out, "Okay, so . . . everybody raise your hand if a flying psycho-ninja copier tried to kill you today." He held up his hand and waited. "No? Me? Only me?" Then, having proved his point, he flipped the envelope to Lennox. "Okay, G.I. Joe, let's go somewhere a little more private so that we don't have to talk about the end of the world while standing in the middle of the street."

iii

Charlotte Mearing, the director of national intelligence, was her typical icy-calm self. Once upon a time, she had had to concentrate on controlling every aspect of her demeanor so as to appear utterly unflappable. She'd learned her lesson the one time, while training in Quantico, when she'd attended a party, let her hair down, and wound up in a romantic entanglement with another spy in training. It had been short, intense, passionate—and by any measure a total disaster. She'd ended it before it could derail her focus and clamped down her emotions for good. By this point in her career, it had become so second nature that she was beginning to wonder whether she was professionally detached or if she had just stopped feeling anything at all.

She certainly knew that she was amused by the astounded looks on the faces of various top army brass, aides, key politicians, and the like. They were standing on one of the upper catwalks of NEST's main facility room. It was cavernous, ringed with observation windows and various rampways enabling scientists and technicians to reach the highest points. The NEST emblem—a circle with a skull in the middle and three protruding triangles, each of which had a lightning bolt embedded in it—adorned a vault door at the far end. The door was partway open, and five pillars—one of them longer than the others and all of them covered with cryptic alien symbols—were being loaded into it.

Of particular interest to everyone watching, however, was the central figure. It was a gigantic Autobot, larger even than Optimus Prime. It was mostly silver but had red trim laced throughout its body. It was suspended on huge girders that almost resembled a throne.

A voice sounded over the public address system, warning loudly, "We are ten minutes to attempted contact. All NEST officials, clear the floor."

Mearing was in the middle of bringing the observers up to speed. Referring to the pillars, she said, "It's some kind of Autobot technology. They say he was the Robert Oppenheimer of their civilization. We're locking them up until we understand more . . ."

Her voice trailed off. She couldn't quite believe what she was seeing.

"I'll be right back," she told the group, keeping her tone as casual as ever. She walked quickly away from them and toward the three people who had caught her attention.

One of them was Lennox. Seeing him around there wasn't particularly unusual. Seeing the other people he was talking to—a young man and woman, presumably a couple since she had her arm looped through his—was, however, unusual. Also a problem. The kind of problem that could wind up with certain people in jail.

As she drew closer, she recognized the young man, although not the woman. But it didn't matter who they were. They sure as hell were not supposed to be here.

Lennox was staring at some sorts of papers that the young man had handed him. "Excuse me," she said sharply, interrupting their conversation. "What's going on?"

The young woman glanced her way, but the young man ignored her, apparently feeling it more imperative to continue whatever narrative he was in the middle of than to acknowledge her presence. That was a dangerous move on his part. "He recognized me," he said to Lennox. "Said I need to warn you. Something about the dark side of the moon."

"Honey," said the young woman, "it's called the far side, actually."

"Yeah, I know." He looked mildly annoyed at the correction.

"He mentioned the moon?" Lennox said, unable to hide his concern. The man continued to have no poker face at all.

The young woman spoke up again. "But why would Decepticons want to kill humans? I thought their war was with the Autobots."

"I'd say they're after what we just found," Lennox said.

Mearing considered grabbing one of the guard's guns and shooting all three of them. It would be really easy.

They weren't even moving. The cold fury of security breach burning behind her eyes, she said sharply, "Excuse me, Colonel Lennox!"

Lennox turned and said, "Director Mearing, this is Sam Witwicky. He's the civilian who—"

"I know his name, Colonel. I want to know who gave him clearance."

"How about Optimus Prime when he landed in suburbia looking for my house?" Sam snapped back at her.

Her lips thinned, making her look like a bespectacled piranha. "Disrespect of a federal officer. Hmm. Maybe that'll get you somewhere." She turned her attention to the young woman. "And who's this?"

"Carly, my girlfriend," said Sam.

She stared blankly at the two of them. "Which makes this . . . what? A date?"

Apparently this Carly was no more easily intimidated than her boyfriend. "Let's see," she said with a toss of her hair. "I was home, cooking dinner. Normal night. Next thing I know there's ten machine guns to my head."

"Carly knows all about the Autobots, Director," said Lennox "I can vouch for her."

"Well, thank you, Colonel," she said, dripping with sarcasm. "Now let's find someone to vouch for *you*."

Sam Witwicky actually made the ill-advised move of stepping right up to Mearing and practically snarling in her face. "How 'bout we talk about the Decepticon that tried to murder me today?"

Mearing fired a look at Lennox that quite clearly said, *Rein him in. Now.*

Lennox gently but firmly pulled on Sam's shoulder, withdrawing him a few critical inches away form Mearing. "Um, Sam," he said in a low, warning voice, "This is the U.S. intelligence director. She can authorize bad things to happen for the rest of your life."

"Well, that sounds illegal," Sam said defiantly.

"Do tell," said Mearing.

For a long moment he met her gaze and then wisely lowered his.

First smart thing he's done, she thought.

Lennox, meanwhile, handed over the collection of papers and photographs that he'd been poring over. "A software engineer at Sam's office was murdered. He was involved with NASA's moon mapping probe."

"Are we trusting national security to teenagers?" she said icily. "Did I miss a policy paper? Are we doing that now?" She let that hang there for a moment and then turned the full force of her patriotic indignation on Sam Witwicky. "I don't care who you are or what you've ever done for your country. You speak a word about what you see in here, you will do time for treason. Do you understand?"

Without backing down in the slightest, Sam said, "I'll take my orders from the Autobots, thanks. I know them. I don't know you."

She brought her face toward him, looking him squarely in the eye. "You will," she said intensely. Then she turned away from him, thinking, *I have got to brush up on my patriotic indignation skills.*

iv

Sam put his hands to his ears as the Klaxon blared throughout the cavernous facility and spotlights were brought up to illuminate the girder throne far below. The huge vault at the far end had been closed, and the ominous skull emblem of NEST glowered at the proceedings.

Carly and he had been escorted to the observation deck on the east side of the chamber. There were armed soldiers all around, although Sam suspected they had been assigned there by Mearing mostly to make a point.

No one really thought that either he or Carly presented any sort of danger. Hell, Sam Witwicky was the first friend that the Autobots had developed when they arrived on Earth a few years back. If he couldn't be trusted to care about their best interests, who could?

Mearing had been all for taking the two of them to a holding facility until they could be thoroughly debriefed. But Lennox had advocated that they be allowed to watch the process, arguing that when it came to the business of the Autobots, a well-informed Sam Witwicky was simply of more value to them than one who was being kept in the dark. Meanwhile, Sam had said he had no intention of allowing Carly to be escorted away, and so after some extended back-and-forth and Mearing ultimately declaring that she had no more time to waste on this, the two young people had been escorted to their current location, where they watched in rapt amazement.

Just when I think they have no more surprises up their mechanical sleeves, Sam thought.

"Optimus," Lennox said over his communication device. "Authorized to attempt contact."

Moments later, a blue and red truck came rolling in. Sam couldn't help smiling. He had never asked for any of this craziness his life had become. Never asked for Prime and his army of Autobots to drop into the middle of his utterly normal existence and stand it on its end. Certainly he'd never asked to be thrust into positions where his life was in constant peril.

Yet for all of that . . .

Damn. It was good to see him again.

The truck slowed to a halt and then began to shift and rearrange itself. In short order, Optimus Prime stood at his full height. Getting down to business, his chest compartment opened to reveal a glowing energy ball encased in what looked like a spherical metal cage. It was inset into a holder that was vaguely diamond-shaped, except either side of it was flared and extended. Overall it had the appearance of a great winged creature with the tip of one wing pointing up and the other down.

"That's the Matrix of Leadership," Lennox informed Mearing, who nodded slowly. "Optimus holds the only thing in the universe that could ever repower them."

"Sentinel Prime," came the deep voice of Optimus, "we bid your return."

Optimus Prime then plunged the Matrix into the chest of Sentinel Prime. Sam felt a rush of déjà vu, for it was in a similar manner that he had once restored Optimus himself to life.

The effect was instantaneous. A pulse of pure energy surged through the being called Sentinel Prime. His back arched, and his head tilted toward the ceiling. And then he cried out in pain and primal rage.

It quickly became evident that his warrior instincts had not dimmed with the passage of time. Apparently, his last memory was of being attacked, and that carried over into the way he came out of his lengthy "death." Barely had he become reenergized than he lunged from his makeshift throne, grabbed Optimus, and threw him to the ground. When Optimus's body struck, it unleashed a clang so loud in the enclosed space that to Sam it was like standing with his head inside the bells of Notre Dame cathedral while they were chiming.

Even as Sentinel Prime immobilized Optimus, his forearm extended into a deadly blade pointed directly at Optimus's Spark chamber.

NEST soldiers all around the room immediately brought their weapons up, but they were uncertain as to how to proceed. Optimus Prime was vulnerable, and Sentinel Prime's capabilities were unknown. When the bullets started flying, they might well end up killing Optimus while simply pissing off Sentinel.

Obviously that was what Lennox was thinking, because he threw his arms wide and shouted, "Hold your fire! Hold your fire! Leave it to Optimus!"

Leave it to Optimus. Worst name for a robot sitcom ever, Sam thought bleakly, trying to fight down the overwhelming sense of fear that he was about to witness his great friend's death yet again . . . and quite possibly forever this time.

And then, the picture of calm, Optimus said, "Sentinel, it is I."

Slowly, very slowly, the words seemed to penetrate the haze of fury that had fallen upon Sentinel. Lowering his sword arm, he started looking around the room. Other Autobots were now gathering, regarding him with reverence and awe.

"The Ark," said Sentinel Prime, putting his hand to his head. Each word was heavy, thick, as if he were relearning how to speak. "It was . . . spinning . . . out of control . . ."

"Yes," said Optimus. "You were crippled by Starscream."

"I locked myself . . . within the crash vault. I did not know . . . if I would ever look upon one of my kind again."

"We are here," said Optimus. "You are safe. I feared the damage would be too catastrophic to revive you. I should have known better."

As one, Optimus, Ironhide, and the other Autobots all genuflected, dropping to one knee in deference to their fallen leader, returned to them long after all hope had been lost.

Sentinel nodded slowly. "The war . . . ?"

"The war was lost," Optimus said.

"And Cybertron? Our home?"

Sam's heart went out to Optimus. He knew that even though the loss was ancient by any human standards, to

Optimus Prime the fate of his world was like an open wound.

"It was left a barren wasteland," he said heavily, "under Decepticon control. It is dying . . . like its whole galaxy. A small band of us have taken refuge here on planet Earth. We have formed an alliance with its human race."

Sentinel tapped his chest and looked momentarily puzzled. "Is this their language I am speaking?"

"One of their languages. It is called English," Optimus said. "Acquired through this world's computer network and imparted by me into you when I brought you back."

The elder Autobot warrior considered all that he had heard, processing it. And then he said gravely, "Stand, young Optimus."

Not young anymore, Sam thought, *but it's all relative, I guess.*

Optimus Prime did as he was instructed, getting to his feet and facing his mentor.

When he spoke, it was like a benediction. "You are, and always have been, the bravest warrior I have ever known."

Sam's heart swelled with pride on behalf of his friend.

Then Sentinel's concerns shifted to another priority. "In my escape . . . the ship was damaged . . ."

Optimus anticipated what his mentor was going to say. "You saved five pillars, Sentinel."

"Only five." Sadly he said, "Once . . . we had hundreds."

"Autobots!"

It was Mearing, calling down to them imperiously from the gantry. Sam winced at her tone of voice. Where did she get off complaining about lack of respect being paid to her when she was speaking to beings that were old beyond anything that walked the earth? To say nothing of the fact that she was apparently immune to the pure drama she was witnessing.

Not knowing what Sam was thinking and probably not caring if she had known, Mearing continued. "What is this technology you were trying to save?"

Secretly Sam was hoping that Sentinel would slap her down for her attitude. But apparently he was far too gracious a guest to do that. "Together, the pillars form a space bridge. I designed it, and," he said with a touch of pride, "I alone can control it. It defies the laws of physics to transport matter through time and space. It was to be our key to winning the war."

Anyone else might have appeared thunderstruck by what Sentinel was saying. Mearing raised an eyebrow, which was apparently as demonstrative as she allowed herself to be. "You're talking about a teleportation device."

Beam me up, Scotty, Sam thought.

"For resources," Optimus spoke up. "Refugees—"

"Or soldiers," Mearing immediately said. "Weapons. Bombs. A means of instant strike. That's the military function, isn't it?"

Sam immediately recalled something his grandfather had always said: *To a carpenter with a hammer, the whole world looks like a nail.* Mearing was someone obsessed with security concerns, with trying to figure out the next way terrorists were going to strike. So naturally, when presented with something as benign as a means of transportation, she immediately started thinking about military applications. It was the kind of moment when Sam felt embarrassed to be a human.

Sentinel tilted his head, regarding Mearing with what amounted to polite confusion. It was as if he couldn't quite fathom how her mind was working. "If my ship had escaped," he said, as if it should have been obvious, "we could have shipped all Autobots to a safe haven."

Then, with a touch of impatience, he added, "It is our technology. And it must be returned."

Mearing didn't seem the least bit inclined to accommodate him. "Yes. When the human race says so. You don't just bring WMDs into our atmosphere. Kinda have to clear customs first. Little formality, paperwork. Separates us from the animals. Oh," she added, "and I wouldn't try to penetrate the safe yourself if I were you. If it's not opened by the proper authorities, such as myself, it has fail-safes inside that will permanently damage the contents. It's for your protection, of course. Just to make sure they don't fall into enemy hands."

Sentinel Prime took this in for a moment and then turned to his protégé. "These 'humans' . . . we call them *allies*?"

Sam groaned. He felt mortified on behalf of his entire race.

But then his great and good friend Optimus Prime stuck up for humanity in a way Sam wasn't entirely sure it deserved.

Without hesitation, Optimus said, "We have fought as one, Sentinel. I would trust them with my life."

There were proud exchanges of looks between the soldiers and Lennox, Carly, and Sam. The only one who didn't look as if she cared was Mearing, who remained as dispassionate as ever.

"Then I am grateful for your alliance," said Sentinel. "But hear me and mark my words: The Decepticons must never know the space bridge is here. For in their hands"—and he was now addressing not Optimus but all the humans in the facility—"it would mean the end of your world."

v

(On the outskirts of Washington, D.C., three Dreads, Crankcase, Crowbar, and Hatchet—the creatures who

*had been skittering around the surface of the moon not
all that long ago—watch in respectful silence as a rusted
oil tanker pulls up on squealing wheels. They bow, and
the foremost of them says, "Lord Megatron, your forces
are assembled and ready.")*

*(There is a pause. These days it takes Megatron a few
moments just to gather enough strength to speak. Finally, he does: "Then upon my command . . . we
strike.")*

vi

Mearing's office in NEST headquarters was cluttered
with boxes that had unique labels, broad enough that
they would give no details to anyone wandering in but
specific enough that Mearing would remember what the
contents of each and every container was.

At that moment, Sam was standing between two of
them, one of which was labeled BAD SHIT and the other
SCARY STUFF. Sam supposed that it was appropriate he
was there: Certainly he'd run from the latter enough
times to find himself landing heavily in the former. Carly
was directly behind him.

He was trying to get up a head of steam in dealing
with Mearing, but she wasn't giving him any sort of opportunity, cutting him off repeatedly before he could get
started.

"What I'm trying to say—" he began again.

She didn't acknowledge that he was even saying anything. "An investigation's been opened. We've sent
agents to your office. You'll be notified if we need anything more."

"And if the Decepticons come after me again?"

"For the time being, we'll be sending you home with
Autobot protection."

In immediate response, Wheelie and Brains jumped up
on her desk and began gyrating about as if they were on

a dance floor. Sam hadn't even realized they were there. Obviously Mearing hadn't, either, because she was glaring at them.

"Whoo hooo! The gang is back together!" Wheelie crowed. "Bumblebee back in da house!"

Sam had seen many strange things in his life, but a robot talking like he just wandered in from the hood was undoubtedly right up there.

Without a word, Mearing pulled out a gun from her top desk drawer and put the barrel to Wheelie's head. "Please take your toys off my desk," she said to Sam.

Wheelie and Brains immediately vacated her desk. Sam mentally kicked himself. If he'd known that was all he had to do to get their cooperation, he'd have visited a gun store long ago. Then he turned his attention back to Mearing. "Look, you don't get it. Where there's one human involved, there could be more. Who knows how many humans have been pulled into this Decepticon plot? There could be—I dunno—a whole network that's—"

"Conspiracy theories?" She looked at him pityingly. "That's what we've got now? Conspiracy theories of people working with alien invaders to pave the way for their incursion? Please try to keep these nonsensical notions to yourself on the way out."

"So that's it? We're just being sent home?"

Carly sounded a bit confused by his reaction. "What's wrong with home?"

He looked at her in surprise, trying to hide his feelings. *I'd have thought that you would be on my side. How can you not get it?* Then he turned back to Mearing. "Who do I have to meet with to get you guys to understand? I can help you here. I can contribute! What, am I just supposed to go back to 'work'? Are you aware," he asked, leaning his hands on her desk, "that I applied for a job here?"

She tapped the barrel of the gun on her desk impatiently. Sam promptly removed his hands from it. Casually she dropped the gun back into the drawer and said, "I am. Denied your application myself. This unit is for veteran intelligence officers and special forces. Not for boys who once owned 'special cars.'"

Sam felt gut punched, being dismissed so casually. For a moment he was at a loss for words. And Carly instantly earned his love all over again when she said, "Well, that's not quite fair, ma'am."

Mearing stiffened. "Do *not* call me 'ma'am.' I am not a 'ma'am.'"

Carly seemed taken aback and then, sounding very suspicious, said, "You *are* a woman, aren't you?"

"Oh, I get it," Sam said immediately. "She's actually one of our brave fighting men. And he's just, y' know, working out some issues. Don't worry, sir," he went on, "nobody is questioning your valor just because this is how you're dealing with your inner femininity. I bet you have a medal. Do you have a medal? Can I see your medals?"

Mearing did not appear the least bit amused. Instead she pointed behind Sam. He turned, and his face fell as he saw a cluttered shelf on the wall next to the door. It was overcrowded with medals.

"You break my chain of command," Mearing said icily. "There's nothing complicated about it. No one works with the Autobots who's not approved by me."

There was the sound of heavy footfalls at the door, and it was pushed open. Soldiers were standing there with the obvious intention of escorting them out.

Trying to put the best spin on the situation, Carly said to her boyfriend, "Sam, you *have* done what you came for."

"Yeah, but there's so much more I can—"

"With all due respect, young man" Mearing said, not

sounding as if she were offering the slightest shred of respect to him, "you're not a soldier. You're a messenger. You've always been a messenger. And once more, your government thanks you . . . for delivering the mail."

He wanted to leap across the desk and slug her.

He wanted to crawl into a corner and die.

Ultimately he did neither. He simply stood there, unresponsive, until the soldiers entered and firmly escorted both him and Carly out the door.

CANADA

In the more northern regions of this continent, we roll through a scenic overpass, through the twisting roads of the mountains, higher and higher toward a place where the snow never melts but instead sits atop the peaks, permanent and glistening and white.

In our camouflaged forms, we reach an overlook and park as innocently as any Earth vehicle would. Yet we might well draw attention were any humans about. I might well not, for my disguise as an Earth truck is ubiquitous. Sentinel, however, has chosen the form of what humans call a fire engine. It is a vehicle dedicated to protection. It was a natural choice for him, although more inclined to acquire notice in such out-of-the-way places as this.

A vast glacier stretches out before us in the distance. After a few moments to verify that we are alone, we shed our disguises and assume our natural states.

We stand quietly for a moment, my mentor and I, taking in the majesty of what we are seeing. Despite our size, despite our power, in this instance we feel . . .

. . . small.

"This planet Earth you have shown me," Sentinel Prime says to me. "I remember when Cybertron was once this beautiful."

I can no longer keep in the truth that has plagued me all these centuries. I must speak the guilt that I have carried, the knowledge that matters could have, should *have, gone very differently on my home world if the right Autobot had been there to accomplish what was necessary. "It should have been me aboard that ship. If you had stayed to lead the fight—"*

"No," Sentinel says immediately. "The decision was mine. We sought a safe haven for our Autobots. And here"—he gestures around—"you have found it."

I do not know that I necessarily agree, but I know my mentor all too well. He will not change his opinion or assign blame. Nevertheless, what is right is right. My chest cavity opens, and I remove the Matrix of Leadership from it. I extend it to him, holding it with the reverence it deserves. "You led us on Cybertron, Sentinel. Let the Matrix be yours . . . to lead us again."

Sentinel makes no move to take it. "And how could I ever lead you? In a world I do not know?" He stares at it for a moment longer and then waves it off. "No, I am no longer your teacher, Optimus Prime. Now you are mine."

His words fill me with both pride and a sense of responsibility greater than I have ever known. I replace the Matrix within me and, for the first time since Sentinel has returned, genuinely feel that I am worthy of it.

Meantime, Sentinel surveys the sky with a noble but darkening look.

"And while I share your faith in these humans," he says, greatly troubled, "there is something about them that I . . . fear."

I am stunned to hear him say this. In my mind, no matter what he says, I am still merely the student, and my reverence for him is unparalleled. Sentinel is the bravest of us all. To hear him speak so . . .

. . . it prompts me to start to see humanity in a different light.

It is not a light that I like.

"*Optimus, if it is acceptable to you, I would like some time to myself.*"

I hesitate. "*I would never question your wisdom, Sentinel, but—*"

"*Perhaps it is possible that your affection for these humans stems from your encountering them on your own terms and on an individual basis. It is my desire to spend some time encountering them on my own without those encounters being filtered through your eyes, if you understand my meaning.*"

"*You wish me not to follow you about, making apologies for them.*"

"*Something like that,*" Sentinel says, sounding faintly amused.

"*But there remains danger to you, Sentinel. The Decepticons have returned, as you know.*"

"*Are you suggesting that I curtail my wishes, plan my life around fears of what the Decepticons may or may not do?*"

"*Of course not, Sentinel.*"

He regards me with patience and forbearance. "*Fear not, Optimus; if danger presents itself, I will inform you. And I will leave my beacon activated so that any Autobot can locate me in time of difficulty. Will that satisfy you?*"

"*If it pleases you, Sentinel, it pleases me.*"

"*A kind sentiment, Optimus, although the fact is that no matter what alliances you may have formed with the natives, we remain strangers in a strange land, and I am not sure that anything will please me anymore.*"

With that discouraging thought, my teacher, my mentor, Sentinel Prime, reverts to the shape of a fire truck.

Moments later, I am alone, and I have never felt more that way in my existence.

WASHINGTON, D.C.

i

You did what you came for.

Those were the words Carly had spoken that kept whirling around in Sam's brain as he lay in bed at night, staring up at the ceiling.

He should have been happy, happier than he'd been in a long time. He'd seen his old friends, albeit mostly from a distance. He'd witnessed a monumentally historic moment in the lives of the Autobots. And Bumblebee was, as Wheelie had put it, back in da house. Well, da backyard, more precisely. Technically, the lawn didn't belong to him but to another tenant in the apartment house, which was why he kept the doghouse on the balcony. Still, the tenant didn't have the nerve to object when the giant yellow robot was walking around, being watchful and standing guard. Besides, as Carly pointed out, they suddenly had the safest residence in the neighborhood. Who was going to try to burglarize the place when there was a giant yellow robot keeping an eye on things?

Yet Sam was more frustrated than ever.

Because he *had* done what he had come to do. And that was the point. That was the whole freaking point.

For the first time in what seemed ages, he'd had a purpose. A goal. He was doing something that he cared passionately about. He had a mission.

And yes, he'd accomplished it, but now he wanted another mission. Something that would be on par with the sort of earthshaking—literally—endeavors that had characterized his life over the past few years. He wanted to do something that would mean something to somebody . . .

That would mean something to *him*.

Instead he had been cast aside, cast out, and was now once again swimming in the sea of aimlessness that was his life. Chased away by that brittle-sounding woman who had systematically demolished him by hitting him with the one thing against which he had no defense:

The awful truth.

Finally giving up on sleep, he rolled out of bed, bare-chested and wearing pajama pants, moving quietly so as not to disturb Carly. He needn't have been concerned; she was sleeping deeply, not remotely filled with the sorts of concerns that were keeping him awake.

He padded across the floor and to the balcony, where Buster was sleeping while Brains and Wheelie were perched on the railing. Bumblebee was in the backyard, and he tossed off a salute. Apparently he'd picked up a few things from hanging out with soldiers all the time. Sam returned the salute. It felt good.

Brains was pointing at the sky and saying, "Ten million, six hundred four thousand and eighty-one . . ."

"What are you guys doing?" Sam asked.

Wheelie said, "The usual. Counting stars."

"I can't sleep. Can you sleep?"

"We don't sleep."

Sam stared up at the stars. In his imagination, several of them were coming together to form an outline of Mearing's face, looking down at him mockingly. "She called me a messenger, Wheelie. You believe that? After everything I've done? How dare she—" His voice filling with emotion, he said, "It was my destiny. The Primes told me so. My destiny to be there for the Autobots. Not hers, no matter how many medals she's got gathering dust. Where the hell did she get off—?"

"I tell you, Sammy, we feel the same way. The disrespect on this rock is criminal."

As absurd as it sounded, hearing that from the robot was oddly comforting. Carly couldn't understand how frustrated he was, but this stupid little pile of bolts was totally sympathetic to his difficulties.

He glanced toward the bedroom and then lowered his voice to a near whisper. "Then how 'bout we do something about it?"

Bumblebee was looking at him with open curiosity. Sam gestured for him to draw closer, and the Autobot obediently leaned forward. Conspiratorially, Sam said, "Bee, I want to know why they're killing humans. If they're after me, I want answers. And I say we call in an expert.

ii

Seymour Simmons, formerly an agent in the employ of Sector Seven, had a burst of realization: He didn't have to put up with this crap, especially this early in the freaking morning.

The obnoxious host of an equally obnoxious syndicated TV program was a guest in his house. *His* house. *Casa Simmons*. But he sure as hell wasn't acting like a guest.

Instead, with the cameraman practically shoving the damned lens down Seymour's throat, the host was leaning forward intensely across the kitchen table and saying, "And what do you say to the claims that you vastly overinflated the importance of your role in the battles between giant alien robots on this world? That you're just some guy who got fired by his government and wound up running a restaurant while living with your mother."

"She lived with me. Big difference," he said heatedly, "and now that I got her her own guest house, I hardly even see her."

The obnoxious host continued relentlessly. "That you are, in fact, not a hero but merely an opportunist who's just trying to cash in on his minimal involvement with—"

Simmons snapped forward like a raptor, his hawklike face looking predatory. "Who said that? Who actually said that, aside from you, huh? Because when you talk about 'claaiiiiimsss' "—he elongated the word as well as putting quotation marks around it—"what I just assume is that it's stuff that you're making up, and you're saying that other people are claiming it because you don't have the guts to make accusations yourself."

"No one's making any accusations."

"Yeah? Yeah? Because I think that's *exactly*"—he picked up a piece of wax fruit from a bowl on the table and flung it at the cameraman, who ducked to one side and nearly dropped the equipment—"what you *are* doing. You see this place? This is my mansion. It might be kind of old and not have much furniture, and it's kind of frayed around the edges, but it's mine! This is *my place!* And I gave you the hospitality of *my place!* Because you said you wanted to do an interview that was fair and balanced! And instead you question my heroism, question my honor . . . I don't have to put up with this!"

He got up and came around the table, advancing angrily on the newsman and his camera guy. The journalist was on his feet, trying to calm Simmons and having no success. The cameraman backed up, working to keep Simmons in focus.

"Where were you when I was dealing with top-secret, white-knuckled intel? Huh? Where were you when I called in an air strike from a navy destroyer *on my own position on top of a damned pyramid?* I'll tell you where you were! You were behind a desk in your nice, safe studio while I was out risking my neck to save this miserable little world that I am forced, by accident of genetics, to share with miserable ingrates such as yourself! Interview's over! Outta my house!"

Simmons pursued them all the way to the door of his sparsely furnished mansion and stood there and watched as they fled down his driveway and out toward their van parked curbside. Then he slammed shut the door and bellowed, "Dutch! *Dutch!*" He stormed into the grand ballroom, looking for him, continuing to shout his name.

His manservant entered from the far end. In his mid-forties, tall, formally dressed, and a bit effeminate, he had a clipboard under his arm, a Bluetooth in his ear, and a smoothie in his hand.

"Yes, Mr. Simmons," he said with a pronounced German accent. "Right away, Mr. Simmons." He thrust the smoothie into Seymour's hand. Simmons hadn't even known he would be in the mood for one. As always, Dutch knew him better than he knew himself. "Your Kombucha shake, sir."

Simmons sucked half of it down through the straw in one shot. Then he lowered it and said, "What's up next? Whadda we got?"

Dutch looked over the clipboard, although, knowing him, he had all of it memorized. The clipboard was simply a formality. "Book signing in Midtown at noon. Then we pitch your reality show to the producers, followed by dinner with . . ." He double-checked the clipboard. "Hugo Chavez and Larry King." He tapped his Bluetooth. "Also, this irritating Witwicky keeps calling. He's phoned five times. Right now I've got him on hold."

Finishing the smoothie, he tossed the empty cup to Dutch, who caught it effortlessly. "The kid? What's he want?" Without waiting for Dutch to respond, he pulled the Bluetooth off his manservant's ear and held it up to his own. "Sam! How are ya!"

"Who was that guy who kept blocking your calls?"

"Manservant. Butler. Basically he's my hired friend. They're way better than regular friends; they don't leave you."

"Aren't they kinda pricey?"

"Not a problem for me, *mi compadre*. This couldda been you. Didn't I tell ya? Shoulda cashed in like me!"

"I was asked by the president of the United Freakin' States to keep a low profile."

"Yeah, well, glad I didn't vote for 'im. See where it gets ya?"

"Simmons, the Decepticons are back. I want to know why." He paused, sounding reluctant to admit it. *"I need your help."*

"They're back?" A grin split his face. "Well, that's good for business!"

"What if I told you I know a government secret that you don't?"

That stopped Simmons cold. "What?"

"You heard me."

Simmons began to feel an unwanted tug toward a road he had deliberately walked away from several years ago. Once he'd milked his connection to the Autobots for all it was worth, he'd gone cold turkey on secrets, the exact kinds of secrets that Sam Witwicky was now dangling in front of him. GiantEffingRobots.com (which he hadn't updated since June 2009) and his alter ego of Robo-Warrior were a thing of the past. So were the copious files he had boosted from Section Seven. He had done so for what seemed at the time a very good reason: Continued involvement would inevitably lead to his personal life, which at the moment was glorious, going totally south. As the song said, you had to know when to fold them, when to walk away, when to run. Simmons had cashed in big at the gambling table of life, and he'd known enough to get out while the getting was good.

He didn't mind the notion of the Decepticons and the Autobots getting into it again. If they became involved in another very public slugfest, then after the Autobots won—as they invariably did—he would enjoy another renaissance of interest in his moneymaking schemes.

None of which necessitated his risking his neck again, especially on behalf of a government that never seemed to have valued his contributions in the first place.

But . . . *secrets*. The chance to be in the know again. The incredible adrenaline flow that accompanied being thrust into the middle of danger. And surviving a near-death experience . . . there was nothing like it. When you came through something like that, the air smelled sweeter, food tasted better, and women . . .

Simmons felt the sweat on his lip beginning to bead. "Do not do this, kid," he warned him in a low voice. "Don't tempt my addiction. I've gone through withdrawal, I've been weaned, to a need to know . . ." He glanced at Dutch. "Is this line secure?"

Dutch shook his head, looking amazed that Simmons would even ask. Obviously it wasn't secure. It was his private cell line.

Immediately Simmons yanked the Bluetooth from his ear and muttered encouragement to himself in a rapid-fire patter, the words tumbling over one another. "You have everything. Don't take the risk. You will not relapse. Stay strong. Do not . . . let the demons . . . win . . ."

Satisfied that he had steeled himself, he shoved the Bluetooth back in, adjusted it, and prepared to tell Sam that he was out, that's all. He was out. He had no interest in hearing any secrets. He had no interest in Sam whatsoever.

Instead, he heard his own voice say, "What kind of government—" He choked. He didn't want to say the last word and fought it desperately even as it hissed out of his mouth. "—sssssssecret?"

"A fifty-year-old alien secret that nobody ever told you."

Simmons's resistance dissolved like sodden tissue. "Dutch! Clear my schedule!" Then, as an afterthought, he added, "Except for the Thai massage. I'm tight," and he flexed his shoulder and winced.

"So you're in?" came Sam's voice.

"Tell Megatron," Simmons said, his heart pounding furiously with excitement, "let's tango."

iii

Sam nearly tripped over his own feet running to the door of his apartment when the doorbell rang. He yanked it open, and standing there was Bruce Brazos, his face a mixture of emotions. He was working on trying to maintain his officious personality, but at the same time there was an air of barely contained excitement in his bearing. His nose had a broad bandage across it, and there was some swelling under his eyes. His gaze darted quickly around the apartment, clearly looking for something, and Sam knew what it was.

Brazos was holding up a thick accordion folder. "Procured your information, Witwicky," he said.

Grabbing it out of Bruce's hand, Sam said, "Fantastic. Thanks." He tried to close the door in his face, but Brazos stuck his foot in the door, intercepting it. "Now," Bruce reminded him, "there was a condition by which I do not sue you."

"Yeah, you were gonna sue me for saving your life just because you got hurt while I was doing it. How do you think that's gonna work out?"

"Considering people successfully do it to doctors all

the time, I'm liking my chances. At least doctors have malpractice insurance. How's *your* liability protection, Sam?"

Sam hated to admit it, but he totally saw such a thing working out in Bruce's favor. How could it be that he had helped to defeat Megatron but now he was being beaten by Bruce Brazos? Bowing to the inevitable, Sam sighed heavily and allowed Brazos in. Bruce looked around eagerly. "Lemme see one."

Stepping to the side, Sam gestured behind himself. Brazos glanced where he was pointing, and suddenly he looked like a band geek who had been invited to be guest of honor at a cheerleaders' convention.

Wheelie was babbling about something or other to Simmons, who was trying not to look bored and failing utterly. Brains was biting the heads off nails because they'd run out of screws. Simmons didn't seem especially happy to see Brazos, but then again, Simmons rarely looked happy to see anyone. He was quite possibly the most dyspeptic man Sam had ever met. But he knew his stuff, and Sam was aware that this simply wasn't going to get done without him. As for Brazos, he was a necessary evil, and Sam was determined to try to minimize his involvement as much as humanly possible.

"Freakin' awesome," said Bruce, slowly approaching them, unable to tear his gaze from them. Then, suddenly apprehensive, he said, "Are they going to try and kill me?"

"We don't take requests," Wheelie said.

Sam tried not to dwell on how unfortunate that was and instead dropped onto the floor opposite Simmons. He reminded himself that once upon a time he had felt as much revulsion for Simmons as he did for Bruce and that his feelings had changed over time. Now he could take Simmons in small doses and had gotten kind of used to him. Perhaps eventually he would regard Brazos in the same way.

Somehow, though, he doubted it.

He sat on the floor opposite Simmons, and they started spreading out the materials pulled from the accordion folder. "Okay, Lunar Reconaissance Orbiter, NASA launched in 2009. Forensics show Wang may have messed with the code, preventing it from mapping a section on the far side . . . aka the dark side."

Simmons was absorbed with the material Bruce had gathered from the late Jerry Wang's office. "My whole career," he said finally, "this is what I've been afraid of. They infiltrate us. Intimidate us. Coerce us to do their dirty work. And when they're done?" He pointed his hand at his head, miming a gun. "*Ba-doosh!* Double tap to the cerebellum." He thought about it a moment. "Kid, I don't think this is about the Decepticons finding something on the moon."

"No? Then what—?"

"I think it's about something they wanted to hide."

"*Hey!*"

Sam turned and saw Brains was busy munching on a small camera. Bruce was pointing in indignation, his finger trembling. "I . . . I was just trying to . . . and it grabbed . . ."

"What part of 'no pictures' did you not get when I told you they were here?" Sam said.

"It was just for me!"

Brains spit the remains of the camera out, and Brazos looked down at the pieces in dismay.

"That's just for you, too," Sam said, trying not to sound as pleased as he felt.

There was the sound of footsteps on the stairs outside, and then Carly walked in, her bag slung over her shoulder. In her free hand she was carrying a blue sequined cocktail dress covered in plastic that she had just picked up from the dry cleaner; once again her "early bird catches the worm" mind-set had her well into her internal to-do list, even this early on a Saturday morning. She stopped in her tracks and looked around, confused and annoyed. "What's going on?"

"Who are you?" said Simmons, and he turned to Sam. "Who is that? Get her out of here."

"*You* get out of here!" Carly said, slamming her bag down on the counter. "I live here! Sam . . . ?" She looked to him for an explanation.

"Carly, it's okay." He uncoiled from the floor and walked toward her, shaking his right leg a bit because it had started to fall asleep. "I'm at work. We're on to something here."

The temperature in the room seemed to dip precipitously when she spoke. "Oh. Of course. You're at *work*."

She stalked past him and headed into the bedroom. Sam watched her go, and Simmons said, "Trust me, kid: Nothing good is gonna come from talking to her right now."

He had the distinct feeling that Simmons was correct, but he couldn't leave matters like this. Besides, it was not as if she'd walked in on him doing something *wrong*. He was on the side of the angels here, working to protect humankind. She should be thanking him. She should be understanding.

So why the hell did he feel so guilty?

He walked into the bedroom, closing the door behind him. She had laid the dress down on the bed, and before he could say anything, she turned and snapped, "It's Saturday, remember?"

"Of course I remember! Which means it's my day off. So don't I have a right to do what I feel like?" He put his hands on his hips as if daring her to disagree.

She rolled her eyes impatiently. "Today is the party,

remember? I told you about it. I even"—she pointed to a piece of paper taped to the bedroom mirror—"wrote down the time and place and put it up here so you'd remember it! We're supposed to be going to Dylan's party. For my job. My *real* job."

He realized she was right. It had totally slipped his mind.

"Oh. Saturday. Right, of course I remember." When he saw her skeptical glare, he decided he needed to take the offensive. "C'mon! After what just happened to me yesterday?"

"You know what I liked about your war stories, Sam? They were stories. As in, 'in the past.' All your life-and-death stuff was over."

"These are my friends! They need my help!"

"Who, those guys?" she said, pointing in the direction of the living room. "The boss you can't stand? That obnoxious guy with the big nose? The little pervert robots?"

From the living room, Bruce called, "Y' know we can hear you through the door, right?"

"And I'll have you know my nose is aquiline!' " came Simmons's indignant voice.

"I meant the Autobots," Sam told her.

"We love ya too, man!"

"Shut up, Wheelie!"

Carly ignored them. "The Autobots need your help? Because of the Decepticons?"

"Of course, because of the Decepticons!"

"What, the Autobots, the CIA, and the military can't handle this on their own? Do you boys have code names? Secret handshakes?"

He knew he should be lowering his voice since they were obviously audible to the group in the living room, but her sarcasm angered him and prompted him to get louder instead. "Look, did I ask to be attacked by a Decepticon? I'm back in the middle here! You think this is what I wanted?"

She hesitated, and then her features hardened. "Yes. Yes, I do. I think this has nothing to do with Decepticons or even the Autobots and everything to do with you. I think you not only wanted this, I think you needed it."

"That's ridiculous! Why would I need it?"

"Because . . ." And for just a moment her lower lip trembled. "Because I wasn't enough."

"Oh, what? Now you're talking in the past tense? That's what we are? Past tense?"

She bit the lip to stop it from trembling and then grabbed the dress. "I don't know." The giant plush rabbit was lying on top of the neatly made bed. She took that as well and headed for the door.

And Sam hurled at her the only thing he could think of: "You said you'd never leave me."

She stopped at the door, her hand resting on the knob. Very quietly, so much so that he almost couldn't hear her, she replied, "You've chosen your path, Sam. And it's not with me. The truth is . . . you left me first." Then she threw open the door. Brains, who had his head pressed against it, fell in and she stepped over him.

Sam followed her out to the car—that superb car dear old Dylan had lent her, parked in the driveway—trying to put some distance between them and the guys in the living room. He tried to get her to stop, tried to think of what to say to avert this.

She was in the driver's side, and Sam leaned in through the passenger side. The rabbit was wedged into the seat next to Carly. In a single move, she grabbed the rabbit and tore the foot off it. Then she thrust it through the window and handed it to Sam.

"Good luck," she said as sincerely as she could. Then

she pulled the car back out of the driveway and, moments later, was heading off down the street.

He heard a footfall behind him. Simmons draped an arm around him like an old grizzled veteran of many battles. "Better off this way, kid. The warrior's path is a solitary one; take it from me." Then, sounding intrigued by the idea, he added, "We'll figure out code names and secret handshakes later."

"Sounds great," Sam said hollowly.

"Sure does." He patted Sam on the back. "Now let's go solve this Decepticon space thing."

NEW JERSEY

i

A caravan of Autobots took Exit 3 off the Jersey Turnpike, merged onto Route 168, and headed for Route 42, which would take them to the Atlantic City Expressway. This was fortunate since they were, in fact, heading toward Atlantic City.

It had been no effort for Bumblebee to summon backup. Simmons, riding in the backseat of his silver Maybach, turned around to make sure that the rest of their caravan was still behind them. Sure enough, the sports car and the Corvette that were the disguised Mirage and Sideswipe were following Bumblebee in his Camaro form. Simmons couldn't help noticing that the distance between them was precise, each exactly one car length behind the one in front of it. Perfect.

"Nothing like going to a gig with Autobot backup," he said cheerily, "right, Dutch?"

"Yes, sir," Dutch said from up front in the driver's seat.

Simmons turned to Sam, who was seated next to him. "Right, Sammy?"

Sam said nothing. He'd been barely verbal since D.C. and hadn't said a word since Delaware. "Kid?" Simmons prompted him. When he still didn't reply: "Kid, you gotta stop thinking about her and get your head in the game. On the off chance she comes crawling back, it won't do you any good if you're dead."

"Whatever," Sam said.

"Oh, good, he speaks." Simmons hadn't brought Sam up to speed yet because the kid seemed so disengaged that he felt it would be best to give him some distance. But now that they were drawing close to their destination, it was time to get down to business. "So . . . okay: Brains came up with three USSR cosmonauts back in '72. Claimed some conspiracy shut down their scheduled manned program to the dark side of the moon. They spoke out, then went into hiding. Defected under Brezhnev. But my Dutchman"—he pointed at his manservant, who tossed a wave from the front seat— "former NSA cybersleuth extraordinaire, tracked 'em down to Atlantic City. Remember, the thing about Russians is they never like to talk."

"Isn't that going to be a problem?"

"Nah." Simmons smiled. "I have a way with people."

ii

At the end of the boardwalk, with all the cars parked and three out of the four of them waiting for something to happen, Sam looked on in astonishment as Simmons and Dutch unloaded their gear from the trunk of Seymour's car. He'd always known that Simmons was a bit overzealous and maybe even kind of crazy, but this was just beyond the pale. He'd traded Carly for this guy?

Sam started picking through the equipment: wireless communications, scopes, night-vision goggles. Night vision? It was broad daylight.

"Is, uh . . . is all of this stuff necessary?"

"Yes, very necessary," Simmons said firmly. "It's gonna take a little of the 'international language.' "

Sam heard a few authoritative clacks of rounds being chambered. Guns made noises like nothing else, and sure enough, Dutch was busy locking and loading several guns. His expertise was evident; he was whip-fast and professional in his movements. It was quickly becoming clear to Sam that when Simmons had mentioned the international language, he wasn't referring to love.

Then Dutch turned and held out a gun to Sam, butt first. Sam held up his hands defensively as if Dutch were threatening him with it. "Whoa! Hey. Hang on."

Dutch looked to Simmons for instructions as to what he should do. Simmons stepped forward, took the gun from Dutch's hand, and shoved it into Sam's. It felt cold and heavy. "You hang on to your cojones," he said, unsympathetic to Sam's discomfort. "Lemme show you how the dirty, filthy espionage game is played."

Then, without bothering to see if Sam was following, Simmons headed toward a nearby social club. Dutch followed close behind. Sam hesitated and then ran after them, shoving the gun in his jacket pocket so that it thumped against his body and felt awkward. But it was better than shoving it into the top of his pants, which he was quite sure would result in vital body parts being shot off.

They approached the back door of what appeared to be a social club. The word "Transformations," which was presumably the name of the place, was embossed on a piece of rusting metal over the door. Sam considered that bleakly appropriate. Simmons strode up to it as if he had every right to be there and knocked briskly on the door. An eye slot slid open, like something out of a Depression-era speakeasy, and a pair of bored but dangerous-looking eyes appeared. Simmons promptly shoved his gun into the slot, making it impossible to close and obviously providing a hazard to anyone within.

"*Dasvidania*, gentlemen," Simmons said confidently.

From the other side they were able to hear a rough voice say contemptuously, "*Dasvidania* means 'good-bye.'"

"Oh." Managing to sound no less sure of himself, Simmons said, "Okay, well . . . what's 'hello?' "

"*Zdrastvueetee.*"

"You're kidding. Is he kidding?" he said to Dutch. Sam saw that Dutch was hurriedly fumbling through a book called *Russian for Dummies.* "Is he trying to get me to say something dirty?"

There was a guttural "Oh, for God's sake" from within, and the door was thrown open so abruptly that Simmons had to yank his gun away to prevent it from flying out of his hand. Sam was almost surprised that it didn't result in Simmons blowing his own face off.

They entered the dim interior. The man holding the door open was in his mid-fifties and looked more annoyed than formidable. Within was an open dingy room populated by three old men playing backgammon at one table and several old Russian women wearing fur coats in the corner. The women cast curious, even appraising, glances in the direction of the three Americans. One cocked an eyebrow invitingly at Sam. It creeped him out; it was like being scoped out by someone's grandmother. The men, engaged in their game, ignored the newcomers completely. The only other furnishing in the place was a dusty portrait of what Sam assumed to be some Russian leader hanging on the wall.

But Simmons was acting like they'd entered a spy stronghold that might be frequented by James Bond, with the same level of potential jeopardy. "Cover the standard-issue henchman, Agent Witwicky," he ordered, pointing at the doorman. The doorman stared at Sam for a moment, then rolled his eyes and shook his head as he closed the door again. Sam didn't even bother to pull the gun out of his pocket. It was like Simmons was operating in his own world. *Why did I even bother?* Sam wondered. *I needed Daniel Craig and I get Weird Al Yankovic.*

"Dutch," Simmons said, pointing with authority, "gimme something tough I can say to them. Y' know, show 'em who's in charge."

Dutch started thumbing through the phrase book.

The men playing backgammon had finally deigned to notice the three Americans. A bartender, heavyset and low-browed, was watching from behind the bar. One of the three backgammon players finally said, "My friend, we speak English."

"*Da?* Do you?" Simmons said challengingly. "Or do you want us to *think* you do?" Snapping his fingers impatiently at his manservant, he said, "Line, Dutch. Line."

Dutch started tossing out random names while he continued to consult the book. "Uh, Kalashnikov! Baryshnikov! *Mein Gott*," and his frustration became evident as he paged helplessly through the guide. "This is not a language!"

Simmons stared at him in disgust. "Dutch, you suck." Dutch, not taking the hint, kept trying to find something useful to say, at which point Simmons, fed up, knocked the book from his hand. Meanwhile, Sam was wondering why it had become his lot in life to stand around feeling embarrassed on behalf of various people— himself, Americans, the whole human race—because of the actions of others.

Turning back to the small group of Russians, who apparently hadn't gotten the memo that they were supposed to be intimidated by him, Simmons announced, "Agent Seymour Simmons, Sector . . . Eight."

Sam was starting to think he should have just waited in the car.

"We know who you are, cosmonautchiks," Simmons continued. "You were supposed to travel to the dark side of the moon. Then it all got shut down. The question is: Why?"

As he spoke, Simmons strolled over to another table, where a half-empty bottle of vodka was sitting open. He took a seat and then, to establish his hardiness, picked up the bottle and threw back a shot. The moment it hit his throat, he started to gag, and then he began choking violently. He coughed several times, and some vodka blew out of his nostrils.

At that point, Sam was finally ready to pull out his gun. Not to show the others how threatening he was but instead to put it to his own forehead and pull the trigger. He would have shot Simmons, but that would have been a mercy killing, and Sam wasn't feeling all that merciful just then.

One of the Russian women appeared to agree with Sam's unspoken sentiments. "This man is an imbecile," she said dismissively. With a leisurely wave, she gestured toward the bartender. "Take him."

Suddenly the bartender had a shotgun in his hand, produced from under the counter.

Sam couldn't believe it . . . and yet, somehow, he also could. These days it seemed like every time he blinked, someone was pointing a gun at him. "Great, this is nice! Save the world twice, get a medal, and die in some gangland shootout. Probably won't even find my body! If I played guitar, I'd end up being the subject of one of those tragic hourlong documentaries on MTV!"

"That's on VH1, idiot," said the cranky Russian woman.

That was when Dutch moved.

He might well have been useless with a Russian phrase book, but there was no denying what he was capable of in hand-to-hand. He was across the room before the bartender had time to react, and he grabbed the barrel of the gun, shoving it upward so that it was aimed at the ceiling. One quick twist and it was out of the bartender's hands and in Dutch's. Dutch then swung the shotgun, slapping the bartender hard across the side of the face, knocking him to the floor behind the bar. All business, Dutch chambered a round and aimed it meaningfully at the bartender.

"Move and I blow your damned head off," Dutch warned him, and he looked so agitated that he might well have fired even if the bartender remained completely immobile.

"Dutch, easy!" said Simmons. "Back in the cage! Safe zone!"

"You said cosmonauts! Not some mafia!" Sam said in agitation.

Simmons scowled. "Russians. One and the same."

The old man, the one who had initially told them that they spoke English, got to his feet. He looked proud, unafraid, in control. In short, the polar opposite of Sam. "We have seen men like you before. Come to try to buy our silence. We did not fear you then, we do not fear you now. So you tell son-of-bitch aliens you work for—"

"Aliens?" Sam was totally bewildered. "We don't work for . . . aliens . . ."

The old man was pointing defiantly to the floor near Sam's feet. He looked down and let out a startled yelp. Brains was standing there, watching the proceedings with interest.

Son of a . . . how the hell did he . . . ? Oh, forget it. "Okay, but we don't work for them. It's more like with them. And not the bad ones. We're with the good ones!"

That seemed to perk Brains up. "Yeah, the good ones! Autobots! Our side!" At which point he rattled off a lengthy string of flawless Russian that seemed to catch the old people off guard.

Then he stopped talking, and Sam said worriedly, "Uh . . . what did he—?"

The old Russian replied, "He say, 'Go ahead. Ask me anything about the universe. How it started, how it will end. Where the . . . ' " He stopped and looked to the woman for help.

"Lame," she said.

"Yes, yes. 'Where the lame planets are, where the fun planets are. Trust me, I am . . . ' What is phrase? 'Good for it.' He say, 'Trust me, I'm good for it.' And he say that all you want to know is what is on dark side of moon."

There was a lengthy silence as the Russians looked at one another. There was no discussion; apparently they had been together for so long that they could more or less read one another's minds.

Finally they seemed to come to a mutual conclusion. The old man said, "My name is Dmitri, and I will tell you what you wish to know, as long as"—he pointed at Simmons—"we do not have to listen to that one's annoying voice."

"Done," Sam said quickly before Simmons could open his mouth.

Nodding in satisfaction, Dmitri walked across the room to the portrait of the Russian leader. He swung it aside to reveal a wall safe. Entering the combination, he opened it. Sam could see there was a stack of large, flat envelopes inside it. Dmitri reached in, pulled them out, and walked back to the backgammon table. The other men stepped aside, and one of them gestured for the Americans to approach.

Dimitri spread the pictures on the table. "America first send man to the moon. But USSR first to send cameras. In 1959, our Luna 3 take pictures of far side and see nothing. But in 1963, Luna 4 sees strange rocks. Hundreds of them. Then Luna 4 lose contact . . . forever."

Sam leaned in to study the pictures. "I've seen those! They're . . ."

Then he stopped, suddenly hesitant, unsure of how

much he should say in front of the Russians. Stepping in quickly, Simmons pulled Sam to one side and looked at him expectantly.

In a low voice, Sam said, "They're the pillars for a space bridge. Our side found five."

"Decepticons must've raided the ship before Apollo 11 ever got there," said Simmons, whispering in deference to Sam's promise to the Russians. "Took the pillars, hid 'em, used humans to help keep 'em hidden. Which means they're still up there."

"But it doesn't make sense! If they found the ship and have all those pillars, why'd they leave Sentinel? I mean, if only Sentinel can use them . . ." Then the realization slowly dawned on him. "He's the one thing they still need." Simmons nodded; it all seemed to make sense. With growing urgency, Sam said, "Let's get Bee to find Sentinel. We've got to keep him safe!"

PENNSYLVANIA

"Allentown?"

Of all places for Sentinel Prime to be, Sam didn't expect it to be somewhere as mundane as Allentown. Then again, it was as good a place as any, he supposed.

It felt great to be behind the wheel of Bumblebee again. He'd ridden with Simmons at Seymour's insistence when they had gone to Atlantic City, but now, with Bumblebee leading the way for the rendezvous with Sentinel Prime, he had made it clear to Simmons that he was going to be reteamed with his old friend, and that was the end of that discussion.

Getting Simmons to wait at the truck stop outside Allentown with the Autobots had been no easy task. He simply didn't need Simmons and his gung ho attitude in the mix, especially since he had no idea what he was going to be dealing with when he encountered Sentinel. Finally he had said to Simmons, "Look, we don't know what we're going to be facing. Could be anything. What if Decepticons are already on the scene? We go in with all our resources in one shot and we fall into an ambush, that's it, game over, end of story. We need to hold the big guns like you in reserve."

He had been thrilled to see Simmons beginning to nod as he spoke and even happier when Simmons patted him on the shoulder and said, "That's a plan. That's a smart plan. You're finally starting to think like an agent, kid. Obviously, I'm rubbing off on you." That was a horrifying notion to Sam, but he kept his smile plastered on his face and thanked Simmons for the vote of confidence.

They moved through the streets of Allentown. A police car cruised past going in the other direction, and Sam could see the cop at the wheel watching him with open curiosity and perhaps even a bit of admiration. Sam suspected they didn't get a lot of Camaros rolling through there. He kept the car moving at the speed limit, and he wasn't weaving, so they didn't have any cause to pull him over, which was good. He didn't feel like answering a lot of questions right then.

"So you still following his beacon, Bee?" said Sam.

The radio flared to life. Sonny and Cher sang, *"I got you, babe . . ."*

"I'll take that as a yes."

Abruptly the wheel began to turn, and Sam removed his hands from it. The Camaro hung a right and headed toward an elementary school or, more specifically, the schoolyard. Since it was Saturday, naturally it was empty.

Then, to his surprise, Bee drove up over the curbside and into the yard itself. He was moving around the school toward where Sam assumed the play area was.

"Bee," Sam said nervously. "We're not supposed to be doing that. They generally like it if you keep off the grass in parks, so this is, y' know, not cool and—"

Bee rolled to a stop. He did not, however, back up. Instead he turned off the engine, and the driver's side door opened.

Taking the hint, Sam climbed out of the car and looked around, unsure of what he was supposed to be looking at. Yes, there was a playground nearby, with swings and a seesaw, a jungle gym, and a . . .

Fire engine?

Not just any fire engine. The words "Port of Port-land" were emblazoned on the side, and below that,

"Airport Fire Rescue." It could not have looked more out of place.

"You're kidding," said Sam.

Slowly Sam walked toward it, watching it carefully, and called out, "Sentinel? Sentinel Prime?"

An instant later he heard the now-familiar sounds that signaled the changing of an Autobot from one form into another. Hundreds of metal plates snapped around, and within seconds the fire engine was now standing in front of Sam, looking down at him.

"Hope I didn't wake you."

"We don't sleep," said Sentinel Prime.

"Right, I should have remembered that. Hi. I'm, uh, Sam Witwicky. I was there when Optimus resurrected you. I'm a friend of his."

"He never mentioned you to me."

That hurt.

"However," Sentinel continued diplomatically, "he has a good deal on his mind. So you and this fine soldier have sought me out." He gestured toward Bumblebee, who promptly changed into his robotic form but remained on bended knee.

Unsure of the protocol, Sam went to one knee as well.

"Oh, stand up," Sentinel said with a touch of impatience. "The both of you. I appreciate the shows of respect, but I do not require constant obeisance from the Autobots. And you, human, are so tiny that I can scarcely see you down there when you're upright, much less kneeling. So please, on your feet."

Both of them did as they were bidden. Sam said, "I, uh . . . I kind of figured Optimus would be with you, actually."

"I desired the opportunity to experience humanity on my own."

"And you did it here?"

"As good a place as any," he said, unconsciously reflecting Sam's own thoughts on the matter. "Small humans climb upon me and frolic. Adults stand near, watching over them. It is curious."

"What is?"

"I have been monitoring your various broadcasts, and there are constant reports of fractiousness among your people: divides along racial lines, philosophical boundaries. Yet children of all races, creeds, and colors cavort upon me, pretending to be firefighters, with no recognition of the differences between them. Meanwhile the adults, also of various ethnicities, engage in casual and friendly conversation and immediately discourage any fights or discord between the children. I have therefore concluded that for your civilization to reach its true potential, what your planet requires is more playgrounds."

Sam smiled at that. "I actually think that's a great idea. I'll suggest that when we get back to NEST."

"And why," said Sentinel, "would 'we' be inclined to do that?"

Stepping forward, Sam said, "Because you're in danger. Terrible danger from the Decepticons."

"I can take care of myself."

"With all respect, sir, I don't think you realize just how much of a target you are. This is all about you. It always has been. And when—not if—when the Decepticons show up, it's not going to be some accidental encounter that's gonna result in a skirmish." He got louder, speaking with greater urgency. "They're going to come at you with everything they've got, because they need you for something. Something big, something that could, I dunno, wind up resulting in the death of everybody on this world, including all the playgrounds and all the children everywhere."

Sentinel Prime considered his words and then said,

"Very well, friend of Optimus. Lead on . . . and I will follow."

Sam couldn't believe it was that simple. "Okay! Okay, well . . . that went way easier than I'd have thought possible."

It was the last thing that would.

WASHINGTON, D.C.

Charlotte Mearing hated having to head up to the Hill on Saturdays. Senators tended to dress down on those days, and she felt that it was inappropriate to the office. If you're going to work, then dammit, look like you're working.

But it couldn't be helped. The late afternoon was the only time the idiot senator she had to see had open, and since he was an idiot in charge of appropriations, that meant she had to accommodate him. Her aides were on either side of her, rattling off some last-minute budget numbers that her steel-trap mind instantly grabbed on to for the upcoming meeting.

And then, as she prepared to cross the street to go up to the Hill, a familiar yellow Camaro came roaring up and cut off her approach. And who else was at the wheel but Sam Witwicky? What the hell had he been up to, and why was he riding around in Bumblebee? And how—?

"How did you know where I was going to be?" she said.

Then she jumped back slightly as Brains suddenly popped up from the backseat of the Camaro. "Yeah, that was me. I checked your appointment schedule on your computer."

"You broke into my *office*?"

"Nah. Did it from an Internet café outside Baltimore."

"That's impossible! How could you possibly hack through all the firewalls?"

"You're kidding, right? Look who you're talking to."

She hated to admit it, but the robot had a point. She turned her attention to someone she was sure would give her less aggravation. "Mr. Witwicky, I thought I was clear." She gestured for the aides to get Sam out of the way. But the aides hesitated, and she immediately understood why. Witwicky was sitting in an Autobot. If he wasn't inclined to move, a couple of aides weren't in a position to make him do so.

"*Listen!*" Sam said more forcefully. "This whole thing's been a trap! The Decepticons *wanted* Optimus to find Sentinel Prime. Because only Optimus had the way to revive him!"

She shook her head. "What are you talking about?"

"Sentinel's the key. He's what they're looking for. We're escorting him back to NEST now. I'm going to meet up with them on the way, soon as I'm done here."

"We? Who's we? Who's them?"

"Mirage. Sideswipe. And"—he hesitated and then said—"some others." Obviously he was hiding something, but he went on before she could ask. "Look, you were right, okay? Obviously, the bridges can be weaponized! And it's something that the Autobots would never do, but the Decepticons sure as hell would, and they need Sentinel for that!"

"But we have his space bridge. It's safe."

"You have five pillars. They have *hundreds*! You've done just what they wanted. They're gonna be coming for Sentinel Prime!"

Oh, my God, thought Mearing. *Oh, my God, what have we done . . . what have I done . . .*

Her phone started ringing. She glanced at the incoming phone number; it was the office of the senator with whom she was supposed to meet. Doubtless they were wondering why she was late.

She hit "ignore" and sent it to voice mail. Then she looked Sam in the eye and said, "Why did you go on ahead to . . . I mean, why did you come to me? To tell me all this?"

He had the answer ready: "Just trying to respect the chain of command."

If Mearing were capable of smiling, she would have done so.

Instead, turning on her heel, she shouted to her confused aides, "We're going to NEST! Now! Witwicky, follow m—!"

But obviously Sam Witwicky, or perhaps Bumblebee, had other ideas. The yellow Camaro whipped around in a sharp U-turn, causing other cars to screech to a halt, and roared off down the road.

VIRGINIA

i

The convoy of Autobots sped down I-66. Simmons was in the lead, Dutch at the wheel, watching the road carefully. The Autobots were behind them: first Mirage, then the long fire truck that was this new guy they were talking about, and bringing up the rear was Sideswipe.

Simmons was feeling damned good about this. The fate of the world was in his hands again, and he really liked how it felt against his palms.

Then, from an on-ramp onto 66, three black Suburbans came rolling on, pulling alongside the convoy. The moment they drew within range, blinking lights atop them began to spin.

"Hey, we got help! The kid came through in spades!" Simmons said to Dutch triumphantly. "Looks like an FBI convoy."

And suddenly one of the Suburbans was no longer rolling.

It was running, sprinting like a large metal lion, keeping pace effortlessly. It was Crankcase, who let out a roar that thundered through the morning air. Cars that were ahead of them sped frantically to get away, and Simmons could see the terrified faces of children looking out the back window of a soccer mom van.

They needn't have worried. They weren't the targets. Simmons knew all too well who was.

"Battle stations!" Simmons shouted, grabbing for a

rifle that was lying on the seat next to him. He hadn't been expecting a Decepticon attack, but it never hurt to be prepared.

He heard a horrific screech of metal, and suddenly the roof of his Maybach was being torn open. Simmons looked up and saw the Dread perched atop the car. Quickly he swung the rifle up to take aim, but Crankcase was too quick. It reached down, grabbed him, and yanked him up and out of the car. The rifle fell out of his hand, tumbling into the front seat.

Simmons slammed his fists into the creature's face even though he knew it would do no good. The Dread roared at him, its mouth wide open, and Simmons tried to pull away but couldn't.

Dutch did the only thing he could: He slammed on the brakes.

The instant he did so, Simmons and Crankcase went hurtling over the front of the car, tangled together. They tumbled forward, rebounded off the hood, and hit the highway, falling to the side, as the Maybach continued to skid past, leaving black tire marks and a smell of burning rubber behind. The impact caused them to separate from each other, and Simmons kept rolling. He heard a horrific crack, and pain ripped down his right leg. He knew immediately that it was broken.

That might well have been the least of his problems, because as he lay there, helpless, he saw the Autobots, still in car form, speeding toward him. Simmons let out a horrified shriek. He rolled frantically toward the shoulder of the road, ignoring the agony that was shooting up and down the entire right side of his body. The oncoming Autobots quickly course corrected and swerved to avoid him, just missing him.

Simmons banged into a railing on the edge of the shoulder that stopped his rolling. He gasped for breath and felt even more pain, now in his chest. He might well have cracked a rib. He heard a low roar and twisted around just in time to see Crankcase coming right toward him, across the highway, and he had no way to stop the thing.

And then, a split instant before the Dread reached him, a vehicle speeding backward slammed into it. It was the Maybach, driven in reverse by Dutch. The Dread let out a screech of protest that was quickly accompanied by a screech of twisted metal as the car ran over the bot, grinding it beneath its wheels. Simmons flinched as he heard an explosion but then realized it was one of the tires on the car blowing out. It thump-thumped over the remains of Crankcase and ground to a halt. The Dread shuddered a few times and then lay still.

Dutch leaped out of the car and ran to Simmons, kneeling next to him. Simmons looked up at him.

"This is what happens when you give in to temptation," Simmons said, and then the pain overwhelmed him and he passed out.

ii

Bumblebee was hurtling up I-66 East when Sam saw the eminently conspicuous red fire engine that was Sentinel heading toward them, going westbound. "Perfect," said Sam.

Then he realized that there was no sign of the Maybach. Simmons was supposed to be in the lead; instead he was MIA. The vehicles were moving much, much faster than they had been before.

The dashboard radio flared to life, and Robert Preston's voice sounded in the car: *"Well, you got trouble, my friend, yes sir, you got trouble, right here in River City . . ."*

It was a divided highway, but there was a break coming up in the median railing that ran down the middle. It had a big sign that read "OFFICIAL VEHICLES ONLY." Bumblebee ignored it, and Sam didn't care about it; the biggest problem they should have at that moment was getting ticketed for making an illegal turn.

Bumblebee canted his wheels, causing himself to fishtail and whip around. He skidded past the break sideways, then gunned the engine and darted forward through the break without slowing down. The move brought them to the forefront of the caravan, right next to the speeding sports car that was Mirage's alternative form.

That was when Sam spotted the two black Suburbans coming up on either side of them. Unlike Simmons, he wasn't fooled for a moment.

He leaned out the window and shouted to Mirage, "Tell Sentinel to get outta here! You guys cover him!"

There was a roar of a powerful engine behind him. It was the fire engine, accelerating like a freight train.

"*Watch out, watch out!*" Sam shouted unnecessarily, because the sports car and and the Camaro were already responding, darting out of the fire truck's way. Immediately Sam saw the wisdom of Sentinel's actions: He was clearing the way for his protectors to be better able to move into defensive positions.

The sports car and the Corvette dropped back, adjusting their speed so that they were coming up alongside the Suburbans. The Autobot vehicles switched out of Stealth Force mode, their weapons coming online. Matching the speed of the Suburbans, the two sports cars opened fire. The Suburbans swerved wildly, trying to avoid the weapons blasts that chewed up the highway around them. The sports cars crisscrossed, coming at the Suburbans now from opposite sides, firing again and this time scoring hits on the enemy vehicles.

The Suburbans abruptly seemed to lose their taste for battle. They suddenly cut hard to the left, approaching the median railing. There was no convenient break in the median strip for them, but that didn't slow them. Instead they vaulted upward, changing in midleap to creatures that looked like jungle cats. It happened so quickly that if Sam had blinked, he would have missed it. And when they landed on the other side of the railing, they instantly changed back into cars. With a screech of tires, they tore off down I-66 in the other direction.

But the Autobots were not inclined to let them get away all that easily. Sam didn't know whether it was because, after many months of their mortal enemies having disappeared from the landscape, the Autobots were eager for a battle or if they were filled with indignation that some Dreads had dared—*dared*—to assail someone as revered as Sentinel. Whichever the reason, they weren't about to let the Decepticons simply go on their way unmolested.

One moment they were a sports car and a Corvette; the next they had left their car forms behind and changed into their formidable robot bodies. They easily leaped the median strip and took off after the fleeing Decepticons.

iii

Crowbar and Hatchet, the two remaining Dreads, moved as quickly as they could, fully aware that the Autobots were bearing down on them.

Mirage and Sideswipe, skating rapidly, came up behind them. Mirage cast a glance toward his battle mate. "Can you keep up with my speed?" he said.

"Easily."

"Good. Wouldn't want you to miss the fight . . . presuming you have the heart for it," he said with just a hint of a challenge.

"I hate the notion of war," Sideswipe said, "but I love the thrill of battle."

With that, Sideswipe actually pulled ahead of Mirage slightly, drawing closer to the Decepticon.

Sideswipe readied the massive swords on his arms to slice at his enemy, but he never had the opportunity. A blast from Mirage's arm cannon ripped right past him and slammed into the speeding Crowbar, striking him broadside. The car spun out, flipping end over end.

"I had that one!" Sideswipe turned back to look at Mirage with irritation.

And then Mirage yelled, *"Duck!"*

Sideswipe turned just in time to see that directly in his path there was an overpass. It was high enough for cars or even trucks but not high enough to accommodate two robots over fifteen feet tall.

The tumbling Dread slammed into one of the concrete supports of the overpass just before Sideswipe and Mirage got there. Sideswipe leaped upward just as Mirage bent his knees and ducked his head. Over and under went the Autobots and then continued their pursuit of the Decepticon Hatchet.

They were operating on the assumption that Crowbar had been put thoroughly out of commission by the impact of the crash.

They were, as it turned out, wrong.

The Dread had used its skills to make the damage it had sustained look worse than it really was. The instant they were out of sight, Crowbar snapped out of his "crumbled" heap of an appearance and took off.

He was heading the wrong way on the highway.

Oncoming cars honked and tires screeched and drivers flung their vehicles to either side to avoid a head-on collision while the Dread continued on its path. Within seconds it had overtaken both Bumblebee and the rumbling red fire engine that was Sentinel and gone past them.

Crowbar prepared for his run at the single Autobot that had been left to guard Sentinel.

iv

Sam was just starting to relax, with Bumblebee having pulled alongside the greatest warrior in the history of the Autobots, leading Sam to believe that the danger was past. Within minutes they would reach NEST headquarters, and everything would be fine.

Then he saw a Decepticon go ripping past them on the opposite side of the road, and things seemed less than fine.

He watched in horror as the Decepticon kept going, leaving an array of swerved cars and multiple crashes in its wake.

"Houston, we have a problem," came over the radio.

"Yeah, no shit, Sherlock."

Sam thought that maybe it wouldn't be so bad. That perhaps the Dread, realizing that it was overmatched, was simply attempting to escape in the most damaging way possible. That would certainly be consistent with Decepticon thinking: Whenever possible, even when retreating, be sure to inflict maximum carnage.

"Carnage," Sam said aloud, and in spite of the seriousness of the situation, he chuckled. "Car-nage. Get it, Bee? That was . . ." Then he shook his head. "Y' know what? Never mind. It wasn't that . . . funny . . ."

His voice trailed off.

Crowbar had doubled back and was heading toward them.

Straight toward them.

"Ah, Bumblebee . . . ?" Sam said nervously.

Bumblebee chose not to reply with either his broken voice or via the radio. Instead he let his actions speak for him.

He sped up.

At that moment, Sam suddenly found himself remembering his high school driver's ed course. He had studied the manual cover to cover and had been impressed by the length and detail in which the manual discussed all the rules of the road. But what had struck him as particularly memorable at the time was a section notable for its brevity. It was the chapter that talked about head-on collisions. By contrast, for instance, the material about three-point turns went on for two pages and the part about how to compensate for rain-slicked roads was even longer.

But the chapter on head-on collisions said this and only this:

Head-on collisions should be avoided at all costs. Chances of survival are not good.

That was it. Fifteen words that said it all. Do whatever is necessary to make sure that you and another vehicle don't come face to face at high speeds.

Granted, the book hadn't been written with the idea that your car might actually be a robot warrior and you weren't going to be given a good deal of say in the matter, but still . . .

"Bumblebee!" Sam shouted, his voice cracking in fear. *"Slow down!"*

Bumblebee ignored him. Or perhaps he didn't, if one could term doing the exact opposite of what you were told ignoring the speaker. Rather than slow down, he accelerated even more. Sam watched in horror as the speedometer rocketed to well in excess of a hundred miles per hour.

And the Dread showed no signs of being inclined to peel off.

He had one final remembrance from his past: his mother telling him, when he was a child, that it was always important to wear clean underwear when you go out because what if you should be in a car accident and they wind up taking you to the hospital? Did you want the doctors laughing at your dirty underwear? Of course not.

Sam, gripping the wheel as tightly as possible, instinctively pushed himself as far back in the seat as he could. As he did, he couldn't help seeing the flaw in his mother's advice. Rescue crews were going to extract him from the twisted yellow metal wreckage that was going to be his coffin, and his parents would come pulling up to the hospital in that ghastly RV of theirs, and they would go running in and be confronted by a doctor who would look at them sadly and inform them that the paramedics were busy scraping the remains of their son into a sandwich-size Baggie, and if they wouldn't mind waiting a few minutes, they could take him with them. And his mother would ask about the only thing that really mattered at that point: *"Was he wearing clean underwear?"* And the doctor would say, *"Well . . . he might have been before the crash. But afterward? Not so much."*

And as that entire worst-case scenario went through Sam's mind, Bumblebee's cannons came online and unleashed a furious barrage straight at the oncoming Decepticon.

If having a head-on collision with another car was a surefire recipe for disaster, so too was having a head-on collision with Cybertronian mortar shells. The cannon fire struck Crowbar straight on while he was barely yards away, and this time the Decepticon was unable to engage in a clever subterfuge to make the damage look less than it was. Instead, the direct hit from Bumblebee's cannons tore through him, and Crowbar was blown to pieces. Debris flew in all directions, and a ball of flame erupted in their path. But Bumblebee went straight through it without slowing down, moving so quickly that none of the flame had a chance to attach itself to the Autobot's exterior. He pushed right past stray bouncing bits of debris, and seconds later the road ahead of them was clear.

Sam let out a sigh of relief that started from somewhere around his ankles. "I love this car," he said softly.

Suddenly the voices of Hall and Oates came over the radio. *"Whoa oh, here she comes. Watch out, boy, she'll chew you up . . ."*

Immediately Sam glanced in the rearview and moaned. "Oh, you gotta be kidding."

The remaining Dread, the one that had been behind them, had doubled back. It was now coming up fast, nearly matching Bumblebee's speed. Mirage and Sideswipe were behind it, Mirage firing off blasts from his arm cannon and Sideswipe from his big guns. But Hatchet was swerving deftly, avoiding every blast while closing the distance between itself and Bumblebee.

Every second that passed brought the Dread closer still, but Mirage and Sideswipe were getting closer as well. Sam was never the greatest at math, but he tried to guesstimate the distances and realized that Mirage and Sideswipe were going to overtake the Dread before it managed to catch up with Bumblebee.

Apparently Hatchet realized it as well.

In what could only be termed a final act of desperation, Hatchet shifted himself into his full robot form and, with a furious screech of anger, fired two missiles.

They hurtled through the air, locked on to Bumblebee.

If Bumblebee had not had a human passenger, dealing with the missiles would have been less problematic. But with Sam on board, it became far more of a challenge.

Sam no longer had his hands on the wheel. He had turned completely around in his seat and was watching in wide-eyed horror as the missiles converged on him.

Brains popped up from the back, glanced around, took one look at what was coming, and without hesitation leaped out the window. He hit the ground and bounced along the asphalt, skidding to a stop as the missiles hurtled past him.

"Thanks for nothing, you little coward!" Sam shouted, and then he saw that the missiles were almost upon him. Moving as fast as he was, jumping out was not an option. The flesh would have been shredded right off his body.

The missiles were almost upon them. They had seconds remaining at most.

And suddenly Sam Witwicky was airborne.

Bumblebee had shifted into his robot form and, using his momentum, had hurled Sam into the air. Thanks to the laws of physics, Sam continued with his forward motion even though he was no longer in the car. Then, in an acrobatic flip that would have qualified him for the Cybertron troupe of Cirque du Soleil, Bumblebee leaped high and somersaulted in the air.

The missiles, which had been tracking him when he was car-sized, streaked right under him.

Sam continued to scream as he began to fall, and then his scream ended in a startled gasp as he landed in Bumblebee's outstretched arms.

Immediately the missiles whipped around in a midair U-turn and reacquired their target, which was now considerably larger. They flew straight at Bumblebee's chest.

Seeing them coming, Bumblebee promptly altered his mode back into the Camaro at lightning speed, tucking the terrified human into the driver's seat as he did so. Once again the target changed shape faster than the missiles could adjust, and they zipped right past the roof of the speeding vehicle.

Witnessing all this happening in a matter of seconds, Hatchet let out a howl of outrage. Then he let out a howl of a very different sort as Sideswipe got close enough to bring his sword sweeping down and through. It sliced right through the Dread, cutting him into two discrete pieces. They started tumbling to either side.

Mirage, right behind him, immediately plucked both halves of the Decepticon out of the way. Then with swift underhand motions, as if he were bowling two balls simultaneously, Mirage sent the two sections of Hatchet directly at the missiles that had missed Bumblebee twice and were now seeking to acquire a new target.

Hatchet's remains provided that target as, thanks to Mirage's perfect aim, the two halves impacted with one of the missiles each, causing them to detonate instantly. Mirage and Sideswipe sped around the explosions—just beyond the blast radius—and emerged without so much as a dent in the fender.

"Hey!" Brains shouted, gesticulating wildly from the side of the road. "A little help here!"

Sideswipe ignored him, but Mirage, somewhat against his better judgment, slowed just enough to scoop up the irritating little robot. He held Brains up to his face and said, "Remember what you just saw in case you ever think about switching sides back to the Decepticons."

"Message received," Brains said. "Loud and clear, at quite a considerable decibel level, I might add. Want to know exactly how many decibels it was?"

"No," Mirage said, and, changing back into his sports car mode, stuck Brains into his interior.

Meanwhile, in the driver's seat of Bumblebee, Sam sat paralyzed, his chest seizing up. It was only when Sting and the Police started singing, *"Every breath you take,"* over the radio that he did, in fact, remember to breathe. He let it all out in a husky gasp. He waited until his heart rate dropped to something approximating normal and then finally managed to get out a sentence.

"Please," he said, "don't ever do that again."

✌

(They think they are safe. The Autobots believe that they have outmaneuvered the Decepticons.)

(They are fools. They have no comprehension of the scope of the Decepticons' plans. They have no idea of the forces arrayed against them.)

(Do they honestly believe that all this time has passed and the Decepticons have merely remained dormant? That what is happening now is something that the Autobots can control?)

(No. Every step of the way has been carefully planned and thought through. Yes, there are some casualties. There will always be casualties. But those losses have been factored into the overall equations and are acceptable within the parameters of a successful mission.)

(The open assault on the convoy heading for NEST headquarters has been thwarted, with no casualties to the Autobots. The irritating human Simmons, however, will no longer be a factor, so that is something, at least.)

(But more Dreads are being dispatched to intercept them. They may succeed. They may not. It is irrelevant. The point is to keep the Autobots confused and off balance and given no time to think ahead. Enemies who are merely reacting cannot act. Enemies who are on the defensive cannot take the offensive.)

(And those defenses must be spread as thin as possible.)

(And so the attacks will come from all sides to draw them off, to distract them. They were fools to set up their headquarters so close to a populous area such as Washington, D.C. Were they in a desert, inflicting collateral damage during a fight would be problematic. But by focusing an assault on the nation's capital itself, the Autobots' determination to protect humanity—and their weakness for the human race—can be fully exploited. They will not know where to look first.)

(When an enemy does not know where to look, it becomes that much easier to slip in from behind.)

(The convergence begins.)

vi

Alarms were screaming inside NEST, and soldiers, who had practiced drills so frequently that many had started to believe the real thing would never come, ran to their stations to be ready to launch into battle.

Colonel Lennox, for whom the days of sitting around in desolate offices chasing down pointless leads now seemed very far away indeed, sprinted down a catwalk, snapping out information and orders to his aides even as he strapped on his combat gear. "We've got Decepticons converging on Washington! Optimus is at Andrews! Get him back here, now! We need to guard Sentinel! Move every NEST team out and spread through Washington! Make a perimeter and send word that if POTUS and V-POTUS aren't at secure locations, now's the time to get them there!"

One of his aides ran up with a telephone, looking reluctant to say what he had to say but having no choice. "Colonel? It's Mearing."

Oh, God. The woman had called him every two minutes since Sam Witwicky had shown up in D.C. telling her what was going on. The fact that she had immediately informed Lennox and put NEST on alert was, naturally, greatly appreciated. The fact that she kept calling back, as if she didn't trust him to handle matters, was not. He grabbed the phone. "Lennox."

"*I'm five minutes out. I won't come in the front; it'll be faster to go to the back NEST gate.*"

"The area isn't secure, ma'am. Decepticon Dreads have been reported in the immediate vicinity."

"*Then send Autobots out to deal with them, Colonel. That's what they're for.*"

"I was about to, ma'am, but I got interrupted by a phone call," he said.

"*Your point is taken, Colonel, but I want a sitrep immediately. And I'm not a ma'am—*"

Lennox snapped shut the phone, dropped it on the floor, and stepped on it as hard as he could. The crunching sound it made was extremely satisfying. "Scramble Ironhide, Ratchet, and the Twins."

"I hate the Twins," one of the aides muttered.

"Shut up," Lennox said.

vii

The convoy with Sentinel was heading straight toward NEST from one direction.

Coming from the other direction at high speed were five fast-moving Decepticon Dreads. Two were still in car mode; the other three were in full fighting array. They were not going to repeat the mistake that had occurred out on the highway. This time they were going to have safety in numbers.

In the driver's seat of Bumblebee, Sam saw them in the distance at the opposite end of the street, barreling toward them. Nightmare reliving of the narrowly avoided head-on collision came back to him, and he had the terrible feeling that this time it wasn't going to simply be a matter of outgunning them.

The safety of NEST's gate was ahead of them, less than half a mile, but the Dreads were going to get there first. Sam could see in his mind's eye what was going to happen next. The Decepticons would get to the gate, pass it, and instead come at the convoy full bore. Here, where the streets were narrower, the Autobots wouldn't have as much room to maneuver, and they would also be hampered by their attempts to minimize damage to innocents in the area. The Dreads would not have that worry.

The distance between the two groups closed, and Sam was right: They were going to get to the NEST entrance and pass it within seconds. At that point, the convoy's easy access to the gate would be cut off.

And just when the Dreads got to the front entrance and were about to speed past, the gates flew open and, with impeccable timing, Ironhide emerged and simply stepped out directly into the path of the oncoming Decepticons.

Ironhide was the quintessential immovable object. The Decepticons discovered this very quickly as, moving too fast to change course, they all plowed directly into him. Their own speed accomplished the rest as they shattered into a million pieces, bits of Decepticon flying every which way. The massive Autobot was rocked back slightly on his heels but otherwise was completely unaffected by the impact.

Sam laughed in relief as he witnessed the outcome of the abortive assault on the convoy.

From within the gate, Ratchet, Skids, and Mudflap looked on. Ironhide turned to them, brushing a few bits of debris from his arm, and said mildly, "They just don't make them the way they used to."

Sam maneuvered Bumblebee in through the main gate. The guards were running forward, but they weren't trying to stop him this time. Instead they were frantically waving him forward. The large ramp way that served as the main Autobot entrance was wide open and welcoming. It was sure different from the last time they came through there, and Sam couldn't help but feel a surge of satisfaction. *If only Carly could see this,* he thought, and immediately the good feelings he was having began to dim.

As he drove past Mudflap, the squat—for an Autobot—robot was gesturing angrily at Ironhide.

"Man, you shoulda saved some for me!" he said.

"If he'd saved any of them for you," retorted Skids, "then I'd wind up saving you from them!"

"Like hell you would!" The offended red robot

shoved the squat green robot, who, other than in color scheme, was identical. "I could take 'em!"

"You couldn't take a dump in a dump yard!" Skids backhanded him across the side of the head, staggering him.

"Shut up, the both of you!" snapped Ratchet, who had had quite enough of the Twins for one day. "Have some respect for the greatest of us all!"

The Twins immediately got in line, because even that fractious pair had some respect for what Sentinel represented. The fire truck rolled past them, and shortly afterward all the Autobots followed him. The final one in was Ironhide, who cast one last cautious look around before striding in, the ramp closing steadily behind him.

viii

Sam had never felt so relieved as when he was finally safely within the main NEST ops center. Once again he was on the upper rampways, alongside Lennox and surrounded by soldiers. But at least this time he didn't have Mearing breathing down his neck; she was nowhere to be seen. Moreover, he felt that this time he had proved his worth beyond any debate. If he hadn't figured out what was going on, if he hadn't tracked down Sentinel, if he hadn't given NEST a heads-up . . .

Don't get full of yourself, Witwicky. You had plenty of help every step of the way. If you'd been on your own, you'd have gotten nowhere. Jeez, I hope Simmons is okay. And if it weren't for Bee and the other Autobots, you'd just be roadkill. Maybe that's part of the point that Mearing was making. It's a cliché, but there's no "I" in "team."

"Ironhide!" Lennox called down from overhead. "Protect Sentinel!"

Sam shouted down to them as well. "Keep him guarded! He's the key!"

"Yes," said Sentinel. And then something in his voice changed, something that Sam couldn't quite identify. "As I always have been."

Before anyone could react, Sentinel turned, faced Ironhide, and produced an odd-looking cannon. Ironhide, the sturdiest of all Autobot warriors—the great friend of Optimus Prime—had no time to react as Sentinel fired a blast of something that Sam had never seen before. It struck Ironhide, the invincible Ironhide, in the side of his head.

When Optimus Prime had first restored Sentinel to life, Ironhide had been one of the very first Autobots to go to one knee in deference and respect to the esteemed Sentinel. Now he went to one knee again, but it was because he was disoriented, confused, unable to stand. He flung his arms out to either side to try to keep his balance and barely managed.

Sam watched, horrified, uncomprehending. He felt like his brain had split—one half witnessing the events, the other half trying to make sense of it and failing. The stuff that Sentinel had shot at Ironhide (*He shot Ironhide! Why the hell would he—?*) was some kind of thick plasma . . . no . . . not plasma . . . it was like an acid rust (*but nothing can hurt Ironhide! And why would he even want to hurt Ironhide, they're allies?*) that was consuming the upper half of Ironhide's head. It worked its way through with appalling speed, and the other Autobots were frozen in place, no more capable of understanding what was happening than was Sam or Ironhide.

"I am sorry, my Autobot brothers," Sentinel said. "But we were never going to win the war. For the sake of our planet's survival, a deal with Megatron had to be made."

Sam's mind locked up completely. He simply couldn't process what he was seeing. In that, he had a great deal of company.

And before anyone else could react, Sentinel fired again, an even larger blast this time. The acid rust enveloped the rest of Ironhide's head and the entirety of his upper body. It seemed to Sam that this time it was working even faster, as if the first blast had been a practice shot to get the juices flowing.

Ironhide wasn't able to do so much as scream because his entire vocal apparatus was gone. Seconds later his torso fell in on itself as his arms tumbled to either side. The acid rust had already worked its way into them, and when they struck the ground, they collapsed into puddles of dissolving metal. The remaining part of Ironhide's body that had been upright now fell over onto the spreading pool of ruin that was already on the floor.

"He's with the Decepticons," Lennox said to his aide. His voice was, astoundingly, icy calm, as if he were assessing a change in the weather. That was the level of professionalism at which he was dealing. Whatever turmoil was going on inside him, for Lennox it was first things first: Follow procedure. "Get all NEST forces back to base."

To Sam it all seemed to be occurring in slow motion. In real time, it was less than five seconds between the second blast of Sentinel's weapon and the final dissolution of Ironhide, leaving him nothing but a lifeless mass, not even recognizable as metal, much less a once-proud Autobot.

Without hesitation, Sentinel turned and aimed his cannon at Bumblebee. There was no way he could miss.

"No! No! Bumblebee, watch out!" Sam screamed.

Sam's cry jolted Bumblebee from his shock, and he started to move, to try to dodge to one side, but there was no way, no time to avoid it. Sentinel simply tracked with his motion and fired.

Skids hurled himself directly in the path of the blast,

absorbing the full brunt of it. A bit splattered to either side, narrowly missing Bumblebee.

Skids staggered, his knees coming together, his torso starting to dissolve. He tried to turn toward Mudflap, reaching for him, but he was unable to move. As he spoke, his voice dropped from its typical brashness to a hoarse whisper. "Sorry, bro . . . guess I wasn't . . . as smart . . . as I thought . . . sor—"

His head fell off, and his lower body fell to the other side. His torso dribbled down the sides of his lower half, and then all of it dissolved.

There had never been a moment when the motor-mouthed Autobot called Mudflap had been at a loss for words. Under ordinary circumstances, Sam would have expected him to say something like, *"Oh, no you did-unt! Oh NO you DID-UNT! Uh uh! You in it now!"*

He said nothing like that. Perhaps it was because of the psychic link that he shared with his twin so that he had actually felt Skids die. Perhaps it was because of the betrayal of a warrior they revered above all others, like finding out the Archangel Michael was on Satan's payroll.

Whatever the reason, Mudflap didn't react the way Sam would have expected.

Instead he howled.

It was a primal agony, torn from that individual bit of Spark that powered all the Autobots. It was the most horrible thing Sam Witwicky had ever heard, and he recognized it for what it was: the sound of a soul dying.

And then it escalated up the scale to a war cry of undiluted fury.

Mudflap leaped into the air, spun, and kicked Bumblebee in one direction and Ratchet in the other as he cried out, then landed, shoved past Mirage, and shouted, *"Run, you guys! Leave him to me! This bastard's mine!"*

Sentinel fired a blast from his cannon with vast calm, certain that he had Mudflap targeted.

He was wrong.

The far smaller Mudflap ducked under it. The spray of acid rust flew over his head, and then Mudflap leaped straight at Sentinel.

He hit the startled Prime in the back of the knees, knocking him off his feet with the sheer fury of his attack. Sentinel crashed to the ground, Mudflap atop him. He pounded upon Sentinel, hammering away with everything he had. Gone was his tactical savvy, gone was his attitude. He was nothing but unbounded, incoherent rage, and many other Decepticons would have been helpless to withstand such a berserker onslaught.

Sentinel was not one of them.

He simply waited until Mudflap provided an opportunity, and then he shoved his blaster cannon into Mudflap's mouth and fired.

Mudflap still kept striking blows at Sentinel, refusing to acknowledge that he was already as good as dead. Then he started trembling violently, and Sentinel shoved him off. Mudflap rolled onto his back and then dissolved, the acid rust eating him from the inside out.

Sentinel got to his feet and looked around.

The others were gone.

He surveyed the area carefully to make sure none of them—particularly Mirage—were in hiding. Then, slowly, he nodded.

"There might be some who would condemn your departure as rank cowardice," he called out, his voice carrying. Obviously, he didn't care if they were close enough to hear him; his words were for the benefit of the humans who were still standing, transfixed at the sight. "But they would be wrong. This one"—he gestured toward the minimal remains of Mudflap—"must have known on some level that his actions were suicidal. The only way in which his sacrifice could have had any meaning is if you attended to his final words. In your survival, you honor him. And you also acknowledge that to which all who are within earshot should attend. When it comes to the question of stopping me, success is not an option. Now," he continued, gesturing toward the great vault at the far end, "open it. Open it in such a way that the contents are not damaged."

He was looking straight at Sam.

Sam couldn't even get a word out. In fact, he could barely breathe as his throat closed up. He simply couldn't fathom the level of betrayal that was being played out here. This would kill Optimus, simply crush him.

It was Lennox who spoke up. "We can't."

"You will not?" There was sadness in Sentinel's reply, but it was tinged with danger.

"No. We cannot. The clearance to do so . . . the codes to open the vault without detonating the fail-safes . . . it's above our pay grade."

"Well, then," said Sentinel, "it appears we have a problem."

MARYLAND

It is an impressive vehicle, this airplane they call Air Force One. *A pity it is inanimate. It would make a formidable Autobot.*

Their president has desired to meet with me for some time, but my coming to his domicile, his White House, offers some obvious logistical difficulties. So arranging a rendezvous at somewhere such as Andrews Air Force Base is the far more reasonable course.

I will be intrigued to speak with him. If any human can comprehend the responsibilities that come with being a Prime, then it would be he.

The main door to the airplane has opened, a stairway with the presidential seal rolled up to it. We have our iconography, and they have theirs. In this, at least, we are alike.

Several men in black suits emerge. They have earpieces and are regarding me with what appears to be considerable trepidation. These men are bodyguards, and it is unlikely that they are happy to see me. This meeting has been long arranged and approved at the highest level, yet still they regard me as a potential threat. And they know that if I were indeed to present a threat—were I to attack them—they would be helpless to stop me. My presence hampers their ability to do their job.

Even after all this time, they still do not understand.

It is the solemn duty of the Autobots to protect humanity. They have nothing to fear from us. Nothing at all.

The president emerges from Air Force One. He looks up at me and salutes me. It is meaningless since I am not in the armed forces. No . . . it is not meaningless. It is a sign of respect, and much appreciated. I return it.

He begins to thank me for my service. He makes a small joke of how he would present me with a medal, but there are none large enough to fit around my neck. And besides, he says, I am made of metal and thus have no need for more. It is a small jest, a play on the two words that sound alike. It seems to amuse him, and I nod in—

What . . .

. . . is that?

A message . . . an electronic message . . . being transmitted to me by Ratchet . . .

It makes no sense.

Sentinel? Has destroyed . . .

. . . Ironhide?

That is impossible. Impossible.

I call out to Ironhide, expecting his immediate response. This must be some bizarre prank of the younger . . .

Nothing.

And not just nothing. Nothingness. Emptiness. It is not that Ironhide is not replying. He is simply not there.

He is gone.

I listen closely to what Ratchet is saying. He is frantic, stunned, shocked. He is telling me that Sentinel has just slain Ironhide . . . that Bumblebee was next, but Skids intervened, laid down his life . . .

I send an immediate message to Ratchet, to Bumblebee, Mirage, and Mudflap, telling them to withdraw. They cannot stand against Sentinel. None can. They must survive until we can determine what has happened.

Ratchet, Bumblebee, and Mirage acknowledge my order.

Mudflap does not. He is receiving it, but his mind is a screaming frenzy, too preoccupied to attend to me.

There is only one conclusion to draw: He is attacking Sentinel. Which means he is dead and simply does not know it yet.

The president sees that something is wrong. He questions me.

"You must leave immediately," I say to him. "You must refuel your vessel as quickly as possible and depart."

His guardians are instantly alert to the threat of imminent danger they discern from my words. The president looks confused. "I . . . I don't understand . . ."

"Something terrible is happening. Something that you need to be nowhere near. Take to the air and leave this area. Your country needs its leader."

Instead of leaving, he approaches me, rife with concern. "And my family needs me as well. They're at the White House. If they're in danger . . ."

"You must help them by surviving. I will protect them. Leave now."

The guardians believe me. "Mr. President, we have to leave. Now. We'll get it sorted out in the air," *says one, and they are already hastening him back up the stairs.*

I switch to my alternative form and roll out of Andrews Air Force Base at top speed, and yet my thoughts are racing even faster.

The explanation is clear to me: Sentinel has been taken over by the Decepticons in some manner. He is not in his right mind. This is entirely my fault; I should never have left him to his own devices. Obviously at some point he encountered Decepticons who brain-

washed him and turned him into an unwilling slave. Somewhere, buried deep within his consciousness, the true Sentinel must be recoiling in horror over everything that he has done. The true Sentinel must be screaming for release from the living trap of his own mind.

The guards at the front exit barely manage to raise the gate before I speed through. Seconds later, Andrews Air Force Base is in my rearview as I speed toward the highway.

As I go, additional messages are coming through. NEST is contacting me. Alerts are everywhere. Decepticons are converging upon Washington, D.C. I immediately send an electronic message to Ratchet, telling them to proceed to the National Mall, which seems to be where the Decepticons are heading. I will meet them there.

We must save the humans from Sentinel.

We must save Sentinel from himself.

VIRGINIA

i

As Charlotte Mearing drove through the NEST complex from the back entrance, she was startled to hear explosions erupting from the area ahead.

Her driver slowed to a halt. "Why are you stopping? Get us over there!" Mearing said. "Lennox has stopped answering the phone, and I have to find out what the hell is going on!"

"Ma'am, your safety is—"

"You're not worried about my safety, you're worried about yours, and I'm not a . . . oh, forget it," she said in disgust. Before the aide could take any action to prevent it, Mearing was out the door. She had already swapped out the hated heels for sneakers, and she sprinted toward the site of the detonations. This was her facility, and she was determined to protect it at all costs.

It was obvious that the Decepticons must have breached the perimeter, and her people were fighting, probably dying, as a result. There was simply no way she was going to be running in the other direction while that was happening.

She reached into her shoulder holster and pulled out her gun, chambering a round as she moved.

The closer she got, the more clearly she saw the damage that had been inflicted. She ran past smoking ruins of helicopters and various land vehicles. Hangar Bay One had been completely demolished, and then she heard explosions coming from within Hangar Bay Two. She started toward it, uncertain of what she was going to see, but never had the chance to get close enough. There was a thunderous detonation that she belatedly realized came from a fuel storage area within, and then a massive fireball erupted from the bay. The concussive force of the explosion blew Mearing off her feet. She flew through the air, her glasses knocked off her face, and then hit the ground hard. If she hadn't been wearing a pantsuit, her legs would have been lacerated. As it was, the skin on her hands was abraded and the fabric of her clothing torn up.

She lay on the ground, gasping, her ears ringing. Her hair had come undone and was hanging in her face. She shoved it out of her eyes, and her hand came away with even more blood, which she realized was seeping from a gash in her forehead.

Then she saw something that filled her with instant relief.

From the smoke, from the flames, Sentinel was emerging. He was moving slowly and steadily, even casually, if such a word could be applied to a being like him. To Mearing, there was only one possible interpretation of what she was seeing: There had been some sort of Decepticon assault, and Sentinel had just finished dispatching them.

Thank God these creatures are on our side, she thought. *What would it be like if only the Decepticons had arrived here?*

Mearing staggered to her feet. She picked up her glasses and saw that the right lens was shattered. Folding them up, she shoved them in her jacket and started toward Sentinel, treading lightly since her left ankle seemed tender. But it could have been worse, a lot worse. Torn clothing, busted glasses, a pulled muscle, perhaps. At least she was alive, so that was something.

"What's happening?" she said to the Autobot. "Sentinel? Report!"

Sentinel looked down at her with as much disdain as his face could possibly convey. "I am a Prime from the great planet Cybertron. I do not take orders from you. But"—his voice softened slightly—"I regret all the harm that must come."

Uncomprehending, Mearing drew closer, and suddenly she heard shouting from nearby. She turned and saw Lennox and Witwicky running toward her. They were gesturing wildly for her to get back, and now she could hear Lennox shouting, "No, ma'am! Stop!"

"Get away from him!" Sam Witwicky was calling to her.

Slowly, understanding dawned upon Mearing. She looked up at Sentinel. "Oh, my God," she said.

"Your God is not here to help you, so you had best deal with me. Now"—he moved around toward Lennox and Witwicky—"return what belongs to me."

"You mean the pillars in the vault."

"Yes. I assume it is within your . . . 'pay grade' . . . to release them to me. Do so."

"Go to hell," she said defiantly.

Sentinel paused, considering her, and then, sounding insanely avuncular, said, "You do not want me for an enemy, Charlotte."

The familiarity he was taking made her skin crawl. "It's a little late for that. You destroyed half my base."

"No. I am not your enemy yet. The destruction I have inflicted thus far is merely to prove a point. Yes, half your base is destroyed, but half remains intact. I have demonstrated restraint."

"*Seriously?*" Sam called. "You trash the place and you're using the 'glass is half full' angle?" Lennox promptly told Sam to quiet down, for which Mearing was grateful.

"Thus far," said Sentinel, "I have merely done what was necessary for the needs of myself and my race. I have stopped short of regarding you as hostile entities to be dealt with accordingly and have restrained myself whenever possible. For you are a young race and know not what you do. You have an opportunity—right here and right now—to maintain that status quo, to keep this war strictly between the two races that have been waging it. If you do that—if you cooperate—you will be saving untold millions, perhaps billions, of lives."

"And if I don't give you what you want, you'll what? Kill me?" Mearing said.

"No. Because right now I require two things in this world: you and my property, locked away in your vault. And so I will simply carry you with me until you agree to do what I wish. And I will kill everyone that I encounter. Men, women, children . . . it makes no difference to me. And you will have to live with the knowledge that every one of those deaths are lives that you could have saved . . . beginning with these two."

And with that pronouncement, he turned toward Lennox and Sam and raised his foot.

She should have let him do it. That was what she would tell herself later. She should have let Sentinel obliterate the two of them with one stamp of his foot. She should have sent him a message right then, right there, in the strongest and most unequivocal terms: The United States did not knuckle under to the demands of terrorists.

But instead she cried out, *"No! Don't!"*

Sam and Lennox had automatically raised their arms to shield themselves against the impact, even though it obviously would have done them no good.

Sentinel remained frozen in that position and then slowly lowered his foot to the side, clear of the two humans he had been about to crush. "That was your instinctive response, Charlotte," he said. "One that was devoid of policy concerns and paperwork. It was your human response. The right response. Follow that instinct, for it will guide you to the proper course. A course that will lead to a destination that you already know. The only question is: How many lives will be ended under my foot before that destination is reached? How many lives will you save? Decide, Charlotte Mearing. Decide . . . now."

ii

Anyone who happened to be standing outside the building that purported to be Health and Human Services would not have found it at all surprising that a fire truck was rolling out through the main gates of the facility. With the reverberations of explosions echoing in the distance, it was obvious that there had been some sort of major conflagration going on. It was impressive that only one truck had been required to deal with it; from the sounds of it and the size of the fireballs that had been leaping skyward, it might well have been a two- or even three-alarmer.

What might have seemed off, however, were the five strange-looking pillars that were lashed to the top and sides, which didn't look like any sort of normal fire fighting equipment.

iii

Sam was a pile of seething emotions: anger over what Mearing had said, frustration because she had a valid point buried in her accusations, and foolishness over having been so utterly deceived by Sentinel that he had—

"It's not your fault," Lennox said as if he were reading Sam's mind. He had released his hold on Sam's elbow and was now moving at double time. Apparently he was expecting Sam to keep up. "Yeah, Sentinel fooled you. But he fooled the Autobots, too. If anyone should have known, it was them."

"I'm not sure they're capable of understanding that depth of betrayal."

"Then you shouldn't be down on yourself. Through here," and he darted down a corridor and out an exit door. Sam followed, wondering if this was some sort of shortcut to the street. He hoped he had enough money on him for cab fare home.

Instead there was a Bell-Boeing V-22 Osprey helicopter sitting about a hundred yards away. The propeller blades were just starting to fire up, and Lennox gestured for Sam to follow. Instead Sam stopped and stood there, looking confused. Lennox, seeing that Sam had ceased following, ran back to him and said impatiently, "Are you coming?"

"I don't think they'll let you land this near my house."

"Don't be stupid. We've got intel the Decepticons are heading to the National Mall. One that we think may be Megatron from the description was spotted near the Lincoln Memorial. With all that going down, what good are you going to be to us if you're sitting at home watching cable news? Forget that: I want you near me when this thing goes down."

"Even though I'm a civilian?"

"You stopped being a civilian the moment you bought a camouflaged robot at a used car lot. Besides, no matter what Mearing thinks, you're probably the foremost expert on the Autobots on the planet." He started running toward the Osprey, and this time Sam fell in behind him. He called over his shoulder, "I mean, c'mon! You brought Optimus Prime back to life, for God's sake."

"Yeah, well, let's hope I don't have to do it again, 'cause I'm not sure how many times I can pull that trick out of my bag," Sam shouted back over the roaring of the Osprey's rotors. He clambered in behind Lennox, and moments later they were airborne.

WASHINGTON, D.C.

i

(*The mighty Megatron strides up the steps that lead to a statue erected in the celebration and memorializing of a famed human leader. It is his understanding that this particular leader was responsible for freeing human slaves during a great war.*)

(*Freedom. What an utterly useless reason for a war.*)

(*War is about domination, not freedom. It is about taking, not giving.*)

(*This man knew nothing of the way of things.*)

(*On eye level with the seated statue, Megatron reaches forward, clamps his hand upon the statue's head, and rips it off with a crunch of stone. Then he calmly sets the head aside and proceeds to shred the rest of the body seated on the chair while taking care to preserve the rest of it, or at least as much of it as possible, intact. He cleans away the remains of the debris and then turns and sits himself in the now-vacant chair. He tests its weight to make certain it will bear up under him and is satisfied.*)

(*He watches as Sentinel busies himself setting up the pillars in a wide circle around the National Mall. The Prime moves with confidence, jamming each one into the ground, affirming that each is prepared for the job it must do. Hanging brightly in the night sky, the moon looks down upon them as if blessing the endeavor.*)

(*Seeing him go about his business with such efficiency*

moves his thoughts to Sentinel's successor. He addresses the bearded statue head in his hand. "Prime never knew. When Sentinel left Cybertron . . . it was to defect. He was to rendezvous with me here on earth . . . before fate waylaid us both. To revive him . . . we needed Prime and his Matrix.")

(Then he hears the sound of an air vehicle approaching. He leans forward and watches with interest as a helicopter descends a distance away. Once, he might have been concerned about such an arrival. The humans have shown considerable resources in thwarting the endeavors of the Decepticons in the past, in conjunction with the Autobots. But there is nothing to worry about this time. The humans, the Autobots, even their leader . . . none of their actions would have any impact on what was about to happen.)

(This time, the Decepticons would win. In fact, they had already won. At this point, it was just a matter of seeing matters play out to their inevitable conclusion.)

(Had he been capable of pity, he would have felt sorry for Optimus Prime.)

(But he wasn't, and so he did not.)

ii

Sam and Lennox emerged from the Osprey on the opposite side of the National Mall. Lennox was busy radioing in their location, while Sam simply gaped at the sight of the revered Autobot warrior completing the array of pillars while Megatron looked on from the Lincoln Memorial.

Seconds later Lennox stepped in next to him. "They used us," he said with cold, dark fury. "Used all of us. Without our space program . . . without Optimus reviving him . . . none of this happens. We handed all this to the Decepticons and practically thanked them for the opportunity. And now he's opening the space bridge."

"To where?" said Sam, still not understanding. "I still don't—" Suddenly he grabbed Lennox's arm and pointed. *"Look!"*

Hurtling across the Mall from the direction of the Washington Monument was an array of sports cars, plus one very familiar blue and red truck. They were barreling toward the site of the pillars at high speed, and then came a familiar series of sounds. The vehicles were far enough away that he saw the changes a second before the sound reached him. But still, he'd never been quite so relieved to hear that distinctive racket, like a series of metal dominoes falling into each other. There came Optimus Prime, moving with the speed and determination of a charging bull, followed by Mirage, Wheeljack, Bumblebee, Sideswipe, and Ratchet.

It's gonna be okay. Yeah, Sentinel obliterated three Autobots like it was nothing, but that's 'cause he's a Prime. And so is Optimus, plus he's got the others backing him up, while Megatron looks like five miles of bad road. Everything's going to be fine.

Sentinel, acting as if he had nothing but time, adjusted the final pillar—the six-foot one in the middle—and then rumbled in a voice that carried across the vast expanse of the Mall: "Power and initiate."

One pillar began to glow, and then the next, each one in sequence, and the Autobots were still too far away to reach it.

NEST forces were now pouring in from all directions. Helicopters, jeeps, even tanks were converging. The air was split by the howls of sirens as police cars and SWAT teams came rolling in, discharging human passengers who were armed to the teeth.

Meanwhile, a dome of light had spread from one pillar to the next, enveloping them like a glowing tent. In the center was the Prime from the moon, standing there like the sentinel that was his name.

The Sentinel . . .

"Oh, my God!" Sam abruptly said to Lennox, speaking all in a rush. *"The Sentinel!"*

"What about him?"

"Not him! It! Look," he said with growing excitement, "the other night Carly and I wound up watching *2001: A Space Odyssey* on one of those classic movie channels. . . ."

"So what? Sam, is this really import—?"

"Listen! There was this old boring guy introducing the movie, and he was going on about how it was partly based on this short story Arthur C. Clarke had written called 'The Sentinel.' About how it turns out there's this whole alien base left behind on the moon that has all kinds of advanced technology, including this object that they based the Monolith on in the movie. But it was, like, this warning beacon, because when humans got smart enough to find it and screw with it, it would mean that we had become a possible danger and it would summon the race that built it so that they would come and maybe destroy us! Don't you get it? *Arthur C. Clarke knew all about this somehow! Maybe he was even trying to warn humanity before it was too late!*"

"So you're saying this guy Clarke can help us?"

"Yes! Wait . . . no." Sam suddenly remembered. "He died a few years ago."

Lennox stared at him. "Yeah. That was useful. Thanks."

THE MOON

(They have been lying dormant all this time, their internal systems operating at such a minimal level that even when the Autobots were inspecting the remains, they did not detect them. They have been waiting for a signal, and if it had never come, then they would have waited for eternity.)

(But now it does come, an inviting pulse sent by five pillars that is received by hundreds of objects just like it. And each of those objects sends a jolt into the beings who are holding them, awakening them, telling them that finally, finally it is time.)

(They emerge from the shadows of the Ark and from the barren soil of the moon. One by one, then by tens, then by hundreds, the Decepticon warriors arise, each of them holding a pillar that serves as a receiving point for the beacons that are summoning them to the verdant world below. Saying, Now, now, come to me now.)

(They obey. The pillars on the moon begin to glow, creating a web of energy that crackles with irresistible force. And in an instant, all the Decepticons are transported from the lunar surface, traversing the distance between the moon and the earth in a heartbeat.)

(The moon is now wholly dead.)

(The earth may soon follow.)

WASHINGTON, D.C.

i

Sam watched in horror as Decepticons poured out of the space bridge. There were dozens, no, hundreds of them, practically falling over one another to scatter in all directions.

The various police and military vehicles that provided transportation and weaponry for the humans now served as templates for the Decepticons. They instantly began transcanning the cars and vans, the tanks and helicopters, and seconds later they were shifting into brand-new earth shapes, driving and flying every which way. It quickly became impossible for the humans to distinguish simple conveyances from robots in disguise that were determined to kill them.

Some of the Decepticons didn't bother to camouflage themselves. They strode forward, proud and lethal, and just started firing away with their onboard weaponry. A millennium is a long time for a bellicose race to sit around and wait for a call to action, and they were taking every advantage of the situation, hammering away at anything they saw.

The NEST and SWAT teams were overwhelmed. They had not been remotely prepared for an onslaught of such magnitude. They returned fire as best they could, but engaging in a sustained battle with a hoard of Decepticons was simply not a reasonable option.

Explosions erupted across the National Mall. Gigantic swards of grass went flying, replaced by huge craters from the Decepticon blasts. The air was quickly filled with vast black clouds and was thick with the stench of incineration. Soldiers and police officers were falling back, still firing, still dying. Even if the Decepticons had been capable of perspiration, they wouldn't have been working up a sweat. They moved anywhere they wished, not in pairs but in squads of a dozen, knocking aside trees to get at the humans who were daring to try to impede them. The humans were like ants squaring off against lions.

Sam, at the outer edge of the fight zone, looked at the battlefield with dismay. *There's too many! They're everywhere!*

And through it all, Sam could see Megatron seated upon his "throne." He was surveying the damage like a proud warrior king, and when the Autobots came through the smoke and debris to face him . . .

Sam Witwicky in his time had seen many expressions on the face of the primary nemesis of the Autobots: arrogance, fury, disdain . . .

But he had never seen Megatron displaying complete, utter, and total confidence.

That was what he was witnessing now. Megatron was acting as if the outcome were so assured, there was no reason to expend concern about it. Any opposition offered by the humans or the Autobots was of no consequence. The victory of the Decepticons, as far as he was concerned, was guaranteed.

And Sam couldn't say he was wrong.

The Autobots charged into battle, firing blindly, firing everywhere. They managed to create a firewall between the Decepticons and the humans, buying time for the desperate survivors to flee the field in the face of overwhelming odds.

"Here we are!" Megatron's voice carried across the Mall. *"Fight us now!"*

Sam, when he was much younger, had once been at a seaside resort when an offshore hurricane caused the waters to swell. He remembered seeing the men gathering at the shoreline, tossing up sandbags, literally trying to stem the tide. But they had succeeded for only a short time, for eventually the ocean had overwhelmed the bags. He would never forget his last recollection of that town, watching out the back window of his parents' speeding car, driving away to higher ground while the ocean cascaded over the bags and annihilated the houses lining the shore.

That was what he was seeing now, except the Autobots were the sandbags and the Decepticons were the ocean.

They had beaten back the initial wave, but now all the forces of the Decepticons, having heard Megatron's defiant cry, turned their backs on their assaults on the humans and converged on the only opposition that truly meant anything to them.

Optimus Prime surveyed the situation and shouted the words Sam never thought he would hear:

"Autobots! Retreat!"

Immediately, if reluctantly, the Autobots obeyed their leader.

Their leader, however, did not follow his own orders. Instead he charged.

The Decepticons, still massing, were caught off guard. As a result, he was able to slam through them like a linebacker, scattering them every which way. That, to Sam, underscored the fundamental cowardice of the Decepticons. They outnumbered Optimus who knew how many to one, yet their immediate reaction was to get the hell out of his way when he charged forward, guns blazing, Energon sword swinging.

Optimus went straight for Sentinel.

Sentinel turned and saw Optimus coming but did nothing in response. He didn't bring up that fearsome acid rust weapon of his; he didn't strike a defensive stance. He simply stood there, waiting.

There were times when the student became the master. When he surpassed his teacher in all ways and thus proved that he was finally, truly ready to assume the title of leader in a way that the previous master never could.

This was not one of those times.

ii

I charge directly at him even as I order the others to retreat. They must live to fight another day, but Sentinel . . . Sentinel must be rescued, here and now. I cannot run from him.

It is not the same for the others.

They were not taught by him.

They were not groomed by him to become the next leader of the Autobots. They did not know him in the days of yore, only the legend that grew around him. But my loyalty is to him, and that loyalty will not allow me to leave him in the clutches of the Decepticons. If he knew what they had somehow done to him—the crime against humanity, and us, that they had forced him to commit—he would simply want to die from shame.

I must rescue him.

He taught me so much in training me, but I have learned much since then, and I must use all of it now against him. I must incapacitate him, take him with us, find a way to undo what the Decepticons have done to him.

I lunge for him, hoping for a quick takedown.

I am a fool.

He sidesteps me and then, as if I am a novice, uses my own forward momentum against me. He twists around and slams me to the ground with such force that it rattles every circuit in my body.

And he wasn't even trying.

I attempt to stand, to come at him again, but before I can, he kicks me in the face, knocking me backward. In the distance I hear Megatron laughing derisively. Then, before I can make another move, Sentinel places his foot upon my throat.

"Sentinel," I manage to say, "you must shake free of their control! Remember who and what you are!"

"Control?" He looks at me oddly and then seems to understand. "You think that the Decepticons have somehow corrupted me? Are forcing me to act against my will? Oh, Optimus, how can one be so old and so utterly naïve?"

"They must have found you . . . captured you . . . when we went our separate ways . . ."

"Yes, I met up with the Decepticons after you and I parted company, but only to finalize our plans. Look into my eyes, Optimus. Hear my voice. You know that I am speaking freely, of my own will. In the depths of your Spark, you know."

And I realize that he is right. In order for the Decepticons to subsume him to such a degree that he would have killed Ironhide and the Twins, that he would have unleashed this hell on earth, there would have had to be nothing left of his true personality. His words would ring hollow, his eyes would be empty.

I was wrong.

He has betrayed us of his own accord. He has slain his own without compunction.

"Why?" I speak the word, still scarcely able to conceive it.

"For Cybertron," he says. "For our home. What war destroyed, we still can save. But only if we join with the

Decepticons." Then, with pity in his voice, he adds, "And I knew you never would. It was the only way."

"This *is* our home. We must defend the humans!"

"So lost you are, Optimus. On Cybertron we were gods. And here . . ." He had been speaking with a sad calm, but now he allows his voice to twist with anger. "Here they call us machines."

And he brings his arm around and aims his cannon at me, the same thing that must have been the final sight for Ironhide. The acid rust against which no Autobot can stand.

"I did not want you to die in ignorance, my old student. You deserved better than that."

He prepares to kill me.

And I have never, in my existence, had so little interest in continuing to live. For if this is the shape of things to come, what place do I have in it?

iii

Do something, Witwicky, something, anything . . .

"The pillars!" he shouted. "It's the only thing he cares about! Go for the pillars!"

"It's a hell of a long shot!" But Lennox was already bringing his walkie-talkie to his mouth. "All squads: Concentrate fire on the five pillars!"

NEST soldiers had managed to come around and draw closer during the brief period when the Autobots had battled back against the Decepticons. The order was quickly relayed from squadron to squadron, and instantly, heedless of the danger to themselves, they converged and started opening fire on the pillars just as Sentinel had his foot upon the throat of Optimus Prime.

What if I'm wrong? What if they don't have any more use for the pillars now that they've transported the Decepticons here?

Then Optimus is finished, and I couldn't help him.

iv

The humans needed me, and I am unable to help them . . .

And suddenly the pressure is released from my throat. No acid rust pours down upon me. I am spared, and I do not understand why.

Then I see, and everything makes sense.

The humans of this country sing proudly of the red glare of rockets, of bombs bursting in the air. For a nation that claims to embrace peace, to sing of war would appear contradictory. Perhaps it is not. Perhaps they would prefer peace, but if pressed to war, then they wish others to know that they are very, very skilled at it.

They prove that now as they rain destruction down upon the one thing that seems to matter to Sentinel Prime: the pillars. They are threatened by the rockets and bombs, and suddenly nothing matters except for saving them.

Other Decepticons race in upon his orders, aiding him in hurriedly gathering the pillars. Then, forming a flying wedge, they lay down suppressing fire, battering the humans back, causing them to scatter. Many of the Decepticons have already fled the vast green sward called the National Mall. Naturally. Why engage in a continued pitched battle when they can insinuate themselves into the world of humans? At any given moment, in any place, they can launch a devastating attack on any target and then return themselves to their alternative form and simply drive away from the site. Humanity will be in an endless war of guerrilla terror, never knowing where the next strike will be or when or how many will die as a result.

"Let the humans serve us . . . or perish!" Sentinel calls as he and the others—his others, his allies, his friends—vanish into the darkening night.

Slowly I get to my feet.

I see Sam Witwicky in the distance, starting to run toward me. He is shouting my name, wanting to ascertain if I am all right.

I cannot face him.

I am shamed.

I have led him astray. I have brought death and destruction down upon him and his kind, and it is only going to get worse. And at the moment when it mattered most, when I needed to stop the individual who was responsible for this calamity, I was fool enough to think that he was under the control of others. My love for Sentinel Prime blinded me to the evil in his Spark.

Humanity trusted me, and I have failed it. I have failed Sam, who has never in his life failed me.

I cannot face Sam Witwicky until I have found a way to make this right. To reverse this calamity.

He deserves better than I have given him—they all do—and I must determine a way to provide it to them.

v

"*Optimus!*" Sam screamed, waving his arms wildly above his head, his throat going raw from the combination of the shouting and the haze of smoke that was stinging the air. "*Optimus! Optimus, what happened? Are you okay? Are—*"

He skidded to a stop, almost falling into one of the craters that had been left courtesy of the Decepticons' rampage. As he stepped back to work his way around it, he watched in astonishment as Optimus Prime shifted into his truck form. The Autobot whipped around, his tires spinning and sending chunks of dirt and grass flying every which way, and seconds later he had driven off into the night.

Sam stood there, speechless, his jaw hanging open. He had no idea how long he remained like that. When Lennox's voice came from behind him, he practically jumped. "What the hell happened?" Lennox demanded. "Why'd he take off like that?"

"I don't know," Sam said.

"Maybe he didn't see you."

"He saw me. He looked right at me. And then he . . . he just drove away."

Lennox nodded. "He probably had to rendezvous with the others. Figure out their next move."

"Sure. That's gotta be it."

"Just wish to God he'd let us in on the plan. Good call about the pillars, though. Obviously, they still must have some kind of use for them."

"Sure they do," Sam said hollowly. "They want to be able to transport themselves instantly all over the world, at any time."

"Could be," said Lennox, sounding annoyed that he hadn't thought of it. "First job in warfare is infrastructure. Be able to move the troops around. Thanks to those things—and Sentinel—they can do that. If they want to overrun Canada, all they need is for Sentinel to get there, and the troops do the rest. On the other hand, maybe they have something bigger in mind."

"Great. Something else to worry about." Sam felt wrung out.

Sensing the young man's unsteadiness, Lennox rested his hand on Sam's shoulder. "Let's get you home, kid. Nothing more to do here."

"Right," echoed Sam. "Nothing more to do."

Lennox quickly arranged for a NEST vehicle to bring Sam home. Just before the car drove away, Sam saw Lennox toss a salute to him. He returned it halfheartedly.

He was pleased that Lennox had commended him for the fast thinking about the pillars, but all he could think of was the way Optimus had just bailed on him like that. The thing was, he had a feeling he knew why Optimus had done it. Optimus had more or less vouched for Sentinel, had trusted him implicitly. And that trust had resulted in the deaths of three Autobots. Indeed, if it hadn't been for the Twins sacrificing themselves, it could well have been more. Optimus had to feel that was on his head, and maybe he just didn't feel like talking to a five-foot, nine-inch monkey descendant about it.

Still, Sam had thought they were friends. Friends were the ones you talked to when things were falling apart. He just didn't understand.

How can you understand? He's an alien, for crying out loud. The whole point of aliens is that they don't think the way we do. We can think we understand them, but we may well be just kidding ourselves. I thought I knew Optimus, but maybe the fact is that I knew as little about him as he did about Sentinel.

He was so wrapped up in his own thoughts that he scarcely realized it when he was in front of his apartment. He muttered thanks to the soldier who had driven him.

He ran upstairs, calling for Carly. But the only response he got was frantic barking from Buster, his dog, out on the balcony. He went out to the balcony and promptly stepped in a present Buster had left for him. The dog whimpered slightly, chagrined.

"Don't sweat it, dude," he said, carefully removing the shoe so he could clean it off. "It's my fault. Nobody's been around to walk you."

That concerned him even more, though. Where the hell was Carly? Wheelie and Brains were nowhere to be seen, but most likely they'd gone to ground with the return of the Decepticons and were probably disguised as merchandise in a Radio Shack somewhere. He tried dialing her number on her cellphone, but she wasn't picking up. So then he tried his parents. On the third ring, he heard someone pick up and he said, "Mom? Dad? Have you guys seen Carly?"

His mother's sleepy voice came back: "No. Not tonight. Why?"

"No reason. Sorry I woke you up."

"Well, it's a Saturday night," she said with a yawn. "You're two young people. You should be out having fun."

Saturday night?

Oh, my God.

Everything that had happened . . . he had completely lost track of not only the time but the day. With all the driving around, the waving of guns, the crazy Russians, the former spies—all of that had prompted him to forget that less than a day had passed.

It was still Saturday.

She was at the party. She was at Dylan's damned party.

Okay, well . . . fine. Let her be there. Let her be with the people she cared about. The people from work. She had made it abundantly clear that she had no patience for him anymore. Hell, the things she'd said to him . . .

Except . . .

They weren't just his war stories anymore. It was everybody's war now. The Decepticons were everywhere, and everyone was knee-deep in it.

"She needs me," said Sam, and he was certain that he was right. Whatever she thought of him, the fact that he *did* have the benefit of knowledge meant that he had the best chance of keeping her safe during what was sure to be a time of paranoia and upheaval. She needed him by her side . . .

. . . and he needed her. That was what it really came down to for him. He knew he needed her, and he knew she needed him, and the only problem was that *she* didn't know it.

And the reason she doesn't know it is because I just haven't made it clear to her.

And I have to. Right now.

He snatched the piece of paper with the address on it from the mirror. "Fine. Let's party."

MARYLAND

As Sam steered his crappy car up the circular drive-way to Dylan's opulent, Old World–style estate in Po-tomac, he could see that the party was winding down by the fact that very few cars were lining the drive. He pulled as close to the mansion as he could manage and forced the Datsun's creaking door open. After he got out, he slammed the door shut behind him, hoping the force wouldn't cause it to fall off the vehicle.

He fully expected servants or security guards of Dylan's to intercept him and stop him from barging in. He was, after all, hardly dressed for it. His hair was di-sheveled, he needed a shave, and he probably still stank from the smoke from the battle at the Mall. It probably wouldn't make any difference to them that he had been invited. It was doubtful they'd believe it, anyway. This was clearly a world into which he had no business in-truding.

To his surprise, though, when he did encounter ser-vants and guys who were obviously security guards, they just smiled and waved him on and even said, "Good evening, Mr. Witwicky." "Glad you could make it, Mr. Witwicky." "Can I get you a drink, Mr. Wit-wicky?" To which Sam replied, "Thanks," "Thanks," and "No thanks," in quick succession without quite un-derstanding why they were not only taking his arrival in stride but obviously recognized him. If he'd stopped to give it any real thought, it might well have set off alarm bells in his head. But he was so preoccupied with Carly that he didn't waste any extra brain cells on it, which, as subsequent events proved, turned out to be an unfortunate lapse on his part.

He had been right in his assumption, though: There were very few guests left, which made sense because of the late hour. Those who were there seemed to be in the process of leaving.

Carly was not one of the ones who had departed or were heading home.

He found her on a patio that was the size of a football field, laughing as if she had just heard the funniest joke in the world. And who was the one who had told that joke? Why, Dylan Gould, of course. Dylan Gould: businessman, Renaissance man, stand-up comedian. The complete freaking package—that was him.

At that moment he had his hand on Carly's shoulder while pouring her a glass of wine. Carly looked so stunningly gorgeous in her blue cocktail dress that it made Sam want to sob.

Their backs were to him, and as he approached, he realized that he was the topic of conversation. That prompted him to slow down a bit so he could hear just what they had to say about his favorite subject, namely, his many shortcomings.

"It's truly a man's greatest challenge to strike that delicate balance between love and career," Dylan said, oozing sympathy from every pore. "If I were him, I wouldn't let you out of my sight."

"Things are complicated for Sam right now," Carly said.

That's my girl. The master of understatement. Or mistress of understatement.

Carly was still speaking. "Look, it's late. I really should go."

Okay, well, that's good. At least she isn't talking about staying over.

"I bet it would help," Dylan suggested, "if I was able to talk to him. Sometimes it just takes a mentor, a big brother, for a boy to be a man."

Right, right. A big brother to help with the younger brother. That worked out great for Cain and Abel.

Sam was now close enough—and annoyed enough—to make his presence known. "Yeah, funny," he said, prompting the two of them to turn around in surprise. "I was just thinking, *'I need some advice from that Dylan.'*"

If Dylan was put out by Sam's arrival, he did a splendid job of hiding it. In fact, he was actually selling the whole notion that he was pleased to see him. "Sam!" he said, spreading his arms so wide that he looked like a cheerleader shouting, *Gimme a Y!* "Welcome! Just the guest I was hoping to see."

Moving forward quickly, Sam took Carly firmly by the elbow and said, "I need to talk to my girlfriend about something important. That okay with you, Mr. Inappropriate?"

"I'm your girlfriend again?" She pulled her elbow away from him, although she didn't seem to know whether to look peeved or grateful.

"I never stopped thinking of you that way, and we really need to discuss this somewhere else."

"You get that I'm still upset with you, right?"

He hated seeing the amusement in Dylan's eyes. He felt like he was providing entertainment for him. To make matters worse, Dylan was still trying to sound conciliatory. "I really think I could help you, Sam. I remember a talk Dad once had with me. About making hard choices—"

"Not a good time," Sam said. "We'll set something up." Then, in a voice so low that only Carly could hear, he said, "Please, you said you were leaving anyway. Leave with me. Don't hang me out to dry with this guy. I'm begging you."

The emotion was so raw that Carly's expression softened to sympathy. "Fine. But we still have a lot to talk about."

"And I swear we will. We'll talk about it all."

She walked alongside him, although she seemed slightly puzzled by the urgency with which he was moving. And Dylan, who apparently hadn't tumbled to the notion that Sam didn't want his damned advice, followed them. " 'Course, that was way back when Dad's firm was in charge of budget review for NASA."

Carly had been moving quickly to keep up with Sam and so was completely thrown off stride when Sam abruptly came to a halt, nearly tripping before righting herself. She looked to Sam in confusion.

Sam felt a pounding starting in his temples. *Aw, you gotta be kidding me.*

"And the thing he taught me," Dylan went on, "was this: When it's not your war, you join the side that's gonna win."

They were standing at the front door, which was wide open. It gave Sam a clear view to the front yard.

Perched atop a branch in a tree, his red eyes gleaming, was Laserbeak. The Decepticon gave Sam a long, slow wink.

Sam hurriedly pushed Carly toward her Mercedes, which was parked nearer than the Datsun. Carly was aware that something had fundamentally changed—that Sam had gone from urgency to barely contained panic— but she didn't yet understand what was going on. It wasn't her fault. There was no way she could, and these weren't exactly the best circumstances in which to explain it. "Get in the car," he said hurriedly.

She jumped into the front seat, fumbling for her keys

in her bag. Sam jumped into the passenger seat, and she looked at him in confusion before casting a glance at the Datsun some yards away. "What about your car?"

"I never liked it anyway! Just drive! Go!"

Dylan was standing at the front entrance of his mansion, doing a superb job of looking wounded by Sam's determination to get out fast. "Too sudden? Too strong? Is it me?" He sighed heavily. "It could have gone the easy way, but it's always the hard way."

He snapped his fingers.

Carly found her keys, but the car started up before she could get them in the ignition. She looked at the keys in confusion and then at Sam.

His heart sank.

Now how did I not see that coming?

"Get out of the car!" he shouted to Carly. "Get out before it's—"

Too late.

The car began to shift, and that familiar clanking sound that Sam found so comforting coming from the Autobots filled him with fear when he heard it now. They had no time to get clear as the car grew and changed and, seconds later, Soundwave of the Decepticons was throwing his hapless passengers onto the driveway.

Carly, on her back, stared up at him, her eyes widening in horror, beginning to grasp the immensity of what she had been thrust into. Then Sam was yanking her to her feet. *"Come on! Come on!"*

Deep down he knew it was hopeless, but he refused to give in to that realization. He charged down the driveway, hauling Carly behind him. She staggered and kicked off her high-heeled shoes, desperately trying to keep up with him. *"That's . . . that's . . ."* she managed to gasp out.

"Welcome to my world!"

With a steady clanking, Soundwave came right after them. He could have overtaken them with a couple of quick steps. Instead he paced them, in no hurry to catch up. Seemingly bored with the chase, though, he leaped, more than covering the distance and landing squarely in front of them in a feral crouch. Carly screamed and Sam screamed even higher, and he grabbed her by the hand and yanked her in the other direction.

They continued to run, and Dylan was just standing there, a short distance away, never having stepped away from the front of his mansion.

And suddenly Carly was no longer there. Soundwave was yanking her away and changing back into his Mercedes form. He shoved Carly into his interior, and when Sam tried to get to her, the Decepticon casually slapped him away just before he finished shifting into his alternative form.

Sam hit the ground, rolled, and came up. Then he saw a guest about to pull away in his car, an older man who was barely glancing at what was transpiring right there in front of him. Frantic, Sam ran toward him, flagging him down, yelling, "Hey, you! Help, please!" In truth, he wasn't sure what sort of help the man could possibly provide in the face of Decepticons, but he didn't know what else to do or say.

The older man never lost a bit of his equanimity. Instead he called to Dylan, in reference to Sam, "He's young. He'll learn." He then waved, said, "Great party, as always," and drove serenely away as if a battle with Decepticons outside a luxurious mansion were the most commonplace thing in the world.

Sam was stunned but tried to recover quickly. He turned back toward Soundwave and caught a glimpse of Carly within, pounding at the window, trying to get out, screaming wildly. Dylan stepped between them, blocking her from Sam's view. "Think you're so special, Sam?

So unique?" he said mockingly. "Really think you were the first man ever asked to 'join the noble alien cause'?"

"Who *are* you?" At this point Sam was so overwhelmed by what he was seeing that if Dylan had suddenly broken down into component parts and changed into a giant robot himself, he wouldn't have been the least bit surprised.

Dylan didn't answer directly. Instead, his hands draped behind his back, he said, "You know why we haven't returned to the moon since 1972? Because that's the year these two"—he indicated Soundwave, who was still holding Carly captive, and Laserbeak, who seemed most amused by the whole thing—"came to my dad. Told him to do some creative accounting. Make it far too expensive to ever go back." He tried to look as if he regretted the events he was recounting but didn't quite succeed. "He and others shut the program down, and a lot of families got to live—and they've been our best client ever since."

Sam pointed at him accusingly. "You've helped them kill people!"

Sounding indifferent to the accusation, Dylan replied, "You think they give you a choice?" This was clearly a man who, if he had ever felt any sort of moral outrage over the things he was doing or the position he was in, had long ago come to terms with it. "It's not like I'm personally participating. I'm a liaison. I . . . liaise," he said with a shrug. "Hostile takeover time, Sam. Alien mergers and acquisitions. Can't coordinate 'human operations' without a human touch."

Sam had heard everything he was going to listen to. He drew back his fist to hit Dylan. Gould remained unfazed, not the least bit concerned about physical threat. The reason for that immediately became clear as the bodyguards, moving so quickly that Sam didn't even see them coming, knocked him to the ground, pinning him.

Sam struggled against them, but he had no chance at all. There were four of them to one of him, but that didn't deter him from continuing to battle back. He even managed to sink his teeth into the arm of one of them, causing the guard to howl in pain and yank his hand away, giving Sam a bit more fighting room.

Carly had been shouting, screaming his name, but suddenly the sound and pitch of the scream changed from alarm to pure terror. Inside Soundwave, the steering wheel was steadily beginning to push toward Carly. At the same time, the seat was shoving her toward it. The ultimate result was inevitable: Carly's upper body was, gradually but inevitably, going to be crushed.

Dylan rapped on Soundwave's hood, and he admonished the Decepticon. "Easy . . . careful now . . . she takes such good care of her skin." He turned back to Sam. "Man, talk about your compact cars. This baby just isn't the right fit for a family of five. The upside is, you won't have to go to the gym to get those flat abs you've been dreaming about." He gave Sam a significant look.

Sam got the message. Instantly he stopped all resistance.

In response, Soundwave promptly halted the process that would have reduced Carly's torso to a bloody pulp.

The guard whom Sam had bit was scowling fiercely, holding a handkerchief to where he was bleeding. Dylan strolled past him and paused long enough to feign concern. "You'll probably want to put something on that." Then he came within a couple feet of Sam and looked down at him, smiling. "Had my eye on you for years, Sam. See, the one spy I could never provide was someone close to the Autobots."

It must have been agony for her to draw in another breath to make her voice heard, yet Carly managed it: "He'll never work for you!"

"No? Never?" Dylan said, feigning disappointment. "As in never *never* ever?"

Then she shrieked, and Sam thought he was going to die as well just from hearing the agony in her voice as Soundwave applied a bit more pressure. Sam shouted for them to stop, and once again Soundwave did so, but there was even less room than before for Carly. One more application of the unyielding pressure from Soundwave, and Sam was afraid the results would be fatal.

"That sounded to me," said Dylan, "like the cry of a young man who would do anything, absolutely anything, to save the life of his lady love. Hmmm?" He cocked an eyebrow. "Am I close? I am, aren't I? Here's the thing, Sam: They *will* slaughter her, do you understand me? In the time that it takes you to blink. They will do it to her, then they'll do it to me. So try to show a little more respect when someone offers you a job."

"You . . ." Sam gulped. "You make it sound like we're in the same fix or something. We're not. Because you're enjoying this way too much, you sick bastard. I can see it in your eyes, hear it in your voice. You would've wound up screwing people over, hurting them, making them do whatever you wanted even if the Decepticons had never shown up. It's just that this way, you have an excuse. You can tell yourself that, oh well, you didn't really have a choice. When the truth is that on your own, you'd've been a sadistic asshole. Now you're just a sadistic asshole with robots."

Dylan's self-satisfied smile never wavered. "Sticks and stones will break her bones, Sammy. You want to roll those dice, or do you want to shut your piehole and listen up? And be grateful. Most people have to work a job twenty-five years to get a special wristwatch. Here you get yours on your first day."

Whereupon Dylan extended his arm and his wristwatch disengaged from it. The watch leaped to the ground, flipping in the air as it did so. Four tiny legs extended from either side of the watch face, eight in all, cushioning the watch's landing. Then it skittered across the ground straight toward Sam.

Automatically Sam started to struggle, until he was halted by Dylan's derisive, "Ah, ah. Wouldn't want to put lovely Carly into an even more pressing situation, would we?" Upon hearing that, Sam immediately halted his attempts to pull free. The guard holding his arm angled it toward the approaching creature. As Sam watched helplessly, it hopped onto his hand and settled upon his wrist. It probed around a little bit as if it were a cat kneading in before making itself comfortable.

As it did so, Dylan circled Sam. "You are to track down Optimus Prime, because you are the only human he trusts."

"Track him down? How am I supposed to track him down?" Sam's voice sounded squeaky to his own ears, breaking with fear for Carly's life. "It's not like I have his phone number. What do you want me to do? Shine a picture of a big truck on a passing cloud?"

"You'll figure it out, Sam. I have confidence in you. You're a clever lad. And once you have accomplished this goal, you will ask him this question: How does he intend to fight back? We want their tactics, strategy, everything."

The spider watch, apparently having found the space it wanted, bit down into Sam's wrist. Sam let out a pained cry and felt like a wimp for doing so. He wanted to be strong. He wanted to show that he could handle anything these creeps could dish out. Instead he yelped at something as relatively insignificant as a bite from a spider watch. But he couldn't help it; it hurt like hell.

"Okay, boys, let him up." Dylan gestured for the guards to release their hold on him and they did so. Sam got to his feet, dusting himself off and glaring at Dylan the whole time. He also fired an angry look at his brand-new jewelry.

"Got a nasty bite, doesn't it?" Dylan said with his typical mock sympathy. "*Very* high tech. Lets us see what you see and hear what you hear. And it taps your nervous system. Electrical feed right to the spine. So if you so much as try to signal Optimus or any of his pals as to what's really going on . . ."

At that point Sam understood why Dylan had let him up.

It was so he could fall down again as more pain than he had ever experienced lanced through his spine. It was like being tasered except, he had to believe, a hundred times worse. His arms flew wide, his legs buckled, and his mouth was open in a soundless "o" of agony. He didn't even feel himself hitting the ground because it felt like every single molecule of his body was being blown apart. Lying on the ground, he spasmed out of control and then lay there gasping as it subsided.

And Carly, ever defiant, even with her own life on the line, shouted, "Sam! Don't do what he wants!"

Sam knew of a certainty that if it were simply his own survival at issue, that would be exactly the course of action he would follow. He would have told Dylan to forget it. He would have taken every bit of punishment that this Rolex from hell was inflicting on him and more besides before he gave up Optimus Prime and risked dealing a lethal blow to the last line of defense humanity might still have. The worst they could do was kill him. It would be a slow and excruciating death, but eventually death *would* come, and he would die knowing that he hadn't let his friends down.

Perhaps sensing the depths of Sam's resolve, Dylan knelt next to him and once again put on that "we're in the same boat" attitude. Like a bartender offering sage advice, he said, "What can I tell you, Sam? Relationships have consequences. I'm here because of my father. She's here because of you."

And then he heard Carly's scream, and he was absolutely certain that it would quickly be followed by the sound of her ribs, her spine, even her skull, snapping like a wishbone at Thanksgiving.

"No! Stop!" In his voice was more than just a protest or a plea for mercy. It was abject surrender to the terms being presented to him.

Dylan had heard what he wanted to. "Soundwave!" he said sharply and with finality.

The steering column retracted, and the seat instantly returned to its normal position. Then the door popped open, and Soundwave essentially spit Carly out. She fell onto the driveway, her arms crisscrossed around her body, alternating between sobs and trying to get her breath back.

"You do your job," Dylan said easily, "and she'll be safe. You have my word."

With pure venom in every word, Sam shot back, "I'll kill you. You have *my* word."

Dylan faked a shudder. "Mmmm. Just got goose bumps. I can see why she formerly used to like you." Then, like a businessman who had just closed a deal—which, as far as he was concerned, he probably was—he informed Sam, "I invest in the future at this company. I'm leveraged heavily in Decepticons. And I just bought you. You go find your Autobots now. How they plan to fight back and all we want to know."

He nodded to his guards, who started to reach for Sam's arms. He shook them off and headed toward his Datsun. The guards followed him to make sure he didn't try anything, although what he would possibly try, Sam couldn't begin to guess. What was he going to do? Make a break for it and run home instead of drive?

Dylan looked to Carly, who was still lying on the driveway, curled up in almost a fetal position, gasping for breath. "I like him," he said cheerily. "Still think you're settling, but hey, your call. Because one thing I value in any employee is a strong sense of what it will take to survive."

And he smiled a crocodile's smile.

WASHINGTON, D.C.

i

The first fingers of dawn were stretching over the horizon. The sun was coming up on not only a new day but a new world. For the first time in the history of the planet, the whole of humanity had to deal with a common enemy.

Lennox had never been in the situation room of the White House before. He supposed it was absurd to be thinking, as he was just then, that he wished it had been under better circumstances. It was the situation room, for crying out loud. When would there be a good circumstance for having to use it? The president was monitoring the situation from *Air Force One;* it was felt that the best option of all the bad ones currently before them was to keep the chief executive on the move.

The joint chiefs and assorted others were grouped around, studying the data pouring in from all over. None of it was giving any of them the warm fuzzies.

Still, considering that they were humans who had been thrown into combat with beings that they should, from an evolutionary standpoint, never have been forced to battle—like cavemen slugging it out with dinosaurs—they were doing their best to stay ahead of the curve.

General Morshower said, "Our combat commands are now at DEFCON 1 around the globe. We'll have our eyes in the sky over the twenty largest U.S. cities within the hour." He cast an expectant glance to his right. "Colonel Lennox?"

Lennox nodded, taking the stage. "We estimate two hundred Decepticons now in hiding. Energon detectors have been triggered as far away as South America. Still no direct sightings, however."

"We assume they're preparing to attack. But so far we don't know when, where, how . . . or why," said Morshower.

An aide quickly entered the situation room and said urgently, "General, the UN's just received an encrypted audio file. They say it is from the leader of the Autobots."

"All right," said Morshower, galvanized into action. "Inform them that the contents of that file are hereby classified top secret. Lennox, I want you to arrange for an immediate special courier to—"

The aide cleared his throat. "Um, General . . ."

"What is it?" he said impatiently.

"The secretary-general decided the circumstances called for a special meeting of the General Assembly. He said that since it was the world's business, the world had a right to know. They're broadcasting it right now, on every channel, on radio, and live-streaming it onto the Internet. They timed it so that it would go hot the exact moment they informed us of its existence."

Morshower went dead white. There were stunned looks from the rest of the brass. "Why the hell did they do that?"

"According to them," and the aide could not have looked less happy about it, "it was because they were afraid we would classify it top secret and have it brought here by special courier."

There were moans from around the table.

Lennox closed his eyes in pain. *Fantastic. Fan . . . freaking . . . tastic.*

ii

("Defenders of Earth: My name is Sentinel Prime, the true leader of the Autobots.)

("For millennia our galaxy was ravaged by a tragic civil war. But now that war is over, and our armies stand as one. We come from a damaged planet, which must be rebuilt.)

("What we need are the natural resources your world has in abundance. Precious metals, iron, steel. We shall use my space bridge technology to transport an equitable share of such material. And then we will leave your planet in peace.)

("However, for such peace to exist, you must renounce resistance. You must immediately exile from this planet the rebels you have harbored, or we will deem it your hostile intent, and, through my space bridge, will come more battalions. And you will know our righteous strength.)

("We want no war with you. Only our planet's reconstruction. Long live Cybertron. Long live Earth. Renounce the rebels. We await your reply.")

iii

There was not a word being spoken by the occupants in the situation room as they watched the General Assembly of the United Nations. It was up on a screen on the wall, which was no great trick since it was also being broadcast into every home in America. The only noises to be heard were the ambient sounds of various data streams still coming in through other control systems. They were being ignored by everyone as they all observed the proceedings.

Lennox didn't know what the generals and the joint chiefs were thinking, but he was getting a bad feeling in the pit of his stomach.

The Autobots have done so much good while they

were here. Going into hot spots where no one else could. Every damned government has come to us at one time or another and asked for the help of the Autobots. Everything from sending them into war zones to delivering supplies and medical aid to nations hit by natural disasters. God may have sent us earthquakes and floods, but he also sent us these metal freaking angels to pitch in.

And that's just going to go right out the window, I know it. The first time the going gets tough, the first time the Autobots need us to have their backs, the UN is going to throw them under the cosmic bus.

The secretary-general slowly rose from his chair to let the whole world in on what was possibly the most cataclysmic decision in the history of the species and one that they would most certainly screw up since fear usually dictated the wrong response to any situation. With a quiet dignity, in words so plain and firm as to command their assent, he said: "For over sixty-five years, it has been our charter to defend refugees from all wartorn nations. Today we are asked whether we shall do the same for those facing an alien war. To stand wth them as they have with us. Whatever danger it may bring to the citizens of Earth, I now ask all representatives who are in favor of allowing the Autobots to stay to stand."

The delegates began to stand. In later days, many delegates would claim to be the first to have gotten to their feet, and historians would devote thousands of hours to studying tapes from all angles—the Zapruder film received less scrutiny—before finally concluding that it was inconclusive.

But everyone could agree on one thing: It started slowly but gained in speed and momentum as a vast majority of representatives got to their feet. The message from the United Nations—from humanity's delegates and representatives—was clear and unequivocal and summarized by a front-page *New York Daily News* headline written in that publication's inimitable style:

UN TO BAD BOTS: GO SCREW YOURSELVES

All of that was to come later, though. At that moment, watching the drama unfolding, the occupants of the situation room were far too experienced professionals to do something as tacky as burst into whoops or cheers. Instead they provided a stately, dignified round of applause for the scene that they were witnessing.

Lennox sagged down into his chair and let out a relieved sigh. *I'll be damned. They got it right. Now all we have to do is survive to write about it in the history books.*

iv

Seymour Simmons stared at his busted leg in dismay as he lay on his back at Washington General Hospital. It was in a cast, and the prognosis for it was good. He had been treated for various cuts and abrasions, and the ribs in his chest, as it turned out, weren't broken but only bruised. So in point of fact, he was one of the luckiest men around since it could have been much, much worse.

But he didn't feel lucky at all. Instead, all he felt was frustrated.

When Dutch walked in with a folder under his arm, Simmons started venting immediately. "I'm missing the whole thing, Dutch! The whole damned thing! The fight on the National Mall! The UN resolution! It's all happening without me, man! The world is passing me by!"

"I think you need to—"

"At least the UN got behind our boys, huh?" He was trying to find a bright spot. "We don't bargain with the bad guys, no, sir. And if—"

"Seymour!" Dutch said, immediately snapping Simmons to attention since typically Dutch respectfully called him "Agent Simmons" or simply "sir." "You need to see this, right now. It started circulating on the Hill almost immediately. Nobody knows about it yet, but they're going to."

Simmons didn't even bother to ask how Dutch knew. That was part of Dutch's job: to know things, particularly where it related to the Autobots. He took the file and started flipping through it. As he did so, he was quickly enveloped by a sense of shock and betrayal. "Are you kidding me?"

"No, sir."

"Are you kidding me?"

"Still no."

"And this is solid? I mean, this is rock solid? This would make Mount Rushmore look like a sponge, it's that solid?"

"Yes, sir. They're convening even now. It's going to happen."

Fury shook his body. "Those ungrateful sons of . . ." His voice tapered off as his mind raced. "But if they were going to, then how would . . . unless . . . oh, of course! It's the only possible way! Dutch," he said, having reached a conclusion that now required immediate action. "Your pilot license up to date?"

"Yes, sir."

"And your plane?"

"Carefully maintained, sir."

"Good. Get me checked outta here. If they try to stop us, get a gun from the car trunk and we'll shoot our way out." He started disconnecting his IV.

Dutch was clearly surprised. "Sir, I brought you this information because I felt you should be kept apprised, but you can't be thinking of leaving . . ."

"Oh, I'm not thinking of it. I'm doing it. I'm gonna need my clothes. Oh, and go boost me a wheelchair from somewhere. If necessary, find a crippled guy who looks like he needs it less than me."

"But, sir!" Dutch tried to reason with him. "You were threatened by Russians, attacked by Decepticons, got your leg broken, suffered all manner of damage. What are you going to do now?"

"I'm going to Disney World."

"Really?"

"No, but damned close. Let's move. Let's get it going. Let's show them how it's—"

Two FBI men walked in. The taller of the two said, "Seymour Simmons?"

"Yeah . . . ?" he said cautiously.

"You're needed."

"Florida?" Simmons said without hesitation.

The agent tried to mask his surprise and wasn't all that successful. "How did you know?"

"The fact that I know is why you need me," Simmons informed him confidently. "Let's get this show on the road. I'm still gonna need a wheelchair, though."

"We have one outside," said the agent. "We took it from a crippled guy who looked like he needed it less than you."

"I like the way you think," Simmons said.

v

There had been many a day in Sam Witwicky's life that he had thought was the worst day ever. And then fate, not to mention the efforts of the Decepticons, always conspired to raise the bar of pure suckiness.

Still, it was going to be pretty damned tough to top this one.

Twenty-four hours ago, he'd been in the living room of the apartment he was now driving up to. He'd been huddled in conference with Simmons, an idiot from work, and a couple of reformed Decepticons, trying to determine just what exactly was going on and how they might go about saving the world. In doing so he had jeopardized, if not outright ended, his relationship with his girlfriend.

So here he was, a day later. Simmons was MIA, the bots were MIA, his dog was crapping on his balcony, and—oh yeah—the very individuals he had been trying to thwart had conspired to turn him into a double agent against his best friends in the world while he'd been forced to watch a killer Mercedes reenact the car-crunching scene from *Goldfinger* with his girlfriend in the featured role of victim. He stared down dismally at his new best friend on his wrist. *I visited Potomac, and all I got was this lousy Decepticon,* he thought with bleak humor.

He pulled up into his driveway, but before he could make it into the garage, the Datsun choked out and died. Naturally. The final insult to be added to injury.

Sam stepped out of his Datsun, and suddenly car doors from up and down the street opened as well, almost in perfect synchronization. He watched in confusion as a half dozen men wearing black suits and sunglasses emerged. He half expected Tommy Lee Jones and Will Smith to be among them.

They approached, coming at him in a half circle. Sam, who couldn't remember the last time he'd slept, was completely tapped out, unable and unwilling to offer even token resistance. He just stared at them lifelessly.

The one closest to him said, "You're a hard man to find."

He found his voice and said gamely, "Good men usually are."

The man somehow managed to resist the hilarity of Sam's quip and didn't crack a smile. "Special Agent Pinkett," he said, holding up identification. "Come with us, please."

"Am I under arrest?"

"No, sir, you are not. Come with us, please."

"If I'm not under arrest, then technically I don't have to go with you."

"Technically, yes. Now . . . come with us, please." He sounded more robotic than Optimus ever had.

Sam leaned back against his car and stared at the agent, trying to see his eyes through the sunglasses. No luck. "Just out of curiosity, what if I say I won't go with you?"

He finally got a reaction from Pinkett: His eyebrow twitched.

"Then I stop saying 'please.' "

Sam considered his options and wasn't finding a whole lot of them.

"Road trip. I'm so there," he said.

He allowed them—if "allowed" was the way to describe something in which he was being given no choice—to lead him to one of the cars. At least they didn't push him in. Instead, they opened the back door and allowed him to ease himself in. He hated to admit it, but it was actually pretty comfortable for a government car.

"Mind if I lean my head back? Close my eyes?"

"As you wish, sir."

Sam did so, figuring that at the very least he would be able to rest his eyes. He didn't really think that, given the stress of all he'd been through, he'd actually be able to get some sleep.

He was wrong. The next thing he knew, an agent was gently prodding him awake. The door was open, and he was someplace else completely, an airfield by the sound of it. Outside the vehicle he could hear the distant thrumming of an engine powering up.

It had gotten sunnier out, and he shielded his eyes as he emerged from the darkness of the car into the full light of day. Sure enough, it was an airfield. It wasn't a commercial one, though. He could see a high fence in the distance and a gate being slid shut. About a hundred feet away was a private plane, which was the source of the engines he had heard. The stairway was down, waiting for him.

He had no idea who was going to be in there. He felt as if he should know and would probably kick himself in retrospect, but as he walked across the field, he remained clueless.

Sam walked up the stairs, which bounced slightly under his feet. He'd heard that once you flew private, there was no going back to commercial jets. That should be the biggest problem he had to face.

He entered the plane and blinked in surprise. Then he took consolation in the fact that there would be no retrospective kicking of himself, because there was no way he could have expected to see the individual waiting for him in the plane.

Charlotte Mearing, all business, was seated with her legs primly crossed in a large, cushioned chair. It was a swivel seat. There was a table in back of her with an open laptop computer on it.

She pointed to a chair across from her that was identical to the one in which she was seated. Already buckled in, she acted as if they had an appointment that he had been inconsiderate enough to be running late for and they'd had to expend energy to go out and correct this lapse on his part. "Glad they found you. We'll debrief you in transit."

Oh, my God, they're bringing me into the loop. At the worst possible time.

He started to back up for the door. "Um, I really don't see how I can be any more help . . . you guys seem so busy . . . we could just do this later . . . *owwww*!"

He clutched at his wrist. The watch was giving him an

ungentle reminder of who was in charge here. Then he saw that Mearing was looking at him with concern and confusion. There was no way he could afford to under-estimate her; the woman was too bright. He couldn't put it past her to figure out something was up with him, something Decepticon-related. And if she did, they would stick him in a room with four white walls some-where so that he couldn't pose a threat, and when they subsequently showed up to question him, they'd find the corpse of Sam Witwicky with his entire nervous system fried. A week or so later, Carly's body would likewise turn up in a garbage dump somewhere, if they ever found her at all.

"Muscle spasm," he said apologetically, and dropped into the chair opposite her.

The door slammed behind them, sealing them in the cabin. Then the plane started rolling forward with no preamble.

"So, uh . . . do we get an in-flight movie? Some mixed nuts? Maybe a barf bag?"

"You seem jumpy, Mr. Witwicky," she said. "I bet I know why."

"Oh, I bet you don't."

She leaned forward in the chair as much as the seat belt would allow and didn't seem to be paying the least bit of attention as the plane built up speed for takeoff. "Sam," she said as the plane lifted off, "I owe you an apology."

"Uh . . . what? No, honestly . . ."

Mearing shook her head, denying both his protesta-tions and a lack of wrongdoing on her part. "You real-ized Sentinel was the key. You warned us they were using humans. We've been conducting investigations, and it seems that Jerry Wang was not an isolated case. There were other people involved, some willingly, some less so. We're only just beginning to get an idea of just how far up this thing goes."

It goes all the way down my arm.

"The fact is," Mearing said, "I underestimated you at every turn. And truthfully, I also unfairly blamed you for some lapses on my own part. It won't happen again."

"No, it's all good. And hey, right back at you. Remember, you totally called it about the space bridge being weaponized. You just nailed it. I didn't see it coming, and you did. I mean, you're the expert," he said quickly. "I'm just a—" He bent his elbow and brought the watch into view, trying to sound casual. "—a walking security risk . . . *ow, ow, ow!*"

"Are you all right?" Mearing said with growing concern.

"What? No—*ow*—I mean, yes. It's nothing. It was . . . I went bowling the other night and overdid it. Strained the wrist."

"Do you want some painkillers?"

Oh, I wanna kill something that's causing me pain, all right. Trying to sound casual, he rotated his hand a few times, "flexing" the wrist as if trying to work through it. "I'll be fine. Really."

The plane was starting to level off.

"Okay, if you're sure," she said. Then she turned the chair back around to face the computer.

The watch began to extend itself, trying to get a better view of what was on the computer screen. He hoped that the thing couldn't split its focus and wouldn't keep trying to zap him while it was busy endeavoring to spy on Mearing's information.

"Okay, just so you know," and Sam struggled valiantly with the watch, trying to shove it back into place or block its view. "I'm a Twitter junkie. Blog everything, total oversharer, no secret is safe . . ."

"I think I'm finally starting to understand your sense of humor, Sam," she said, her back still to him. "It took me a while, plus I had to have a briefing memo drawn up so I could read an analysis of it. But I get it now. Say what you want, but we both know that you can be completely trusted with matters of security, particularly where it comes to the Autobots and the current difficult situation we now have to face with them."

"Yeah, that's me, Mr. Trustworthy." He pounded with a fist on the watch. It snapped back at him and almost took off his little finger. "But y' know, the situation, the current one, it's not that difficult. I heard on the radio about the UN telling them—"

"The UN resolution means nothing, Sam. Not a damned thing." For a woman who kept herself wrapped as tightly as Mearing did, it was surprising to hear the bitterness in her voice.

Sam didn't understand. Neither, obviously, did the creature on his wrist, which ceased its struggling so that it could hear better what she was saying. "What do you mean it doesn't mean a damned thing? That's, y' know, practically the whole world standing up and saying that the Autobots can stay."

"A resolution that has no meaning, no force of law. The Autobots are here in the United States. That makes them our problem, and the decision as to whether they stay or go is no one's business but ours. And apparently when it comes to Congress, they never miss an opportunity to get it wrong."

"What are you talking about?"

"They finally found something they agree on, Sam. Democrats, Republicans alike. They converged on the Hill, like lemmings, in an emergency session. House and Senate, united as one, speaking with a single voice: Get the Autobots the hell out of here. The special dispensation allowing them to remain has been revoked. The military alliance has been severed. If they're not out of here in twenty-four hours, the orders are that they are to be attacked on sight. I swear to God, if they were standing in the middle of Detroit, a nuke would probably be dropped to wipe them out along with the entire population of Michigan and some of Canada. That's how terrified the government is."

"Okay, well . . ." He tried to find words. "If they have to leave the States, then other countries . . ."

"You think it's only happening here? You think other governments give any more of a damn about a show of support from the UN than ours did? Nobody wants them anywhere near their territory. Which means we're going to wind up on our own against an enemy we're not remotely prepared to fight without the Autobots on our side. Which brings us to the reason you're here, Sam."

"It . . . it does?"

"Yes. If there is anything more you know, anything at all, about the enemy's intentions, it's time to tell."

The watch promptly dug its teeth into Sam's skin as a reminder of what he could and could not say. Sam jumped slightly and bit down on his lower lip, trying to shift the conversation away from discussing things like—oh—the lethal little creature on his wrist. "But wait I don't understand. The Autobots have no way to leave the planet—"

"That's where you're wrong."

"I . . . I am?" He looked out the window. He'd assumed that they were taking a short hop over to NEST headquarters, but he saw the coastline below them and stared down in confusion. "Where the hell are we going?"

"Florida."

"Florida? What's in Florida? Aside from theme parks and old people?"

"The Kennedy Space Center," she said. "And *Xantium.*"

"Xantium? It sounds like a remedy for stomachaches."

"It's a remedy," she said. "But not one any of us is going to like."

vi

In the shipping bay of Dylan Gould's office building, Carly watched as the loading of an armored Decepticon truck was completed. The gate in the back was pulled down, and she had one final glimpse of the cargo—strange pillars stacked one atop the other, nearly to the ceiling—before it was shut tight. Dylan, who had been overseeing the entire procedure, banged a fist twice on the side of the truck to signal that everything was locked down, and then the vehicle rumbled away from the loading dock.

She was fortunate that she had changed from her more casual clothes to her party clothes at Dylan's. It had provided her with something to change back into at his house so she wouldn't be standing around on loading docks wearing a cocktail dress. If nothing else, she didn't have to feel creeped out over the prospect of Dylan staring at her with that grin that she had once found charming but now was repulsed by.

Dylan strolled back to her, that insufferable smile on his face. As Carly watched him, she felt her gorge rise. Everything Sam had said had been absolutely right. This was not a man who was being forced against his will to do terrible things. This was someone who was doing terrible things and was enjoying having an excuse for it.

"One woman's adversity is another's opportunity," he

said. When she continued to glare at him, he continued. "You really need to see this as more of a partnership."

Then he led her off the loading dock, heading toward where she knew the helipad was. "Where are we going?" she said.

"To help build a bridge."

FLORIDA

i

When he was a kid, Sam had, like many children, dreamed of what it would be like to be an astronaut. Before they stopped broadcasting launches, he remembered sitting cross-legged in front of the television, watching raptly as the mighty vessels would tear free of the earth's gravity and hurl themselves into the air. It didn't matter whether it was something as relatively mundane as a satellite or as pulse-pounding as a shuttle or a trip to the space station. There was just something that fired the imagination about the infinite possibilities that space had to offer.

He had often wondered what it would be like to be one of the people sitting in the distant bleachers, watching and cheering as the rockets blasted off for the depths of space.

It had never occurred to him that he might someday be walking around on the field itself, the bleachers far off in the distance, staring at a shuttle on a launchpad that was preparing for liftoff. There was no countdown yet, nor were the engines even firing up.

But unlike those previous occasions where he'd been watching the launches on television and waiting with breathless anticipation as the countdown dwindled toward zero, here and now he prayed that the thing would never take off.

Xantium.

He hadn't known about it and couldn't help but wonder why he hadn't. Why had Optimus never mentioned it to him? Why hadn't any of the others? It also made him wonder what else they might be keeping from him.

It looked like no other shuttle in the history of the space program, which naturally made sense since it was not of this world. It looked battered and beat up, but from all accounts it was still functioning, and now it was standing upright on the launchpad, ready to be pressed into service once again.

Mearing had brought him up to speed on the flight down. The *Xantium* had been the vehicle that had brought the second wave of Autobots—Sideswipe and all those guys—to Earth years ago. It had been under NASA's care and study ever since. Fortunately enough— or unfortunately, depending on one's point of view— they had left it intact. *With the U.S. government harboring aliens,* Mearing had told him, *we've always wanted an exit option.*

Now she was standing next to him as they watched work proceeding apace to get the vessel prepped for takeoff. Sam could sense the damned creature on his wrist scoping out everything he was seeing. He was strongly starting to consider finding a power saw and hacking off his forearm just to get the thing off him. "Um," he said as he gestured toward the rocket in the distance, "this seems pretty top secret. I should really have clearance."

She actually patted him on the back. She did it awkwardly, as if she were inexperienced with simple human contact, but it was an attempt, at least. "Sam, you have clearance with me."

Well, that's just terrific.

The field was a hive of industry. Technicians were making last-minute checks, working in close contact with the NASA scientists at launch central to make sure that everything came together correctly. Mearing was able to walk forward without breaking stride, radiating confidence, and somehow all the technicians and scientists and engineers moved right around her and avoided her. Sam, by contrast, endlessly seemed to be in everybody's way as he was bumped into or even shoved aside by people hurrying to do their jobs.

"I'd think that even with years of studying it, this would be kind of out of their comfort zone," Sam said tentatively.

"That would be true if we purely had humans working on it. We also have the Wreckers."

"Wreckers?" He was confused. "You mean there are guys tearing it apart or . . . ?"

"Not guys. The Autobot engineers; they're known as the Wreckers. We never let them off the base because . . . well, they're not very nice."

Seconds later, Sam had the opportunity to judge for himself firsthand as three Autobots came out of a nearby hangar at high speed, wielding various tools that Sam didn't recognize (and which he assumed to be of Autobot design) and arguing furiously. Their basic designs were close to one another, but one was blue, the second red, and the third green.

Mearing pointed to each one as they approached and said in quick succession, "Leadfoot, Topspin, and Roadbuster."

For their parts, the Wreckers were paying no attention to anyone who might be in their way. Even Mearing, who so easily exuded a sense of dominance that made everyone else automatically keep clear of her, felt the need to get out of their path as they neared. Ignoring Mearing and Sam, they converged on the NASA technicians, expressing increasing ire with accents that sounded like a vague blend of Australian and Irish. They seemed particularly irate with one technician in particular, a short, squat fellow who was becoming increasingly pale the closer the Wreckers drew.

"Gonna be ten thousand pounds of torque on that itsy-bitsy hold!" Roadbuster was saying with clear frustration. "So it better get twenty and a quarter rotations! *Not* nineteen! Did I say bloody nineteen?"

"Yah, either yer deaf or yer an idiot," said Topspin, and Leadfoot chimed in with, "Or a deaf idiot; ya might be that!"

Roadbuster was poking the short fellow with his finger. "Ya gonna risk the lives of all me mates over one and a quarter screw rotations? Thought we were working wid professionals. Oh, what now?" he said when the technician tried to stammer out a response and was unable to manage it. "Ya gonna start crying?"

Sam could see what Mearing had been talking about. It was bad enough when he had had Mearing insulting him so thoroughly that it made him want to crawl into a hole somewhere. But being ragged on by three huge robots in front of everybody you worked for? That had to stink.

And then salvation for the beleagured technician came from a most unexpected source, albeit a familiar voice.

"Back off, you greasy gearheads! To your pits!"

Sam turned and saw that, yes, it was exactly who he thought: USAF Master Sergeant Robert Epps, who had fought so valiantly beside Colonel Lennox during previous smackdowns with the Decepticons. But he was most definitely out of uniform, clad in overalls with NASA patches on the arms. Nevertheless, he had such a strong personality that even the acerbic Autobots seemed to recognize his authority. They didn't back down, but at least they stopped haranguing the technician.

The NASA technician—O'Toole, according to his name tag—who had been the main focus of the Wreckers' ire, really did seem a bit ready to cry. But it quickly became evident that it wasn't out of his feelings being hurt so much as from frustration. "I . . . I just can't work under these conditions," he complained to Epps. "Every day, they're always changing their specs!"

Epps did his best to calm the frustrated technician down. "It's okay. Deep breaths. You just gotta focus on his positive intentions. Remember, it's their metal asses on the line if something goes wrong. He's just trying to protect their interests. And you," he said, rounding on the Wreckers while pointing at the technician. "That's a human being you're working with! He's got feelings, doubts, and emotions. He's trying to do the best he can!"

Unfortunately, the Wreckers didn't seem particularly moved by Epps's appeal to their gentler side. "Tough shite," Roadbuster snapped. "It's a cold, cruel galaxy! Either the job gets done or it don't."

O'Toole was getting upset again, and by that point Epps had clearly had it. He shouted loudly enough to get the Wreckers to take a step back. "Strap a muffler on it, you hear me? I'm here to mediate your ass!"

Sam couldn't hold in his surprise any longer. "Epps? What're you doing here?"

Because he was deep in the middle of trying to stop a fractious situation from blowing apart completely, Epps looked with pure irritation at what he considered merely the latest interruption. "What the—" But then he saw who it was, and his face lit up. "Sam! Sam Witwicky?"

The uttering of the name instantly caught the Wreckers' attention as well. All eyes went to him, and Topspin said with what actually sounded like reverence, "*The* Sam Witwicky? The Sam Witwicky who is an ally of— who, indeed, restored to life—the great Optimus Prime himself?"

"Um . . ." He didn't have a flip retort. "Well . . . yeah."

" 'Ey!" said Roadbuster, slugging Topspin on the shoulder. "It's the kid!"

Immediately all three Wreckers were shouting out variations on "Good on you, mate!" Just that quickly, he had instantly become their new best friend.

As the Autobots immediately started sharing Witwicky stories with one another while Mearing looked on with as close to amusement as she ever displayed, Epps approached Sam and shook his hand firmly. "Imagine seeing you here," he said.

"Yeah, well, I'm with her," Sam said, chucking a thumb at Mearing. "But I don't know what the hell *you're* doing here."

"Retired from the air force," Epps said. "I just consult, run interference. I kinda know how to talk to them." He nodded toward the Wreckers, who were still busily comparing notes over things they'd heard about Sam. "No more combat or aliens shooting at me. It's a dream job."

Abruptly the Wreckers decided that they'd spent enough time dwelling on the legendary exploits of Sam Witwicky and turned their attention back to where they'd been when they'd been interrupted. "Now yer just standing there!" Roadbuster growled at O'Toole, and he pointed in the direction of the *Xantium.* "Check 'em again! Every weld on those liquid hydrogen lines! Sealed. Up. *Tight!*"

"Hey, hotshots!" Epps said, clearly fed up. He was pulling something that looked like a television remote control from his pocket, but Sam didn't understand why he'd need that. "I said to your pits!" With that declaration, he clicked the "on" button of the remote, and from the direction of the nearby hangar, Sam heard what sounded like race cars roaring around a track.

Instantly the technician, the *Xantium,* and Sam Witwicky were forgotten. The three Wreckers nearly tore one another apart, trying to clear one another out of their way, as they sprinted toward the hangar that presumably was the location of their "pit." O'Toole and the other technicians breathed a collective sigh of relief while Sam looked in confusion to Epps.

"Daytona 500," Epps said. "It's like catnip to them, so we keep a looped feed on a TV set in there, 24/7. When they get too obnoxious, this just sends them off to la-la land. So"—he indicated the shuttle craft with a nod—"you believe this is really happening?"

"It's happening whether I believe it or not, but . . . jeez." Sam shook his head. "Where's it supposed to take them?"

"Any planet but here," Epps said ruefully.

"My God, I don't believe it," Sam said.

"Yeah, I know. It sucks big-time," said Epps.

"No, not that. *That.*" Sam pointed.

Epps looked to see what he was indicating.

Rolling toward them in an electric wheelchair was Seymour Simmons. His manservant, Dutch, was right behind him. His right leg was in a cast and elevated, and he had a crazed look in his eyes. Well, a more crazed look than usual in his eyes. He was shouting, "Clear a path! Outta my way! I wanna talk to whoever's in charge!" Then he rolled within sight of them. "Well, well, Charlotte Mearing."

"Former agent Simmons. I see you managed to survive Washington."

"Washington, Egypt, heartbreak. I survive. It's what I do." The comment about "heartbreak" seemed directed at Mearing, but Sam instantly dismissed the idea as being simply too ludicrous to contemplate.

"Would you mind telling me how the hell you got in here?" Sam said. "And how are you even functioning? Aren't you in like ten kinds of pain?"

"Guys like me laugh at pain. As for how I got in, I got

fans down here, kid. Fans who appreciate how a real American hero goes about his business. Fans who are willing to wave our rental car right through the main gate because none of them are any more thrilled with what they see warming up on the launchpad than anyone else, and they're hoping that I'm gonna find a way to make it not happen. Fans who believe that I am the last, best hope for integrity that America has left."

Sam was amazed. "Really?"

Simmons let it hang there for a moment and then said, "Nah, not really. I'm flying on so many painkillers that you could chop off both legs with a pair of rusty scissors and I wouldn't feel it. I'm popping oxycodone like M&Ms."

"Aren't those addicitive?"

"We should be so lucky that the world survives long enough for me to become addicted. As for how I got here, they're bringing everybody in, kid. Putting all the intel on the table. And what I gotta say is this." He shifted his chair back so that he was facing Mearing. "If you think deporting the Autobots solves a damn thing—"

She didn't let him finish the sentence. "This has gone way above my pay grade, agent. If there's a war for Earth, humans will fight it. It doesn't matter if I agree with it or not. That's the play my government has called, and it's my job to execute it to the best of my abilities. And I think you know that."

"Here's what I know: If humans are fighting this war, it won't be much of a fight. Spent my life studying this alien species." His voice rose. "This is what I know. This is who I am. Those Autobots are the only chance we have."

"They might be," Mearing admitted, "but it's out of my hands." With that pronouncement, clearly feeling that that was the end of the discussion, she turned and walked away.

Simmons angled the wheelchair to face Sam. "Tell her she can't let this happen. Tell her everything you know about 'em!"

He's right. Clinically insane but right. I have to make her realize what the stakes are. I have to tell her everything I know, and I have to start with what's on my . . .

. . . wrist?

He looked down at his wrist and saw that the spider watch was gone.

Sam gaped, unable to believe that it was over that easily, but he wasn't about to waste the opportunity. He opened his mouth . . .

And suddenly he had no air.

He clutched at his throat and discovered that the spider watch had taken up residence there, reshaping itself. It obviously didn't want to take any chances that Sam would listen to the blandishments of Simmons, but it also apparently had decided that shocking him into submission—or perhaps even killing him outright—would be counterproductive. So instead it re-formed itself into something resembling a broad silver necklace and, having wrapped itself around the bottom of his throat, proceeded to clamp down on his larynx.

Simmons stared at him quizzically. "Uh . . . what are you wearing?"

Sam was able to clear just enough space in his throat to gasp out, "Choker."

"You're a weird one, kid," said Simmons, which Sam had to think sounded pretty strange, considering the source. "Thanks for nothing! Charlotte!" He rolled off after her. "Charlotte!"

Epps had already headed off to deal with the Wreckers, so Sam was alone. Yet the creature remained around his throat a moment or two longer, as if to remind him who was in charge and that daring to fly in the face of the Decepticons could be a truly fatal mistake.

For him . . . and for Carly.

"Message received," he whispered, and the creature promptly released its hold and skittered back down his arm. It wrapped itself back around his wrist and sat there, waiting for him to do what he was supposed to do.

ii

Mearing was walking as quickly as she could, yet, annoyingly, Simmons was able to catch up with her. What the hell was with that chair? Was it turbocharged?

Bringing him here had been a mistake. A huge mistake. A mistake of epic proportions. She was absolutely sure of that, and knowing Simmons, he was going to go out of his way to prove it.

She could not have been more correct.

"So, Director," Simmons said, driving his chair alongside her. "Moving up in the world."

"Yes, I am."

"Which of course enables you to leave people like me behind."

"Not everything is about you, Simmons. In fact, almost nothing is about you. And I didn't leave you behind. I went my way, and you went . . . yours," she said with obvious distaste. "Your own, unique, totally insane way. The choices you made, the direction you decided to head with your life . . . aren't my problem or my responsibility."

"Right, right, I can't argue that. In fact, I never said otherwise. But just for the record, I want to say: You still smell nice. Great ass still."

She stopped dead and turned around, halting the forward roll of his wheelchair with her foot. Her voice low, her eyes glancing around to make sure that no one was within earshot, she said, "If you *ever* speak a word to *anyone* about what happened that night in Quantico, I will cut out your heart."

For one moment, just one, Simmons set aside his usual bombast. His voice perfectly flat and sincere, he said, "You already did."

She had nothing to say back to him.

Then, stiffly, he said, "Thank you for bringing me here, *ma'am*," and then he pivoted the chair around and headed off toward Dutch, who was waiting for him.

And she never would have admitted it to another living being, but she loved it when Simmons—and only Simmons—called her "ma'am."

iii

Sam kept waiting for something to happen to avert the inevitable. Some sort of presidential pardon, even though the Autobots hadn't actually done anything wrong. Or maybe Congress would come to its senses. Maybe the population of America would arise as one and storm the nation's capital, demanding that their elected officials do the right thing.

But if any of that was happening, word of it wasn't getting to them there in Florida.

Instead, what got to them was the Autobots.

It reminded him of that moment in *The Right Stuff* when the Mercury 7 astronauts were moving toward the camera in slow motion. The Autobots, walking side by side, standing proud in the face of such despicable behavior as the humans had displayed. So many times had the Autobots been there to protect humanity, and so many times had they come through. And now, the first time the Autobots needed someone to stand by them . . .

Get off your high horse, Witwicky, he scolded himself even as he ran toward the Autobots who were heading toward the shuttle. *Yes, a bunch of totally lame politicians stabbed the Autobots in the back. But you're their friend, or at least their supposed friend, and here you are trying to catch up with them solely so you have the chance to do the exact same thing.*

Where do you get off thinking you're any better than anyone else, when by any reasonable measure you're worse?

He caught up with them as they were approaching the bottom of the launchpad. The gantry had been set up for them to have easy access to the shuttle, which was mounted on what looked like a two-stage Saturn V rocket. "One side," came an unexpected voice from near the ground.

He looked down in surprise. "Brains? Wheelie? You're here, too?"

"If the Decepticons are running the joint, we wanna be anywhere *but* here," said Wheelie. "Planet's not big enough for the both of us."

"But how did you know that—?"

"They'd be here? I figured it out," Brains said. "Of course I figured it out. Got a brain the size of a planet."

"Been a pleasure working with you," Wheelie said.

They moved past him, and then Sam approached a familiar, looming figure. "Optimus!" Sam called out to him.

Optimus halted his approach. The rest of the Autobots kept going, continuing to make their way to the shuttle that served as their means of departing Earth.

The gigantic robot looked down at him, but Sam couldn't hold his gaze. After all, he had this . . . this thing on his wrist that was determined to make him betray the Autobots, and he wasn't sure he had the strength to resist it.

"Look, Optimus . . . I don't know if anyone has actually said this to you, but on behalf of, y' know, the whole human race, I want to apologize for what they're doing to you."

"It is I who should apologize, Sam." Sam could barely stand to hear the utter defeat in the Autobot's voice. "This was all my fault. I told them whom to trust. I was wrong."

He started to walk away, but Sam ran around him so that he was standing in front of him. He looked up at the Autobot leader and said insistently, "That doesn't make it your fault. Just makes you human for a change."

Now ask him. Ask him what they need to know.

Again he flinched inwardly, and again he looked down at the tarmac.

"Remember this, Sam. You may lose faith in us. But you must never lose faith in yourselves."

Once more Optimus started to head for the shuttle, and suddenly the creature on Sam's wrist bit him even more insistently, and there was serious meaning in that bite. It seemed to say, *Do you think we're joking around? Do you think Carly is going to make it through the day? Your last chance to save her is about to head up that gantry. You either betray him or you kill Carly. Come on, Witwicky. This is a no-brainer.*

But you have a brain. Think of a way around it. Think of a way to—

And again another bite, even sharper than before, and Sam shouted out, "Optimus, I need to know how you're gonna fight back!"

Optimus stopped once more, and when he turned to regard him this time, there was what looked like something . . . Sam could only think of it as determined curiosity.

He knows something's up. Or at least he suspects it. Sam could practically sense the spider bot on his wrist pausing, waiting eagerly. Sam's mind raced. He had about a half second to figure out how to warn Optimus in a way that wouldn't destroy Carly.

"You're coming back, right? You have some plan? You'll . . . bring help. Reinforcements? Something? What's the strategy?" He paused, because Optimus was still just staring at him, his head slightly tilted to one side, clearly far more curious about the way in which Sam was asking than why he was doing so. And suddenly, pitching his voice in a more nasal, wheedling manner, sounding like a shady used-car salesman and hoping that the spider bot picked up only on words rather than intonation, he said, "You can tell me. No other *human* will ever know."

For a second Optimus's gaze flickered to Sam's wrist. Sam couldn't tell whether he was imagining comprehension dawning in the Autobot's eyes. *Drive it home, Witwicky! Drive it home!* "You know we'd never be able to live with ourselves if we just *do* what *they* want."

He wasn't sure what he was expecting Optimus to do. Grab his arm, maybe, and pluck the thing off his wrist, squishing it between his fingers as if he were popping a pimple. Instantly dispatch the Autobots to head full speed back to Washington to rescue Carly.

Instead, after a long moment, Optimus said, "You are my friend, Sam. You always will be. But your leaders have spoken. From here, the fight will be your own."

With that, he turned away for the last time and headed up to the *Xantium*.

The last Autobot in line was Bumblebee, and Sam shouted, "Wait! Bumblebee! Bumblebee!"

Bumblebee crouched so that he was as close to eye level as he could get to Sam. The damage to Bee's voice capacity had been such that he could indeed talk, but it required a great deal of effort. Since the radio required none, and since there always seemed to be *something* available to express what was on his mind, it was his preferred method of communication with Sam.

Not this time, however. Clearly he had no desire to

have another voice, no matter how melodious, speak on his behalf. Slowly, laboriously, he said, *"I will . . . never . . . forget you . . . Sam . . ."*

"This is your home," Sam said insistently. "Earth is your home."

Touching Sam's chest, Bumblebee said, *"I will always be . . . here . . . fight them . . . forever . . ."*

Then he rose to his full height and, still looking downcast, went to join Optimus and the others.

Technicians were already starting to clear the area. Sam knew he had to do so as well, because nothing was going to be served by standing close enough to the engines to get fried. Even so, he remained as long as he could before he started to walk away.

Suddenly he felt a cessation of pressure on his wrist.

He looked down. The spider bot had leaped clear and was skittering away, moving so quickly and being so small that nobody was noticing it. Sam wanted to run after it, to try to grind the miserable little thing under his foot.

But somehow it just wasn't worth the effort. Despite Bumblebee's admonition never to stop fighting, at this particular moment in time, Sam simply didn't have it within him. The spider bot didn't have any interest in him? Fine. To hell with it.

To hell with everything.

iv

In the launch control facility, feeling as if they were watching a piece of human history coming to an end, the onlookers monitored the countdown as the primary ignition sequence in the main rocket fired up. The shuttle *Xantium* clung to the outside, waiting for its lift out of the earth's atmosphere.

"Saturn V?" said Sam.

Epps was standing at his side. "It was when it got

started. The Wreckers completely redesigned it, though. It's more theirs than ours by this point. Made it forty percent more efficient. At least that's what they claimed, and who am I to tell them they're fulla crap?"

"The *Xantium* couldn't just, y' know . . . take off on its own? I mean, it's just hard to believe it would be dependent on us."

"It's not," said Epps. "But according to the Wreckers, the engines are too powerful. It's not constructed to function on our world. If they ignite down here, they'll tear a hole in the atmosphere that'll make the one we already have in the ozone layer look like a gopher hole. So the Autobots felt it would be safer if, should a departure ever become necessary, we enabled them to piggyback out of here."

"So they were watching out for us, even to the end."

"Pretty much," Epps said, not sounding any happier about it than Sam was.

Simmons had a ringside seat by the wide windows at the front of the facility. As the countdown reached its inevitable conclusion and as the booster rockets fired up to their full capacity, he spoke out in a voice that rang out above the technicians who were monitoring the impending launch. "Years from now, they're gonna ask us: Where were you when they took over the planet? And we're gonna say we just stood there and watched."

Mearing was near him when he said it. She glanced at him, her jaw set in a determined line, but she said nothing.

"Three . . . ," intoned the voice of mission control, ". . . two . . . one . . . ignition."

Nothing happened, and for a second Sam rejoiced inwardly, thinking that there was some sort of malfunction and the Autobots had been granted a reprieve, even if it was only in the form of mechanical failure. But then a roar filled the area, and despite all its shockproofing, the launch facility trembled slightly as a mass of smoke and flame erupted from the bottom of the rocket.

It was the fulfillment of a lifelong dream for the child still living inside Sam Witwicky: He was getting to watch a rocket liftoff and had a ringside seat for it. How cool was that?

The adult in him, however, felt no joy. The words "end of an era" were commonly bandied about, but never had they had a meaning that was both as significant for the whole of humanity and as deeply personal for one young man as they did right then.

Sam followed the trajectory as the rocket hurtled skyward. Within moments the first-stage booster dropped away, the ignition of the secondary booster propelling it higher and faster now that the weight of the first booster was gone. Against the bright blue cloudless skies, the rocket remained clearly visible.

His cellphone rang.

Sam pulled it out and looked. The caller ID read CALLER UNKNOWN, but it didn't matter. He knew who it was going to be. He stepped away from Epps, who didn't even seem to notice that Sam was trying to distance himself from them. Once he was sure that he was unobserved, he brought up the phone and spoke tersely into it.

"Well? You get what you wanted?"

Dylan's voice came back to him. "That Bumblebee, God, so friggin' adorable. But that Optimus . . . come on! Guy needs to learn to lighten up!"

Sam was in no mood to bandy words with this jerk. He thought about how he had said to Optimus that no human would be privy to what they were saying to each other. It had been his way of trying to warn him that he, Sam, was a direct pipeline to the Decepticons, but technically he had been lying since Dylan was listening in. Then he decided that, no, he'd been truthful. As far as he was concerned, Dylan had voluntarily burned his human race membership card ages ago. "You wanted an answer, you got one. There was no strategy. They're gone."

"We thank you, Sam. We just needed to be sure."

"Sure of what?"

"That they'd go without a fight," Dylan said, as if it should have been the most obvious thing in the world. "An Autobot tight . . . clean . . . package."

Sam knew that Dylan, in his smug, superior way, was conveying something to him, but he couldn't for the life of him figure out what it was.

And then, above the distant thunder of the ascending rocket, Sam heard a new sound, closer and more urgent. It went from distant rumble to thundering roar in a matter of seconds.

Clicking shut his phone, he ran to the observation window, scanning the horizon. Simmons and Mearing were looking at him questioningly, both seeing the urgency that had seized the previously despondent Witwicky. Sam kept looking for the source of the noise, and then suddenly he saw it.

So did they.

"What the hell is that F-22 Raptor doing out there!" Mearing demanded, and sure enough, the sleek black plane was hurtling at high speed across the field before suddenly taking off in a nearly vertical manner. It streaked after the hurtling rocket ship, slowly but steadily closing the distance between the two.

Sam realized it before Mearing did, and Simmons realized it before either of them, because he said it as the horrifying thought was still coming together in Sam's mind. "That's not a Raptor," Simmons said, as if speaking from beyond the grave.

Sam watched its rapid ascent with horrified eyes. *"Starscream! No!"*

Naturally Starscream did not, could not have heard him, nor would it have made the slightest difference if he had.

Starscream couldn't quite overtake his target, but he didn't need to. All he had to do was get within range, and having achieved that, he let loose with his cannons.

His targeting was precise.

Seconds later, in a massive explosion, the stage two booster erupted, and a fireball ripped through the sky that twisted back upon itself and enveloped the *Xantium*. It took a few seconds for the sound to reach the launch facility, but when it did, windows shook and coffee cups shuddered and in some cases skidded off the countertops and crashed to the floor.

No one paid attention to any of that. Instead, all horrified stares were upon the rolling conflagration high in the air. It was an explosion that nothing could possibly have survived.

The Raptor descended quickly and overflew the air base. As it did so, its wings waggled at them mockingly, as if to say, *Well? Did you enjoy the show? I sure hope so.* Then it angled up once more and hurtled off into the sky, leaving the stunned observers behind.

Mearing was one of them, standing there with her jaw agape. Then, slowly, she turned and looked at Simmons.

He was the only one in the room who didn't look the least bit surprised.

"And now you know what happens when you do what the Decepticons want," he said.

ILLINOIS

Carly had never been much of a fan of helicopters. She'd ridden in them any number of times, particularly when she'd been with the British embassy. It was just part of the job. But she wasn't wild about them. They were often cramped, they were noisy as hell, the ride wasn't always especially smooth, and she wasn't ecstatic about the fact that a single rotor was keeping them in the air. At least jets had more than one engine. If a helicopter engine crapped out on you, that was game over.

Now she had one more thing to dislike about them: Henceforth, presuming she managed to survive all of this, they were always going to remind her of Dylan Gould.

He was seated opposite her in the tight quarters of the Gould corporate helicopter. She tried to twist her lower body around in the seat so that her knees wouldn't bump up against his. She would just as soon have thrown herself out the door and taken her chances with gravity, but that didn't seem to be a viable option.

"Y' know, I just read this great book," Dylan said cheerfully. "*The Power of Now.* Know how you live for that moment? 'Cause this is like that moment." He sounded eager, as if he had just had some sort of major personal revelation that he was anxious to share. "I love New Age shit."

She looked at him with all the disdain she could muster. "You could have stood up to them. You're a smart, resourceful guy. You could have outthought them. Hell, you could have just told them that you're not going to betray your entire race. But either you couldn't be bothered or you just didn't want to. You're a coward."

"No. Just business, Duchess." He smiled and sat back in his seat. "Welcome to the New World."

Out the front window of the chopper, the skyscrapers of Chicago loomed on the shores of Lake Michigan.

FLORIDA

i

In the launch facility, people were moving like zombies. Mearing had a phone pressed to her ear, looking grim, nodding. Simmons just sat there, saying not a word, waiting for her to finish her phone call. Epps was gazing out the window at the sky, where there was still a thick smudge of black smoke that probably would be there for some hours yet, until the winds finally dissipated the last visual reminder of the Autobots.

Finally she clicked the cell shut and said, without looking at him, "President's ordered us back to D.C."

"You happy now, Charlotte Cuddlebear?" Simmons said bitterly. "What if the Autobots weren't just the target? What if they were the trigger?"

"The—?" She stared at him blankly. "I don't know what you're—"

"The starting gun. The opening whistle."

"Seymour, you're not making any sense. I think you're too hopped up on painkillers to know what you're talking about."

"Then you should take some of what I'm taking, sweetheart, because it might help you see things the way they are. You think the Decepticons don't have some kind of endgame beyond 'Oh, we just want some materials and we'll go on our way'? If so, you're delusional. They're Decepticons, for God's sake. They got 'deceive' right in their name! They got something cooking, and the Autobots were the only thing stopping them from setting it into motion. One countdown may be over, but another's started, and it's a countdown toward the end of the world as we know it."

"I hope you're wrong, Agent Simmons," she said, and walked away. But he could tell by the sag of her shoulders that she knew he was right.

He was about to go in pursuit of her when Sam Witwicky ran up and interrupted him, holding up a cellphone. Simmons was immediately irritated; he was a busy guy, and he wasn't thrilled with the notion of having to stop and pose for Sam snapping a picture of the moment with his cellphone camera.

But then Sam immediately grabbed Simmons's full attention. "I need your help to track a phone call. There's another man out there. He runs their whole human operation. His name's Dylan Gould, and he took my girlfriend hostage!"

"What? And you're just sharing this information *now?*"

"Like I told you: hostage! I couldn't say anything before! Now I can. So are you gonna help or not?"

Simmons's eyes lit up with excitement. "Dutchie!" he shouted, and Dutch promptly materialized by his side in that bizarre way he had. "Let's play! As in"—he dropped his voice to a chortle—"dirty."

ii

Sam watched, fascinated, as Dutch jacked the cellphone into his laptop computer and started typing. His fingers were moving so quickly that Sam could scarcely follow them.

"What are you doing?" he finally said.

Without glancing at him, Dutch said, "I'm calling back the last number in your call history."

"The number was blocked."

"Not to me."

"But . . . look," he said with growing concern. "If he knows you're calling him back, it could tip him."

Dutch did not look or sound the least bit worried. "He won't know. I'm simply sending a pulse through. Undetectable."

"Is that possible?"

"Not with any software that you know of, no." Dutch smiled grimly. "But there are things in heaven and on earth beyond your philosophy, Horatio."

"My name's Sam."

Dutch stopped smiling and gave him a pitying look. "Sorry. My mistake," he said, sounding sarcastic, although Sam wasn't quite sure why.

Simmons, in the meantime, was working on his own flat-screen pad. "So your girlfriend works for Dylan Gould, huh? Let's just call up all his assets so we can start kicking his assets, if ya know what I mean."

"Triangulating now," Dutch informed them. "He's in Chicago, moving horizontally and at some elevation. Way it's tracking, probably a helicopter . . . wait. It's slowing down."

"Chicago, huh?" said Simmons, consulting the list of assets he'd pulled up. "Okay . . . his company owns a building on Wacker Drive. Overlooks the Riverwalk. Also, he rents a penthouse in Trump Tower . . ."

Epps was listening with interest. "Trump Tower have a helipad?"

"It does indeed," Simmons said.

"Chopper is stationary. I assume it's landed," Dutch said. "Got the coordinates. Let me run it through an address matrix . . . I've got it at . . . 401 North Wabash."

"That's the Trump Tower, all right," Simmons said triumphantly. "Our bird's gone home to roost."

"This is a kidnapping," Dutch said immediately.

"That makes it an FBI matter. You could inform Mearing and—"

"And she'll what, Dutchie?" Simmons said. "You got any idea just how full the FBI's plate is right now?"

"That's not the big problem," Sam said. "The problem is that Dylan's got Decepticons backing him up. I saw at least two while I was there; there might be more."

"Exactly," said Simmons. "Just how much experience has the Chicago field office had with handling Decepticons? I'll tell ya: Nada. Zip. Zilch-o. They'll go in there and they'll be dead in seconds. Not to mention poor Kaley—"

"Carly," Sam said.

"Whatever. Dylan knows that we know where he is, one of two things happens: He kills her outright and dumps the body, or he takes off again. Maybe even ditches the cellphone 'cause he's figured out that that's how we found him. Hell, he might have snuffed her already."

"No. Not him." Sam's face twisted in disgust. "I saw the way he was looking at her. He's gonna keep her around for as long as possible." Steeling his resolve, he said, "I'm going. All she's ever done is try to help me. And this is what I've done for her? I can be there in . . ." He glanced to Dutch.

"Eighteen hours, twenty minutes," Dutch said briskly. "If you regard speed limits as only guidelines instead of the law, then probably fifteen hours."

Sam started to head out. He had no idea where he was going to find a car, but one thing at a time. Before he went even a few feet, however, Epps was in his way. He expected Epps to try to stop him, to talk him out of it. Instead, Epps said firmly, "You're not going alone."

"What?"

"NEST is out there, preparing for war. They'll never

sign off on going after one guy even if there's a kid-napped girl involved. Lemme make some calls, round up whoever I can to help."

"Why are you helping me?"

"Because," Epps said, "those assholes just killed my friends, too. And if Gould is connected to them, then I'm making sure he's going down in the same kinda flames the Autobots did."

iii

Mearing had spent the last few minutes getting in touch with various NEST forces and briefing key individuals on the tragedy that had just transpired. Now she was heading to her airplane, never more anxious to leave someplace than she was right then.

And then she heard a by now all too familiar whizzing of wheels and knew who was coming in fast behind her.

"I want in the mix!" Simmons called out. She stopped with one foot on the stairway leading up to her plane. But she didn't board the plane, and he sped around her so that he could face her. "Two outs, bottom of the ninth, you send your DH to the plate and you go down swinging."

"Do you have any idea how much I detest sports metaphors?" she said. There was no energy to her voice, however, no real snap in her protest.

He rolled closer. "I have dedicated my life to beating these . . . bastards. Not you. Not your yes men. *Me*."

It would have been so easy for her to climb the rest of the way into her plane and get the hell out of there. It wasn't as if he could follow her up the stairs.

Instead she remained where she was, looking deeply into herself. Every instinct she possessed told her to leave this lunatic behind. But lately her instincts had been pretty lousy. Maybe it would be smarter for her to start acting in a manner contrary to what her instincts were telling her. She might be able to save some lives that way.

And then Simmons said, "Plus I'm good for all kinds of stuff. If you don't want me riding up there with you, strap me to the plane's belly. I double as landing gear."

She laughed. Despite everything that had happened, despite all the uncertainty, she actually laughed. Not long and not loud, but enough.

Simmons grinned lopsidedly. "Admit it: I'm still the only guy in the world that can get a chuckle out of you."

"Shut up and have your bodyguard"—she pointed to Dutch, who was standing behind him—"get your ass into the plane."

"Yes, ma'am. By the way, does it still turn you on when I call you ma'am?"

"You realize I can just shoot you, fill out some paperwork to explain why it was necessary, and no one will question it, right?"

"Dutch! I need a lift!" Simmons called.

CHICAGO

In an underground loading dock at the Hotchkiss Gould Building in Chicago, Illinois, Carly watched in silence as Dylan supervised the strange, ornate six-foot-long metal pillar being off-loaded from an armored car.

Off-loaded by a Decepticon.

It was the one Sam had referred to as Soundwave, the one who had nearly crushed her to death. As it carried the pillar on its shoulder, it cast a glance toward her and slowly closed its fist, apparently to remind her just what it had done to her—and could still do if she tried something cute like running away.

She shuddered. Dylan seemed to notice and naturally grinned upon seeing her discomfort. He gestured for her to follow him, which she did reluctantly, trying to decide whether, if she had the opportunity, she'd have the nerve to strangle Dylan with her bare hands. She decided that the longer this went on, the more likely it was.

Moments later the Decepticon, Dylan, and Carly were in a freight elevator, heading upward. Deciding that silence would serve nothing where information might actually be of use, she said, "What does that mean? Their planet needs our 'resources'?"

"You haven't figured it out yet? You're a smart girl. Work on it." He waited a few moments and then prodded her. "Got it yet, Duchess?"

"No."

"Whaddaya think those resources really are?" he said.

"Iron? Metal? Steel? They could mine all that from the you-name-it galaxy. Not to mention Mars. Why here? What's here and nowhere else?"

The dime dropped. "Us . . ."

He nodded. "Can't rebuild without a slave labor force," he said cheerfully. "How many rocks out there in the universe offer six billion workers? I asked. It's a short list."

"But . . . you can't transport people. We wouldn't survive . . . would we?"

"Probably not," he said reasonably. "I hear that the energies unleashed . . . for a human, it would be like sticking your head into a blast furnace. Anyway, it doesn't matter. They're not gonna be shipping people. They're shipping their planet here."

"That's ridiculous," she said. "That can't possibly . . ."

The freight elevator opened, and Dylan stepped out onto the roof of the building, locking the car as he did so so that she'd have no means of heading back down. The sun was setting, night creeping over the horizon. Far below was the Chicago River, with a series of drawbridges stretching across it. The one closest to them was the one on North Wabash Avenue, although she could also see the ones at North Michigan Avenue and North State Street from where she was standing. Under other circumstances, it might have seemed beautiful. With Sam at her side, it would even have been romantic. There was one day in particular, in spring, when the tall boats would come sailing up the Chicago River from their winter boathouse homes on Lake Michigan. As they passed through, the drawbridges would go up in waves to let them through and then close in their wake. Months later, in autumn, the process would reverse itself. It was as if the city were saluting the passing of the seasons.

But there was nothing romantic in what immediately drew her attention.

Tall, even majestic, two gargantuan robots stood on the far end of the rooftop, waiting. If they hadn't been living symbols of the end of everything, she would have been awed instead of struck with fear.

The Decepticon proceeded to erect the pillar in the middle of the roof, and now Dylan saw where she was looking. He came to her side as if they were sharing some mutually wonderful and inspiring sight, such as the Grand Canyon. "Sentinel," he said, "and Megatron. Look at those two. Takes your breath away, doesn't it? Their war destabilized their galaxy ages ago. Destroyed their planet and half its stars. Whole thing is doomed. So these two worked out a secret deal."

"A deal . . . to move their whole planet?"

"Yup. Bring it right here. A neighboring world."

"That's insane," she said, facing him. "You can't just . . . just drop another planetary body next to ours. It has mass, for God's sake! Its own gravity! Think, Dylan! Think of the effect the moon has on the tides! And that's just a . . . a ball of rock. Another planetary body within range of us . . . it'll wind up tearing our world apart!"

He waved dismissively. "I'm sure they've got it all worked out."

"You're crazier than they are!"

"They're not crazy at all," he said. "They're organized. They're spreading hundreds more pillars across the earth so they can launch them into orbit by morning. That," he said, smugly pleased with his knowledge of these matters, "that's the control one. It needs to stay anchored by the earth's magnetic core." Then he hesitated. "I think it's magnetic. Or kinetic. It's something." He shrugged. "When you're born rich, you're just not into science. Anyways . . . tomorrow morning? Bang!" It was appalling how enthused he seemed about it.

From a distance, she could hear the howling of police sirens. There was no doubt in her mind why that was. The Decepticons had been spotted. No surprise there. They were impossible to miss.

Dylan was grinning, watching the approaching flashing lights with as much eagerness as if he were sitting in the bleachers at a baseball game. "Yeah. Those guys are gonna make a big difference."

"You want this to happen!" Carly said.

Suddenly Dylan snapped. It was as if his personality had undergone a complete transformation in a matter of seconds as he shouted, "No, I want a world of happy children, laughing, singing, nibbling on fields of cotton candy, but that's not what I'm dealing with right now!" She was taken aback, and just as quickly as he had flared up, he reined himself in once more. The same cocky smile returned, and he continued with a forced calm that didn't match his expression. "I want to survive. I want forty more years. Every slave labor force needs a hierarchy. They'll need human leaders—"

"And a CEO," she said drily.

He wagged a scolding finger at her as if admonishing a child. "Duchess! Don't jinx it for me. We had a good long run, we really did. But we don't own this planet. We've just been renting."

Suddenly the building shook.

For the first time, Dylan showed genuine alarm. Explosions had begun in the distance, but they were coming closer and closer, one set of buildings after another erupting in flame. There was so much smoke billowing upward that at first it was hard for Carly to make out what was happening, but then she saw it.

Decepticon battle cruisers were hurtling down from above, threading their way through Chicago's concrete canyons, firing everywhere, seemingly at random. They weren't selecting targets. They were just firing everywhere, both at things that were in their way and at things that weren't.

Pedestrians were running desperately to get out of the way, but it wasn't as if there was a safe haven. Buildings were blasted apart at their foundations, crumbling into vast piles of rubble. Cars were struck with stray blasts and promptly erupted, causing massive fires to start rolling down the streets. From North Columbus down to LaSalle, as far as Carly could see, Chicago was under an assault that seemed to be ripped straight out of *War of the Worlds*. And this time germs weren't going to be sufficient to take down the aliens.

She grabbed Dylan by the shirtfront and screamed in his face, *"Didn't tell you about this part, did they? You inhuman monster! You—!"*

His hand swung fast, taking her across the face, knocking her off her feet. She stumbled back, landing hard on her backside, and Dylan was shouting, *"Hey! You think I'm in every meeting?"* His hands were clenched into fists. And they were trembling. "Look, I'm safe! They said I'm safe, which means if you stick with me, you are, too. You have to stand on the side of progress if you want to be a part of history! Even if it means you stand alone."

At that moment, she truly wanted to leave him alone in every sense of the word by bolting toward the edge of the roof and throwing herself off. That gave her a nice mental picture: swan diving while Dylan was left behind, shouting after her, cursing her name. It would give her the final word, of sorts.

Because she was positive that Dylan was deluding himself in accepting the word of the Decepticons. He had to be. He was just a means to an end to them, and there was no way he was going to come out of this alive. Which meant she wasn't going to, either. At least she could choose the manner of her death.

But she didn't.

She didn't because of one thought that kept going through her mind:

Sam will come for me. He'll save me. Somehow.

It was ridiculous. In her own way, she supposed she was as insane as Dylan was. Yet it was that firm belief that kept her right where she was and prevented her from ending up a splotch on the sidewalk far below.

As the city of Chicago was hammered with death on all sides, Carly dared to dream of life with Sam, as thoroughly unlikely as that was.

INDIANA

From the moment Sam had hit the road with Epps behind the wheel of his sporty Mustang—which Sam half expected to turn into a robot—the ex-soldier made phone call after phone call. Three dozen phone numbers he went through, and most of them didn't answer, and some of them did and offered apologies . . .

. . . but half a dozen of them were in a position, both healthwise and geographywise, to say yes.

"How the hell many mercs do you know, anyway?" Sam said at one point.

"How many mercs do you think I know that are giant robots?"

"Uh . . . none?"

"Right. So however many mercs I *do* know, it's not enough. But we'll make do with what we've got."

The rendezvous point was a rest stop just north of Indianapolis. They pulled in, and Epps killed the engine. Sam looked around. There were a couple of cars there, but they were filled with families that were sound asleep, using the rest stop to grab some shut-eye and break up a lengthy trip. "Where are they?" he said.

"They'll be here. When they're ready for you to see 'em, you will."

Epps exited the car, going into the station to use the restroom and returning with an assortment of candy bars and soda he'd gotten out of the vending machines. When he returned, Sam went to the restroom as well, splashed water on his face, and returned to the car. It was four in the morning, and he was functioning on a combination of adrenaline, Kit Kats, and Red Bull. Presuming he survived this, he was going to crash and sleep for about a week and a half.

He prayed that Carly would be at his side.

She had to be.

"It was my fault."

Epps, who had been about to eat another square of chocolate, turned and looked at him. He didn't seem any the worse for wear after having driven all night. He was geared up for whatever they were going to have to face. "Dude, there's plenty of blame to go around. Way I see it, you have the least reason to—"

"No, you don't get it. I had this . . . this thing," and he pointed to his wrist. "A spiderlike Decepticon that could also make itself look like a watch. Gould put it on me, and if I didn't do what it wanted, then it would bite into me or even shock me. It could've turned my nervous system into Swiss cheese."

"Ouch."

"Not to mention that Carly's life depended upon my doing what they said."

"Okay. But I'm still not seeing . . ."

"Don't you get it?" Sam said, feeling mortified but compelled to tell someone what was eating away at him. "The Decepticons were tracking me the whole time. I led them straight to the space center. They wouldn't have known where the Autobots were and wouldn't have been there to—"

"Whoa, whoa . . . slow down, chief. You didn't lead them there."

"But—"

"I checked around immediately after the . . . after the incident. That F-22 was there since the previous day."

"Are you sure?"

"Positive. And don't think I didn't ream some people out for that. No one questioned it being there. Everyone just assumed that everyone else knew about it. Considering we're dealing with beings that can shift into alternate forms, that's exactly the kinda crap that should be setting off bells everywhere. Point is, they were there ahead of you."

"How, though?"

"You said it yourself. They've got eyes and ears everywhere. They could have found out any one of a dozen ways. Hell, for all we know, they had someone staked out at every major facility in the country equipped with rocket science, hoping to get lucky."

"Lucky?"

"Well, lucky for them. Sorry." He shrugged. "Probably wasn't the best word for me to use."

Sam waved it off. "No sweat. You didn't mean anything by it. And besides, if it weren't for you, I'd probably still be back in Florida trying to bum a ride, so—"

Then he jumped as a hand rapped firmly on the door.

Someone was standing outside, a large, bulky man with a face so pockmarked and scarred that it looked like a road map of a life of warfare. Behind him there were other hard-to-see figures. They seemed to have emerged from the darkness like shadows come to life.

"Took your sweet time," said the scarred man. He scowled at Sam. "Who's he? Your boyfriend?"

"Sam," Epps said, "this is Hardcore Eddie. And over there"—Epps gestured toward the shadowed figures—"is Tiny . . . and that's Stackhouse . . . and that's . . . is that you, Rakishi?"

"Yeah."

"That's Rakishi. And standing over there by himself because he's got this whole go-it-alone thing is Ames."

"Okay, well . . . I'm Sam Witwicky. My girlfriend is

the one Dylan Gould grabbed and took with him to Chicago."

Rakishi spoke up with a deep and impressive voice. "He's a dead man."

"No," Sam said angrily. "I made a promise. He's *my* dead man."

Hardcore Eddie nodded approvingly. "Kid's starting to grow on me. Okay, then: Let's go to Chicago and blow some stuff up."

Moments later Epps's Mustang, followed by three low-slung, nondescript vehicles that Sam would've sworn just a few minutes ago weren't there, pulled out of the rest stop and started rolling down the highway.

Every single one of the drivers was an experienced mercenary, and they also happened to be among the best wheelmen in their singular line of work. Hyperaware of their surroundings at all times, they would have staked their lives on the notion that they were not being followed.

They would have lost that bet.

CHICAGO

Normally, on a regular morning, I-65 heading into Chicago was choked with traffic, filled with people on their normal morning commute. Southbound, on the other hand, was fairly light.

This morning was, as Sam might have said when he was a kid, Opposite Day. On this day, the southbound traffic was so heavy that it was scarcely moving. Northbound, on the other hand, wasn't simply light; it was nonexistent. Nothing was headed toward Chicago.

It was easy to see why even from less than a mile out. Epps, Tiny, Stackhouse, Hardcore Eddie, Ames, Rakishi, and Sam had all pulled over and emerged from their cars. They simply stood there, staring, and even the hardened mercs appeared stunned into silence by what they were looking at.

Large portions of Chicago had simply been blown away. The skyline had literally been decimated; at least a tenth of it was no longer there. A vast cloud of blackened smoke hung over the city, and there was some sort of huge shape that was visible in the lower sections of the smoke. Sam wasn't sure, but he suspected it was some sort of Decepticon vessel. An airship, maybe, or a base from which Decepticons could launch smaller attack ships. It could be the equivalent of a floating aircraft carrier.

And oddest of all, the city was glowing. It was as if it were suffused with some sort of energy, or perhaps energy that was starting to build up to something. Had the Decepticons nuked the place? Sam got a mental picture of Carly dying from radiation poisoning, her skin covered with sores, her eyes glazing over . . .

He closed his eyes a moment but then gave up when he realized that it would do nothing to block out the images in his mind.

"You ever get the feeling there's something you don't want to know about?" said Epps.

"You have no idea," Sam said.

Stackhouse seemed to be checking something on what looked to be a palm-sized computer. Meanwhile, Tiny had removed some manner of device with a flat wand attached to it and was waving it in the air. Sam tapped Epps to get his attention and then pointed to Tiny. "He trying to cast a spell?"

"Taking readings. What've ya got, Tiny?"

"No rads. Or at least nothing beyond what's normal these days," Tiny said.

"No communications, either," Stackhouse informed them. "We can stay in touch with shortwave, unit to unit, but forget about cellphones."

Epps shook his head at the prospect of what they were facing. "My God. We came here to find one guy . . . in the middle of *that*?"

"We going into that, Epps?" Tiny sounded dubious about it.

"No one's going in," Epps said flatly.

"Are you kidding?" Sam couldn't believe what he was hearing. "I thought you guys were mercs! I thought you were badass! This is just . . . it's a city that's been messed up by war! You've never been to places like that?"

"We've been to plenty of places like that, runt," Hardcore Eddie said. "But we got prep time, we got access to way more equipment than what we have with us, and—oh, yeah—we got a paycheck."

"Eddie's right," Ames said. "Don't mind doing no pro bono for old time's sake to help out Epps, but this? With a week or two to plan, maybe . . ."

"Well, we don't have a week or two! The damned planet may not have a week or two!" Sam said angrily. "You're not going in? Fine! I am. With or without you, I'll find her."

He started to stalk away, but Epps grabbed him firmly by the arm. Sam tried to pull away, but Epps's grip was solid iron. "You'll get yourself killed. That what you want? Come all this way for that?"

"She's here because of me!"

"If she's in there—if she's even alive—there's no way you're ever gonna reach her. I'm sorry, but it's all over."

Sam relaxed, and in response Epps did, too, easing up on his grip. It was exactly what Sam was waiting for, and when he yanked free, Epps was caught off guard.

He started running toward Chicago. He was hoping that Epps would simply shrug and say that if he wanted to throw his life away, he was welcome to do so. Instead, Epps immediately went in pursuit. Sam tried to put on as much speed as he could, but within thirty seconds he was gasping for breath and could tell from what he was hearing that Epps wasn't even breathing hard.

And suddenly from behind them, Hardcore Eddie shouted, "*Incoming!*"

A Decepticon fighter was howling through the air in their direction. Sam hoped for a moment that it hadn't spotted them, that it was just hurtling past on its way to somewhere else. That notion was quickly dashed when the fighter angled straight down toward them and opened fire with a strafing run. The mercs, Sam, and Epps scattered in all directions, and it was just Sam's luck—or maybe it was by design—that the fighter appeared to be zeroing in on him. It chewed up ground behind him, and he knew that it was catching up. It was only a matter of seconds before it overtook him, and there was nowhere for him to hide.

And suddenly the fighter exploded, blown right out of the air.

The concussive force knocked Sam off his feet, and he fell flat onto the highway. He threw his arms over his head to protect it as huge chunks of the fighter bounced all around him. He saw the head of a Decepticon, the pilot, go rolling past, and—with the sound of the explosion still ringing in his ears—he looked around to see where the blast that had destroyed the fighter had come from.

He couldn't believe it.

Optimus Prime was standing ten feet away, smoke still wafting from the discharge of his arm cannon. Arrayed behind him were all of the Autobots, the ones who were supposed to have been blown to cinders.

The mercs were gaping at them, exchanging glances as if to ask one another, *You ever see anything like this?*

"Perhaps your leaders will now understand," Optimus said. "Decepticons will never leave your planet alone. And we needed them to believe we had gone."

It took Sam long moments to recover his breath. "They . . . they were watching me." He pointed to his wrist even though the miniature spy was long gone. "I couldn't tell you . . ."

"You told me enough for me to know that something was wrong."

"But your ship . . . They blew it up . . ."

Roadbuster strode forward with his characteristic swagger. "Designed the damn thing, didn't we? First booster rocket to separate . . . that was our splashdown escape pod!"

"Thing was a bucket of bolts anyway," Topspin said dismissively.

Roadbuster agreed. "Never woulda made it outta the atmosphere."

Optimus looked toward the city. There were explosions in the distance, and Sam watched with dismay as another building collapsed. He prayed that there was nobody in it but was afraid he was wrong. God, what if it was the one that Carly was in?

Why? Why the hell are they doing this?

"If they're destroying the city," Optimus said, answering the unspoken question, "it's to make a fortress so no one can see what they're up to inside."

"Then I think I know how to get a look," Sam said. He turned and pointed to the fallen alien ship. There were chunks of it all over the place, but a considerable portion of it was still in one piece. "Can we sneak in with that thing?"

Without hesitation, Roadbuster called out, "Get to work, boys! I want this enemy ding-wing shipshape top-tight ready!"

The Wreckers pounced on the ship, moving in perfect synchronization in their efforts. They kept up a steady stream of chatter, talking so fast and furiously that Sam couldn't tell what the hell they were talking about. But, he reasoned, it didn't really matter whether he understood, as long as *they* did.

The way that they were moving . . . it seemed familiar somehow . . .

Suddenly he laughed.

Considering the circumstances, it certainly seemed an odd reaction. Epps stared at him questioningly, and Sam said, "Don't you see it?" He pointed at the Wreckers.

"See what? What're you—?" Then he realized, and a broad smile crossed his face. "A pit crew."

"Yeah. They're moving just like a pit crew."

"Who says television isn't educational?" Epps said.

"So, ah," Sam said uncertainly, "are you guys, y' know . . . outta here? Like you said you were gonna be?"

"You kidding?" Epps pointed toward the mercs, who seemed engaged in endless, fascinated discussion with the Autobots. "This is going to be *the* heavyweight fight of the world. If you think we're going to wanna be anyplace other than ringside, you can just forget it. We'll stay under the El tracks, use subterranean roads. We'll be fine."

The Wreckers were finished in less than an hour. Once they were ready, Bumblebee climbed into the cockpit. Sam followed right behind him, although it was somewhat cramped since Bumblebee was taking up most of the space within.

Sam glanced around. He did not for one moment think he was remotely qualified to render judgment on the quality of the work the Wreckers had put into slapping this thing together. But to his untrained eye, it sure looked like it was being held together with spit and baling wire.

"You think it'll fly?" Sam said, trying to keep the uncertainty to a minimum.

Bumblebee gave a confident thumbs-up.

That helped ease Sam's concerns a bit, and then, almost as an afterthought, he asked, "And you *do* know how to fly it?"

The hand that was holding an upwardly pointed thumb flattened out and wavered side to side, conveying the sign recognized throughout the galaxy: *So-so.*

"Whoa, wait, what does that mean?" Sam was suddenly less sanguine about the whole notion. "Bee, explain that—"

Bumblebee declined to do so. Instead, the ignition of

the engine and the liftoff of the fighter ship were almost simultaneous. Sam was thrown back hard against the seat as the fighter hurtled into the sky, banked hard, and headed at top speed toward the smoking remains of Chicago.

VIRGINIA

i

The situation room at NEST headquarters, while not quite as impressive as the one in the White House, was capable enough when it came to dealing with an emergency. Also, because of the fact that the walls were entirely curved, it had been given a whimsical nickname by NEST personnel: the Egg. Mearing, annoyed by anything having to do with whimsy, had actively discouraged and then outright forbidden it. Naturally, this had caused the name to become so entrenched that by this point even she was using it.

Fortunately enough, the Egg had not been in one of the sections that Sentinel had annihilated during his rampage through NEST confines. Having remained unbroken, the Egg was now serving as accommodations for General Morshower, Director Mearing, Agent Simmons, and the titleless Dutch.

General Morshower initiated the bad news by saying that was only the first salvo of what seemed an endless stream of setbacks. "Our high-range bombers were knocked out of the sky. We can't get through the enemy air defenses over the city."

There was a speakerphone set up in the middle of the table, and Lennox's voice came over it. "All NEST teams are on stand-down, holding at Grissom ARB. We're ten minutes outside the battle zone."

Simmons was all business, not at all in a frenzied

state, which was a bit of a relief to Mearing since she never quite knew which Simmons she was going to be dealing with. "Can we get any eyes in there at all?"

"Radio silence. Comms are jacked," Lennox said.

"Just a couple of surveillance UAVs," Mearing said, referring to unmanned aerial vehicles. "Only link to that whole city."

Morshower looked grim. "They want us out. They want us blind."

Simmons wasn't listening to Morshower. Instead, his entire attention was on Mearing, and he was leaning forward eagerly. Or at least as far forward as his busted leg would allow him to. "Whoever's manning those UAV drones, can we try to navigate them toward Trump Tower?" When he saw her puzzled expression, he continued. "The kid was on his way to Chicago. He thinks that Dylan Gould is a point-man human op. If I know anything, I know this: That kid's an alien bad-news magnet."

There was just enough of that manic energy in Simmons's voice to prompt a skeptical look from Morshower. "Gould? Old money, long-standing industrial business partner. You're saying he's in on it?" When Simmons's head nodded so furiously that he looked like a bobblehead doll, Morshower said to Mearing, "You vouch for this man?"

She considered it a moment. "Today. Maybe. We'll redirect the drones."

But that wasn't sufficient for Simmons, who rapped the speaker box on the table as if Lennox were inside it. "Lennox, listen up. You have the only guys close enough who know anything about how to fight these things."

"Sending combat teams now . . . it's a suicide run!" Morshower said sharply. Then he paused, considering. "But it's your team, Colonel. Your discretion. I'd back you up as best I can."

Simmons leaned in closer "Can't tell you what to do, soldier. But if I wasn't in this wheelchair, I think you know where I'd be."

"I absolutely do, Agent Simmons," Lennox said. "And I think we're on the same page."

ii

The technician had set up shop in the Egg and was expertly controlling the drone as it maneuvered its way through Chicago. Its point of view camera sent the digital feed directly to the view screen on the Egg's curved wall. Mearing and Simmons watched in stunned silence, surveying the scenes of utter destruction. Simmons felt as if he were looking at the middle of Baghdad after a night of shock and awe.

"Are you telling me," Mearing said with astonishment, "that Sam was headed there?"

Simmons shook his head. "Poor kid. Probably never got close."

CHICAGO

i

Carly sat in Dylan's penthouse apartment in the Trump Tower, looking out at the smoking ruins of the Windy City. Some of the destruction had been caused by, she thought, army planes trying to launch assaults on the Decepticons and having no luck. Some of it was the Decepticons destroying things simply because they could, and they were sadistic monsters who enjoyed inflicting damage.

And Dylan was in their hip pocket. No . . . Dylan was their best pal. Their best flunky. He wasn't the Devil. He was, as they once described someone on *The West Wing,* the guy who ran into the 7-Eleven to get Satan a pack of cigarettes.

And she had defended him to Sam. That was the most humiliating thing. Sam had been absolutely right about him, and she had been absolutely wrong. She could not believe how badly she had misjudged him. Although, to be fair, even if she had believed Sam that there was something up with Dylan, she would have just thought Dylan wanted to sleep with her. The notion that he was aiding and abetting an alien takeover would never have occurred to her. It hadn't even occurred to Sam, and he was Mister Alien Invading Takeover Guy.

She walked back across the living room, pausing only to cast an angry glance in the direction of the vindictive little watchdog Dylan had left behind to make sure she stayed put while he grabbed some sleep in the next room. He had not so subtly suggested to Carly that it might be wise on her part if she chose to join him. She made it clear in no uncertain terms that that would never happen. That left her walking around the living room in a daze of fear and frustration.

The fear she could handle. The frustration, however, was going to continue to eat away at her until she managed to find something to do to occupy her time other than worry about Sam, Dylan, Decepticons, and the end of the world.

Carly glanced out a window. More pillars had gone up all over the city. Purely as a guess, she supposed that there had to be a preponderance of them here in Chicago in order to focus and disperse the energy that was going to emanate from the anchor. It would then be projected around the world to other pillars, and then . . .

Then what? A celestial neighbor pops in?

She could readily believe Dylan's protests that science wasn't his forte. How long would it take for the earth to be shaken to pieces by the arrival of the Decepticons' home world? Minutes? Hours? Days at the most? All they needed to do to relocate the Decepticons was get a few pillars to the new world, and boom, off they'd go. But what about the humans for whom the bridge might prove too demanding a means of transport?

Then it dawned on her. She had seen hints of a vast ship hovering above, although it was hard to make it out clearly. What if it was some sort of ark? What if there were more of them around the world? Perhaps they intended to cram as many humans as they could into the ships and bring them to Cybertron as a brand spanking new slave race, just as Dylan had said. She had a mental image of Dylan standing there, on a perch, snapping a whip and encouraging all the pathetic slaves passing below him to move faster, damn it, faster. It was not a pretty picture.

Feeling the need to move, as if she could leave the mental image behind her, she noticed a telescope standing out near Dylan's balcony. It was angled downward, which made her tend to think that he was far more interested in using it to go all Peeping Tom on surrounding windows.

She looked south across the river and spotted the two giant robots, Megatron and Sentinel, right where they had been last night, on the same rooftop.

Desperate to engage her mind, she swung the telescope around and focused it on the two titans to see what she could see.

ii

("The city is secure," Megatron says with confidence. "The humans cannot stop us.")

("Very soon, the rest of the pillars will absorb sufficient solar radiation to reach full capacity," Sentinel replies. "Then they will be placed into launch position.")

("This is the victory I promised you, Sentinel, so many years ago. A victory where, in the end, we rebuild Cybertron together.")

(Sentinel's next words are laced with disdain. "I have deigned to work with you . . . that our planet may survive. I will never work for you.")

(Abruptly Sentinel's hand lashes out, and he wraps it around Megatron's throat. With a twist of his upper body, he is suddenly dangling Megatron over the sheer drop from the top of the building to the street far below. He shakes Megatron several times like a cat worrying a mouse, Megatron's feet treading nothing but air. "And

you would be wise to remember the difference," Sentinel warns him.)

(His point having been made, he tosses Megatron carelessly not to the street but back to the roof next to him. Megatron looks utterly stunned and says nothing.)

iii

Carly had many talents, but tragically, being able to read lips wasn't one of them, even when the speakers had huge metal mouths.

Nor, as it happened, was it a talent that she required. It was abundantly clear to her that Megatron had just been bitch-slapped by his supposed ally.

She walked back across the living room, turning over in her mind what she had just witnessed. It seemed unlikely that there would be an occasion for her to use this information or turn it to her advantage in any way.

On the other hand, if it did present itself, she knew one thing for sure: She was going to be ready.

"Shhhh! Carly . . . !"

Her head snapped around, and her eyes widened in shock.

"Sam!"

He was standing in the middle of the living room in a half crouch, looking exactly like what he was: someone who had managed to, somehow, sneak into enemy territory to effect a rescue. He had one finger to his lips, and with the other he was gesturing for her to come to him.

For a moment, she was totally stunned, trying to figure out where he had come from and how he could possibly have gotten here. It overwhelmed everything else only for a second, but that second was all that was required for the stereo system to change into Laserbeak. The malicious Decepticon launched itself straight at

Sam, and Carly barely had time to scream a warning even as Sam caught the motion out of the corner of his eye. He tried to avoid the assault but failed utterly as Laserbeak slammed into him, knocking him headfirst over the couch.

The shouting, the falling—all of that would have been sufficient to wake the dead, much less Dylan. He charged into the living room from the adjoining bedroom, shoving the sleep from his eyes and studying the scene in astonishment. Sam was just clambering to his feet behind the couch, and Dylan locked eyes with him. "How the hell—?" he demanded, which admittedly Carly was also wondering, and then he bellowed, *"Kill him!"*

Laserbeak aimed his guns straight at Sam, who ducked back behind the furniture to avoid the blast.

Dylan threw up his hands in alarm. *"Not the couch! It's Ralph Lauren!"*

Clearly annoyed but under orders to accommodate the ridiculous human whenever possible, Laserbeak turned and shot out the doors leading to the balcony. Wood and glass shattered and splintered, providing plenty of clearance. Laserbeak then came around the couch, grabbed Sam by the ankle, and dragged him unceremoniously toward the balcony.

"No!" Carly screamed, and she lunged toward Sam to try to head it off. But Dylan moved too quickly, coming in behind and putting her into a crude but effective headlock. She struggled, kicking at his shins, trying to pull free and failing.

With one quick throw, Laserbeak hurled Sam the width of the living room and over the balcony. Carly's scream mingled with his own, and then Sam was gone.

Dylan shoved Carly aside, sending her tumbling onto the couch. Laserbeak was heading over to the balcony to double-check that Sam was nothing but a puddle of bloody mess on the sidewalk, but he was distracted when an angry Dylan bellowed, "Would you please tell me how the hell he got in here? What were you, sleeping on the job? Could you be any more useless?"

Carly saw Laserbeak's angry red eyes focused on Dylan, and Dylan was distracted by Laserbeak, and all she could do was look with despair at the balcony where she had just seen Sam Witwicky thrown to his death. She choked back a sob.

Suddenly Sam's head appeared just beyond the balcony. His head and then his shoulders, and she could see that he was crouching on something flat and broad: the top of an air vehicle. He was frantically gesturing for her to drop down, and then she saw the guns, bristling and ready. She instantly rolled off the couch and hit the floor, lying facedown and covering her ears.

Laserbeak glanced her way, unsure of why she had just done that. Dylan, at the wrong angle, didn't see her and hadn't yet looked off to the side to see what was arriving on the balcony.

The guns aboard the fighter plane cut loose, strafing the penthouse apartment, blasting Laserbeak against the wall.

Dylan threw himself backward, hitting the floor on the opposite side of the living room from Carly. He let out a scream and cowered behind a Louis XIV chair.

The guns stopped firing. Carly, sensing her moment, jumped to her feet and bolted for the balcony. Sam was just beyond the edge, his hand outstretched. A sheer drop yawned below, and she still had no idea how he'd come to wind up atop a combat vessel or whether they would make it down safely. It was, in every way, a literal leap of faith.

She didn't hesitate to take it.

She hit the balcony and kept going, clambering up the railing and over in one smooth motion. With a confidence and smoothness that would have been the envy of a trained acrobat for a Ringling Brothers trapeze act, Sam caught her and pulled her to safety atop the ship.

The cockpit was wide open, and Sam eased her in behind Bumblebee. He was about to climb in himself, but suddenly he was being pulled backward.

Carly let out an alarmed shriek.

Laserbeak was behind Sam, on the fighter. He was pockmocked with bullet holes and a sizable chunk of his body had been blown away, but he was still determined to inflict as much damage as he could, like a berserk shark in the throes of a feeding frenzy.

Locked in a life and death battle, Sam managed to angle himself around and grab Laserbeak's neck, twisting the robot around so that he couldn't bring his blasters to bear. Laserbeak fought back furiously. They tumbled toward the edge of the ship, Sam barely managing to stay on.

Carly tried to clamber out of the cockpit to get to Sam, but Bumblebee firmly pulled her back in. Apparently one human running around on the outside of the ship was more than enough.

Sam cried out in pain as Laserbeak managed to seize the leverage and push him onto his back, slamming him down. Sam lashed out with his foot, kicking Laserbeak back, but it wasn't far enough as Laserbeak swung his blaster around and fired. It wasn't point blank, but it was close enough that a miss was highly unlikely.

And out of seemingly nowhere, an incredibly small vessel came zipping in and intercepted the blast. Carly had no idea what it was. She'd never seen anything like it before. Whatever it was, it was blasted sideways, spinning out of control, and sent crashing into the ship's stabilizers.

The ship was barely holding together as it was; the damage to the stabilizers was more than enough to cripple it beyond repair, or at least beyond what Bumblebee could fix on the fly. He struggled to control the rocking, tossing ship, and it began a slow, spiraling descent.

The ship tilted backward, and Sam, back on his feet, was catapulted directly at a startled Laserbeak. He collided with the robot, and the two of them went down in a tangle. This time Sam was on top and shoved Laserbeak back across the deck.

Laserbeak had clearly had enough. He angled his blaster around, and now he was indeed point blank. One discharge of his weapon and Sam Witwicky would never bother the Decepticons again.

Suddenly Sam shouted, "Bumblebee! *Fire!*"

Looking to the side, Laserbeak realized too late that Sam had maneuvered his head right in front of one of the ship's cannons. Laserbeak let out an alarmed croak, and that was all that he had time for before the cannon blew off his head.

Releasing his hold on Laserbeak, Sam allowed the headless robot to slide off the ship and crash to the street below.

The problem was that when it came to hitting the street, the attack ship wasn't far behind. Sam flattened himself, bracing for the impact that came seconds later. The jolt was so violent that he was sent tumbling off the ship and landed on the street next to it.

Carly climbed out of the cockpit and, trying not to collapse in a fit of the shivers, ran to Sam and crouched next to him. Placing her hands on his face, she said in loving wonder, "You . . . found me."

"Yeah, well . . . I had some help," he managed to say, and then he pointed behind her.

She turned and saw the most motley assortment of humans and robots ever collected.

Carly spotted Wheels and Brains among them, and naturally she knew Bumblebee as he hauled himself out of the ship's cockpit. "Y' know how they say that any landing you can walk away from is a good one?" said Wheelie. "Don't believe it. That was one sucky landing." Then he swiveled his attention to Carly. "Hey, sweetheart. Couldn't stay away from our boy, couldja."

"I guess not."

One of the men with the guns, a black man, approached. He wasn't in uniform; instead, he was wearing khakis, and he had a rifle tucked under his arm. "You Carly?" She managed a nod. "Name's Robert Epps. You're gonna be fine."

" 'Ey!" Roadbuster was holding up the object that had intercepted the blast that would have killed Sam. "Check this primitive dingus."

"That's a UAV! A NEST UAV! It's an unmanned probe. Was it working before?" Epps said.

"Y-yes," Carly said. "In fact, it flew into Laserbeak's path. It saved Sam."

"Then that means that someone back at NEST was controlling it. And maybe they can see or hear us." Immediately he grabbed it out of the blue robot's hand.

"I weren't finished with that yet!" the robot protested.

"Shut up, Roadbuster!" He started shouting directly into the probe. "Flight control, copy? Repeat, do you copy? Acknowledge transmission . . . somehow. Rotate! Do something!"

At first the drone did nothing at all. But then the center ball, the one with the lens, nodded up and down.

Carly and Sam immediately darted in front of it. "If you hear us, this is ground zero!" Sam shouted.

And Carly, remembering all the things Dylan had told her—boasting in his confidence that nothing he said would go any further and enjoying his position of being in the know—said, "Sentinel's here in Chicago, getting ready to launch!"

VIRGINIA

The exuberance in the Egg over the technician's deft maneuvering of the probe that had saved Sam's life quickly gave way to frustration. No one was doubting that it was worth sacrificing the device in order to buy Sam Witwicky even a few more minutes of life. But now their main source of information was down for the count.

The general had left the room to return to the White House, but Mearing and Simmons were still there, desperately trying not to let frustration overwhelm them. At first the screen had gone out completely, indicating that the camera was offline. Mearing snapped orders to the technician, telling him to do whatever he could to bring the device back online. After a minute of tinkering with it, he managed to get a partial image. It was grainy and indistinct, but it was something, and it seemed to indicate that the drone was on the street somewhere. There was a good deal of noise from nearby multiple voices and shouting, but it was garbled and hard to hear.

"Is that the best you can do?" she said to the technician.

"So far," he replied tersely, continuing to adjust a control bank that was a truly staggering array of dials.

Then the drone abruptly shifted position in a manner that told them that someone had picked it up. A face appeared, pixillated into what seemed a thousand squares.

Mearing squinted. "Is that . . . yes! It's Epps! And . . .

oh, my God . . . behind him . . . that's . . . Ratchet and . . . Bumblebee . . . ?"

"Autobots! Haaaahaha!" Simmons was thumping one of the armrests of his wheelchair in undiluted glee. "I knew it! I knew they survived, those mechanical miracle workers!" Then he quickly turned his attention to the technician. "Can you let him know we can see him at least? And get the damned audio fixed!"

The technician fired him an annoyed look, clearly not pleased about Simmons barking orders at him. Then he twisted a dial, and the picture abruptly moved up and down.

"What're you . . . oh, my God, that's brilliant," Simmons said. "You're making the camera nod! Good going!"

"Can you boost the audio?" Mearing said.

"Working on it."

Garbled words began to come through. Two faces appeared: Sam's and a female whom both Mearing and Simmons knew instantly.

It was hard to make out, but it sounded like Carly was saying, "Sentinel's pillars . . . atop building . . . Hotchkiss Gould," while Sam was telling them "to open . . . other . . . space bridge."

"We gotta get this in front of Colonel Lennox," said Simmons.

Mearing didn't disagree. "Feed it through to him at Grissom." As the technician prepared for the relaying of the images, she shook her head in quiet amazement. "He actually got to her. Hard to believe."

"Never underestimate the lengths that a man in love will go to for his woman," Simmons said.

She stared at him. "You really need to stop talking now," she said.

"Got it."

INDIANA

i

Grissom Air Reserve Base was situated approximately sixty-five miles north of Indianapolis. Named for the late astronaut Gus Grissom, it was home to the 434th Air Refueling Wing.

At that particular moment, it was also home to Colonel Lennox, who was seated behind a desk, feeling frustrated and uncertain. Time was ticking down, and he had no play. Instead he was left sitting there, staring at an array of monitors on the wall that were providing him with nothing. He had a collection of rumors, of half leads, but nothing definitive. He needed to be able to see, he needed rock-solid intel from someone on the ground, and he was being relentlessly deprived of all that. Technicians were monitoring the screens, constantly trying to find some sort of live feed, but nothing had come through.

Suddenly an image appeared on the screen, causing Lennox to jump to his feet.

He was reasonably sure that it was Bob Epps standing in the background, and in the foreground . . .

Sam. Of course, Sam. Who else *but* Sam?

"*. . . will . . . transport . . . Cybertron here!*" the girl was saying.

And Sam was now saying, "*Have to . . . destroy . . . control pillar! Shoot it . . . down . . . !*"

There were GPS readouts coming through as well, localizing where the broadcast was originating from. In the meantime his fax machine came to life, spitting out a rushed transcript of the entire broadcast for reference.

"Is this coming out of Chicago?" he called out.

"That's the point of origin, sir, but it's being routed through NEST!"

Another technician was holding up a telephone. "NEST on line one, sir!"

Lennox immediately grabbed the phone and jammed it against his ear. "This is Lennox!"

"You getting all this, Colonel?" came Simmons's voice. "If you're going, the time is now!"

ii

An array of extremely capable soldiers stood at ease in front of Lennox, having just been informed of the situation to the best of his knowledge and what was expected.

He saw the eagerness in their eyes. Not a one of them was displaying the slightest hesitation in the face of what could well be overwhelming odds. Lennox wasn't sure whether it was unstinting bravery or if they simply didn't understand what it was they were going to be facing. It could well be a combination of both. How could you explain to anyone what it was to square off against the walking death machines called Decepticons? At least they'd been given the welcome news that reports of the Autobots' deaths, like that of Mark Twain a hundred years earlier, had been greatly exaggerated. So they wouldn't necessarily be all on their own in attempting to get into Chicago. But still . . .

"If we want to hit back, we'll have to wing-suit in," Lennox said. "I'm not promising a ride home. Anyone with me? The world needs you now."

One young soldier immediately stepped forward. His nametag read "ZIMMERMAN," and he was bristling with youthful certainty. He reminded Lennox of himself when he first became an army ranger. "I can find my own ride home, sir."

In no time at all, every single one of them—nearly forty in all—had volunteered for the hazardous assignment.

Lennox thought about his wife and daughter waiting for him back home. This job wasn't going to be about making it back because failing to do so meant that his wife was a widow and his little girl would grow up not remembering her father.

No, this was about succeeding so that they'd have a planet to live on.

The stakes were slightly higher this go-around.

CHICAGO

i

It was a difficult notion for Sam Witwicky to wrap his brain around and certainly there was no circumstance under which he would consider the loss of human life to be a lucky thing, but the harsh truth of the matter was that the Decepticons might well have done the opposition a favor by bombing the living crap out of Chicago.

If they had not taken such an aggressive posture—if they had continued to perpetuate the myth that they were not going to inflict any harm and waited to deliver their masterstroke until it was too late—they would have had a couple million hostages at their disposal to use in any number of ways to hamper the efforts of Sam and his allies. But the majority of the population either was dead or had gotten the hell out of Dodge, which simplified the problem of collateral damage tremendously.

Except now Sam was prepared to do some serious damage of his own.

The predator had been packing a Hellfire missile. The Wreckers had managed to cobble together a launching cylinder that they assured Sam definitely, positively, abso-fraggin'-lutely had an 89 percent chance of firing, take that to the bank, mate. It was, under the circumstances, going to have to be good enough.

Between the buildings that were still standing and the massive distribution of debris, there were still plenty of places for them to hide, enabling them to get as close to their target—the anchor—as they possibly could.

The Autobots had formed a protective circle around the humans, acting as the most formidable escort in the history of crowd control. They moved from spot to spot, trying to minimize their exposure to any prying eyes. In the distance, across the way, towering above the skyline, was their destination with the anchor pillar atop it. Except from this angle, although they had a decent view of Sentinel and Megatron, there was no clear view of their actual target.

"I say we just blow up the whole shebang," Hardcore Eddie said.

"Won't get the job done," said Mirage. "Let's say you manage to blow out the building's foundation. It's going to require more than that to take care of Sentinel and Megatron. They'll just grab the anchor pillar and leap clear of the collapsing building."

"He is correct," Sideswipe said. "We need to target the anchor itself. And we can't do it from down here; the angle is wrong."

Sam abruptly looked down at the Hellfire missile he was carrying in his arms. When the Wreckers had thrown together the launch device so that it was functional— more or less just to see if they could—they'd then handed it off to Sam with a dismissive " 'Ere, mate! Make yerself bloody useful! Carry something!" But now he was coming up with a plan of action that he was starting to like. "With this rocket, could we shoot that control pillar down?"

Epps did some fast calculations of their position versus their target. "Eight blocks away. Gotta get closer for the shot, and it's across the river. Gonna have a hell of a time sneaking up."

"Forget getting closer," Sam said. "Think higher. All we need is a direct line of fire."

Epps studied the area and muttered a profanity to himself. The destruction of Chicago had been accomplished in the same manner as when a tornado sweeps through a town. Some areas get clobbered while others escape unscathed. Buildings that would have been ideal for height had been destroyed altogether, whereas buildings that were too short remained standing. All except for . . .

He pointed. "If we got up into that one there, maybe . . ."

Sam looked where he was indicating and wasn't thrilled with what he was seeing. About a half mile east by the River Esplanade was a tall glass building that kind of reminded him of Nakatomi Plaza from *Die Hard*. But at least Bruce Willis, for all that he had to deal with in that film, had been in a structure that remained resolutely vertical even when the shit was being blown out of it. This thing was tilting. Geometry wasn't Sam's strong suit. Apparently his strong suit was hairbreadth escapes from killer alien robots, which wasn't a skill that looked good on a résumé, as he'd found out. Still, it appeared to be, to his math-challenged eye, at least at an eighty-degree angle from the ground. Common sense told him that anything short of ninety wasn't the best use of real estate.

Epps saw the look on Sam's face. "So it's leaning. So what? That tower in Pisa, it's been leaning for years, it's still upright."

Sam called, "Carly, how much does the Leaning Tower of Pisa, y' know, lean?"

It just seemed to be the kind of thing she'd know. As it turned out, he was right. "About four degrees," she said.

"Okay, so that thing's leaning more than the Leaning Tower of Pisa. That's got to be at least five, six degrees more lean, I'm thinking."

"You got a better idea?" Epps said.

"Yeah. Waking up. Waking up right now, safe at home, finding out I'm dreaming all this and none of it ever happened. That's my plan A."

"Sam! Time for school!" Epps said as he reached over and pinched Sam hard on the ear, causing him to let out a yelp. Then he stared at him sardonically. "How'd that work out for you? Wake up, didja?"

Sam shook his head to ease the pain and then said, "So, plan B, then."

"Looks like."

Quickly they informed the Autobots of their new destination and their plan, such as it was. "It is a worthy endeavor, Sam," Optimus said gravely. "We will see you through to your destination. We would enter the building if that were feasible, but I think our height and, of even greater concern, our weight"—he looked dubiously at the tilting structure—"would make that inadvisable."

"Gotta agree there. All I ask is that you keep an eye on Carly while we—"

Without hesitation, Carly said, "No way. I'm coming in with you."

He looked at her in surprise. "Are you crazy? There's no reason—"

"I'm not leaving you again. Not ever. I love . . ." She hesitated and then, seeing the look in his eyes, switched tracks and continued, ". . . nothing about this plan, but it beats sitting around on ground level and feeling helpless. You go, I go."

Wheeljack rolled forward, producing assorted high-tech equipment from wherever the hell he always managed to pull it out from (truthfully, Sam didn't like to think about where he stored it). "Urban combat. A classic. Don't forget my prototypes. Grapple gloves for climbing; release is a little tricky, but you'll get it. And everyone take yourself a boom stick." He lay down a set of intricately designed metal rods about two feet long. One end looked like a flare; the other appeared to be covered by what almost looked like a metal fist with the fingers clenched. It was like a combination of a mace and a lightsaber. Wheeljack pointed to the flare end. "Safety off, arm, ignite, thirty seconds, boom." The way he was doling out the equipment accompanied with wry understatement, Sam half expected him to conclude, *And do try to bring it all back in one piece this time, Double-Oh-Seven.*

Sam lay down the Hellfire missile long enough to pick up a grapple glove and a boom stick. The glove looked like segmented metal, running up to his elbow. On the top side of it was a launcher that would fire a grappling hook and a retracting line, which he thought would come in particularly handy if he was endeavoring to escape from the Joker. He shoved the boom stick through his belt and secured it.

Epps looked down at the missile. "Too bad we only brought one shot."

"One shot?" Sam replied. "That's all we'll need."

ii

(Megatron is still flush with humiliation from the manner in which Sentinel addressed him, grabbed him, slung him about as if he were nothing. His emotions are torn between wanting to prove his worth and wanting to lash out at the Prime for treating him so. He ultimately rejects the latter, because this is a time for unity, not fractiousness. Besides, he doubts that if it came to it, he could defeat Sentinel, anyway. So it is the former, then. Proceed with such efficiency and professionalism that Sentinel has no reason to question his capability again.)

(And then something catches his eye. Something running over the bridge connecting the north shore to the south, waving a white piece of cloth. That is the typical

human gesture for surrender. He decides to target it for amusement and blow it to atoms, just to show how highly Decepticons value such concepts. His sight zooms in and his audio locks on, and then he realizes that, no, it is the human Gould. What is he shouting?)

("Autobots! They're here! Alive!")

(Megatron is staggered. He glances toward Sentinel. Has he seen, heard, what Megatron just heard?)

("Remind me again," Sentinel says, glowering, "what exactly your army is good for.")

(That answered that *question.)*

(And Megatron sends out an electronic message to all Decepticons within range: "Decepticons! Defend the pillar!")

(Gould just manages to clear the drawbridge before it starts rising. Within moments the Decepticons make sure the rest of the drawbridges are upright as well. The castle has raised the bridges and decided to rely on both the knights in the field and the moat to protect it.)

(The siege is on.)

VIRGINIA

It seemed to Mearing as if the Egg had become her second home. She then realized bleakly that if circumstances didn't change and soon, it might well be her last home.

As she studied frustratingly limited satellite photos, she felt a hand patting her on the back. "I just want you to know," Simmons told her, "whenever I imagined the end of the world, I always pictured being with you."

She turned and looked at him. "You're making it worse. You're making me start to feel that the world can't end soon enough." Simmons wasn't big on taking hints, but even he could handle this one, and he removed his hand from her back. She returned her attention to the photos. "We've got to be able to see what's going on around that building from the ground."

Perhaps eager to make up for being stupid enough to bring up his feelings at a time like this, Simmons immediately jumped to the task. "Get NSA to send server specs for any cameras in that area. Traffic lights, ATMs, anything. Then"—he indicated Dutch—"let the Great German Hope hack us in."

Dutch flexed his knuckles, and the crack they made echoed in the Egg.

CHICAGO

i

The Autobot convoy, having changed into their car incarnations, barreled around the debris that littered the landscape and sped as quickly as they could toward the streets of the north side of Chicago.

Optimus was in the lead, of course, an unstoppable juggernaut, or at least Sam hoped that he was unstoppable. Sam was at the wheel of Bumblebee, Carly at his side. The Hellfire missile was secured in the back; they certainly didn't need it rolling around randomly. The rest of the Autobots were behind them in a steady stream of cars, and Epps and the various mercenaries were hitching rides within them. Despite the seriousness of the situation, he couldn't help but smile; the Wreckers were all race cars.

Carly was studying Leadfoot, the closest behind them, in the side-view. "I just have to say, was it really the best idea for that one to have a large white target painted on him? Isn't that kind of asking for trouble?"

He hadn't thought of it that way. Now that she had said it, though, he couldn't think of it any other way.

Wheeljack was bringing up the rear, and suddenly there was a violent shaking, and before anyone could react, a huge crevice split the earth, creating a chasm directly in front of Wheeljack.

He cut hard to the right, but momentum had him. Unable to regain control, he jumped the barriers and headed straight into the Chicago River. In midair he shifted back to his robot form, and then he plummeted into the water and disappeared beneath the surface.

ii

(Wheeljack feels more foolish than anything else as he sinks to the riverbed and lands, his feet kicking up a cloud of silt. He had reacted like a car instead of an Autobot disguised as a car. He had been caught off guard and has wound up looking like a right fool because of it.)

(Once he has his footing solid, he begins to move toward the shore. It should not take more than a few moments for him to—)

(Then the water begins to swirl around him.)

(He looks behind him, in front of him, and to either side.)

(Decepticons are converging upon him.)

(He unleashes fire in all directions, but in the water the blasts are slowed while the Decepticons move even more quickly, easily avoiding his attack.)

(Then they are upon him, bearing him down to the dirt. He fights back furiously, and at close range he blasts apart one of the Decepticons, but then two more are upon him to take its place.)

(His last thought before final darkness falls upon him is that he should have come up with a more efficient means for the others to carry weapons.)

iii

They drove to the shoreline, the Autobots still in their car forms, and waited for Wheeljack to emerge. When he did not do so immediately, Carly said, "Should it be taking this long?"

It was Optimus who answered. "No, it should not." He started toward the water. "It should not be at—"

Suddenly he froze, and his voice was empty as he said, "He is not responding. I am sending him a message and he . . . is not there . . . he is—"

"There!" Ratchet suddenly called out, pointing in alarm.

"Bloody hell," said Topspin.

Large pieces of what had once been Wheeljack floated to the surface, one by one at first and then several at a time. The river's current started to carry them away, and Sam's heart sank as he looked on.

"Why didn't he call us? Why didn't he summon help!" said Sideswipe.

"Because he was a warrior and he disliked the lay of the battlefield," said Optimus. "He didn't like the odds of our survival and felt that he might well be summoning all of us to our deaths. It is the only answer that makes sense."

"Then we gotta make sure his death wasn't for nothing," said Epps. "We gotta take down these—"

Once more the ground beneath them began to shake. The humans looked around. The Autobots looked down.

"I don't suppose there's any chance that could be natural causes?" Sam said with not much conviction.

"We need to get the humans clear of here, immediately!" said Optimus, and he immediately began to change into his robot form.

It wasn't fast enough.

The street trembled and then ripped open, practically right under the feet of Optimus Prime. He was sent hurtling into the air in midconversion. He landed safely on his feet, but his trailer, complete with the valuable weapons and tools within, was flipped high in the air and then crashed to the ground, upside down, at least a hundred meters away.

They're separating us from weapons! Sam thought

frantically. *First Wheeljack! And now Optimus's armory! They're trying to make sure we have no resources.*

Even as Sam realized the immediate strategy of the Decepticons, the earth vomited up a mechanical nightmare. It was a gigantic metal snake of a creature, towering over the Autobots, letting out a screech that would have been at home being issued from the throat of a Jurassic-era dinosaur.

"Drillers! Why did it have to be Drillers!" Leadfoot shouted.

And it was not alone.

The cockpit upon its back opened, and Shockwave emerged from it, not as huge as his mount but no less intimidating.

We are so screwed, Sam thought.

Optimus tried to make a move toward his weapons cache. But Shockwave had the high ground and used it to maximum advantage, unleashing a series of blasts that created a virtual wall of explosions between Prime and his arsenal.

"This way!" Optimus shouted, and herding the humans in front of him, he steered them to shelter within a partly crumbled train station. The other Autobots were returning covering fire at the Driller, driving it back, but it wasn't about to relinquish its position and let Optimus anywhere near his weapons.

They crammed into the train terminal, knowing full well that this was a temporary solution at best. Shockwave was in no rush. Time was on his side; he didn't have to destroy them. All he had to do was keep them occupied until the pillars had been activated. After that, it was game over.

"Things just got a lot worse," said Optimus, an assessment that Sam was hard put to argue with. "We have no weapon that can match Shockwave's. We've got to outflank and get behind him."

"We'll circle around to the bent glass building. You guys can draw his fire," said Epps.

Wheelie rolled forward and said, "Can I just maybe put in a vote for doing it the other way around? I'm not big on the whole drawing fire thing."

"Right," said Carly, "because if you guys go out there, the one they're *really* going to shoot at is you."

Wheelie gripped her leg firmly. "You understand me. You are my new warrior goddess." Then he started to thrust himself repeatedly against her shin.

She kicked him away and said to Sam, "If I die in the next few minutes, at least I won't have to live with that memory for long."

Sam considered that the most desperate attempt to find the bright side of all this he had ever heard. But he would take whatever he could get.

LAKE MICHIGAN

Five V-22 Ospreys streaked through the skies above Lake Michigan, hurtling toward the smoking remains of Chicago.

Lennox's Osprey was bringing up the rear. Counting himself, there were forty soldiers in all, eight in each plane, each of them clad head to toe in specially modified wing suits. Aerodynamic cloth stretched from their wrists to their hips and between their legs. Zimmerman, seated next to Lennox, brought his arms around himself, enveloping himself in the stretched cloth. His voice low, he whispered, "I'm Batman."

"You're Rocky the flying freaking squirrel, is what you are," said Perkins, another soldier.

Lennox permitted them to engage in the lighthearted jabs because he knew what was really going through their minds. Their enthusiasm and bravery were not at all in question, but they knew what they were about to head into. Keeping it light until the go moment prevented them from dwelling too much on what they had to deal with.

But the go moment was nearly upon them, and Lennox started issuing orders through his comm unit. His words sounded in the radio sets of all the soldiers and the pilots as well. "Use Willis Tower for cover. We get altitude, we jump. Aim your descents toward the river. Follow tight. Wacker Bridge."

"Clarification, sir," came the voice of one of the pilots. "Willis Tower?"

"Formerly the Sears Tower."

"Copy that."

First it was the Sears Tower; now it's the Willis Tower. Everything changes, Lennox thought. Then he remembered the nature of the beings they were going to be fighting and realized just how apt that thought was.

Lennox looked out the front of the Osprey, and even though they were at the back of the diamond formation, he was able to see the ruins of Chicago spread out before them. There was still a thick black cloud hanging overhead, and . . .

"What the hell is that?" he said to the pilot. "At two o'clock?"

"Can't make it out, sir," said the pilot. "Big sucker, though."

Their flight path wasn't going to bring them near it, but whatever it was, it was drifting closer and closer to Chicago. One thing that Lennox knew for sure: It wasn't going to be anything good for—

"Bogeys incoming!" the pilot suddenly shouted.

Hurtling toward them were several Decepticon airships, moving with incredible speed. Certainly far faster than anything the Osprey could achieve. They darted forward, and suddenly the air was alive with the alien ships' firepower.

"Evasive maneuvers!" Lennox called out, but the pilot was already on it. The Osprey darted hard right, just barely avoiding a diving attack by one of the Decepticons. The Osprey to their right wasn't quite so lucky. An incoming wave of fire from the Decepticons' attack ship ripped away its port wing. Undoubtedly the pilot within tried to compensate, but he failed utterly, and like a crippled bird the Osprey veered off course, colliding with one of its fellows. The two planes erupted upon impact, sending a fireball that cooked the air around Lennox's ship and resulted in a ball of twisted wreckage plummeting down into the waters of Lake Michigan. It hit, sending up a huge splash of water, and then vanished from sight.

One of the Decepticons was darting downward to avoid a collision with another of the Ospreys and cut directly into the path of Lennox's aircraft. Their onboard weapon, an M240 machine gun, cut loose at it, shredding the Decepticon, sending it spiraling out of the way and carving a path. The other two Ospreys leaped toward the gap and hurtled forward, reaching Chicago with Lennox's own ship close behind.

"Where are the remaining Decepticon ships?" Lennox called out.

"Not picking them up, sir! Maybe they disengaged!"

Maybe. But he wasn't buying it for a second. The Decepticons were relentless. There was no choice, though, other than to stick with as much of the plan as they could.

At least Chicago, or what remained of it, was providing them with some cover. The Ospreys hurtled with almost reckless speed through the concrete canyons, approaching the Sears Tower, which was, miraculously, still standing.

There was no more joking among the soldiers in Lennox's ship. They were all grim-faced, determined, knowing not only what was at stake but that sixteen of their fellows had just met a horrible death without having the slightest opportunity to face the enemy in battle. They were aware that it could just as easily have been them.

And it could still be.

The Ospreys kept low, trying to stay below any tracking that the Decepticons might be doing of any incoming hostiles. Lennox watched on the array of monitor screens, looking for some sign of life on the battered streets below. He wasn't seeing anything. "God," he breathed.

"Not even sure God's listening right now," said Zimmerman. It was a rather depressing attitude to have, but Lennox couldn't entirely blame him.

They were rapidly approaching the Sears Tower. The first two Ospreys had already reached them and rotated their wings, enabling them to begin the vertical ascent up the side of the building. On reaching the top, the ships would hover within visual distance of each other and Lennox would give the order to jump.

With any luck, this mission was still going to be salvageable.

ii

(The lead Osprey reaches the top of the tower. The pilot rotates the craft ninety degrees in order to allow the men a clear jump path. And as the plane turns, he comes face to face with Starscream, standing on the roof.)

(Starscream is amused. He lets the look of shock register on the pilot's face. He wants the human to realize that he is dead and that there is nothing he can do to prevent it. He can almost taste the deliciousness of the moment. Then he reaches out and easily breaks the propeller off the Osprey. Whirling out of control, the vehicle crashes into the side of the building, raining fire, steel, and glass on the street below.)

(The second Osprey barely manages to avoid the debris that is filling the air around it. It is a formidable bit of flying. Starscream acknowledges the talent of the human pilot by personally blowing the vessel out of the air with his arm cannon. What better way to reward such skill than by giving it the honor of being disposed of by the mighty Starscream?)

(*He then turns his attention to the third vessel and sees with mild annoyance that it is already darting away, heading as quickly as it can back out toward the body of water called Lake Michigan. He scowls at the cowardice of the pilot. In contrast to the other vessel, this one is not even worth the effort of firing his arm cannon at it. Not worth it, and not worthy.*)

(*Then he notices something, and there is a deep growl of annoyance within him. There are eight flying humans, hurtling away with amazing speed. They are wearing some manner of flight suit with black wings stretching along the sides. Quickly he tracks and fires at them, but he is unaccustomed to such puny targets. As a result, the blast explodes near them, and the subsequent shock wave sends two of them tumbling. But instantly they recover and seconds later have sped around the corner of the building and out of sight.*)

(*"Thunderation!" Starscream snarls, and immediately sends out an electronic command to the nearest attack ships. Seconds later they are in pursuit of the annoying humans.*)

(*Starscream remains at his station, scanning the sky to look for any further foolish intrusions on the part of the humans. He is confident that the attack ships will dispose of the remaining intruders. How difficult could it be? They are, after all, only humans.*)

(*The attack ships speed after the fleeing humans, trying to pick them off but running into the same problem that plagued Starscream: They are too damned small. It is difficult to lock on to them, plus they display an almost supernatural ability to get out of the way of any shots fired.*)

(*The humans have no way of knowing that in a strange way they are replaying a sequence of events that occurred millennia ago. Back then it was Sentinel keeping out of the way of assailants. It had all been a ruse, of* course, designed for the benefit of any onlooking Autobots. They had to believe that Sentinel was truly dead, his supposed mission an utter failure. It was part of the grand scheme to both demoralize the Autobots and lay the groundwork for the eventual triumph of the Decepticons on whatever world the Ark eventually landed.)

(On that day long gone, Sentinel had performed a series of daredevil maneuvers and the Decepticons had harried him and several were actually sloppy enough to die.)

(History repeats itself. That is a truism as real for the Decepticons as it is for anyone else.)

(The men dart and weave, moving through spaces between fallen or angled buildings that become smaller and smaller, making it an increasingly greater challenge for the attack ships to keep up with them. They fly around a sharp corner, and one of the attack ships banks hard to follow and crashes into a dangling overpass, exploding upon impact. A second ship tries to avoid the explosion and fails, erupting in flame when it comes into contact with the detonated vessel. The third attack ship moves quickly past the remains of the other two vessels and angles into an increasingly narrowing space between two buildings that are leaning, tops nestled against each other like a pair of lovers. The humans hurtle through the canyon, which becomes smaller and smaller. The attack ship has to turn sideways in order to fit, and then one of the flying men fires something, some manner of weapon. It strikes a building just ahead of them, and as the men pass under it, a huge chunk of the angled building's upper section is blasted loose and tumbles down.)

(It strikes the attack ship as it attempts to get past it. The impact knocks it hard to the side and causes it to strike another building. The attack ship blows up. The building remains resolutely where it is.)

(Just like that, the attack is over.)
(Now comes the hard part.)

iii

All seven of Lennox's men landed atop the roof of a parking garage.

All seven? Lennox couldn't quite believe that those words had played through his mind. Eight men in total had survived, including him. He'd lost thirty-two men already. And if he hadn't gotten off that shot that brought the building collapsing upon their pursuer, it was entirely possible that none of them would have survived. All seven? They weren't "all" of anything, and he told himself that he would do well to remember that.

"Weapons status," he said briskly, giving no indication of the feelings roiling within him. "What have we got left?"

Zimmerman was right on top of it. "Twenty nine Bot Busters. Twenty piercing D-bots. Frags, but no rockets. No launchers." That seemed a bit of a downer, but Zimmerman immediately rallied. "But ass-kicking attitude, *sir.*"

Despite the overall seriousness of their situation, Lennox couldn't help but permit a small smile to let the soldier know he appreciated his enthusiasm. Then the smile faded, and he gestured for all of them to come closer. "Listen up," he said. "For our brothers, let's make this trip worth it."

"Hooah!" the soldiers shouted, and Lennox returned the shout.

They ran out into the streets of Chicago.

CHICAGO

i

It was called the Galileo Building. Apparently they specialized in producing equipment for astronomical endeavors, but now it had an additional meaning that was remarkably appropriate: Galileo, according to legend, performed a famous experiment involving the dropping of objects of varying weights off the Leaning Tower of Pisa.

Now it's going to serve another purpose, Sam thought. *It's going to help us stop an alien race from beyond the stars. Galileo would have liked that. At least I hope he would have. Hell, for all I know, he was a disguised Decepticon. I don't know what to believe about anyone anymore.*

Sam, Carly, Epps, and his merry band of mercs were making their way up as quickly as they could. Naturally, taking the elevator was out of the question. The power was out, and even if it wasn't, this was not a situation in which to trust oneself to some rickety contraption.

So they took the stairs.

This was not the easiest of endeavors. First, clambering up forty flights of stairs was something of a challenge in and of itself under ordinary circumstances. The building's angle served to make gravity an additional factor.

Sam felt as if he were perpetually on the edge of falling over. He clutched on to the railing with a death grip, making his way up the stairs, hauling the Hellfire missile, which seemed to be getting heavier by the second. Others offered to carry it, but Sam, through gritted teeth, insisted that he could do it. It was a matter of pride by that point. Foolishly stupid pride that had meaning to no one but himself, but pride nevertheless.

Pride goes before a fall . . .

He glanced down the dizzying stairwell and gulped. *Don't think about falling.*

"We have a problem!" came Hardcore Eddie's voice from ahead of them.

"Just one?" Epps said sarcastically.

Up ahead of them, the way was blocked. Not only was there massive debris, but a sputtering power line was dangling in front of it, swinging gently back and forth, seeming to invite them to take a whack at trying to dodge it.

"We're at the thirty-fifth floor," Carly said, tapping the entrance door next to her. Sam couldn't believe it. She didn't seem the least bit out of breath. He was starting to think that maybe she was part machine. That would explain a lot of things.

"It'll have to do," Epps said. "Open it."

She pushed it open and almost slid right out. With a startled yelp she grabbed on to the doorknob, her feet nearly going out from under her.

"Carly!" Sam shouted.

"I'm okay! I'm okay! But boy, thank God I'm not wearing stilettos . . . Sam, you know the ones I mean."

"Yeah . . . yeah, I do." He grinned, his mind suddenly going to a much happier place, and then he yelped as someone hit him on the shoulder.

Ames scowled at him and rumbled, "Focus, kid."

"Right, right. Sorry."

One by one, they made their way out into the office. It was the most surreal thing Sam had ever seen. It was an open area so that he had a clear view of the skewed office landscape.

Carly was now in a crouch, as if she were tentatively making her way down the side of a mountain. "Nobody move too quickly." She made her way out the door, crab walking as she went. The others followed suit.

It appeared to be some sort of graphics design office. A vast bullpen area stretched out in front of them, dotted with art boards and high chairs. There was also one long, flat table that might have been used for conferences or perhaps simply as a communal gathering place to eat or discuss things. Some of the offices, presumably those of the higher-up guys, had glass partitions.

There was an entrance to another stairway off to the left. Sam made a mental note of its location, just in case.

The rest of the determined band followed Carly's example, except for Rakishi, who must have been born on a mountain since he simply walked forward with utter confidence, apparently unbothered by something as trivial as gravity.

At one point Sam stumbled, and he grabbed on to a nearby chair for support. The chair promptly sped away from him, and he would have fallen if he hadn't shoved himself against a desk. Stackhouse said to him, "All the chairs here are on wheels. Not exactly anchors."

"Thanks for the safety tip," Sam said.

Then the phone rang on the desk that Sam was leaning against. Incredulous, he picked it up. "Hello?" he said tentatively.

It was an automated message informing Mrs. O'Shea that she had a dental appointment at Doctor Friedman's office tomorrow.

It was such a trivial, mundane thing, yet it struck an odd chord for Sam. It reminded him of how people had simply been trying to live their ordinary lives, and then all this insanity had happened. It made him all the more determined—as if he required any more incentive—to beat those bastards and return at least some semblance of normality to their lives.

Load-bearing columns dotted the tilted landscape, and that quickly became their main means of support as the group made its tentative way across the office. Minutes later, they reached a wide window that opened up on the cityscape and gave them a clear view of the Hotchkiss Gould building.

"Okay, Sam, we'll take it from here," Epps said.

His determination to contribute having been satisfied, Sam handed the missile over to Epps. Epps and Tiny then brought it close to the window and started setting up the makeshift launcher cobbled together by the Wreckers. Sam couldn't believe it, but he actually missed the arrogant, crazed bots. He missed all of them and continued to have a deep fear in the pit of his stomach that they wouldn't survive the day even if somehow the humans did manage to stop the Decepticons' plan.

Suddenly there was a groaning of metal from deep within the bowels of the building, and everything shifted.

Sam banged up against a desk, the impact of which caused the desk to slide a few inches. Carly threw her arms around one of the pillars, and the other mercs braced themselves against whatever they could find.

The launcher started to tip over, and Epps barely managed to catch it.

Hardcore Eddie seemed to be getting far less hardcore by the moment. He was actually starting to sound frazzled. "This whole thing's unstable! We gotta get outta here!"

"If we don't do what we came for, nothing else matters," Sam said. He pointed to the anchor pillar positioned on the roof of the Hotchkiss Gould Building across the way. "That's our target."

"All right, everybody," Epps said as Tiny started to reposition the launcher. "No sudden movements."

Suddenly Carly pointed and shouted, *"Watch out for the ship!"*

A Decepticon attack ship rose into view. It was moving in what seemed a leisurely manner, just sort of drifting along. It might not have necessarily known they were there. Or else it had a general idea of their whereabouts but wasn't sure.

The humans tried to find hiding places to obscure themselves, Tiny grabbing the missile launcher to protect it. But it was too late. The attack ship caught sight of their movements and wheeled around to face them. Now it was no longer a matter of hiding; it was a matter of trying to find shelter before the inevitable assault.

The attack ship cut loose, blasting through the windows, shattering them. Sam fell behind a desk, bullets chewing up the furniture around him. He saw Carly positioned behind one of the support pillars. Bullets or whatever the hell it was shooting blasted off overhead sprinklers, sending water cascading everywhere. *Great. Just what we need. The floor's tilting* and *it's wet.*

"The stairwell! Over there!" Sam shouted frantically.

The mercs, from their makeshift hiding places, saw where he was pointing. The moment the firing ceased, perhaps so that the Decepticon could determine how much damage it had done, they broke from cover and dashed for the exit. The Decepticon started firing again as the mercs dodged and wove through the tilted floor, banging through the exit door.

"Go, go, go! Next floor up!" Epps was shouting, gesturing wildly to Sam and Carly. He wasn't going to leave until they were clear. Sam made a break for it, grabbing Carly by the wrist as he went.

There was another crashing sound near the window, and Sam saw to his horror that the Decepticon who had been piloting the vessel had leaped in. The ship was drifting away; he must have set it to land itself. Unlike the Autobots, he was small enough that he was able to maneuver within the confines of the office and didn't seem to care what effects his weight might have on anything. Water cascaded down upon him from the busted sprinklers, serving to disorient him temporarily.

The motion of Sam and Carly must have caught his attention, though, and he started toward them, glass crunching under his feet.

Sam and Carly bolted into the stairway and up the flight of stairs so fast that Sam barely felt them underneath his sneakered feet. Epps followed them, and as he sprinted up the steps, the door below burst open and the Decepticon stood framed in the doorway.

In an instant Epps's gun was in in his hand, and he opened fire on the Decepticon. The bullets hammered home, blasting away at its chest, shredding a portion of it. The Decepticon's body swayed back and forth from the series of impacts, but its face remained impassive.

The trigger of Epps's gun clicked on empty.

The Decepticon, aside from having sustained some upper torso damage, looked none the worse for wear from the barrage.

And then slowly, deliberately, it lifted its hand and extended one clawlike middle finger upward at Epps in an unmistakable and familiar display of contempt.

Sam, watching from the doorway above, had no idea where the Decepticon could have picked that gesture up from.

"Oh, *hell,* no!" shouted Epps, and as the Decepticon advanced on him, he snapped a grenade off his belt, yanked the pin from it, and flung it at the Decepticon. As if it had eyes, the grenade lodged itself in the hole that had been created by the bullets from Epps's gun.

The Decepticon reached for the grenade but in its haste knocked it into its own innards.

Epps dashed for the door, bellowing, *"Fire in the hole!"*

He flung himself through the door, and Sam slammed it shut behind him just as an earsplitting roar thundered from within the stairwell.

The door wasn't designed to withstand that degree of impact. The blast tore it off its hinges and sent it flying across the office space, which was similar in design to the one on the floor below. It smashed through a far window and out.

Between the pounding from the Decepticon attack ship and the explosion from within the stairwell, the building started to give way even more. It jolted violently, angling even more sharply. Desks, chairs, everything, started sliding, and that included the desperate humans inside the office. They grabbed for whatever support they could as anything that wasn't nailed down skidded past them.

Sam threw one arm around a column and the other around Carly, barely managing to prevent her from falling away from him. *I am never watching* Titanic *again*, he thought grimly.

Then, above the groaning of metal and the crashing of furniture, Sam heard an alarmed shriek. He turned just in time to see Ames, arms pinwheeling, plummeting headlong out the window at the far end. The man who had preferred to be by himself apparently hadn't been close enough for anyone to grab at him, and he hadn't been able to snag on to a support fast enough.

And then he was gone.

ii

(Shockwave does not see the human coming. He does, however, hear it. It makes a heavy noise hitting the

ground, like a sack of wet cement, and Shockwave turns toward it and regards it with curiosity.)

(Then Shockwave looks up toward the tilting glass building from where the human had just fallen. Knowing where the human landed, he easily charts the trajectory and determines precisely what level the human must have been on before it began its terminal arc.)

(He turns to the Driller and indicates the human's point of origin. "Eliminate," he says.)

(The Driller moves to obey.)

(Shockwave returns his attention to his initial mission: finding the Autobots. They have proved elusive, which is particularly annoying. Rather than stand and fight as one, they have headed in all different directions. Cowards. How can they not realize that they are simply prolonging the inevitable?)

(Best to return to Optimus Prime's weapons cache. He has deliberately left it there as bait for the Prime to return and try to reclaim it. He has also left six Decepticons there, camouflaged, who will ambush Optimus Prime and bring him down should he be foolish enough to try to retrieve it.)

(It is a solid plan and sure to work.)

(Because this is the Day of the Decepticons, and nothing is going to stop their inevitable triumph.)

iii

Sam, Carly, and the mercs had slowly edged toward the far end of the building, Tiny still clutching the missile. They made sure to keep themselves anchored to anything that seemed stable enough to support their weight.

Then they heard a distant roar.

As much as they would have preferred not to, they looked down.

In the distance, but approaching fast, was the slithering metal creature that Leadfoot had referred to as a Driller.

"Holy Mother . . ." Tiny whispered.

The mercs looked stunned. Epps looked envious. "Man, the Decepticons always have the best shit. Just unfair."

The building swayed slightly beneath them. There were collective gasps, and then it stilled again.

Hardcore Eddie came up alongside Tiny and quickly started helping him set up the Hellfire, using a desk to brace the weapon. The desk slid in response, and Eddie said, "Guys, you gotta keep me steady!" Tiny and Stackhouse quickly pitched in, crouching to try to achieve some traction while bracing the desk on either side.

"Targeting for ninety meters!" Eddie said as he sighted on the pillar. Sentinel was standing nearby. Sam hoped that if Sentinel got in the way, it wouldn't make a difference. That he would be blown to hell along with his precious anchor. "Wind five knots . . . almost . . . locked . . . almost . . . *there*!"

Just as he fired, the Driller slammed into the building far below, shaking it violently.

The missile blasted out of the tube, knocked off course by the sudden impact of the Driller against the building. The Hellfire hurtled across the Chicago skyline before blasting apart the structure half a block over from the Hotchkiss Gould Building.

"*Goddammit!*" Epps shouted. "Plan B! Lemme hear it!"

"The stairs! Get back to the stairs!" Rakishi shouted. "We gotta go down!"

Sam was already there, looking down into it through the doorway that the door had vacated. The grenade had done its job and more besides. The stairwell was a showcase of wreckage. "They're blocked!"

Then they heard a distant and constant thudding, starting from ground level within the building and drawing steadily closer. "Oh, *now* what?" Eddie said.

"It's the Driller," Epps said. "It must be coming up the center shaft of the ventilating system."

Of course it is, Sam thought bleakly. *Where's an Autobot when you really need him?*

iv

When he looks back upon the ruin of this day, I believe that Shockwave will realize, in the final analysis, that his greatest mistake was to underestimate me.

He mistakes compassion for weakness. He thinks that my concern for humans, my time spent among them, has somehow made me less than what I am.

He is wrong, and he will discover that.

The minions that he left guarding my weapons have already learned that harsh lesson.

They lie scattered in pieces. This was not some murky, underwater environment where they could wait in ambush. This is a war-torn surface, the type of which I have known for far too long. Six of them against me? Some might consider those to be unfair odds, and in a way they were. It was unfair to them. But I will certainly waste no time weeping for them.

I reach the weapons pack, still in the alternative form of a truck trailer. Upon my touch it changes into its true form.

I affix it to myself. It takes a moment to power up, and then the thrusters kick in. Within moments I am airborne.

v

(The Driller reaches the top of the building. There is nowhere else for it to go. It feels cramped within the confines, and its tentacles reach out in all directions. It

requires room to see what it is doing and so makes some through the simple expedient of ripping off the top twenty or so floors. The entire section of the building tumbles with a howl of twisting metal and shattering glass, slamming down onto the roof of a building across the street. It leans awkwardly against it, glass falling everywhere, and winds up sagging like a fallen tree but still remaining miraculously intact.)

(Paying it no mind, the Driller emerges, looking around and down.)

(How fortuitous.)

(The troublesome humans are down below, in the section that has just been knocked aside.)

(They are clutching on to whatever they can, since they have no floor: pieces of columns projecting from the ceiling, stray dangling wires. Anything and everything they can. But they will not be able to do so indefinitely.)

(Still . . . why let them dangle there, far above the ground, waiting for the inevitable? Why not simply dispose of them now?)

(The Driller moves toward them, preparing to slap them from their perches, ending this farce.)

(Let no one ever say that the Decepticons are not merciful.)

vi

"I won't let you fall! I won't let you fall!" Sam was shouting.

The grappling glove of the late, great Wheeljack was the only thing allowing Sam to cling, batlike, to the remains of the support column.

He had no idea how the thing worked. Whether it was static electricity or a zillion little suction cups or whatever. But the surface and texture of the material permitted him to hold on to a perch that should never have sufficed.

Unfortunately, he had only one, and the other hand was grasping on to Carly's wrist. She dangled below him, a sheer drop yawning beneath them. He tried not to think about the fact that the muscles in his shoulder were screaming at him, or that his arm was starting to cramp up, or that his palm was starting to get sweaty. He just needed to hold on to her until . . .

Until what?

He spotted a fire escape attached to the building that they were leaning against. He wasn't sure if it was too far or not, but it might provide hope for Carly if he could get enough momentum before—

Then he saw the Driller emerging from the remains of the building across the way, coming straight at them.

Oh, God . . .

Carly's back was to what Sam was seeing, but she saw the terrified look on his face. She must have realized that he was seeing nothing good, yet she didn't twist around to try to see it. That was fortunate, because Sam would almost definitely have lost his grip on her.

Instead she screamed up at him, *"Sam! I love you!"*

He thought, *Now? This is what it took?*

"I love you, too!" he shouted back. "But your timing sucks!"

And as the Driller moved toward them, preparing to finish them off, that was when shots exploded against its surface, causing it to rear back and howl in protest.

"Optimus!" Sam shouted.

The mighty Prime dived toward the Driller, continuing to fire away at it with his onboard weaponry. The Driller writhed and screeched, its attack on the humans seemingly forgotten.

Sam took the opportunity being presented to him before his arm gave out entirely. He swung her back and forth, shouting, "The fire escape!" so she would know what the hell he was doing. She cast her glance toward it, and then Sam saw the Driller twisting away from Optimus and trying to resume its heading toward the humans. *Now or never,* he thought, and released her, praying that he'd built up enough momentum.

She came up short of the fire escape, banging into it and almost tumbling away toward the street. She reached up desperately, and her fingers wrapped around the railing at the last second. With a grunt, Carly pulled herself up and found safety—a relative term, to be sure—on the landing of the fire escape.

But that left Sam, Epps, and the mercs still dangling perilously, and the Driller was making another attempt to move toward them. Sam wasn't particularly inclined to admire the creature, but if he were going to, it would be for its single-mindedness.

Optimus swung around again and fired another series of concentrated blasts just behind the thing's head. Apparently that was some sort of weak spot, because the Driller writhed and twisted as it hadn't before, howling like the damned. Then it collapsed, flopping about helplessly, even pathetically, before the spasms finally ceased.

Then, from below, he heard, "Need some help?"

Below, on street level, was Mirage. He was already lowering Carly gently to the street and now started climbing up the side of the adjacent building so he could get to the others. "Unless you just want to keep hanging around."

Within seconds Sam and the rest of the group were safely down on the ground. Hardcore Eddie looked like he was ready to kiss the sidewalk.

Sam couldn't believe it. For once—for *once*—things were going their way.

Suddenly Mirage was yanked upward, off his feet. Looming behind him was Starscream, one arm across

Mirage's chest and the other across his neck, immobilizing him.

"Run!" Mirage managed to get out.

"I never had much patience for you," Starscream said to Mirage. "You were the one who preferred hiding to fighting. You should have stayed hidden."

With one quick twist he ripped Mirage's head clear of his shoulders. Then he tossed the head aside, allowing the lifeless body of the Autobot to slump over. He looked around for the humans.

They had taken the advice of Mirage's last word.

It would do them no good.

vii

(Shockwave is furious. It was not supposed to happen this way. Optimus was supposed to have been destroyed by his troops. The Driller was supposed to kill the humans. The slate of their greatest opposition was to be wiped clean in preparation for the impending triumph of the Decepticons.)

(Yet now the Prime had shown up and killed the Driller before it could finish disposing of the humans?)

("Outrage!" says Shockwave. He targets the damnable Prime who is hurtling through the air toward the humans—those precious, infuriating humans—and fires. The blast is well aimed. It destroys part of Optimus Prime's flight equipment, and Prime hurtles out of control, crashing into a distant building that is still under construction. Caught up in rebar and cables, he struggles like a fly trapped in a web. Unable to gain any sort of leverage, he cannot free himself. At least not immediately. And later will be too late.)

(High above it all, Sentinel watches all that has transpired. He finds the entire business mostly sad, if not vaguely amusing. Then he turns his attention to matters of greater importance.)

("The magnetics are aligned," he announces. "Activate assembly.")

(All over the world, the pillars lift skyward from wherever they are. They form a gigantic ring of light around the entirety of the globe. Were that light not serving as a signal for the end of the human race, some might actually consider it quite lovely.)

(The light burns away the dark cloud hanging over Chicago and reveals, there in the beauty of the last day of life as humanity knows it, a Decepticon battle cruiser. Crafted in secret over many years under the auspicies of such individuals as Dylan Gould, a combination of Terran and Decepticon technology, it floats high above, a glorious symbol of a brand-new world to come . . . in every sense.)

viii

Sam scarcely had time to process the horrible death of Mirage before he and Carly were running like mad.

In the twisting and turning piles of rubble and debris that now constituted Chicago, it was easy to get separated. Sam and Carly remained together since they were clutching hands as they ran, but within moments they had lost track of Epps and his team.

Unfortunately, Starscream seemed to have taken a particular interest in them. Ignoring the scattering mercs, he remained focused on the two young people, rampaging after them, tossing aside buses and cars, smashing walls aside to keep in pursuit of them. They were able to dart through narrow holes that kept them out of Starscream's grasp for precious seconds, but it required no effort for him to clear a path after them.

"Thought you were working for us, boy!" Starscream said mockingly as he kept right on their tail.

They turned a corner and skidded to a halt. Rubble was piled a mile high, blocking their path. There was nowhere for them to go. They turned to try to back-track, but Starscream stepped into view, a sneer on his metal face.

"Nowhere left to run," said the giant. He could simply have stepped on Sam Witwicky, ground him to a pulp under his foot. But he wanted to see the trouble-some human up close. He wanted to see Sam's face as he squeezed the life out of him. So he leaned in close to reach down and grab him.

That was a mistake.

Sam brought up his arm, the one with the grapple glove on it, and fired the grappling hook. *"That's for Mirage, you son of a bitch!"* he shouted as the business end of the hook buried itself in Starscream's right eye, like a harpoon into the side of a whale. *"And for trying to crush my girlfriend!"*

Starscream let out an earsplitting howl and reared back. It was at that moment that Sam abruptly realized that he had no idea how to disengage the line. Wheel-jack hadn't mentioned it, and the damned thing didn't come with an instruction manual. He tried to yank it clear from his hand, but it remained fastened tightly around it, as it was designed to do.

As a consequence, Sam was hauled upward, with no more control over his fate than a yo-yo at the end of a string. Starscream didn't realize he had the human dan-gling from his eye; he was in far too much pain, thrash-ing and flailing about, half-blind.

Sam desperately tried to reach the boom stick he had jammed in his belt. Unfortunately, it was over his right hip, and his right arm was busy being Starscream's pull toy. He attempted to reach it with his left, his fingers brushing against the tip, but he was being thrown around too much to be able to grasp it.

He let out a yell as he saw himself heading right toward the wall of a building and braced himself to wind up as a smear. But Starscream, as it happened, had punched a hole in it, and Sam landed inside it. It had been someone's apartment, and he crashed into a kitchen table and some chairs, scattering them.

It provided him the stability he needed just long enough to yank the boom stick out of his belt. He gained his feet, and it was at that moment that Starscream saw where he was and his face loomed in the hole, bellowing his fury.

Perhaps he thought that doing so would cause Sam to cringe in fear. Instead, Sam did the exact opposite, charging forward and jamming the boom stick between Starscream's jaws. He slipped off the safety and ignited it, then tried to fall back enough so that he'd be out of the blast range, whatever that was.

Starscream tried to reach for the boom stick to pull it out, but his fingers were too large and thick and he couldn't get his fingertips around it.

The door to the apartment banged open behind Sam, and he twisted his head around to see, to his astonishment, William Lennox, with another soldier right behind him. Now, *that* was timing.

"Sam, get outta there!" Lennox shouted as he and the other soldier opened fire. The bullets pinged off Starscream's face, and he shouted in fury.

"I can't! Cut the cable! *Cut the cable!*" Sam pointed frantically to the cable that was keeping him anchored. Lennox, seeing the problem, grabbed the glove with one hand and brought up his knife, ready to hack through the cable and free Sam.

That was when Starscream tried to take off.

He activated his jets, and Sam was yanked right toward the hole. The knife flew out of Lennox's hand. Lennox did the only thing he could do. He tried to anchor Sam, to pull back. He failed, and instead Sam, with

Lennox holding on, was hauled out of the building and into midair.

Starscream endeavored to gain elevation, but he was still half-blind and instead smashed into a building just across the way. He was still grabbing at his jaw, trying to get at the boom stick, and he kept on trying until the boom stick detonated. Wheeljack had struck at his enemy from beyond the grave as the weapon he'd created performed precisely as designed. The explosion was so fierce that it tore Starscream's head off, which was only appropriate considering what he had done to Mirage.

Unfortunately, it left Sam and Lennox with nothing securing their position. They started to fall to the street several stories below.

But there was Bumblebee, vaulting down the street, leaping over piles of debris as if they were hurdles on a track. He leaped through the air, his arms outstretched, his hands cupped, like an Autobot filming a commercial for Allstate Insurance. He caught them and slammed to the ground, absorbing the shock with his body.

Sam and Lennox lay there for a moment, gasping for air, looking at each other with mutual surprise, as if each of them couldn't quite believe that they were still alive. Then they both turned to Bumblebee and said in unison, "Nice catch."

Bumblebee grunted what sounded like thanks.

They clambered out of his hands, and then Wheelie suddenly came rolling up to Bumblebee. "Bee! Ya gotta see it! Ya gotta see what we found! C'mon! Quick!"

Bumblebee hesitated, looking to Sam. Carly had just run up to him, throwing her arms around him and kissing his face repeatedly. From nearby Epps and the mercs were coming back together and heading their way. "Go. See what the little lunatic wants," Sam urged, and Bumblebee immediately set off after Wheelie.

Epps and his team came forward as Lennox and his people assembled as well. They could not have looked more different, the battled-hardened mercs and the young, well-trained soldiers in the black uniforms. But in the nods, the silent greetings, the slight tilt of the heads—there was a quiet but obvious mutual respect between the two.

Lennox and Epps fist bumped. "So this is retired, huh?" Lennox said teasingly.

"Don't start with me," Epps warned his old partner. "I'm armed and I'm angry." He pointed to the top of the building, where Sentinel and Megatron, clearly confident in their power, stood above the city like gods. "We can't get across to the building."

"We have to," Sam said. "We have to find a way. I mean," he said, looking with an odd degree of triumph at the remains of Starscream, "we got one. Now we gotta stop that space bridge."

ix

The attack vessel whose Decepticon pilot had fallen prey to Epps's grenade was now lying on the street, engine idling, waiting for its pilot to return to it. Brains was in the cockpit, doing some enthusiastic rewiring as Wheelie came rolling up with Bumblebee in tow. "Ya got it ready to go, Brains?"

"Yes, yes, no question. It was hardwired to respond only to its previous pilot, but I've got it. All taken care of," Brains said in that rushed, manic way he had.

Wheelie turned to Bumblebee and pointed skyward, toward the Decepticon battle cruiser that hovered far above. "Brains and me, we're sick a seeing everybody else making a difference and we just sit around like we don't matter. Plus Wheeljack was a good guy. We're looking for some payback, and that looks like as good a target as any. Think you can get us up there, big boy?"

Bumblebee gave him an enthusiastic thumbs-up.

Moments later the attack vessel was arcing upward, closing in on the battle cruiser very quickly. Had Bumblebee gone in with guns blazing or attempting some manner of suicide run, he doubtless would have been attacked on sight. But since he was proceeding as if nothing was remotely unusual, it tripped no alarms on the cruiser and so he was able to draw extremely near.

There was a wide deck below, and Bumblebee angled near it.

"Thanks for the lift, Bee!" Wheelie said, and a moment later both he and Brains had leaped out. They landed safely below, and then Bumblebee angled the ship back toward the ground.

He was rather pleased with the situation before him as he flew toward the city streets. He had an attack vessel at his disposal. It was certainly in better shape than the one he'd been flying before, and that had worked out. He might well be able to do some damage.

In fact, he knew exactly where to go.

He turned the vessel in a leisurely maneuver and angled straight toward the building where Sentinel and Megatron were standing, looking skyward toward the coruscating energy being generated by the control pillar. With a grim smile, he charged up the attack ship's weapons and targeted the pillar. Sentinel and Megatron weren't even looking at him.

He was going to save the day.

x

(Bumblebee's ship is suddenly hit broadside by a devastating blast accompanied by sound so overwhelming that Bumblebee thinks his brain is going to fry.)

(Bee recognizes the pitch of the weapon that struck him instantly: a sonic cannon. He fights to regain control of the vessel, but there is nothing left to gain control

of. The engines are sputtering, about to die, and the helm is useless. Yet he keeps valiantly battling and by the end is attempting to steer it by means of sheer mass, throwing his body this way and that to try to control where and how it is going to come down.)

(The ship hits the ground, chewing up asphalt and annihilating parked cars. It bounces several times, rolls over, and finally skids to a halt.)

(The world is spinning around Bumblebee as he tries to recover his wits, and suddenly he is being yanked out of the cockpit. He is hauled to his feet by several Decepticons. His struggles are unsuccessful.)

(What he sees then utterly crushes his spirit.)

(Leadfoot, Topspin, Roadbuster, Ratchet, and Sideswipe are being held immobilized by other Decepticons. Standing directly in front of Bumblebee, holding up the sonic cannon that he used to blast Bumblebee from the sky, is Soundwave. And behind him is a human who looks familiar to him, but he is not sure from where.)

("Nice landing," Soundwave says. He then addresses the other Decepticons. "Take him to the other side. Use the tunnel that the Driller carved for us so that we could pass under the lake. Take him with the others to Megatron and Sentinel.")

("As what? Prisoners?" says the human. "You better teach them some respect. Especially that cuddly little yellow one who blew up my apartment.")

(Ah. Now Bumblebee knows. It is that Dylan Gould. He had seen him only briefly, when Gould was busy cowering in a corner.)

("No prisoners," Soundwave assures Gould. "Only trophies.")

VIRGINIA

Simmons surveyed the area with the variety of cameras at his disposal. "Whatever's set to happen, with those pulses getting faster, it's gonna happen soon. How long," he asked Mearing, "before the SEAL team arrives?"

"Your guess is as good as mine, Agent Simmons," she said brusquely. "They were coming in through Lake Michigan and should have made landfall fifteen minutes ago. We're assuming there's going to be the same communications jam across the board that we've been having, but Colonel Lennox is equipped with a GPS homing beacon, and the plan is that they'll be able to lock on to him with that and rendezvous."

"None of which is gonna mean a damned thing if they can't get across the lake." He looked in annoyance at Dutch, who was silently hammering away at his computer. "C'mon, you overgrown side of kraut. Gimme some good news."

"I believe . . . I can give you exactly that." He punched the "return" key with a flourish.

Watching through the traffic cameras, Simmons grinned in triumph as the drawbridges began to lower.

When Mearing didn't comment, Simmons couldn't let it pass. " *'Pleasure working with you again, Seymour,'* I believe is what you're supposed to say."

She actually smiled at him.

Then she said, "Good job, Dutch."

CHICAGO

i

Sam felt like he was dying, standing on the other side of the river, helpless to intervene.

On the roof of the Hotchkiss Gould Building, the building on which it seemed the entirety of his life had come to be focused, a new element of torture had been added to his witnessing the impending end of the world. The anchor pillar was still firmly in place, generating energy that was linking it to all the others around the world. Megatron and Sentinel were standing there like the smug prigs that they were. And above them, looming over all of it, was what was now clearly some sort of battle cruiser. Attack ships were suspended under it, held in place in preparation for use as needed.

But worst of all was the sight of the Wreckers, Sideswipe, Ratchet, and Bumblebee—his car, his friend—surrounded by Decepticon warriors. They were struggling in the grasp of their captors but were outnumbered, to say nothing of the fact that the Decepticon warriors towered over them. Watching over the whole proceedings was Soundwave, and he seemed to be taking particular delight in tormenting Bumblebee. He was holding some sort of long rod and was jamming it into various of Bumblebee's joints. Every time he did so, Bumblebee would shake and shudder, all in frightful silence.

One of the Wreckers, Leadfoot, suddenly managed to pull free, but Soundwave promptly unleashed a blast from his sonic cannon. Leadfoot screamed as his right leg was blown clean off, and he went down.

Carly was by Sam's side, and she could sense him living and dying with everything his friends were feeling. "They're going to be okay. You'll see. I mean, since the army's gotten here . . ."

She gestured toward the reinforcements who had arrived several minutes earlier.

"Navy," he said. "They're navy SEALs."

"Whatever. They're here, and they're going to help."

From what Sam had overheard, they had crossed Lake Michigan in a boat that had gotten annihilated by Decepticon drones. But the SEALs had, miraculously, survived, although they'd managed to salvage only some of the arsenal they'd brought with them. At the moment they were conferring with Lennox, who was going over the weapons they had brought with them and planning strategy. "Okay, lose those. Keep those. Use mic-mics and frags, go full auto, vibrations jam their circuits. Snipers, hit their eyes." He didn't bother to point out what the target was. It was hard to miss.

Unable to stand watching Bumblebee's suffering anymore and feeling the need to take his anger out on someone, no matter how undeserving, Sam broke away from Carly and stormed toward Lennox, who looked startled. "Why the hell are they over there and we're stuck over here?"

"Maybe one of them turned into a submarine, Sam," Lennox said. "I don't know for sure."

"Then let's find out for sure so we can do it, too!" he said in frustration. "I mean, these guys are navy SEALs, and no one thought to bring a few rafts to get across the water?"

One of the SEALs looked at Sam with great irritation. "Colonel Lennox, what purpose is served by having this civilian here?"

Lennox gestured for the irritated navy man to step back, and then he said placatingly, "They were destroyed, Sam, but don't worry, I'm working on a plan."

"A plan! Great!" Sam said, not placated in the least. "Why not just wave your arms"—he demonstrated—"and shout, 'Close, Sesame!' "

At the exact moment he did that, seven hundred miles away, Dutch hit the "return" key on his computer keyboard.

The bridges promptly started lowering.

Sam stood there with his hands still in the air, looking bewildered. So did the navy SEALs. Even Carly seemed impressed.

Only Lennox took it in stride. "That, Lieutenant, is the purpose in keeping the civilian around. He makes things fall our way. People!" he said, raising his voice, "we're moving out! Two by two!"

Seconds later the navy SEALs, the NEST soldiers, and Epps's crew of mercenaries were hustling over the bridge, determined to make it across before the damned thing opened once more. Following behind them were Sam and Carly. Neither of them had the faintest idea how they could be of any help, but both were determined to manage it somehow.

ii

(On the bridge of the battle cruiser, towering Decepticons watch the lights in the skies, enraptured, sharing in the impending triumph of their race and knowing that nothing—absolutely nothing—can stop it.)

(Meanwhile, two former Decepticons, so small that no one notices them, are apparently unaware that nothing can stop the impending triumph and are going about the business of trying to see just who is correct.)

(Wheelie reads a control array very carefully. "Do not use in flight," he says aloud.)

("Better not use those. We're in flight.")

(Wheelie rolls his eyes counterclockwise. For someone with the name "Brains," his associate can be somewhat dense at times. "Exactly, idiot," he says, and reaches for the controls.)

(On the rooftop far below, even as Wheelie deliberately violates the explicit instructions on the array, Soundwave is saying to Bumblebee, "I've brought something along. I thought you would want to see it." He gestures toward one of the Decepticons, who hurriedly brings forward an object immediately recognizable: the remains of Mirage. They dump his body to one side. Soundwave takes the head and then starts waving it around like a puppet. "Look at me. My name is Mirage. I am a cowardly Autobot who would much rather hide than fight, and my death was a small, pathetic, meaningless thing, which matches the way I lived.")

(Bumblebee, noiseless, tears free from the Decepticons holding him. Except he doesn't really; they release him for the entertainment value. Even though his arms are pinioned behind him, even though he saw what happened to Leadfoot, even though he knows that he cannot possibly succeed, still he charges.)

(It plays out exactly as one might expect.)

(Soundwave swings a roundhouse kick that takes Bumblebee in the side. Bee goes down, falling among the wreckage that was his friend.)

("I'm saving you for last, Autobot," Soundwave tells him. "You've earned special treatment." He pauses to look at the vast wall of attack ships nestled beneath the battle cruisers. With firepower such as this, any remaining resistance from the Autobots, from humanity—from anyone or anything—would be brief. "Better have our fun while it lasts.")

(He steps forward and kicks Bumblebee viciously several more times, and still Bumblebee does not cry out.

Then Soundwave looks toward Megatron to see if his lord is entertained by his actions.)

(Megatron gives him a pitying glance and then looks away.)

(Suddenly the enjoyment of his actions ends for Soundwave.)

("I thought I would have some fun with you," he says, "but now that it comes to it, I feel bored. Time to die.")

(And then he hears a whistling through the air, as if something not unlike a bomb is heading his way.)

(He looks up.)

(Battle cruisers are falling from on high, released from their supports by two small former Decepticons who are busy pushing controls on the bridge that they shouldn't be touching. With no one aboard controlling the ships, they are plummeting like rocks.)

(Megatron and Sentinel immediately take up protective positions around the anchor and start opening fire, picking off any cruisers that look as if their trajectory might bring them down upon the anchor pillar. Their heavy-duty weaponry is more than up to the task.)

(But there is chaos all around, including Decepticons on the ground who are scrambling to get clear of the ships that are raining down upon them like a meteor storm. The attention of the Decepticons on the roof is distracted, and the Autobots seize the opportunity to strike back at their captors. They tear free from the Decepticons and then, moving as one, reverse themselves and slam directly into them. Autobots and Decepticons go tumbling off the roof, spiraling toward street level.)

(The Decepticons bear the brunt of the impact, and the violence of the landing jars loose the bonds that are imprisoning the Autobots' arms and suppressing their weapons systems. They tear loose froom their restraints

and come straight at the Decepticons who had only moments earlier been lording it over them.)

(Bumblebee brings his arms around as Soundwave aims his sonic cannon. It is an old-fashioned cowboy showdown, and Bumblebee wins the draw as he fires into Soundwave's torso, cutting him in half. Soundwave's top half, lying on its back like a flipped-over turtle, continues to struggle, determined to fight back. Bumblebee places his cannon to Soundwave's head.)

("Time . . . to . . . die," Bumblebee manages to say, and fires at point-blank range.)

(There is no less chaos on the bridge of the battle cruiser. The Decepticons onboard are having a maddening time with Wheelie. They chase him around, trying to grab him, trying to shoot him, trying to do something, anything, to stop him. He moves so quickly that they appear to be standing still. They do not realize that there is a second small former Decepticon there, and he has taken over both helm and navigation. By the time they do, it is too late. The battle cruiser is spiraling down, down, and moments later crashes into Lake Michigan.)

(All the large Decepticons are crushed upon impact.)

(Two small former Decepticons swim away.)

(Throughout all of this and more to follow, Sentinel remains calm. He is waiting for the light beams to peak, to come together, and he knows exactly what he will say. He will say: "It's our world now. Commence transport." And it will be glorious.)

iii

The light beams that will form the space bridge are about to converge upon each other. They will wrap themselves around the earth in its entirety, and then Cybertron will be brought here, and the abominable fantasy of the Decepticons will be made reality.

I cannot allow this to happen.

I have been struggling to free myself from this mass of crossbars and metal for what seems an interminable amount of time. And then, as pilotless attack ships plummet from the sky for no reason that I can discern, several of them strike the building in which I am inextricably entwined, jarring loose the rebar that has been restraining me. It is not by much, but it is all I require. I tear loose from them and drop to the ground, darting to the right to avoid an attack ship that smashes down to the street.

Within moments, the energy beams will come together. At that point, the transportation will commence.

I draw near and see soldiers, human soldiers, displaying that determination of spirit that so impresses me about these small beings. They are fighting Decepticons.

No. Not just any Decepticon. They are assaulting Shockwave. One soldier has draped a parachute over his head to block his view while others are firing upon him, trying to slow him, hurt him, kill him.

For a moment I am back on Cybertron, thinking that he has destroyed my mentor, unaware of the vast charade that must have been staged for our benefit.

Then I am back in Chicago, back in the world that is my home now, and just as Shockwave pulls aside the obscuring cloth, just as he is about to annihilate these humans who have dared to hamper him, I am upon him and punch him so hard that I break off his jaw. He staggers, tries to speak, obviously fails. Shockwave lunges at me, trying to bring his laser cannon to bear upon me. I sidestep him and bring around my Energon sword, driving it into him up to the hilt. He glares at me, shuddering. His eye offends me. I pluck it out, throw it down, and crush it beneath my foot.

He sags against me, but still he tries to twist his laser cannon around to aim it at me. I grab it and aim it up-

ward, toward the anchor pillar, just as I hear Sentinel declare that the transportation should begin. I look up. The light beams have come together, the connection finalized.

I fire Shockwave's laser cannon for him.

It strikes the anchor pillar on the roof above just as Megatron is reaching forward to trigger it and send the final pulse of energy through. The blast knocks the pillar off the roof. Sentinel grabs for it, but it is too late as it tumbles away from his grasp and to the streets below. He looks down to see the source and spots me just as I yank out my Energon sword, reverse the direction, and bisect Shockwave vertically. The two halves of him fall to either side, and I turn and point at Sentinel.

"Face me!" I shout, and my voice thunders up and down the streets. "Face me, traitor! Face me and pay the ultimate penalty for your betrayal!"

iv

("How dare he!" says Megatron. "Let us destroy him together, Sentinel! Together we can—")

("I do not need you to annihilate Optimus Prime. I will dispose of him myself.")

("No! I will not sit by again! Not this time!" Megatron becomes even more insistent. "This is Optimus Prime, and I must be at your side—")

("You useless piece of scrap! You weren't even able to prevent him from shooting the pillar! You will never stand by my side. Never. And this," he says as he slams Megatron in the face, sending him stumbling backward, "is for your presumptuousness, you nothing! Be grateful I do not melt you into a puddle!")

(Unable to catch himself in time, Megatron hits the edge of the roof and falls.)

(Sentinel gives him no more thought as he leaps to the ground to confront his wayward student.)

v

"My God!" Carly said. She and Sam were hiding behind a pile of rubble, and there was so much noise and so many explosions, and from the other side of the building, they were sure that they had just heard Optimus shouting some sort of challenge to Sentinel. But this particular exclamation from her was prompted by what she had spotted lying amid one of the many piles of rubble all around them. "*Sam! That's it!* The control pillar, the anchor thing!"

"Are you sure? It's not just one of a hundred others?"

"I was ten feet away from it! That's definitely it!"

He saw that she was right, and not only that, it was still generating the energy that was connecting all the others. It was down but not out.

He nodded and said, "Stay here. I have to do this." He kissed her quickly and dashed out into the open, running for the pillar.

She stood, about to follow him, because she saw no point in remaining where she was. What good was that going to do for anyone?

But once on her feet, she spotted something off to the side: a huge and yet familiar shadow in an alleyway.

"It can't be," she murmured.

She left Sam to deal with the pillar, a plan already forming in her head to address what she thought she might encounter less than a hundred feet away.

vi

He lands in front of me in a crouch and then slowly stands, uncoiling to his full height. "Decepticons!" he calls out, and I have no doubt that he is broadcasting his command in addition to giving it voice. "Trigger the pillar!"

We circle each other warily. "You were the one who taught me that freedom is everyone's right," I say.

"And survival is the right of the fittest."

He telegraphs his move before he makes it, producing his devastating weapon of acid rust. The instinct of self-protection would prompt most to back off, to flinch, to hesitate for just long enough that he would unleash a blast of the same devastating formula that destroyed Ironhide and the Twins.

But he has trained me too well, Sentinel has. Rather than retreat, I immediately move forward, stepping inside the sweep of his arm before he can take proper aim. With the flat of my sword I slap the blaster from his grasp, sending it bounding away.

When we met in battle on the National Mall, I was still in denial. I refused to believe that the Autobot I revered above all others could be in his right mind. There is no denial within me anymore. I look upon him as if for the first time and see only an enemy.

For a moment we are pushing against each other, weight against weight, strength against strength. With incredulity in his voice, he says, "When only one world can survive, you would choose their race over ours?"

"Over you," I growl back at him, and then, with a quick twist at my waist, I upend him and slam him to the ground.

But he has lost not one bit of speed or fragment of his fighting ability. On his back, he sweeps his leg around and knocks mine out from under me. I go down and, cat-quick, he leaps upon me, trying to grind my head into shards. I twist my head away and return blow for blow, jarring him loose. I kick out, connecting with his chest, sending him crashing into a nearby building. Brick and mortar go flying, and the building collapses.

He springs to his feet and comes at me once more.

This could take a while.

Sam wasn't entirely sure what he was going to do with the pillar once he got to it. Shut it off? If he did that, someone could just turn it back on again. Destroy it? How? Pound it with some debris? Haul it to Mount Doom and toss it in the lava?

It was good enough for another Sam, so . . .

Suddenly he saw someone sprinting from the other direction, heading straight for the same pillar.

The other guy was faster. The other guy was closer.

The other guy was Dylan Gould.

He reached it before Sam and threw his arms around it, embracing it like a lover, his hand coming down on top of one round glyph in the middle that was protruding above the surface of it.

Instinctively Sam knew what it was and, worse, knew what it was going to do. He stopped, put up his hands as if he were trying to talk down a jumper on the edge of a building, and said, "Stop! Dylan! Please don't! The future of the world—!"

"There's only one future for me," Dylan said, sounding strangled.

He slammed the glyph home.

A pulse erupted from the pillar, leaping skyward, and the energy unleashed knocked Dylan backward. It was as if, for a moment, the entire city was buckling from a sonic boom.

Sam looked up and saw something that he would remember to his dying day, which was very likely today.

The curvature of Cybertron was beginning to emerge through the space bridge.

So many times Optimus Prime had spoken with reverence of his home world. Sam had lost track of how many times, in his sleep, he'd had dreams of Cybertron in which he was walking along its metal surface and seeing the Autobots in their home environment.

He was struck by the fact that it looked just as it had in his dreams.

Except this was no dream. This was a nightmare.

The realization broke him from his momentary paralysis, and he charged at the pillar, trying to get past Dylan, who was blocking his path. Dylan grabbed a piece of rubble about the size of his fist and threw it. Sam attempted to dodge and was only partially successful as it slammed against his shoulder, knocking him off his feet.

Dylan came at him, having extracted a length of rebar from the rubble and waving it threateningly. "You chose sides, Sam. You chose wrong."

viii

(The remaining Decepticons are arriving from all over the city. They know the bridge has been activated; their aid is no longer required for that. Instead, now they come to help Sentinel in his battle against their mortal enemy. A number of attack ships are still functioning, having been on routine patrol when the battleship was destroyed, so they are moving in as well.)

(They converge on the battle site where the two Primes struggle. Within seconds they will be there to aid Sentinel and dispose of the hated Optimus. They will not intercede, but in the exceedingly unlikely event that Optimus is triumphant, it will be his last victory. It is clear, though, that that is not going to happen. Sentinel is handling everything that Optimus endeavors to dish out and more besides, and every assault is beaten back.)

(And suddenly missiles are firing upon the attack ships, blasting them apart, sending them spiraling down into the Decepticons who are on foot.)

(Human soldiers are everywhere, opening fire with weapons of devastating potency. And they are side by side with half a dozen Autobots, charging into battle,

cutting a swath through the Decepticon attackers and annihilating everything that stands in their way.)

ix

Carly couldn't believe she was doing what she was doing. But she felt as if she had to do something, and this was what was available to her. She was banking everything on the idea that she had properly interpreted what she had seen via the telescope, but she was fairly convinced that she had. Years of work in the diplomatic corps had made her very adroit at seeing past what typically met the eye.

She entered the alley and saw exactly what she was expecting to see: Megatron, seated among the garbage, his back against the wall, looking about as pathetic as anyone ever had.

There was a wrecked bus wedged into the alley near him. Carly climbed up on the hood and from there onto the roof, bringing herself to eye level with the Decepticon. "So, Megatron, may I ask you a question?"

He looked up at her upon hearing his name. This was the moment of biggest risk. He might just reach over and crush her with his fingers immediately just to get her out of his face. If she survived the next few seconds, she might actually succeed in what she was trying to accomplish.

He did nothing except sit there.

Carly gulped and said, "Was it worth it? All your work to bring Sentinel back. When clearly he now has all the power." When he didn't respond, she spoke faster and with more determination. "I just find it ironic. Almost tragic, really. Your Decepticons finally conquer this planet, and yet their leader won't be you."

His face twisted in anger. She could just imagine what was going through his head. *Who is this little insect to speak to the mighty Megatron in such a manner?* Yet he was listening to her instead of swatting her.

In the distance, sounds of the battle between Sentinel and Optimus raged.

Carly went for broke.

"Any minute now," she said in slow derision, "and you'll be nothing. But. Sentinel's. Bitch."

Megatron was on his feet in an instant, his fist clenched, and he brought it slamming down toward Carly. She let out a scream, and the fist came down to her immediate right, crunching the front of the bus and sending her skidding to the ground. She looked up, and Megatron towered over her, glaring.

Then, without another word, he stormed out of the alley, and Carly wasn't sure what she had just unleashed. But considering the fact that she was alive, she was liking the odds.

x

Sam and Dylan struggled in the rubble, pounding on each other, and Sam was taking the worst of it. One eye was already swollen shut, and the other wasn't in much better shape. His lip was split, and he was tasting the salty bitterness of his blood in his mouth. Meanwhile, searing energy was pouring from the pillar. Even from a distance, Sam felt like it was going to burn off his eyebrows.

Dylan, much to Sam's annoyance, simply looked disheveled. Sam was giving the mogul his best shots, and Dylan didn't seem fazed.

He felt his resolve failing until he saw the curve of Cybertron continue to draw closer, to assume form and substance. He pictured his world being ripped apart, the remaining humans enslaved by the Decepticons, and the image gave him new strength. He lashed out, knocking

Dylan back, swinging a series of jabs and punches as fast as he could, driving him toward the surging pillar.

Dylan brought his fists up in a boxing stance to protect himself, and Sam charged forward, focusing all his strength in one last-ditch effort. He pounded Dylan around the midsection, feeling his solid abdominal muscles absorbing the impact. He swung a roundhouse punch and missed completely as Dylan sidestepped, and then Dylan brought his fist down on the back of Sam's neck, sending him to his knees.

Sam was gasping for breath, and Dylan stood over him, triumphant. "You see that planet up there? I just rescued a whole other world. Think you're a hero? You think you're a hero?"

"No," Sam said raggedly. "Just a messenger."

And Sam leaped upward and slammed his foot into Dylan's solar plexus. Dylan stumbled back, unaware until the last possible second just how close he had allowed himself to get to the pillar.

By the time he realized, it was too late. He fell into the powerful beam that the pillar was generating and was instantly incinerated.

Sam fell to his knees, gasping, unable to believe it was over. Then he realized that, of course, it wasn't. He grabbed for the glyph that had sunk into the surface of the pillar, the one that, if he could just extract it, would shut the thing off and end this madness.

No chance. It was smooth against the pillar, and there was no way to extract it, or at least none that he could find.

"*Lennox! Epps! A little help!*" he shouted, not knowing where they were and not really expecting to be lucky enough to be heard by them.

To his astonishment, he turned out to be wrong.

Seconds later, Lennox and Epps were attaching charges to the pillar. Carly was at Sam's side, trying to tell him something about Megatron, but he was too distracted to listen. He was busy watching the impending destruction of the earth by means of another world. "Guys! A little faster!"

"We good?" Epps said to Lennox.

"We're good! Now let's go! Go, go!"

They got.

xi

I have battled with as much determination as I can. I have no excuse this time. He has simply outfought me. There is no dishonor for me in that. Unfortunately, there is no victory, either.

I lie upon the ground, trying to gather myself for another assault, but my body ignores the commands of my mind. I tell it to stand, and instead I remain prone. Sentinel, who moments before knocked me onto my back, stands near me and shakes his head in what can only be considered pity. "Always the bravest of us, Optimus. But you could never make the hard decisions. Our planet will survive. Thanks to me."

He reaches down and picks up the fallen blaster, the one containing the acid rust. He points it toward my head, and now I feel strength returning to me, but too late, too late . . .

And suddenly Sentinel's arm is wrenched back, and the blaster goes flying. He turns in confusion and is astounded to see who has committed such an unexpected act.

"Megatron?" he says.

"Lord Megatron," he announces, and strikes Sentinel Prime a mighty blow in the face. Sentinel staggers, and Megatron fires a blast from his cannon, lifting Sentinel off his feet and sending him crashing to the street some distance away. "Three will stand, and one will fall!"

Megatron spins and puts out a hand to me. Not a hand cannon. Not a weapon.

A hand.

I take the hand of him who once slew me, and he hauls me to my feet. Side by side, we face Sentinel.

We charge into battle.

And still he beats us back. Still he thwarts us. He moves faster than anything I have ever seen, and we pound upon him and exchange blows at dizzying speed. The air rings with the repeated impact of metal on metal, and stray explosions blast apart everything within range of the battle, and still Sentinel is on his feet, and still we are not able to overcome him.

"We were gods once, all of us!" Sentinel bellows, "but here . . . there will be only one!"

He slams into me, and the speed of it carries us through another wall, pulverizing it. I manage to toss him aside, but he lands upon his feet and is ready to come at me again.

Then Megatron charges in, skidding on his side, akin to images I have seen of a baseball runner sliding into base. The slide takes Sentinel's legs out from under him, and as Sentinel falls, I leap over him, landing on the street behind him. Sentinel is instantly on his feet, ready to fight, ready to end the battle.

So am I.

And I happen to be the one holding the acid blaster.

He has taught me well what to do in just such a situation. For this one instant, the student truly has surpassed the teacher.

Sentinel Prime freezes.

It is all I require as I unleash a blast of acid rust.

It strikes Sentinel Prime fully in the chest. He staggers, clutching at the rapidly expanding hole in his torso, looking bewildered that such a thing could possibly be happening to him, and then he sags to his knees.

"All I ever wanted," he gasps out, "was the survival of our race. You must see . . . why I had to betray you."

He reaches up with a trembling hand, which I ignore. "You did not betray me. You betrayed yourself."

His hand sags, falls to the ground, and dissolves. Moments later, so does the rest of him.

I feel as if I have just slain a part of myself. Just as humans who have lost limbs claim that they still feel phantom pain from the missing body parts, so too will I always know the sensation of the absent part of my life called Sentinel.

Except . . .

I lost him once.

I can lose him again.

Suddenly I hear several explosions, and the coruscating beam originating from the control pillar, wherever it has fallen to, sputters and then goes out. Someone has destroyed it. Knowing their resourcefulness, it is probably the humans.

Megatron lets out a long, high cry of protest as, with the anchor destroyed, the beam is broken.

I have just enough time to glimpse my home world. I reach up, imagining that I am holding it in the palm of my hand. And then the space bridge collapses, and just that quickly, the planet of my birth is drawn back to its point of origin.

All is silence.

Slowly I turn to face Megatron.

"You felt it," he says to me. "You must have felt it. The draw of our world. It called to you just as forcefully as it calls to me. The difference between us is that I was willing to answer that call."

"No," I say. "It was never about Cybertron, any more than it was about Earth now. It was always about you. Whatever nobility you may have had once, or think

*you've had, was long consumed by your overwhelming
need to dominate all you see before you."*

*"Such pompousness from you, Prime. Your sanctimo-
niousness would be more impressive if we did not both
know that the two of us are very much alike."*

"We are nothing alike."

*"I wanted to control Cybertron because I thought I
was right. You fight me because you believe you are
right."*

*"I," I tell him, preparing for battle, "am tired of your
control."*

"And I . . ." He hesitates.

*And he sags to the ground. "I . . . am tired of fight-
ing."*

I have no idea what reply to make. So I wait.

*"I sue for peace, Optimus," he says finally. "I will
order all Decepticons to stand down. It is over. All
this"—he gestures around us—"is over. Even endless war must end sometime. Our world calls, and
I will devote my existence—and the existence of all
Decepticons—not to attacking you or humans but to
returning to our home world. I have spent far too long
destroying, and it has brought me nothing. Nothing. So
I wish to try creating for a time and see if that brings
me . . . something."*

*"And I am supposed to believe your words? I am sup-
posed to accept this call for a truce? After all the lies
and deceits? After all the attempts to lay waste to an entire world?"*

*He stares at me for a time and then says, "Honestly,
Prime, it does not matter to me what you believe. You
still hold the weapon of Sentinel Prime. Use it. Annihilate me. I no longer care what you do. All I ask is that
whatever decision you make, make it quickly."*

*I look at the blaster in my hand. How easy it would
be to destroy him. To put an end to it once and for all.*

I glance toward the sky. Cybertron is gone. But as loath as I am to admit it, he is right. It calls to me. It calls with the song of what it once was, and what it could be again if only we, as a race, were capable of living up to the potential we once had.

"*You are wrong. I am not like you,*" *I say at last,* "*because if I were, I would destroy you for showing what any Decepticon would define as weakness. Your own people may well tear you apart for this change in your attitude. For your sake as well as theirs, control them.*"

"*I will.*"

Slowly he rises, trying to display some measure of dignity, and then he says, "*When I do return to Cybertron and when I do make things right, I will send for you and yours. And we will join and be one race again. A race of peace. We will once again have a home.*"

I say nothing as he walks away.

I want to believe it will be peace.

I want to believe that he can truly transform.

And I will hold out hope . . . because in the end, that is all we have.

xii

"You said it, you know," Sam reminded her tiredly.

Bumblebee was seated on the ground while Sam leaned against him. Carly was busy using some towels she'd found to try to clean Sam's face as best she could. "I said what?"

"You used the L word."

"That didn't count," she said. "That was under duress. You say crazy things under duress. You're not in your right mind, endorphins get released—"

He put a finger to her lips, silencing her, and he tried to smile except it hurt, so he settled for a wince. "I love you. You're all I'm ever gonna need. And all this?

This blowing stuff up and war and everything? I promise I'll make it up to you."

"You promise?"

"Promise. If *you* promise me that you'll say the L word to me, not under duress, within the next sixty seconds."

"Well, that's a pretty steep requirement," she said. "Be specific: Just how are you going to make it up to me?"

Sam stopped, unsure what to say.

Bumblebee abruptly coughed up a gasket ring. It dropped down and into Sam's open palm.

He looked down at it and what it symbolized and suddenly felt a decline of nerve. "Okay, hold it . . . hang on . . ."

Carly plucked the gasket ring from his palm and slipped it onto the third finger of her left hand.

Sam looked up at the robot, flustered. *"Bumblebee!"*

And Carly reached over, took Sam's hand in hers, looked at him with total adoration, and said, "I love . . . this car."

In any war, there are calms between the storms. There will be days when we lose faith. Days when our allies turn against us . . . but the day will never come when we forsake this planet and its people. For I am Optimus Prime, and I send this message to the universe: We are here. We are home.

Read on for an excerpt from
TRANSFORMERS: EXODUS
by Alex Irvine

Published by Del Rey Books

The Hall of Records in Iacon was closed to the public. In the archive stacks, at a workstation where he had been installed following the tradition and practice of his caste, sat a monitor named Orion Pax. He was tapped into the Communications Grid that invisibly spanned all of Cybertron, monitoring and recording every communication that passed through the Grid. Those that met certain criteria, he listened to, annotated, categorized, and saved in a different sector of the DataNet.

Like much of the rest of the great city of Iacon, the Hall was constructed of a golden-hued alloy that lent itself to the curving architectural style that predominated elsewhere in the city. The architects of Iacon had favored towering, monumental buildings topped by conical structures that looked as if they might take off. The entire city was a monument to aspirations . . . only there were no aspirations among Cybertronians anymore. They were born into a caste, a place that they would maintain for their entire lives. The civilization of Cybertron existed in a perfect stasis. It had been that way for millennia. Iacon was in some ways a memorial of a Cybertronian culture that had not existed in the memory banks of any existing Cybertronian.

Inside the Hall of Records, another kind of stasis existed. The history of Cybertron, from the mythical ages of battles among the Thirteen Primes across the billions of cycles, to the latest transmissions on the latest bands Orion Pax was charged with monitoring—all of it was here. All of it was categorized, cataloged, stored, indexed, and cross-indexed. After that, save for when the High Council or another authority got interested in a threat to civic order, the ever-growing collections in the Hall of Records were ignored.

Once—or so Orion Pax understood from reading in the older records—Cybertronian civilization had maintained links with other planets that surrounded other stars. Via a network of Space Bridges constructed with technology long abandoned, populations of Cybertronians on far-flung planets had stayed in contact with Cybertron. Gigantion, Velocitron, even the Hub, all were once part of a greater Cybertronian culture. Now the Space Bridges were all long since collapsed and degraded. The last of them, which hung in the skies between the two moons and the Asteroid Belt, had not been used since a long, long time ago. Even Orion Pax, who could ordinarily dig anything out of the records of Teletraan-1 and the DataNet, was not sure exactly how long it had been.

Now a Cybertronian like Orion Pax would not go to the stars. He would not fight nobly for the great ideals of the Primes. A Cybertronian like Orion Pax would monitor, assess, and catalog transmissions on the Grid because that is what Cybertronians of his caste did. Other castes built and engineered, governed, made laws . . . or fought in the gladiatorial pits.

From there, oddly enough, came some of the more interesting transmissions Orion Pax had heard lately. He was not a great follower of the arena, but even he knew of the most recent champion Megatronus. Quite a bold action, to assume that name—it was not just any bot who could carry the weight of one of the Thirteen Primes, whose deeds still echoed across the megacycles of history. This Megatronus had not lost a match since the early days of his career in the arena. The gladiators began with no names, and most of them ended that way as well; Megatronus had claimed not just a name, but a name that could not help but capture the attention of even those castes who pretended to pay no attention to such degraded entertainments as gladiatorial combat.

The sight of two—or more—Cybertronians tearing each other apart was something that few would admit enjoying. Yet the pits in the lower levels of Kaon were one of Cybertron's most popular tourist destinations, and the Grid was alive with broadcasts and rebroadcasts of the various tournaments that were constantly going on. The only industry in Kaon that could rival gladiatorial entertainment was recovery and reconstruction. The mechasurgical engineers of that city—and its gladiatorial rival, Slaughter City—were without peer. Arena combat was illegal across Cybertron, but the High Council in its wisdom understood that a population confined by caste needed certain outlets. So the pits in Kaon, which had begun long ago as a diversion for the workers in the great foundries there, were now entrenched, even if technically outside the law of Cybertron. In Slaughter City it was much the same.

So it was odd that from Kaon and Slaughter City, Orion Pax should be hearing and seeing arguments he could only call philosophical. And they were coming from the greatest of the illicit champions of Kaon's pits: this Megatronus.

The transmissions were fragmentary and distorted, originating as they did from deep inside the metallic bowels of Kaon. Between those lower levels and the Grid receptors, they picked up enormous interference from the industrial processes that drove Kaon . . . and, Orion Pax knew, the civilization of Cybertron. Nothing could be created without the raw materials first being refined. That happened in Kaon and the Badlands that stretched between it and the Hydrax Plateau. As long as those Badlands fueled the needs of Cybertron, the High Council would keep turning a blind optic to the gladiator pits.

Orion Pax wondered how long that would continue. He listened to the most recent of Megatronus's transmissions, fingers hovering over the interface that would determine where he cataloged it.

"Are Cybertronians not all made of the same materials? My alloys are the same as those in the frame of a High Councilor; my lubricants are the same as those that lubricated the joints of the Thirteen themselves!" Megatronus's voice scraped and rasped like one of the great machines in the factories of Kaon. Orion Pax looked up and down the row of other Cybertronians of the same caste as he. All of them would spend their careers monitoring and cataloging, feeding the vast databases of Iacon. This was the way the civilization of Cybertron had been since long before the creation of Orion Pax.

And yet they were made of the same materials as the Archivist Alpha Trion, or any member of the High Council.

Would a Councilor spend his life monitoring transmissions?

"We are individuals! Once we were free!" Megatronus's voice scraped through Orion Pax's head. What would his fellow monitors think if they could hear?

They would report this Megatronus in a nanoklik. That's what they would do, Orion Pax thought. As if in reply, Megatronus said, "The High Council, if they heard me now, would quietly render me into slag. Do not doubt it. They may be listening now. If I vanish, carry on my work. Soundwave, you and Shockwave will carry on. You are my trusted lieutenants."

A second voice came in. "Lieutenants? Are you now the general of an army, Megatronus?"

Orion Pax listened harder. He ran a check on the new voice—it was neither Shockwave nor Soundwave. He had heard them before, and had records and database entries for each.

But this new voice was not in the index he maintained to keep track of Megatronus's associates. Who was it?

It was not part of Orion Pax's job to investigate. He monitored, observed, recorded. Investigators were of another caste.

He could, however, report to Alpha Trion, the overseer. Orion Pax sampled the new voice and spent a few cycles compiling a report. It wouldn't do to present himself to Alpha Trion without a good reason, and proof of how good the reason was.

The Archivist of Iacon, Alpha Trion, was far older than Orion Pax, who had heard stories that he had existed since the great age of the Space Bridge–fueled expansion, the high point of Cybertronian civilization. What that must have been like, to be able to ride the dimensional bridges to other stars . . .

"Orion Pax," Alpha Trion said. "What brings you here to interrupt my work?"

"I seek advice." Orion activated the recording of Megatronus. Alpha Trion put down the antiquated stylus he used to make entries in the single book that sat on his desk. The Archivist of Iacon had databases and endless hard-copy records of virtually everything that had ever happened in the history of Cybertron, yet he chose stylus and book as his interface. Like many of the older Cybertronians Orion Pax knew, Alpha Trion had grown eccentric.

When the recording had played out of a wall-mounted speaker and Alpha Trion had taken his standard moment to tap his stylus on the desk and think over various potential responses, the Archivist said, "Megatronus."

"Why has he named himself after a mythical being?" Orion Pax asked.

"If the old stories are true, Megatronus believed until the end that he would be vindicated," Alpha Trion said. "He believed himself to be doing what was right even if his methods destroyed much of what he professed to believe."

"Not much of an example if you're plotting a revolution," Orion Pax said.

With a dry chuckle, Alpha Trion stood. "Indeed not. But perhaps that is not the only example to be taken from the deeds of Megatronus. Who is this upstart?"

"He has been a gladiator in Kaon. Like all of them, he began without a name, a worker who took to the arena as a way to glory. He has never lost, and his fame has grown to the point that few other gladiators will fight him one-on-one. Now it seems that he is no longer content to be the greatest gladiator in Kaon; he has grander ambitions."

"Ambition," Alpha Trion echoed. "That is not a quality encouraged on Cybertron. As you know." He fell silent, and Orion Pax thought he had detected something of a wistful tone in the Archivist's voice.

He waited, and after several cycles Alpha Trion spoke again. "Go back to your post, Orion Pax. Continue to listen. When you know what this Megatronus is planning, return to me and we will consult further."